THE
DRAGON
QUEEN

BY ALICE BORCHARDT

Devoted

Beguiled

The Silver Wolf

Night of the Wolf

The Wolf King

The Dragon Queen

THE
DRAGON
QUEEN

ALICE
BORCHARDT

THE BALLANTINE PUBLISHING GROUP

NEW YORK

A Del Rey ® Book
Published by The Ballantine Publishing Group
Copyright © 2001 by Alice Borchardt

www.delreydigital.com

Library of Congress Cataloging-in-Publication Data

Borchardt, Alice.
The dragon queen / Alice Borchardt.—1st ed.
p.   cm.
ISBN 0-345-44399-3
1. Cornwall (England: County)—Fiction.   2. Arthurian romances—Adaptations.
I. Title.

PS3552.O687 D73 2001
813'.54—dc21
2001037970

Text design by Holly Johnson

Manufactured in the United States of America

First Edition: November 2001

10   9   8   7   6   5   4   3   2   1

PROLOGUE

OW ODD THAT I SHOULD WRITE A BOOK. AND write it now when I have ceased to believe in them. When I was young, I loved books: the coiled paper rolls in copper casings, the bound parchment kind whose leaves turned one at a time. They revealed all the world to me.

Or so I thought.

This is what the Christian church has done to us: made us people of the book. Now I think that is perhaps not such a good thing.

Before Patrick came to Ireland we were people of the wind, the storm, the spring flood filling the rivers. We marked the turning of the seasons and the sun's journey through the halls of heaven. We struggled with the famine in the spring and feasted when the autumn poured out its abundance at our feet. By day we lived in the sun when it shone and the gray rain and wispy mist when it didn't. We sang to one another of the paths taken through the heavens by sun, moon, and stars and watched them when they rose and set above the chamber tombs to carry with them the souls of the dead. And we sought truth, enlightenment, love, and beauty in each other's faces, hands, hearts, and bodies—not in the shadowed, crackling pages made of paper and parchment.

We were a people of music, and we sang and danced, the thunder and whisper of tides on sand and shingle, the roar of the wind speaking in a forest making love to moor and meadow or the shrill lament of a cold winter storm. When hungry, we ate—if we had the food. A lot of times we didn't. When cold, we huddled about the fire and wove magnificent tales of love, conflict, good, evil, gods and heroes, who were sometimes more than gods in their steadfast courage and sacrifice.

Oh yes, I admire books. I *still* do. They can preserve a truth for twice a thousand years and teach it to any who has the skill and cares to read it. They can also fix a lie in stone forever. But worse still, they—the books— can be about nothing at all.

Nothing real.

And men and women can pour out their lives, brooding over shadows that never existed except in some madman's mind. Men can wear away their lives searching for the kernel of truth they think can be found in the disordered ravings of a fool. For you see, the turning spindle twists thread, the shuttle flies between the warp and weft, and the jewels of mixed colors light cloth, the adze smoothes wood, the knife cuts it, and the scraper cleans hides. But a mass of words may mean nothing at all.

So we must return to the music, the dance, the songs, to hunger, desire, and love, lest we forget who and why we are. We must sit around the fire and tell the tales, the stories of gods and men, so we might know how to behave properly. In work and war, in life and death, we are instructed by the deeds of others. In wisdom and courage, skill and truth, by music and the dance.

I am myself a creature of the dance, the imitation of the movements embraced by the dialogue between earth and sky. The dance of power, the steps I trod on the edge of a mountain so long ago.

CHAPTER ONE

Cornwall, England
Tintigal, Year of our Lord 470

THE SHIP PULLED UP TO THE QUAY.

Above the fortress, rock frowned down on the two men standing on the deck. "It has never fallen to assault," the captain told Maeniel.

"This I can believe," Maeniel said, studying the formidable stone and wood walls at the top.

"Even Caesar did not care to besiege it," the captain continued. "Or so it is said."

Though spring had come to the continent, the wind in Britain still had a bite to it, especially the sea wind. Maeniel pulled his mantle more tightly around himself. He knew the captain was eaten alive with curiosity about him and his mission. He had declined to say more than absolutely necessary about it to the man. The people he served needed as much protection as they could get. Not simply from the imperial tax gatherers but also from the barbarian warlords who so willingly served the interests of those who monopolized the remnants of Roman power. The captain probably had friends in every port where the Veneti called. A man now might be hard put to get a letter to Rome within a year, but gossip spread like a brushfire.

3

"I was surprised when they gave me permission to bring you here," the captain continued.

"I have business with Vortigen," Maeniel said.

The captain laughed. "I love the way you say that, as though you were a man stepping out to a fair to purchase a horse. A small matter of business, nothing extraordinary. Vortigen is the high king of Britain, and he seems to know your name. Oh no, my lord Maeniel, nothing unusual about this situation at all. Big doings up there tonight, though. I have been ferrying important people out here all day, one after another. You will be the last. Enjoy yourself at the feast, my lord."

Maeniel nodded and smiled.

"High king or not, I hope he knows what he's doing—all those Saxons," the captain said, spitting the word *Saxon*.

One of the sailors reached out with a hook and pulled the boat up against the quay, while two others began mooring her fore and aft to iron rings set in the stone.

"No!" the captain shouted. "Don't. We will sail with the tide. I won't remain here. Not tonight at any rate." He looked up at the fortress through narrowed eyes.

The man holding the boat to the dock gave him a puzzled glance. "I thought you enjoyed the king's hospitality."

"Not tonight, I won't," the captain said. "And don't ask me any questions about why."

Maeniel jumped over the gunwales to the stone quay. "You are returning to Gaul, then?" he called back to the captain.

"Yes."

"Come," the man said. "All this trouble for nothing. We could at least stay the night. We might pick up a cargo."

"No," said the captain. "We will be in Vennies by sunrise. I'd prefer it that way."

A dozen men were at the oars. The mate shrugged and pushed off with the boat hook.

"Put your backs into it!" the captain shouted to the crew. "We will be home by morning. You married men can chase your wives' lovers out the window and get some sleep. We were paid in gold for this day's work. Everyone will have a share."

Then they were gone, drawing away on the evening tide.

Maeniel's eyes closed. The sea wind brought a mixture of odors to his nostrils: salt, roasting meat, and other savory cooking smells; pitch from the torches being lit on the walls above him; the human odor of infrequently washed bodies living in close quarters on the rock, perspiration and perfume, the diverse odors of linen, silk, and wool. This was going to be an aristocratic gathering.

And something else was borne on the wind to him, something he didn't want to intrude on his consciousness just now, a warning. Yes, a definite warning. Sometimes humans sense things also. Yes, he'd paid the captain in gold to bring him to Tintigal in the kingdom of Dumnonia, but the man might as well have remained and tried to pick up a cargo. In fact, the captain had not done too badly once Maeniel was in Britain, picking up other travelers along the coast and ferrying them out to the rock. But come nightfall, he began to grow nervous. Maeniel knew the signs very well. The hair on the back of the captain's neck began to stir, as had Maeniel's when he first saw the fortress. And the captain didn't know why any more than Maeniel did. Left to himself, Maeniel the wolf would have cleared out. He wouldn't have run exactly, but that "not right" feeling, when it wouldn't leave yet wouldn't be resolved, was something the wolf wouldn't have wanted to play around with. But humans— as he was now—with their predetermined appointments and planned meetings left little room for a response to the shadowy awareness that haunted him, that haunted the wolf.

A serving man appeared at his elbow. He bowed. "My lord." He was responding to Maeniel's silk woolen tunic and heavy velvet mantle. "My lord, are you here for the feast?"

Maeniel nodded.

"The stairs are to your left. They will bring you to the citadel; but before you go, if you would be so kind, I must have your sword."

Maeniel felt even more uneasy. He was tempted to say no, but in the growing gloom he saw two indistinct figures behind the serving man and realized they must be part of the king's guard. "Will I be the only one who must yield up his weapon?"

The servant bowed again. "No, my lord. No one may bring a weapon to the king's board, not tonight. They will be held in the strong rooms under the fortress and will be returned in the morning. They will all be under guard through the night."

Maeniel unbuckled his sword belt. "I want to see where you take this," he said.

The servant smiled, a little bit patronizingly, but said, "Certainly, sir."

Then his eyes widened slightly at the sight of the hilt. It was wrapped in gold wire. A lot of gold wire, more gold than the servant had ever seen in his life. "It looks old," he said.

"It is old," Maeniel answered.

"The hilt—"

"The hilt is nothing. The blade is everything." So saying, Maeniel drew half its length from the sheath. The torchlight shining down from the ramparts above woke rainbows in the steel.

The two soldiers behind the servant peered over his shoulder to look into the blade, for indeed, they could see their reflections there.

"Only the gods could make such a weapon," one of them said.

Maeniel looked down at it sadly. "Not the gods but men made and wore it before the Romans came to Gaul. But no matter, please take care of it." He handed belt, sword, and scabbard to the servant. "My teacher bestowed weapons on me. I cherish them."

Then he turned and began climbing the stair. The servant walked ahead with the sword, the soldiers behind.

From the stair, Maeniel could look out over the ocean. The sun was only a salmon glow among the purplish-blue clouds on the horizon, but since a feast was in the offing, torches blazed everywhere. The serving man paused before they reached the top.

"The fortress was built in the form of rings, each higher level above but inside the lower."

Here Maeniel encountered magic. He always seemed to do so when he least expected it. This ring had a broader area of open ground than the others, and it had been turned into a garden. Large square clay pans held

6

food crops, and giant urns housed small trees and shrubs. A waist-high wall surrounded the garden, and the trees and vines flowed from troughs at the edge, hanging down so far that they almost reached the next level. There were roses—many roses—white, yellow, and red. Pomegranates, hazel trees, and berry vines, their long thorny canes draped over the rail. They were not in fruit but in bloom, white flowers scattered like stars among the vines. The clay pans were filled with herbs—rosemary; mints, which will grow anywhere if they have water and sun; pennyroyal; spearmint and the hairy apple mints—onions, leeks, garlic, cabbages, and mustards, their cross-shaped yellow flowers open to the night wind and sea air.

"A garden in the sky," Maeniel said.

"Yes. Are you then an adept?"

"Adept?" Maeniel said, mystified. "Adept at what?"

"Magic, sir," the serving man answered, then pointed to the soldiers. They were climbing the last flight of stairs to the inner keep above. "They don't even know we are not with them, though they will announce your presence to the king. He will thank them for it. He is always polite and will not warn them that they are deceived.

"Most can't see this garden at all, and those who can only think it is a quaint concept of the high king to keep a few pots of flowers and vegetables near his front door. I will conduct you to the hall of weapons."

"Yes," Maeniel said. "Beneath the rose."

"Behind it," the serving man corrected, for there were pots of white roses all along the inner wall.

Maeniel saw the wall and the entrance hidden by magic, and he and the serving man—by now Maeniel was sure he was no ordinary servant—stepped into it.

Was it morning or was it evening? He couldn't be sure, and the wolf did not inform him. The sun was just over the horizon, driving long shafts of light into the mists drifting in the vast hall.

Vast, Maeniel thought. *Why vast?* The drifting mist was so thick he could barely make out the doorway behind him. Yet he had the sense of enormous empty space, a high roof, and giant windows looking out over a cloud-filled sky, of winds that drove sharp downdrafts, cold and moist, and updrafts, hot and reeking of jungle, forest, and marsh, and a sense of latent lightning hovering just out of being but poised to rend both earth and sky. The mists around him were not fog or dew but clouds drifting over the summer country of an earth below.

"You are no natural man," the servant said.

"No," Maeniel answered as the clouds, dark, now bright blue, silver, and bloody with the new—or was it the old?—sun boiled around him. "I am a wolf who is sometimes a man. Tell me, is it twilight or dawn here?"

"There is no *here* here," the servant answered, "and it is neither one nor the other, each and both at the same time. Do you wish my master any harm?"

"No. I came in hopes of his help for—"

The servant raised his hand. "I need know nothing more. There are those here who do wish him ill. He has been warned, but he balances the need for peace with the danger they pose. I can do no more than advise caution." He extended the sword before him. There was a chime as though a great bell had rung. The sword vanished. "It will be returned in two days. Wherever you may be, you will receive it. The blade is warm with the love its maker put in it. His blood went into the molten steel as an offering, making it resistant to any magic but your own. No matter what I do, I cannot retain it here for long. It is yours in more than one sense."

Seconds later they were both climbing up the steps to Vortigen's hall.

"Not even the dead can remain long in the halls of the sky," the servant continued. "Birds alone rule it. That's why they are sacred to her—she who gave you face and form. She has always had only one name, The Lady."

They reached the top, and Vortigen's hall stood before them. When Maeniel turned to look, the servant had gone.

The feasting hall occupied the top of the fortress, a dome of fitted, unmortared stone.

Vitrified, Maeniel thought, *a house of glass.*

He'd heard of the process but had not seen it before. The walls had originally been made of wood, the dome of sand and other silicates framed within it. A hot controlled burn fused the sand into a mass like obsidian, and when the wood was burned away a glass bubble remained. This was Vortigen's hall. The exterior and interior walls were polished, with openings drilled for a door and smoke hole in the roof.

It was beautiful.

Maeniel stepped through the arched door. The glass dome at the top near the smoke hole was transparent, but since it was night only the stars shone through. They were reflected in a cataract of brilliance on the polished stone floor. The hearth was in the center; three steps led down into the fire pit, where a fire blazed, warming the room. It was a very big room, but still the firelight was reflected by the black, polished floor and the matte-finished walls. In addition, there were candles, many candles, each in a tall holder behind a table that encircled almost the whole room.

A good many people were already present; and they wandered about, sipping wine from Roman glass beakers and visiting with friends and acquaintances. Maeniel had lately encountered the new invention, the fireplace with a chimney, on the continent. He liked the central hearth a bit better, but it used a lot of fuel. He had no doubt a world warmed only by fireplaces was approaching. Yet, there was something very democratic about this ancient hearth. People could gather around it and all be comfortable, whereas with a fireplace those few who were able to get the seats closest to the fire harvested most of the warmth and light, while the rest were consigned to increasing levels of cold and darkness. It was rather like what was happening all over the dying Roman Empire.

Someone offered him a cup of wine, a very attractive serving girl with very blond hair, blue eyes, and fair eyelashes. The cup was glass blown over a gold frame, but when she drew near to pour the wine, he found himself immersed in a stink of fear. Then he saw the collar she wore and noticed all the other women were similarly collared. She offered to conduct him to the king. Maeniel followed.

A man he took to be Vortigen was seated at the table directly opposite the door. When he reached the king the girl turned and walked away to attend to other guests. Maeniel knelt.

"Get up," Vortigen said. "All I can see of you is your eyes. Please, come around and take a seat on the bench beside me."

Maeniel rose and nodded, seeing that the table—a work of art itself, being made of old oak and carved along the edge with the dragon motif of the royal house—was not one table but six sections with openings so that guests could pass between them. The woman who had led him to the king was walking along with her crystal pitcher, filling the cups of a few seated guests.

"She is beautiful," the king said. He sounded uneasy. "Want her?"

"No." Maeniel's answer was a resounding one, a little too vehement.

The king made a quick keep-it-down gesture. Maeniel apologized immediately. "I'm sorry," he said more softly, and then, trying to sound regretful, he said again, "No."

"If what the letter said about you is true," Vortigen said, "I can understand why you might find her disturbing. They are all slaves, you know, purchased for the occasion by my sons and brothers-in-law of Anglia, Sussex, and Essex. No women were invited to this feast. The women are for the convenience of the guests. That, and that only, is the reason they are here."

"Yes," Maeniel said. He studied the people, who were still crowding into the room. Each man seemed to have from one to four Saxon warriors in his entourage. Maeniel walked around the table and seated himself beside the king, saying, "With your permission, my lord."

Vortigen waved away his apologies and placed a hand on his knee. "And how is my old friend and correspondent, the bishop of Aries?"

"He's well," Maeniel said, "and sends you his greetings."

"And is he still involved with the Bagaudae?"

"Yes, and it is on their behalf that I have come here. I have been told their activities are even more prevalent in this country."

"They are," the king told him. "It is for this reason that the Saxons have been imported here by my relatives along the coast and the Saxon shore . . . to suppress the brotherhood of the Bagaudae."

Maeniel nodded. "The same way the Gauls used the Franks to collect taxes and suppress rebellion among their own people."

The king nodded sadly. "As high king I have warned them that the raids along the shore would cease, the land grow more profitable, if they remitted taxes rather than trying to crush their own people by employing the Saxons as mercenaries. But all they learned from the Romans was how to destroy and how to take. They are loyal only to their own interests. Hence, we are overrun with tribesmen from the continent, and the people abandon their lands and flee. This has not happened in the north. We stood fast."

He sighed. "I am a weary man. All my life I have fought the long defeat."

And indeed, to Maeniel's eyes he did look weary. Though Maeniel knew him to be only forty, the king's hair was lightened by streaks of gray and his face was deeply lined by a fatigue no sleep could ever banish.

"All the Romans did was steal," Maeniel said. "And all they accomplished was to rupture the ties that bound the chieftains to their own people and destroy any ability of the ordinary man or woman to call even the least of these rich high lords to account for their actions. The landowners are the tyrants and the barbarian warriors are the instruments of their pleasure. The smallholder, the craftsman skilled or unskilled, is nothing to them. The Romans appreciated beauty, but they turned to their slaves to create it; and indeed in Roman lands the singer, the musician, the dancer, the sculptor, the painter are all slaves, as are the thinkers, prelates, and any others who do not devote themselves to the arts of war and oppression. This is and was their legacy, and we are left to struggle along with this curse as best we can."

"You say it well. I can see where the good bishop finds many of his arguments," Vortigen said.

"I have had a long time to think," Maeniel said. "But perhaps we can stop the rot here. Even in Gaul the Bagaudae keep the dream, the hope of resistance, alive."

"I have no help to offer you," Vortigen said. "If my family ever knew I had entertained an emissary from the Bagaudae and a follower of Pelagius, I would have a great deal more troubles with my subkings than I have now. I greatly fear I have neither men nor money to offer your distinguished patron. But we will speak about this later, and perhaps I can find something to offer you. One thing I cannot give you is a seat by my side, but I will place you at the end of a table near the door."

Maeniel nodded. "I am honored to be here at all," he murmured.

The throng in the hall was growing. A big man wearing a sword and accompanied by three large Saxon warriors swept into the room. The servant who had placed Maeniel's sword followed.

"He's armed," Maeniel said.

Vortigen studied his guest sadly. "Of course. No one would take *his* sword. This is Merlin, or rather the merlin. Just as I am Vortigen and the vortigen."

"You confuse me," Maeniel said.

"It is a riddle, a riddling question," Vortigen said.

"I have heard of Merlin, though. He is the chief druid of Britain and the archbishop of Canterbury."

"Yes."

"He is a young man to hold so high an office," Maeniel said.

And indeed, the man Maeniel looked on did appear young. He was dark, as many north Britons were, and yet fair at the same time with white skin fine as alabaster and wide-set, piercingly blue eyes. His hair was black and worn to his shoulders. He was dressed magnificently. His rank demanded no less. He wore dark suede riding pants, cross-gartered leggings, a tunic of midnight blue silk embroidered with stars in gold. His sword belt was heavy with moonstones, opals, and gold. He wore a scarlet velvet mantle.

"He is the midnight realm of Dis Pater come to earth," Maeniel whispered.

"Don't speak so," Vortigen answered and made a sign against the evil eye.

Merlin left no doubt who and what he was, for he immediately strode not around the fire, as ordinary mortals do, but through it, down three steps and into the flame. Maeniel and Vortigen rose to watch his progress as he walked across the bed of seething coals.

It may not injure him, Maeniel thought. Sometimes those without un-usual powers can walk through fire and not be harmed if they are quick enough; however, clothing usually did not share the immunity of the flesh under it. *Surely that silk tunic and mantle will catch.* But they didn't, and as if to laugh any doubts about his magical prowess to scorn, Merlin paused to kick a heavy flaming oak butt aside.

A fountain of sparks rose into the air surrounding him like fireflies in the summer twilight, but Maeniel could see that they did him no harm. Nowhere was his skin scorched, or even his clothing, and had he been merely mortal they would have, must have, but they didn't. When he reached the other side and climbed the three steps up, he presented himself to Vortigen, now standing in front of his chair at the table. He did not bend his knee to the king, and Maeniel remembered that there was a law in some Celtic lands that not even a king could speak before his druid. A murmur of awe filled the room, closely followed by applause.

Merlin frowned.

"Greetings, Merlin," Vortigen said. "And are you here to amuse us with your conjurer's tricks?"

Maeniel could see the man was stung. "Conjurer's trick, my lord Vortigen?"

Maeniel heard the subtle insolence in the *my lord*.

"And why are you wearing your sword? I believe you promised to leave it behind when you attended this gathering. Our agreement was no arms."

And then the servant was standing behind Merlin. He seemed to have gotten there without anyone quite knowing how. He bowed low. "My lord?" he asked. "I believe we had a similar conversation on the stairs."

Merlin turned and looked at the servant; his back was to Maeniel, but he saw the results of the look as the man took two steps back. To Maeniel this was a new kind of power.

Merlin turned to Vortigen. "What is this, my lord king, no trust?"

"No," Vortigen said. "No exceptions. Your weapons." He pointed to the door. "Or go."

Merlin unbuckled his sword belt.

"Give it to Vareen."

The servant bowed and took the belt from Merlin's hand. As he did, Maeniel saw his face twist in pain, and Maeniel heard a hiss and smelled a stink of burning. Vareen's face went white.

"There is no need to punish my servants because you are angry with me," Vortigen said.

"I think there is," Merlin said, "a need to discipline any who would try to make themselves greater than they are by trespassing against those of infinitely higher station."

Vareen's face smoothed out. "A small matter," he said, "a trifle, really." He smiled into Maeniel's eyes, turned, and departed.

Merlin scanned the room, evaluating then dismissing each man he saw until his gaze fell on Maeniel. He made as if to dismiss him in a perfunctory manner, but his eyes returned to rest on Maeniel almost in spite of himself.

"I believe I know everyone here . . . but this one. It seemed when I entered you were in close conversation with him. Am I interrupting anything?"

"No, he is simply a messenger from an old friend, Cosmos, the bishop of Aries. He brought me news and a letter from my friend."

"And his name?" Merlin demanded.

A strange tension thrummed in the air. Maeniel opened his mouth to give the answer himself, but Vortigen forestalled him. "He is called the Gray Watcher."

Merlin smiled, or rather demonstrated he had teeth. "Watcher? I thought you said he was a messenger."

"Sometimes that, also," Vortigen said, "but I think we might be seated. The feast is about to begin. My lord Merlin, you will have the seat on my left, the seat of honor. The Gray Watcher will have the seat on my right."

Maeniel felt mild surprise. Vortigen had said he must sit at the foot of the table. He wondered what caused the change of plans.

Merlin showed his teeth again. Maeniel felt right at home. Did humans really think those smiles fooled anyone? Maeniel understood now why he was uneasy. There was enough hatred packed into this chamber to begin a conflagration to burn all Britain.

He was prescient. He just didn't know it. And again he wondered at the willingness of humans to use social lies to cover the fact that they loathed one another. Had he felt the same way about someone, or even some thing, the way most of these humans did, he would have gone fifty miles out of his way to avoid that person or thing. But here they were, all together and contemplating how quickly they could find a way to cut one another's throats. He felt a rather dismal certainty they wouldn't do it here, but aside from that, he knew all bets were off.

One of the mountainous Saxons who arrived with Merlin was seated on the other side of Maeniel. "That is the woman's seat," he said, pointing down to the place on the bench where Maeniel was sitting.

"Indeed," Maeniel said.

"If the queen were here, she would be seated where you are."

"Since she is not, I will keep it warm for her."

"You are not insulted?" the Saxon asked. "Most men would be insulted to be told they are seated in a woman's place. They would be afraid someone might think to treat them like a woman." The Saxon gave a sly smile.

"I'm not interested in being insulted," Maeniel said. "I'm interested in being full. I'm hungry. Insult me after dinner, then I will have time for you."

"Maybe I will insult you after dinner," the Saxon said, "and treat you like a woman, too." He laughed at his own sally and elbowed his other seat mate, another of Merlin's big Saxons.

Maeniel, who wanted no fight at a king's table, looked over at the Saxon, a long, slow, considering sort of look.

"You have eyes like a wolf," the Saxon said. The smile dropped from his face. "I have killed wolves."

"And I," Maeniel said, "have killed men."

He felt the weight of the Saxon's hand on his leg. Maeniel's hand dropped, and a second later the hand that had been on his thigh was twisted up between the Saxon's shoulder blades. The Saxon's other hand was groping for his table knife.

"Put it down," Maeniel said. "I can, and will, break your wrist."

The Saxon was quiet. No one else seemed to be taking any notice. The servants were passing out cups and the women were following with downcast eyes, filling them. Vortigen was looking straight ahead, a small smile on his lips; next to him Merlin was watching Maeniel from the corner of his eye.

"You will respect the king's peace or I will slit your throat with your own table knife," Maeniel said softly.

The Saxon made no answer.

Maeniel brought the man's shoulder almost to the point of dislocation. Perspiration broke out all over the Saxon's face.

"You will do as he says." The voice was Merlin's, speaking from the other side of the king.

"Yes-s-s-s." The word hissed out, like steam escaping from a kettle.

Maeniel released the Saxon's arm. The Saxon let out a low groan of relief.

Vortigen murmured softly, "And left-handed, too."

Maeniel was silent, but something about Merlin's face bothered him. It was almost as if the man—priest, druid, or whatever he was—seemed satisfied, and Maeniel didn't like that. No, he didn't like that at all.

A cup was placed in front of him by Vareen. The girl following him was collared like the rest but either she didn't mind her status or wasn't afraid, because she smelled to Maeniel of the clean, fresh breeze coming from the water and of something less universal, rosemary perhaps. She smiled at Maeniel when she filled his cup, and he knew when he met her eyes that she was something unusual.

Ah, he thought. *I am ever susceptible. Many things I dislike about humans, but their women—never.* She had a smile for him in her eyes. The bishop had warned him about women. He hadn't heeded the warning, but then he never did. *But for them, the fair ones, I had rather been a wolf. The gray people are far less complicated to deal with,* was his thought.

"I don't recognize her," the Saxon muttered. "She wasn't one of the ones I rounded up."

He was speaking to his friend seated beside him. The anger Maeniel felt when the Saxon had touched him without his permission had extended his senses full stretch.

"Damn," the other whispered back. "She might be one of Vareen's people. The old fox is a sly one. I wonder how many he managed to plant among the dinner guests?"

"I don't know," the Saxon said, and shuddered.

"Someone walk over your grave, Crook Nose?" the other warrior said. "Surely the British pig eater didn't twist your arm that hard."

Maeniel realized they were speaking in low voices and in their own language, and he was sure they felt secure. Not only did they think their whispers wouldn't be heard, but even if overheard, they would not be understood. He reached for the wine before him, lifted the cup to his lips, and drank.

Very good, he thought. "From one of the Roman villas in Gaul."

"He shouldn't have been able to do that," Crook Nose said. "He's not that big or strong."

"You see magic everywhere."

"That's because it is. Those drui—"

"Be quiet."

Maeniel felt Crook Nose jump as his companion kicked his ankle.

"Don't even speak of that."

Maeniel took half a cup of wine, then he stopped because he was beginning to feel it; but he noticed no one else did. They all drained their cups with a right good will. The women made the rounds again with the wine. Merlin rose. He was holding a cup in his hand. It was large, bound at the edges with expensive filigree work, and set with rubies. Something about the rubies bothered Maeniel's eyes. They seemed to stand out from the cup in a strange way.

"Let us drink to our king and the hard-won peace we now have all over this island." Merlin stretched out the cup toward Vareen and commanded, "Top this off."

As Vareen came forward, Maeniel saw it before anyone else. It was not a cup Merlin held in his hand but a glowing golden serpent with ruby eyes. Vareen screamed as the serpent lashed out, embedding its fangs in his wrist. At the same moment, Maeniel felt the steel in his own body. He turned. Crook Nose had driven a long knife, the sort the Saxons were named for—a sax—into his belly below his ribs. Maeniel slammed one hand into the Saxon's shoulder and the other into the side of his jaw, twisting the Saxon's body one way and his head the other, snapping his neck.

All over the room screams rang out as men died. As the first Saxon fell away, Maeniel saw another driving a sax into Vortigen's back. Maeniel pulled the sax out of his own side and eviscerated the king's assassin.

The wolf reared and leaped out of his brain's darkness, slamming Maeniel into the change to save his life. A second later, the gray wolf cleared the table and landed on the floor in front of the king's chair. The wolf's mind was a whirl of confusion. He knew no one here other than Vortigen and he was dead. Before Maeniel killed him, the assassin had done his work. This was Merlin's doing. He was sure. The wolf lunged for the druid's throat.

Something like a club slammed into Maeniel's body, sending him reeling. The snake was on him, its coils wrapped twice around his body. The head drew back and two glowing red eyes looked into his. It struck, burying its fangs to the hilt in the wolf's shoulder.

If Maeniel could have screamed, he would have. Instead, he became human. Even Merlin was stunned by the sight. A powerful, naked warrior stood between him and the fire, his skin gleaming with the ripple and play of iron muscles under it.

Vareen's dying brain took in the sight. Vengeance! The gods themselves would demand vengeance for the British druid's actions this day. Merlin had thrown his lot with the Saxons and the chiefs who would sell out their own people and laid vile hands on a high king. He used the last of his energy to reach out and drive a message like a sliver of light into the gray wolf's mind. *Throw it into the fire.*

Vareen lay in the arms of the slave girl who had served Maeniel's wine. She smelled of the sea.

They both heard Merlin scream, "No!" He threw up his arms and crossed them over his face, as Maeniel ripped the golden serpent free, taking a lot of his own flesh and blood with it, and hurled the serpent into the heart of the fire. The fire seemed to explode, sending logs and parts of the serpent flying up toward the roof. It went splintering into shards of glass, coming down like smoke-colored knives on the guilty and innocent alike.

The falling glass sheared away part of Merlin's arm and sliced into his face.

The wizard screamed and fell, as did dozens of his men, some dead, some yet living, in their own blood and guts, dying among their victims.

The girl, cradling Vareen's body in her arms, smiled and made a strange gesture toward Maeniel.

The wind took Maeniel. Feeling as if he were caught in the rapids of a wild river, he hurtled into nothingness as the venom of the magical creature burned out of his body—and then he was in the wind above the clouds, for seconds looking down on a sea surging, moving, foaming by moonlight. He was so high he couldn't tell if he were flying or falling.

He yielded up everything—will, memory, and, finally, at last, consciousness itself—into nothingness.

She was, Maeniel thought, a beautiful thing, to a somewhat battered wolf stretched out in a thick copse of rowan. He had landed here sometime in the night. At least that was his first thought when he awakened among the trees.

Thirst had brought him up from the primal sea of darkness. The events in Vortigen's feasting hall seemed like a dim memory or the shadow of an unhappy dream. Dreaming is a thing men have in common with all other warm-blooded creatures, and even as a wolf, Maeniel had been familiar with nightmares. He staggered to his feet, his shoulder still terribly painful, and went to look for water.

He found it at the foot of the hill, a spring that emptied out of the rock into a stone basin.

He drank. Thirst was a burning torture, but at first he drank too much and his stomach shot it back into a patch of bracken on the stream bank. He lay down for a few moments while raw terror flooded his brain. He remembered the golden snake with its glowing red eyes. Had it killed him? It had killed Vareen. And, indeed, Merlin had been at pains to kill Vareen, believing him more a threat than Vortigen.

Oh, god, suppose he couldn't eat or drink and simply vomited until he died. Died in torment. Thirst was a glowing coal in his mouth. What if he could never assuage it? But he was a solid creature. Most canines are, and he did not easily give way to panic. *Rest now and let your stomach rest.* He did so, and in a little time he drank again, this time exercising more moderation, and the water stayed down.

He lay there for the remainder of the night, alternately sleeping and drinking until he felt stronger. He was awakened by first light stealing across the downlands below. He had heard of Hadrian's great wall; it marched from sea to sea across the neck of Britain. It took Maeniel a few moments to realize he was looking at it—or what remained of it—built across open country. Wall, bank, and ditch, with a mile castle overgrown by weeds and small trees on a hill nearby.

He worried for a few minutes about how he could have gotten so far from Tintigal, almost at the other end of the country. Then he was distracted by a serpent that came to drink. Every hair on Maeniel's body stood up, and he let fly with a savagely menacing growl. The serpent, a normal green-striped individual, was profoundly intimidated and drew back into the grass. But it remained, peering at him through the red stems. He remembered his own overpowering thirst the night before and felt sorry for the creature, so he lay still and made no more threatening noises. At length the serpent, emboldened, returned, slid out of the sedges where it was hiding, lowered its head into the water, and drank.

Maeniel was further disturbed when the serpent turned, faced him, and said, "Be quiet. Wait here."

Fine, Maeniel thought. *Now I'm hearing things.*

No, you are not, the wolf half of his divided nature told him. *Shut up and obey.* He was so injured and so weary that all he *could* do was obey, and he drifted off into a light sleep.

He was aware the moment a doe and her fawn stopped to drink and when one of the wild stallions that roamed the downs showed up accompanied by three mares. But he didn't move and remained near the wild rose thicket where he was resting. He was too weak and weary to go after any of them for food. Especially not the horses, who were in a dither about something. They reeked of fear.

Then she came and was a beautiful sight to his eyes. A young she-wolf, her teats swollen with milk and a load of meat in her belly for her pups. She drank and her eyes met his over the pool. She gave a slight start, then walked around the well to look down on him.

"Mother," he said, "give me some of what you have in your belly. I am in great need."

"I have my young to think of," she replied.

"I will repay you when I regain my strength."

She made her decision. "It is not every day I find a strong stranger lying under a bush. Will you remain with me or return to your kin?"

"My kin are far away and I cannot think I will be able to find them."

"You temporize like . . ." She didn't quite know what to compare him to.

He lifted his head. She was life. "I will remain."

She lowered her muzzle and he licked it. She regurgitated all the meat in her belly for him. He ate and felt the life returning to his body the way longed-for rain soaks into the dry earth. When he stood, he was lean but whole and hungry.

She had sat and watched him gulp the meat down. "Well," she said.

He remembered the four horses that had been so afraid. He was pretty sure he knew why. The wind told him a number of things.

"Bear?" he said to the she-wolf. (Wolf is laconic.)

"Yes." (Translation, yes we have bear here.)

"Come."

She hesitated.

"I will protect you."

"You look as though you might be able to." And she followed.

Not far from the spring the hillside had fallen away, leaving a low bluff. The bear had killed by driving the horses over the bluff.

One had not survived.

The bear fed on the haunch, then left to seek his cave. There was plenty of meat on the carcass. The she-wolf sat, then lifted her muzzle to the sky—a notification song.

She and Maeniel began to feed. He chose the haunch where the bear fed, leaving the shoulder to her. By wolf law, she was entitled to as much as she could consume for herself and her pups.

Her two brothers arrived somewhat later. By then Maeniel was finished. He was full and grooming himself.

They looked at him.

The she-wolf lifted her head and spoke to the two of them. "Don't even think about it. Besides," she continued, "I need a husband. He will do."

The brothers studied Maeniel. He studied them. At best, at the very best, they were yearlings. So was she; in a well-realized, prosperous pack she wouldn't even be thinking of motherhood, but something had happened here.

"Men?" Maeniel asked.

The brothers looked at each other. "Yes."

"I will join you. I can provide some wisdom."

"You know men and can predict their strange ways?" one of the brothers asked.

"Yes. I am very good at it." Maeniel was patient as they sniffed him nose to tail. Afterward, they joined their sister at her meal.

Maeniel sat, and from time to time his tail thumped on the ground. He considered his options. Why not? They needed his help. Wolf love was less satisfying than human but, oh my god, the complications involved in human desire. He had other obligations, but he had no idea how to work his way back to France or if he could do so at all. Even if he could, it would take months or years of dangerous travel across a war-torn land. If last night's events were an indication of how things stood on the island of Britain, there was no help to be found here. In addition to owing the she-wolf a debt of gratitude, he was very tired of humans.

I want a rest, he thought. *I did all I could for the Bagaudae. I have no more to give. I will remain.*

With that, he was decided. He rose when she finished and accompanied her as she left for the den to feed the pups. *It will be nice having a family again. It's been a great many years.* In spite of some soreness and fatigue, he found her company lifted his spirits, and he was greatly cheered.

CHAPTER TWO

OU CANNOT WRITE ANYTHING IMPORTANT down."

I told him—my teacher—I thought that was ridiculous. He only nodded, shook his head, and looked wise. I hate it when they do that. We were lying in the grass and heather on a beautiful, warm spring day watching the gates. They loomed high, cloud shadows, or perhaps clouds themselves, not far from the western horizon. On this day they formed a V, open at the top and joined near the water. Birds floated against the high-topped clouds massed inside the gates, and the sun on its journey to the western horizon shone onto them and formed a rainbow.

The dragons played on the beach and in the shallows at the foot of the cliff where we were lying, and farther out they caught fish for their young, who were crying in the nests below us. They were beautiful, blue below and silver as the sea at dawn above. As we watched, the males contended in tests of strength. They wound their long necks together and then, heads facing each other, each tried to push the other down. This is the way snakes prove their mettle, and so it is with the serpents of the sea.

The females fished, a wonderful sight. They glided through the water like giant swans, large eyes looking down into the sunstruck sea for schools of fish. When they spotted one, the head would drop like a lance tip, followed by the wide-flippered body. If you were lucky and the water was clear, you could follow them in the depths as the fish moved in unison up then down, flashing around rocks and kelp like so many living, shining needles, the shadow terror of the dragon always following, taking her prey until she was gorged. Afterward, they would surface and return to the beach to regurgitate their catch for the tiny ones calling in the nests among the dunes.

"Can you write this down?" my teacher asked. "The way the cool, fresh salt air smells, the colors of the flowers blooming around you?"

"No, I probably couldn't," I was forced to admit. "I could try."

"Yes, and never fully succeed," the old man said, "and the fascination of the attempt might bring you back again and again, battering your mind, heart, and spirit against the impossible. As the poets do. For that *is* what they do. And indeed a life such as that is no bad thing. But I cannot think it is the life for you. No, the movement of the stars, the flight of the birds, the falling of sticks, the shadows in the water when I looked, all predicted a different fate for you.

"Indeed, I felt you cry out to me in your mother's womb, and so I brought you here. No, nothing that is important for you to know can be written down. I can tell you what you need to learn, and I can place you on the pathway to knowledge, but the only real way to learn about war is to fight a battle. And even then you will not know all about it, but the choices of command will be a lot more clear to you and the only way that you learn about love is to love and be loved. And then you may count the cost of knowledge too high.

"So for now I bring you to see the dragons and the gates that they may give you happiness as they do me, and because I'm a lazy old man and I want to see the dragons once more before I die. They don't come to their old nesting grounds now very often, and the gates open only on increasingly rare occasions."

He was speaking to himself as though he were an ancient, but even as a child I knew he wasn't really that old, only incredibly learned. And I was often told that I was lucky to have him for a teacher. Dugald was his name. He took me to watch things often. He showed me mother birds caring for their young in the nest. We walked behind the plow, and the plowman told us how he knew the earth was ready for the deep steel horn, how he could feel with his feet if she were warm enough, dry enough, to be plowed so the soil would turn and not scour, and how when he saw the plowshare cut its first smooth furrow, his heart leaped with joy. We visited the armorer at his forge. I learned to ride even if we had no horse, and I began weapons training before I can remember. These were the chief things I needed to know because, as he told me and it seemed I knew even before I was told, I was born for war, and I would spend my life practicing my trade. I knew this to be true, and it has governed my every waking thought for as long as I can remember. How it all began is my first memory, and though I have been told I should not remember that first day, I do remember, and it is not only the first thing I remember but the most important memory I have or ever will have.

He was coming home, his belly stuffed with food for the pups, when he heard the alarm yip. It was high and sharp, really out of the range of human hearing. It brought him up short. He had not been paying as much attention to his surroundings as was his wont, and momentary confusion was the result. Wolves cannot say "what!" All the yip said was *trouble— watch out*. His belly was loaded with several pounds of meat, and he thought a few human curse words because he was groggy and slow. But he moved into a thick growth of bracken and the remnants of a fallen pine; had a human been watching, he would seem to have disappeared. None of the fronds moved more than a few millimeters as he went belly down among them.

The den was set just below a hilltop. He and his mate had chosen the spot because the ground was so broken that even the shepherds avoided it, but as far as a wolf was concerned it was a high road. He circled the den coming up on the hilltop. He looked down and saw the child.

She was not a newborn but a toddler, and began to squall and stretch out her arms to the retreating backs of three adults. However, once they were out of sight, she fell silent.

Good practical intelligence, the wolf thought. *Why screech when there is no one to comfort you?*

As he watched, she turned and crawled toward the den. The warning yip he'd heard had come from inside, where his mate and the pups had taken cover. One of the pups, probably the oddly marked one with the dark leg, had ventured toward the entrance. The baby stuck her head inside and their noses touched.

Both reacted with shock. The child drew back quickly, and he heard a scrabbling sound as the pup crawfished down into the earth, returning to its mother. Then the baby sat quietly—after the manner of good children—playing in the pebbles at the den mouth. She was not a fat child, but one of the lean, rangy ones who learn to crawl early and walk even before they begin babbling because they are not carrying so much weight as their plumper confreres. They behave as though they were in a hurry to reach independence.

She was not particularly pretty.

As he watched, his mate stuck her head out. He loped easily down the hill to join her.

"Why is it here?" he asked in laconic wolf speech.

"Possibly they do not care about it," she answered.

He gave her a look that expressed skepticism. Wolves are not birds. They do not see the need to chatter a lot. He ducked into the den to leave his belly load of food for the pups. Then he came out again.

"I will see if they are truly gone," he said. "Don't harm it."

The she-wolf gave him a razor-edged glance of contempt as if to say what am I, a fool that you must instruct me in the obvious? He trotted away, ears down, to track the people who brought the child.

Three of them, two men and a woman, had come directly to the den, climbing up the mountain and then, after leaving the child, gone directly back down. Probably guided by the woman. He knew her: Idonia.

He returned to the den. The she-wolf was suckling the three puppies and the human child. He looked long.

"I have plenty," she said, and put her head down and began to doze in the sun.

After their meal the puppies and the child began to roughhouse. Two other wolves belonging to the pack arrived, and but for a few raised wolf-ish eyebrows no comment was made. By then the sun was low in the sky and beginning to set. The wolf puppies were weary and began to yawn, as did the child. She turned to the she-wolf but was nosed firmly away. Then she crawled hopefully toward the pack leader and found better hospitality.

She began to explore, and a few times he was forced to do what parent wolves sometimes do—place a heavy paw on the toddler to keep her fingers out of his eyes, nose, and ears. But after a time she got two handfuls of fur in her grip, crawled partway up his back, and fell asleep, her head pillowed on his side. The pack leader rested his head on his forepaws and dozed.

The puppies were similarly placed on the female. At dusk, when the wind began to turn cold, she shook off her children, threw an ironic glance at the male and his sleeping charge, and herded her three sons into the den. The pack leader looked annoyed. He laid back his ears, then flipped them forward. Since he was not entirely a wolf, he did not leave his charge alone. One of his brethren might mistake her for supper, a fatal mistake and not just for the child. Whatever powers the priests of these highland peoples were invoking, they would not ignore the child's death at the teeth and jaws of his pack, however much they would seem to have invited it.

The she-wolf came out of the den and gave him another ironic glance—she was a sarcastic bitch—and joined the other two males. It was time to hunt. But she paused for a moment before the entrance to the den, head down, waiting. One of his sons was growing very insubordinate. Sure enough, when a short interval of time passed, the puppy's nose appeared at the entrance to the den. Surprise, dismay, and apprehension chased each other across the baby wolf's face. His mother didn't do anything. She stood there, head down, meeting his eyes; but it was enough. The puppy crept back into the den with a soft whimper of apology, and the three grown wolves started out on the night's hunt.

The big gray continued to sit in the gathering dusk, the child asleep against his body, until he heard the distant sounds of humans making their way through low trees and scrub covering the mountainside. Then, easing away from the child so slowly and carefully that she did not awaken, he merged with the cover of the pale mauve-flowered bushes that carpeted the rocks at the hilltop. A few minutes later the humans arrived, carrying torches, and stood looking down at the sleeping child.

Two men and one woman had emerged from the forest into the clearing in front of the den. One of the men was middle-aged with dark hair and beard sprinkled with gray. The other was magnificent: young, blond, lean, and powerfully muscled with narrow hips and waist, broad shoulders, and the pale, fair skin of the northern peoples. The woman, Idonia herself, was old, but the wolf knew she was not as old as she looked. Her face was deeply lined, her eyes sunken and deeply hooded. Her body was lean and spare, her skin leathery and weather-beaten. She wore an underdress of deep blue and an overtunic decorated in complex patterns of flame and gold, a rainbow of reds at the bottom fading into deep blue at the top.

The dark-haired man went to one knee and picked up the child. She didn't awaken.

"I cannot believe it," said the blond man. "She has taken no hurt."

"Hush," Idonia said. She extended one brown finger and touched the child's lips. "Milk," she said. "She was suckled at a wolf's teat."

The woman raised her arms toward the sky in what seemed a ritual gesture, and the wolf saw she held a long blackthorn staff in her right hand.

"She is chosen," the woman said.

"You are all mad," said the blond man. "So the wolves didn't harm her. What does that prove? Those stories are all nonsense."

"So you say," the dark man said. He didn't seem inclined to dispute the matter.

"Hush," the blond man said softly. "Don't move, either of you. I'm going to see if I can get a shot at him. He's watching us right now." He had a crossbow, a small one, hanging from a loop on his belt.

The wolf knew he'd been seen. The blond man was looking into his eyes. The wolf flattened his body lower against the heather and cursed himself for a fool. His eyes had flashed in the torchlight and alerted the man. He was young and looked fast. In a second his hand was on the bow. The wolf knew he had miscalculated. He'd believed the man would raise the bow to fire, giving him a second or two to leap right or left, giving him a fifty-fifty chance to escape the bolt, but the bastard was going to shoot from the hip.

But just as he touched the weapon, the bolt, without any pressure on the trigger, discharged into the ground. The wolf went straight up and came down in a small grove of poplars just below the hilltop. The blond man swore.

"I lost him. My hand must have slipped. Never mind." He reached down to free the bolt embedded in the soil at his feet.

"Do not reload," Idonia said.

The blond man looked mightily offended. "Are you presuming to tell me what to do?" The blond man looked dangerous.

"I believe you are a guest of my people," Idonia said. "Does a guest offend his host?"

"No," the dark-haired man said. "He doesn't. Not if he's smart." His eyes met the blond man's.

"That was a wolf."

"That was a wolf," the dark-haired man repeated.

"That was the Gray Watcher," Idonia said. She reached down, picked up the crossbow bolt, and tossed it out into the darkness.

The blond man looked annoyed. "What?" he asked. "You give the pests who steal your sheep names?"

"These wolves never take sheep or children, either," Idonia said. "Let us return. It's getting cold."

The child stirred in the dark man's arms. He wrapped her in his mantle very tenderly.

From his spot among the trees the wolf watched them walk away. He didn't think for one moment that the blond man's hand had slipped. Too many strange things happened around Idonia for him to believe that. The gray wolf's tail waved back and forth and then back, a sign of agitation. He returned to the den and checked the pups. They were all asleep, even the adventurous one. His mate and her brothers were perfectly capable of keeping them fed. The wolf moved downhill toward the Hall of the Hawk.

He moved at the wolf's smooth gait, recalling that he'd left his weapons and clothes in a hollow tree. He hadn't used them in years. He'd hoped he wouldn't need them again, but he let fly with a few human curses—purely in the mind, as a wolf couldn't speak in that way—a waste of energy really. He lowered his head and kept going.

Idonia saw him sitting in the hall at a low table near the door. He had a truculent expression on his face and a cup of beer before him. She knew him at once, though she'd seen him only a few times, and many years ago. She had just returned with her two companions and the child . . . she realized he'd beaten them back. Idonia asked her steward who he was, wanting to know what the man was calling himself.

"He says his name is Maeniel, and he is a vagabond by his clothes and a hero by his weapons. He smells of damp mold, and I cannot but wonder if he has risen from a grave somewhere to visit you."

"Thank you, Crerar," Idonia said. Then in an unheard-of gesture of recognition, she walked over to Maeniel and saluted him. "Maeniel," she said. "I always called you the Gray Watcher."

He rose and bowed politely, then asked, "What are you playing at, my lady, to place a child in such a dangerous position? Well you know I would not harm it, but I cannot speak for others of my family."

"When they wanted to bring the child to the wolves, I thought of you immediately."

"I would thank you, but I cannot think why I should," Maeniel answered.

Idonia chuckled. "Join me at the high table. Your rank demands it. Besides, you must meet Dugald and Titus. Dugald is the dark one. He has charge of bearing the child."

"And Titus?" Maeniel asked.

"A Romanized Saxon." Idonia's lips curled. "Dugald is convinced he can still treat with the barbarians despite their treachery."

"Thank you for defeating his crossbow," Maeniel said.

" 'Twas neatly done, wasn't it?" she said sweetly.

The big hall was dark. The fire in the pit at the center was an incandescence shining through a thin covering of light ash. Outside, the wind began to rise and in the distance they could both hear the sea. The tide was going out; it roared and muttered in the distance. The wind from the coast battered the building with hammer blows.

"A storm?" Maeniel asked.

"Yes," Idonia said. "I have called one each night since—" she spat on the stone floor "—that blond Saxon snake came. I would rather dine with wolves," she sneered. "Wolves may claim their share of the prey, but you need not watch your back among them."

"You did dine with us, more than once," Maeniel said.

"Yes, and feared no treachery. Crerer—seat my friend at my side at the high table," she called out to the steward. "Come see the baby."

He tossed back the beer and followed.

When they returned, the hall was lit for supper. Torches shone on every wall. The big table had been set up to form a horseshoe around the fire pit. The wall hangings that told the history of the hawk clan glowed on the walls of the round room, their colors blazing in the shadows. The woodwork sang with freshly painted images, strange beasts and plants coiled together with Celtic knot work, all enameled in red, green, gold, blue, orange, lavender, violet, and other colors the wolf couldn't put a name to. Behind the high seat at the closed end of the horseshoe, the hawk screamed, wings outspread, head lifted, beak open.

Idonia, Dugald, and Titus the Saxon sat together under the protection of the hawk's wings. The rest of the clan sat at the lower table to take their main meal of the day.

"I can provide for all of my people one meat meal daily," Idonia told Maeniel with some pride. "This year and the last were very good."

One of the girls serving beer and mead gave a squeak and stepped quickly away from the table. Idonia fixed Titus with a cold eye.

The young blond man laughed. "She's a beauty," he said.

The girl blushed. Idonia reached over and took the girl's hand. The girl put her head down near Idonia's face. The old woman whispered something and the girl nodded and departed.

"A bit of advice for you, if you care to take it," Dugald said to the Saxon.

"What?"

"The ladies of this house are all girls of good family. They come here to make proper matches."

"That girl's father's eyes are probably on you right now," Idonia said. "He is seated among my people, so unless your immediate plans include marriage, I'd strongly advise you to keep your hands to yourself."

The Saxon's face went red with anger. "She should be honored," he muttered.

"Possibly," Maeniel said, "but perhaps not. And even if she is, her menfolk might not share her sentiments. Pay attention to Idonia. She's trying her best to avoid trouble."

The Saxon smiled and said in Latin, "The pretensions of these savages. Everyone knows they have no morals. Even Caesar said they hold their women in common."

Maeniel answered him in even better Latin. His dialect was much purer than the one the Saxon had been taught. "What? Do you fancy yourself a Roman? In their time the Romans I knew would have consigned you to the arena, where you would have been required to die bravely for their entertainment."

The Saxon went white, and his hand dropped to his sword hilt.

"And, as for Caesar, he was wrong. True, the customs of this wild people are not yours or those of the Romans, but in their own way they respect and greatly honor their women—especially young girls like that one."

The Saxon's hand tightened on his sword hilt.

"Don't," Maeniel said. "I'll take that sword away from you and make you eat it." Then he smiled at the Saxon, a smile that showed all his teeth.

Idonia was sitting between the Saxon and Maeniel. Maeniel knew she didn't understand what he was saying, but she caught the undercurrent of hostility and sensed the Saxon was being told off. The expression on her face was one of grim satisfaction.

Dugald's face was averted, so Maeniel believed he must be grinning. Just then the food arrived and everyone was preoccupied with getting their favorite. Maeniel was solemnly served the champion's portion by the pretty young girl the Saxon had been pawing. Dugald looked amazed, the Saxon simply annoyed. Idonia looked smug. It was pork, a whole shoulder of wild boar cooked with quince, honey, and carrots. A buzz of talk broke out among the people seated at the big table. Maeniel rose. He bowed first to the assembled company, then to Idonia, then to the girl, who curtseyed in return. He sat down, carved a portion of the meat for himself, then resigned it to the rest.

Idonia took a piece for herself. Dugald did the same. The Saxon refused.

Maeniel was pleased. He smiled at the girl. She curtseyed again. As she passed him, her fingers fell on his wrist, slid slowly up his arm to his shoulder. Then she walked away to take her seat at the table among her kin.

His eyes followed her admiringly as she passed behind him. She was beautiful, with dark brown hair like old oak and very pale, fair, almost milky skin. "Mmmmmm," he said.

Idonia laughed, then whispered, "She's yours for the night. I made the necessary presents to her family, but you will be expected to be generous in the morning."

It was Maeniel's turn to blush.

The wild boar vanished quickly, but there was venison, woodcock, fish, three kinds of soup, roast mutton, oatcakes, and barley bread.

Maeniel, who liked pork but would now only eat it cooked, particularly enjoyed the roast and occupied himself with trying to figure out how to be generous in the morning. He certainly wasn't going to turn down Idonia's hospitality. The brooch holding his mantle at the shoulder was all the jewelry he had with him. It was cloisonné gold set with ruby, garnet, and amber, big around as the palm of a large man's hand, and easily the price of enough land to feed a family—a hundred acres or so. Yes, that would do.

The crowd in the hall occupied themselves with the serious business of eating as much as possible, but after a short time he noticed the Saxon studying him covertly, and he was not the only one. Everyone in the room looked at him from time to time. Idonia had seated him in a place of honor at her side, given him the champion's portion, and shown him many marks of favor. If he was any judge, at least half the people gathered at the table knew he would have exquisite company in his bed tonight. But Idonia hadn't introduced him or even told anyone his name. Everyone, even the nasty-tempered Saxon, must be dying of curiosity.

At length even the oldest and slowest pronounced themselves satisfied. Drink was now distributed by the same girls who had served at the beginning of the meal. The dark-haired girl came to Maeniel's seat carrying a silver pitcher filled with mead. She poured some into his cup and smiled at him, then brushed his cheek lightly with her fingers in a possessive gesture.

He returned her smile and offered her the cup. She drank and returned it to him. He kissed the spot her lips touched, then drank. She tossed her head, throwing back her long dark hair, then stepped down from the dais and went back to sit among her kin.

Maeniel sighed deeply.

The Saxon threw him a poisonous glance.

Dugald averted his face again, too well-mannered to laugh openly.

Idonia rose. It was time for business. If there was a serious dispute among her people, a large transaction, an important marriage pending, or even the birth of any child, it was at this time that the matter would be brought before her. It might not be settled here and now, a full assembly might be required, but it would be brought up now and she would be made acquainted with the situation.

She began walking along the outer edge of the big table, greeting all her people one by one from the eldest graybeard to the youngest child.

Maeniel sat back in his chair and watched her, wondering how many years had passed since they'd first met. She had once been a young beautiful girl. He had never bothered to count the years, but she was old now—yet the shadow of what she had once been remained. He knew he had outlived most, if not all, humans and all wolves. It was a source of some disquiet to him, especially when he met someone he had known as a child who had become an elder, bent and withered with age. He felt his years acutely.

The elderly seem often to come in only two sizes, scrawny and lumpish. Idonia was one of the scrawny ones—long, lean, and leathery. Her face was cadaverous, eyes sunken, but her mouth was still mobile and happy. She had most of her teeth.

She made a circuit of the room while everyone drank, then came back to stand before the high bench. She lifted both arms and stood silhouetted against the blazing central hearth fire. "Let us drink to our guests and a fine meal."

Idonia had finished speaking and those around the table hammered the wood with their cups, plates, and fists. Only the wolf heard the *quark!* from among the rafters.

Maeniel leaped to his feet. His sword was out of its sheath before he thought to pull it. He was going to kill the Saxon first, but then held back for a second.

His eyes met Dugald's. He was staring open-mouthed at Maeniel, as was Idonia.

"Didn't you hear it?" he shouted into the sudden silence.

Then the raven flew, circling the hall just above the heads of the people seated at the tables. Ravens are big birds. The shadow it cast touched everyone.

"To the walls," shrieked Idonia. "We're being attacked."

The Saxon leaped to his feet. "I swear—" he began.

"You treacherous bastard," Maeniel said, but he was loath to use the sword in his hand and breach Idonia's hospitality.

Dugald killed the Saxon.

Maeniel never knew how. He only saw the man drop like a fallen rag to the floor at his feet.

"Thank you for distracting him," Dugald said quietly. He was wiping his knife on his sleeve.

War was constant; weapons were never far from anyone's hand, man or woman. Everyone rushed from the hall's four doors into the yard. The attackers were coming over the palisade that surrounded the hall.

Idonia had a moment to spare for Maeniel and Dugald. "Get the child," she said. "She is more important than our lives. She is more important than anything."

Maeniel and Dugald prepared to charge the attackers, but Idonia lifted her hand and shouted, "Wait!"

"Wait!" Dugald screamed. "Wait for what? In a moment they will have us."

"Wait," Idonia commanded, her voice a whip crack.

The attackers covered the wooden palisade, swarming the way a wolf pack does when the pursued deer finally loses its footing and goes down.

Idonia turned and lifted both arms, and the wall burst into flames. The attackers jumped away, some of them on fire. Idonia's people charged, carrying anything they could grab up in a hurry. One man dashed past Maeniel holding a spit with a bird on it. The whole palisade was aflame, a ring of fire around the Hall of the Hawk. Idonia's people slaughtered the few attackers able to get past, but from beyond the walls arrows began to fall like a deadly rain. The defenders took cover as well as they could.

"Help me," Idonia screamed, and ran to a patch of turf in front of the hall's main door. She began to roll the turf back like a thick carpet. Maeniel and the other men helped, and a second later he saw a grating set flush with the ground. Even before they got the turf clear, he could feel cold sea air rushing past him with the force of a gale, drawn by the heat of the blazing palisade.

The flames gulped up the air rushing past them and leaped skyward with renewed force. The arrows, like flocks of birds caught in a firestorm, caught fire, tumbling harmlessly to earth. All but the dead ran from the heat of the burning wall.

"Hurry," Idonia shouted. "There is no time to waste."

She was still moving fast, followed by Maeniel, Dugald, and the rest. She uncovered three more tunnel entrances, one at each compass point. When they were all open, the fire began spreading to the bank and ditch below, so that the timbers bracing the earth at the palisade posts were burning.

"Are you mad, woman?" Dugald shouted. "You will kill us all. We will be roasted alive here."

The fire burned white hot. Nothing could get past it. The arrows shot by the attackers outside simply vanished, whiffing away into flame as they reached the superheated air above the posts.

"I've always said the worst old women are men," Idonia said. "Fool, look at the roof of the hawk's nest."

Dugald looked. It wasn't the conventional thatch but turf that in the cool, wet climate of northern Britain would grow as well on a house top as on the ground. The low walls had wood in them but were reinforced by stone. The women in a disciplined fashion were already cooling the posts with buckets of water from the well.

"Everyone knows what to do," Idonia shouted. "And, Dugald, if you are worried about becoming overheated"—she pointed to one of the tunnels—"go stand in the breeze."

The raven who'd given the warning appeared just above their heads, swooped down, and landed on the grass near Maeniel. It let fly with a long series of hisses.

"He sounds like a bag of snakes," Dugald said. "Is it a real bird?"

"Only too real," Maeniel said, giving the raven a dark look. "And *I told you so* doesn't sound any more pleasant coming from a bird than it does coming from a human."

"How did they get here?" Dugald asked.

"Ships," Maeniel answered, listening intently to the raven.

"What kind of ships? Where did they come from?" Dugald asked rapidly.

"It's a *bird*," Maeniel pointed out.

The raven made a raucous sound, almost like a laugh, then made a wing-assisted jump to Maeniel's shoulder. She pecked with her beak on Maeniel's shirt, then made some more sounds. Maeniel translated.

"She and her friends found a stranded skate about a mile down the beach. They were enjoying their dinner, the deceased fish, when the men landed, carried in by shallow-draft vessels at low tide. More of them than the feathers on her tail and both wings. That's still not a lot," he said to Idonia.

Men were returning from the hall more conventionally armed now— mail shirts, boiled-leather armor, swords, spears, shields. One by one, they were climbing down into the tunnels.

"They lead to sea caves nearby," Idonia explained. "I imagine our un-invited dinner guests are waiting for the flames to die down so they can rush us. Won't they be surprised when they find a gang of angry men be-hind them?"

Maeniel ran out, as close to the flaming ramparts as he could, got one of the corpses by the leg, and dragged it into the shelter of the hall. It was only just recognizably human, but the equipment was familiar.

"The legions are gone," Dugald said, "but the memory lingers."

"Roman," Idonia grunted.

"Auxiliaries," Maeniel said. "Saxons?"

Dugald shrugged. "Saxon, Frank, Vandal—who knows? They come to serve the landowners, who have a taste for life as it was under the empire, and to snatch up anything they can get."

The raven swooped down from Maeniel's shoulder and began to investigate the corpse's arm.

"Seems he has a taste for roast meat," Idonia said and laughed.

"Actually, it's a *her*," Maeniel said, and made a sharp sound in his own throat at the raven. She turned her back to him, flipped her tail feathers into a fan, and bent over.

"That looks like—" Dugald began.

"It is," Maeniel told him.

"Then leave her alone," Dugald said. "This roast pig was no more than a scavenger himself come to try to pick the bones of my beloved Albion. Let him serve the same purpose now. At least he's useful. You can't say the same for most of them, not while they're alive."

The hatred in his voice sent a chill down Maeniel's spine.

"They aren't important," Idonia said as a steady file of well-armed men descended into the tunnel. "I'll wager most of them will be dead before dawn, but, Dugald, you must flee with the child. Whoever sent those men will send more. We are too few to ensure her safety, and she is important. I feel it. No, that is a weak word, *feel*. I *know* it. She must be protected. Flee to the north beyond the great glen where no Roman foot has ever trod."

"But, Idonia, I wanted her to be civilized, to know Roman ways even if she never decides to adopt them. Idonia, whatever we may think of them, they did wondrous things. Things that will never be forgotten, much less surpassed. Their books, poetry, music, magnificent sculpture—houses with marble and cedar, mosaic floors—smooth-surfaced roads a carriage just flies along. She needs to know, to understand, these things.

She must be taught Greek so that she might dip into the great learning of that people and—"

"Be as blinded by the folly as those fools who sent these murderers here to butcher my people and end her life before it has a chance to begin?" Idonia shouted. "Have you forgotten what they did to your order? The destruction of the sanctuary at Mona?"

"They were pagans," Dugald said piously. "Until we received Patrick's word, we were all—"

"You weary me," Maeniel said. "We could have been killed and the child lost, but immediately when there is a lull in the battle, you fall into a dispute with each other—a great weakness among your people. Tell me, when they flee—and they will in the end—where will they go?"

"Back to their ships, I suppose," Idonia said.

"Yes," Maeniel said. "And when they do, I will be waiting for them."

The raven was feeding ravenously. Maeniel kicked the corpse. "Come on," he said. "You will have all you want."

She flew up with a cry of outrage, cursing Maeniel in tolerable Third Raven.

"Why don't you learn Second Raven?" Maeniel said.

"I'm not from there," she said.

CHAPTER THREE

HE NEXT DAY THE WOLF MET DUGALD TRAVEL-
ing through the wilderness alone. He held the child in
his arms. Maeniel stopped, sat down in the middle of
the trail with his tail curled around him.

Dugald paused, considering him, and then walked over to a flat
lichen-covered rock nearby. He sat down. The child was asleep against
his shoulder. He eased away part of his mantle, spread it on the stained
stone, and placed the child tenderly on the fold of cloth. She did not
awaken but continued to sleep quietly, thumb in her mouth.

The sky was almost clear. The breeze was gentle. Far away, below a
nearby cliff, both Dugald and the wolf could hear the sounds of the sea.
He and Dugald could tell the tide was coming in simply from the sound it
made when the waves struck the shingle and rocky outcrops on the shore,
and they would both be able to tell when it was at its height and when it
began at last to ebb.

The wolf placed his forepaws on the rock, raised his head, and sniffed
the child. Healthy, and though she was dressed as a boy with her hair cut
raggedly short, she was female. The wolf could tell from the information
his nose conveyed that one day she would be formidably female, a crea-

ture to be reckoned with. There were no telltale signs that would tell him she was somehow wrong, that there was hidden weakness that would carry her away before she attained her growth or stunt and cripple her before she could reach her full potential. No, this creature, given decent food, access to clothing and shelter, would be as vital at eighty as she was now. He knew these things, knew it in the same way he knew, when he tested a group of deer for weakness, which ones were vulnerable and just how vulnerable they were.

He dropped back to the ground, loped away, and vanished into the patches of sweet heather, long grass, and scrub oak clothing the cliff. Dugald remained where he was, sitting beside the sleeping child.

A few moments later, a man strode out of the brush, sat down beside Dugald, and began to do up his leggings. He wasn't wearing a sword.

"Idonia and I quarreled," Dugald said. "A serious quarrel—she threw me out."

"Yes," Maeniel said. "I know."

"That's interesting," Dugald said. "How do you know?"

Maeniel gave him a long, slow look, a wolf look. "My nose tells me—among other things."

"Yes, of course. You can scent anger. Even dogs can do that."

"Don't flaunt your ignorance or try to insult me. I don't suffer fools gladly and insults irritate me."

Dugald colored. "I'm sorry. You took my remark amiss. I apologize."

"You aren't sorry and don't apologize. Do you know what I find most annoying about your order?"

"What?" Dugald snapped.

"Your presumption of superior knowledge. The idea you have firmly lodged in your skulls that the rest of mankind are a mass of beasts only waiting with openmouthed awe for your superior knowledge to direct their lives. In that, you are like those Romans you so much admire. You both walk in an absolute certainty of your right to rule, to enslave, to exploit all those others you see as beneath you."

Dugald's cheeks burned. He felt fury rising in his heart. He reached down to snatch up the child and leave.

"No," Maeniel said, catching his forearm in an iron grip. "You will remain here and so will I—and we will discuss your plans for this child between ourselves—because I have known Idonia for a long time and she says this child is important and I believe her. You called me by placing the child at my den, by threatening my wolf sons. Well, I am here and won't and don't care to leave quietly, druid. I thought here in this wild sanctuary I had escaped the troubles of the world, but I can see, and in fact saw when I met Idonia, that I hadn't. So, I am moved to become part again of the human struggle. It would seem since I conceived an affection for Idonia and her husband, Malcolm, I must."

Then he released Dugald's arm.

Dugald made the sign of the cross and let out a ragged sigh of relief. "It seems it doesn't do to underestimate you."

"The converse is also true," Maeniel said. "Please, put up that nasty little knife in your left hand. I assume it's the one you killed the Saxon with."

Dugald looked down at his hand. "Oh, sorry. I wasn't aware I was still holding it." The knife vanished somewhere into his clothing. "I'd prefer you didn't use that name."

"What?"

" 'Druid,' and don't play at pretense with me. We don't call ourselves that any longer. Not since Patrick came to Ireland bearing Christ's message."

"Yes. Now you're just Christian monks." Maeniel grinned.

"Yes."

"Very powerful Christian monks, but holy men all the same."

"Yes. One bearing the word of God is very powerful indeed."

"You stole the child."

Dugald's eyes darted in every direction, but he would not meet Maeniel's gaze.

"You stole the child and have fallen out with your master, Merlin. It is he who hunts you."

"Yes and no and yes and yes."

"And that adds up to . . . ?"

"Merlin took the boy. He will be king. But the girl's mother sent for me. She is of Bodiccia's line, the great warrior queen of the Iceni. She will not abide the Roman way. Until not so many years ago, she rode armed and led her men in battle. But the girl was an unexpected child of her middle age, and she would not yield her up to Merlin to be brought up to be a proper wife to the son of Uther Pendragon.

"Because this is what Merlin wants. It is his wish and that of the faction of priests he leads to unite the great British lords and the Saxon warriors that dominate their defenses against the Picts, Irish, and the tribes beyond the wall and across the water. Turn their faces away from the old ways and toward Rome. He says it has worked with the barbarians on the continent and will work here. I disagreed."

"And why would you not face him down openly?" Maeniel asked.

Dugald laughed. The child lying next to him stirred. Above their heads the high overcast was growing thicker, hazing the sun's eye. The wind was chilly.

"The stone is cold," Dugald said.

The baby was lying on most of Dugald's mantle. Maeniel contributed some of his own to cover her.

"When Patrick of beloved memory came to Ireland to bring us the word of Christ, Patrick's opponent, the king of Connacht, died. He fell, so the story goes, from a high place. There are wheels within wheels, rules about the formation of rules, and laws about other laws," Dugald said.

"And?"

"You have accused me of arrogance," Dugald said. "Well, I am. We are. But there are reasons. For our order to function at all, there must be unanimity among us on certain important matters. The loser in such a debate must perish and take his faction with him."

"Patrick won, Christ and the word of Christ was accepted, the loser was thrown from a high place?" the wolf asked.

Dugald turned his face away from the wolf into the wind. High up, a hawk cried out to its mate, a fierce rasp telling him she was in the hunt.

"Not thrown," he replied. "Oh no, not thrown. No one would lay hands on such a man. The blood guilt would drown the assassin. But the loser knows what to do—what will and must become of him."

"How do you know?" Maeniel asked. "You can't have been there."

Dugald looked bleak. "Was I not? Was I not indeed?"

Maeniel felt his skin crawl slightly. He knew these men undertook studies that involved a return to former lives. He wondered if he was in the presence of such a man. "I see."

"No," Dugald replied. "No, you can't. Not until you have made such a journey. But to continue, I found myself in this position vis-à-vis Merlin."

"I imagine the person in such a situation might find himself very lonely, since the loser must take those of his opinion with him. Not many would wish to share it."

"Not any." Dugald nodded.

"So, you find yourself here, alone with a stolen child, pursued not only by Saxons but also by the powerful head of your order."

"You've a nice turn of phrase, my friend. Yes, he sees her as the mother of misfortune, disaster waiting to happen, her birth from Bodiccia's line. She is most royal but, like the tragic queen's line, most unlucky, most doomed. So, if I perish, she will die with me. I cannot turn back now because her mother was the first sacrifice that she might live. A great lady, who died trusting me."

"I will offer you what help I can," the wolf said. "Come with me. Stay at our home. My gray lady has milk to spare."

He never knew what Dugald might have answered because at that moment the warriors appeared all around them. The leader, a grinning blond youngster, was holding the point of a sword to Maeniel's throat.

"A fair child," the youth said. "And which of you is her mother?"

Maeniel smiled. "That would be me."

The young man grinned back. "Surprising that you would own yourself not a man." He drew the sword back slightly, and Maeniel could read the thrust in his eyes. The young warrior moved forward. The sword should have entered Maeniel's throat, but he wasn't there. A second later, Maeniel came up, the youngster's long, blond hair in his fist and his opponent's sword in his hand, holding it to his throat.

Dugald had snatched up the child and was watching with anxious eyes.

"Back off, the lot of you," Maeniel said, "or I will hand you your leader's head."

"Fools," the blond man said. "You have your orders. Kill him."

Maeniel jerked his head back and the sword in his hand bit into the man's neck. Blood ran down his opponent's throat and stained his white shirt red. "Stay where you are," Maeniel said.

A darker young man with a strong family resemblance to the man Maeniel was threatening shouted, "Dugald, you refused the jump so we are here to see you ride the wind. Call off your hound."

"Hound, indeed," Dugald yelled. "He is the hound of Cullain and was as my hound is—a great hero."

Maeniel smacked his captive on the side of the head with his own sword. His captive's eyes rolled back in his head, and Maeniel released his hair and let the war leader fall at his feet.

The dark-haired man charged him without hesitation. Maeniel didn't parry his sword strike. A really fast man doesn't have to; he simply wasn't there when the stroke landed and sparks flew from the rock as the sword's edge cried out against it.

Dugald reached out and, it seemed, caught the spark in his hand. He gestured at the dark-haired man, who was wearing a cuirass of scale mail. Suddenly smoke began to rise from his clothing, and Maeniel felt the thermal warmth on his face as the metal began heating. The dark-haired warrior screamed, dropped his sword, and began clutching his body as the heat cut through his padded undercoat and began to sear his skin.

The rest of the war band backed away, staring openmouthed in horror at what was happening to their leader.

Dugald yelled, "Run!" and suited his actions to the word. Maeniel threw down his captured weapon and followed.

So I began my life suckled at a wolf's teat while Dugald and the Gray Watcher fled north into the land of the Picts. His wife—for that is what she was, four legs, gray coat or not—went with us, and also his three sons and her brothers. We were a family. A strange one to be sure, but a family nonetheless.

The first night out I heard Dugald trying to explain magic to the Gray Watcher. We had concealed ourselves in a cave overlooking the sea. The wind screamed and waves lashed the rocks in the darkness beneath. When the tide came in I could taste the salt spray on my lips even high up as we were, for I had crawled toward the mouth of the cave and tried to look out and down.

"Watch her. She's a bold one," he said as he gathered me up and placed me within the curve of the wolf's body.

The wolf laved me with her tongue and I laughed. Then I crawled toward the source of all pleasure, the teat on her warm belly.

"She will need to be bold," Dugald said, "for many will seek her and for a variety of cruel reasons. If the war band catches her, they will give us to the sea, I along with her. And that may be the kindest fate she might meet. Others would rather have her sold to the Saxon raiders to be taken away to the golden horn at Constantinople that she might perish or wear out her life whoring in the streets of that or another Greek city. Others would send her to Rome to be a cloistered nun given to the church, as some are, before she can learn to speak her name and, all unknown, live and die devoted to prayer and good works."

The Gray Watcher snorted. "Very romantic, old man, but convents and monastic orders keep records. If she comes from a great family, as you claim, I think some ambitious bishop would probably make sure she doesn't get lost. Best she be properly prepared for the life she will probably lead. Now, stop evading my questions. I have offered myself and my family to you, and we have entered your service."

"Your family," Dugald choked out. "Six wolves!"

"Just so," the Gray Watcher snapped.

His wife, the she-wolf, gave both Dugald and the Gray Watcher a rather sardonic look. The pups at my side—I was working that teat, it had been an active day—were too young to care that they were being talked about, but the she-wolf's brothers raised their heads. They were lying at the back of the cave far from the fire and gave Dugald disapproving yellow stares.

"Begging your pardon, please." He bowed in their direction. "Yes, I suppose they are your family, and I suppose you have entered my service."

"Fine." The Gray Watcher continued, "Now, first, what did you do back there to the warrior who attacked us and what is this all about?"

"What I did back there was magic."

"Real magic?" The wolf's eyebrows lifted.

"Yes, real magic. One of the few tricks I have left because I am old and my travels and troubles have wearied me. I will tell you something that probably will be new to you."

Maeniel nodded.

"The proverbial magus is always seen as an old man with a long white beard, but this is a lie, no doubt promulgated by some antic practitioner who wished to appear venerable. In truth, magic is a young man's—or for that matter, a woman's—game. The old lack both the erotic drive that powers its chancy operations and the energy to sustain them. There was a time when I could have sent every one of those fools hopping and howling—though even then it would have cost me dear—but that day is long gone. All I succeeded in doing was catching a few sparks from his clumsily wielded sword and turned them against him. And even so, I was burned by my efforts." He extended his hand to Maeniel, who saw several small but obviously deep burns on the old man's hand. "You pay for every trick you pull; the difference is when you're young, you don't notice it as much.

"Now, as for my quarrel with the head of my order." Dugald took a deep breath. "When the great queen failed against the Romans, her kin—all her kin—and people were marked down for extermination. The brutality of the Roman commander's revenge was so terrible that the Romans themselves recalled him lest he ruin the province."

Maeniel nodded.

"But there were survivors," Dugald continued. "There are always, it seems, survivors. They fled to Ireland, assisted by the Veneti, who were guest friends of the royal house. Their mother was legend, and her daughters were able to marry well. They made matches appropriate to their rank." He indicated the child sleeping among the pups at the wolf's belly. "Did you know that once this was not an island? Did you know there were people here before it was an island?"

"What has that to do with anything?" Maeniel asked.

The old man gave a start. "Why?" He looked astounded. "Why, I must have been dozing. Please, pardon me. I'm very tired."

"You just broke off the story of the Iceni to tell me that this island was once not an island and I asked what that had to do with anything."

Dugald smiled a beautiful smile. "Why, everything and nothing. But, please, I'm very weary," he said and yawned. "Let's get some sleep."

The Gray Watcher rose and went to the back of the cave. "Not us," he said. "It's time for the hunt."

A few seconds later there were three wolves where only two had been, and then there were none as they slipped through the crack in the rock that was the entrance to this den. Dugald yawned again and then tried to pull me away from the she-wolf. She bared her fangs silently at him and stared him full in the face.

As for me, I was just as happy to stay where I was. She was warm as a blanket. So Dugald, his face a mask of fatigue, not readily understood by a child, sank down on an improvised bed of dried grass and went to sleep. I snuggled down among those I was already beginning to think of as my brothers and slid into darkness.

But—and this is why I remember that night so well even though I was very young—I woke again deep in the night. It was very late and I am sure the world was preparing for morning. The fire was burned down to a heap of red coals. We had, in the trust and wisdom of sleep, drawn close to-gether for warmth. Dugald, the she-wolf's pups, and I all shared the pile of dried grass. The she-wolf's muzzle lay across Dugald's outthrown arm. The pups and I lay pressed between the bodies of the two adults, wolf and man. A pair lay at my back, but one, the largest, most strongly marked one, lay in my arms, but he was not a wolf at all, but a dark-haired boy who slept, long lashes against his cheek, fist in his mouth, nestled in my embrace.

They never agreed on what to teach me, but I learned a lot anyway just from listening to them argue, because they both knew a lot. In be-tween, I ran wild. Mother—because that's how I thought of her, the Gray Watcher's mate—and my brother, Black Leg we called him because he had one forepaw darker than the others, remained together. The gray brothers went off to found their own packs and find their own hunting grounds. The next spring she had more pups, and eventually they also left. When I think about it now, I must have been a nuisance to Mother, because I was nearly seven before I gave up the comfort of her teat, or rather before she finally pushed me away for good.

Dugald and the Gray Watcher got into one of their usual arguments about it, Dugald thinking it unnatural for me to be so affectionate with a creature like a wolf, and the Gray Watcher telling me I must grow up. I ended by running down to the beach, one where the dragons didn't nest, and crying to myself. But Mother joined me, and my brother, also.

"You have too many teeth," Mother said.

I don't know when I began to be aware she was speaking with me, but by seven I could understand her very well.

"A wolf pup would have been grown and gone by now," she told me, "but because humans are backward, I put up with you, but now no more. Your teeth are a trial to me, and besides, you eat very well of everything that cannot run faster than you." She poked me with her nose and said, "Go, catch me some fish."

They come in at low tide to feed in the shallows. She and Black Leg taught me how to hunt. You stand where the sun will not throw your shadow across the water. They will come in to nibble at your toes. Simply sweep your two fingers down through the water and catch them behind the gills, then toss them up on the beach.

Mother usually took them in the air. Black Leg could fish for himself. He had been doing it since he was a puppy. He was also a scourge of the sea birds, because he liked eggs and could go places a wolf usually couldn't climb to get them.

At first I had thought my experience with him was a dream, but the Gray Watcher could go back and forth, and it seemed he had passed on the trait to his son, though he was loath to use it. But climbing among the rocks, it gave him an advantage, and from time to time on our forays I would see a laughing human face attached to a lithe, sun-bronzed human body slipping into places a wolf could never go. But he didn't seem to want to use his powers except to satisfy his desire for fresh eggs and on the rare occasions when he had something to say that wolf speech wouldn't cover.

So, we all danced and played in the surf, enjoying the sweet largesse of the great untouched world around us, when something dark appeared on the billowing clouds at the horizon. Mother saw it first and paused.

"Something moves," she said. She was staring out to sea at the far horizon.

I looked and saw a sail. It was fully unfurled and filled by the winds. The dark part was the design dyed into it: a raven. I was used to ships—

the smaller, hide-covered craft used by fishermen and other clumsy mer-
chantmen glimpsed in the distance beating southward toward Roman
lands. But this ship moved swiftly, skimming like a bird over the water.
Sail alone could not account for such speed.

I first thought to tell the Gray Watcher but then remembered he and
Dugald were gone hunting. Beyond the headland, to my left, was a village.
The people fished and farmed a small valley nearby, grazing their flocks
among the mountains in the summer and overwintering them with hay cut
from the meadows on the lower slopes. It and a dozen others like it scattered along the coast were the only human presence among these peaks
forming the extreme land's end of Britain looking out across the north sea.

Dugald and Maeniel talked. Oh, how they talked, more than enough
to make up for mine and the wolves' long silences. And what they most
often talked of was how these villages were vulnerable to raids both by
their fellow Picts closer to the wall—the great wall of Hadrian that flowed
across the downs in the south—and by pirates with oared, shallow-draft
vessels. They came for what little gold or silver was taken from the mountain streams by the people, wool—the fabulous long wool of the mountain
sheep combed out by the women every spring and dyed to rainbow colors
in their workshop—and, most deadly of all, for the women themselves.

When he cautioned me to be wary of strangers, the Gray Watcher
told me that there were places where a captive woman skilled in weaving
was a unit of value, where women were compared to so many pounds of
silver or gold.

The raven, sister to the wolf, like the one who accompanied Gray
Watcher, was not a bird of good omen. She was the war bird.

"It has a raven on the sail," I told Mother. "We should flee."

She made the low sound in her throat that passes for agreement
among wolves.

"No," Black Leg said. "War band." Then he grinned, tongue lolling.
"Girls."

Mother laughed also. "They have been telling me they were here for
the last two hours in the wind. The boys in the war band and the girls."

This said it all to me.

The villages along the coast supported the war band. It was made up of young men from all the villages. In the summer they watched for raids along the coast and from the south. In the winter they dispersed back to their homes. They were out now, running wild, and they paused to flirt, or sometimes a lot more than flirt, with the girls of the village. They were not loved by the more prosperous farmers and artisans but rather tolerated. Most of the members were surplus males with little or no prospects. Potential disaster for a family with a marriageable daughter.

But since they lived off the land six months of the year and provided a modicum of protection from raids by land and sea, the village chiefs tried to keep them at arm's length without driving them entirely away. They were kept under control because they needed shelter through the winter, and any of those wild enough to make serious enemies among the settled farmers and fishermen would find himself a hunted outlaw skulking through the coverts without shelter from the cold, with every man's hand against him. The boys were tough enough, but few were so foolish as to risk this fate. Most looked to distinguish themselves in battle and be taken into the household of a man of property or marry a woman who was heir to land and a clever cloth worker, or, best yet, seize a fine bit of plunder and be able to buy their way into the cattle- and sheep-grazing privileges of one of the chiefs' houses. An opportunity to do this was not to be missed, and the ship rapidly approaching might be one.

I could have simply run away and hid, but that never occurred to me. I found them at the edge of the forest. They were scattered among the trees. The two oldest with the best weapons were together with a brace of the village girls. One, I was surprised to note, was the village chief's daughter, Issa. The leader of the war band was tall, blond, muscular, and handsome. I still remember his name: Bain. As usual, they had paired themselves with two plainer people that they might show off their good looks to the best advantage. The other boy, Bain's friend, was dark with thick, coarse hair, arms that seemed almost too long, and a strong, rather squat body. Issa's friend was a very skinny, wiry redhead.

Issa was smiling up at Bain, looking totally entranced by whatever he was saying. When I spoke, it was obvious he didn't want to be interrupted.

"There is a sail," I said.

He spared me a quick glance. "There are always sails," he replied. "Go away." Then he turned his attention back to his adoring Issa.

"Listen to me." I picked up a pebble and shot it past his face. It snapped against the trunk of the cedar he and Issa were leaning against.

He turned angry eyes toward me. "You little scruff, you're lucky you missed. Otherwise, I'd be teaching you a lesson about how to treat a warrior."

"I didn't miss," I said, and sent another pebble sailing in his direction. This one took him square in the middle of the forehead.

He let out a yell and began to draw his sword, but his long-armed friend clapped a hand on his wrist and kept it in its sheath. "Are you mad, Bain? That's a child."

"He's no one of note," Issa said. "He belongs to the madman and his servant. They live near the shore."

They thought me a boy. Most people in the village did, because Dugald and the Gray Watcher dressed me that way and kept my hair cropped.

"Will you listen?" I asked. Somehow I knew the time was short. "That's all I want you to do. Listen."

"Very well," Bain's friend said. "Bain, we don't need trouble with these people. Keep your sword in its sheath."

"You needn't worry about them," Issa said haughtily. "It's likely as not they are runaway slaves."

"Slaves," I said, outraged. "I'll give you slaves," and began reaching for another pebble.

"You stop that now," Bain's friend said. He got between me and Bain and strode toward me. He was fast. I saw that at once. I barely evaded his grip and made a quick dash toward the hilltop. He slowed when he saw Mother and Black Leg appear from the brush, one on either side of me. I noticed the thin redhead had followed him.

"Ahh," she said. "The child has friends."

Mother was showing her teeth in a most unpleasant snarl.

"To be sure, Anna," the dark one answered. "Large, unpleasant friends. Very well. Show me this sail."

We were only a few steps from the bald knob of rock that formed the hilltop.

"Look!" I said, pointing out to sea.

The sail was a lot closer. The ship could be seen clearly now, oars lifting in and out of the water.

The dark one could see it just as well as I could from where he was standing. His skin turned pale under his swarthy complexion. "Mother of Christ, pirates!"

"Yes," I crowed triumphantly. I saw the skinny redhead had gone as white as he with fear.

"Gray, Gray," she whispered, "are you sure?"

Bain and Issa had come up behind them.

"Oh no," Issa said and moaned. "I'll catch a hiding. Bain, protect me."

Bain didn't look as though he wanted to protect anyone. His blond good looks had abruptly faded and he seemed, if possible, even more frightened than Gray. "We will need more men," he said.

Gray sighed. "Bain, there isn't time. Not another hour will pass till they are ashore. We must meet them with the dozen or so we have."

"Are you crazy?" Bain shouted. "There will be three times that number on the ship—and professionals, too."

"What's a professional?" I asked from the hilltop.

Gray took the trouble to answer. "The men aboard that ship make their living by raiding. They will almost certainly be experienced fighters."

"And better at it than you?" I asked.

"Probably," he said.

Bain was blowing his horn to summon what force he had.

"I'll get a beating," Issa said petulantly. "They will be able to see the sail from the village. We don't need to warn them."

"No, they won't," Anna said. "The village is beyond the headland, and it faces northwest. The sail will be hidden by the cliffs. They won't know they are under attack until the pirates are among them. Now, come on." She snatched her friend's wrist, and both women began running downhill.

"You think that's what they will do?" Bain asked Gray.

"It would be what I would do were I captain of that ship. I would land my people on the beach. They can go around through the rocks and fall on the women—it's early afternoon and most of the men will still be in the fields working—and you well know it's the women they want. And the new wool. The houses will be full of it."

"We need more men," Bain insisted.

"No. The band is scattered all along the coast. By the time we collect enough of them, Issa and Anna both will be standing on the auction block in London."

"Very well. Where do we meet them? On the beach?"

"No and no," Gray said. "Down there, in the rocks, between the beach and the village. There are some very narrow, steep places and we will stand some chance."

I jumped down from my perch on the rock. Mother and Black Leg joined me. I crouched between the two wolves and looked up at Gray.

"Run home," he said. "Or better yet, if your kin are not there, hide in the woods and don't come out until you are sure they are gone."

Then lightning struck. That's what I have always called it since. There are many ways to see into the future. Many magics. But this is the swiftest and best, the most sure. When it has struck and illuminated the world, it has never guided me wrongly. Always in the light of the flash I have seen the world as it is in truth. Seen not only my choices, but the choices of others. Seen the path that I must follow to reach my goal, however difficult it is, however dangerous. And at that moment I first felt the stone in the belly that is fear, and I saw the choice and chose now and forevermore the thing that would be my life.

"No," I said. "No, I cannot go. You will need me." My eyes met his for an eternal moment, and I knew he felt the power. He might not acknowledge it, but he felt it.

"Yes, I will."

Then he turned to the rest—there were seven or eight there by now and more arriving. I was ignored. As Gray began explaining his plan to them, I sent Mother to find Maeniel. I knew the boys would need him. The boys followed Gray without a word, and they waited in the rocks just beyond the beach while the oarsmen brought the ship into the shallows.

I went with them, but Gray lifted me to the top of a rock, a big boulder, taller than a man's head. I crouched there with Black Leg. I didn't know how he got to the top, but I could guess.

They didn't beach the boat. She rode rather low in the water. They weighed anchor by dropping a big piece of granite overboard. A rope was attached to it by an iron ring set in the stone. They secured the rope to a stanchion near the stern, then the pirates jumped overboard and splashed through the shallows toward the beach.

"They have captives on board already," Gray snarled below me. "Brace yourself, boys, here they come."

The first to reach the rocks almost ran into Gray before he saw him. Gray drove his sword through the man's throat. The man behind Gray's attacker, I took to be the leader. He wore boiled leather and metal armor and carried a shield and ax. He swung the ax at Gray's head. Gray parried with his shield, and the ill-made thing disintegrated. His first sword thrust skidded on the leather armor. His opponent shoved his shield boss, a bronze spike, into Gray's face, almost taking an eye. But in the hand he'd been using to hold the shield, Gray held an improvised mace, a big rock tied to a split tree branch. The descending ax struck the rock and the ax head broke, shards flying into the air like a swarm of glittering needles. The pirate overbalanced and fell forward. Gray swung his mace and emptied the pirate's skull in a splatter of red.

The one behind him was better armed. His long sword gave him a reach that Gray didn't have and he was bigger, a man grown. He drove straight for Gray's belly with the blade. Gray pivoted and the blade rang out a deep challenge when the mace hit it, but it didn't break the way the ax had. He slammed his shield into Gray's body to pin him against the big boulder and spit him with the sword. Taken by madness, I jumped, dropping from the top of the boulder onto the pirate's neck. Blindly, Gray thrust forward, and his short sword, a Roman gladius, punched through the quilted cloth his opponent was wearing and drove through the ribs into his heart.

All along the line I could hear and even feel the shock of combat as the very thin line of young and worried boys met the older, experienced fighters and tried to hold them back. And at least for a short time succeeded. The pirates drew back; the narrow passages between the boulders were death traps for an attacking force. The boys had, thanks to Gray's intelligence, caught them by surprise, weapons undrawn, and killed or incapacitated a half dozen. But this couldn't last, and I knew it.

Another leader waved his arm and the force moved forward, to Gray's right to turn his flank. Once behind the rocky scarp, they could slaughter us at will. I heard Gray grit his teeth and moan. In the broken ground, we could still make a fight of it, but we were doomed.

Many peoples' proverbs say it is better to be lucky than smart—and we got lucky. The pirates ran into Maeniel, the Gray Watcher, when they tried to turn our flank, and he is as deadly a man as I have ever known. Two of the pirates staggered back, dying, from the notch in the rocks where he'd stationed himself.

At almost the same moment the boys got reinforcements from the village. Not all the men were working in the fields. Some of the women came along also, and they'd armed themselves with anything they could carry: clubs, kitchen knives, hay forks, even the hot soup and porridge for the evening meal. Another force from the village came rounding the headland, a fishing boat loaded with all those who hadn't the stamina to climb the steep, rocky headland. The oarsmen pulling frantically, men and women standing in the boat ready to attack from the rear. The pirates decided the pickings weren't worth the price and ran for their ship.

I was standing beside Gray, and he lowered his mace and sword, saying, "Not a bad day's work," as he cast an eye on the corpses scattered on the shingle. They were mostly raiders, and they wore their plunder on their backs. Armor, weapons—fine weapons—gold rings on their fingers, gold and silver belts, bracelets, torcs, all decorated their bodies. He and his men were rich.

As we watched the first of the raiders splash into the water, we both saw something was happening on the ship. Her cargo had shifted, as it were, and the captives streamed onto the deck. They were all women. They went bare-handed for the men left aboard. As we watched, some of the women died, but not enough, not nearly enough, and the men on the boat went down under a squirming mass of bodies.

Then one of the women pulled free. She had a knife in one hand and an ax in the other. She cut the anchor rope. One of her eyes was gouged out, but she didn't seem to feel the wound; the moist, red socket glared out of her face at me across the narrow strip of water between the boat and the beach.

Panicked, the pirates tried to catch at the gunwales with their fingers and pull themselves aboard. But the one-eyed woman cut fingers and hands off, sometimes using the ax as a long-bladed cleaver, sometimes simply slicing with the knife. She also seemed to find it fun to ignore fingers and take ears, noses, and even lips from the men trying to clamber aboard.

At first I thought she would surely be overwhelmed, but then the other women joined her and they got into the spirit of the thing. The long boat drifted quickly into deeper water, and a few of the pirates tried to make a stand in the shallows. The boys from the war band and the villagers, howling like the legions of the damned, charged in to finish them, but the final blow was dealt by Dugald. He stepped out from behind a rock and gave an exemplary demonstration of power.

Cobbles, large gravel, and water-worn pebbles rose from the beach and began to fly at the pirates with the force of sling stones. Within moments half the remaining men were down and the others were fleeing in all directions. The rest was just revenge. I cannot think any of them escaped. They were hated everywhere along the coast. As to the women aboard the vessel, they had seen their fathers, brothers, husbands, and sons killed by the slavers. Many had been raped, some repeatedly, and those pregnant or with babies at the breast had seen their newborns killed, because a woman with a child at the breast was worth less than one without. They showed no mercy.

The fishermen hauled the ship ashore and beached her above the tide line while the erstwhile captive women drowned the few remaining wounded pirates in the surf after they deprived them of their eyes, ears, noses, and other offending body parts. For when women take revenge, it is with all their hearts and souls, not to mention considerable inventiveness and ingenuity.

The sun was low, casting a lurid light over the beach, the surf foaming like stained lace against the violet water. The killing was finished. We went to the chief's hall to undertake a division of the spoils. It was then

Gray gave me the head, the head of the leader of the pirates. He placed it before me in a bag as I sat between Dugald and the Gray Watcher in the chief's hall. I opened the bag and looked at the face. The pirate chief looked annoyed at being a trophy, as though he were about to protest his slaying at the hands of rank amateurs, boys only. He had not expected to die today.

Odd how I remember his face. I cannot now call to mind the faces of those I have loved all my life, those for whom more than one time I would have sacrificed everything.

Dugald, shivering next to me, drained with the effort of his magic, said, "That's no gift for a child."

Maeniel studied the head. "We will place it in cedar oil and dry it in the smoke from our hearth fire."

Gray nodded. "She was the one who first saw the sail and warned us. Without her, we would have been taken by surprise."

The one-eyed woman was spooning soup into Dugald's mouth. She spat in the chief's face. "He died too easy. I wish I'd gotten my hands on him. He gouged my eye out because I fought him when he tried to have me. He said one eye was all a weaving woman needed. He promised me worse this night." And she laughed. "Seems he won't get to keep that promise."

"The ones who did live long enough to meet you regretted it," the Gray Watcher said.

It was a good feast, and we all drank our fill, even the captive women. They remained because none of us knew how to send them home. None of us had any idea where they might be from. The boys from the war band all got good offers from the people in the village, though Bain strutted and preened as though he'd won the battle single-handed.

When we left to go home, the one-eyed woman went with us. She told Dugald, "Look at the three of you, dirty, dressed in rags." She twisted my head toward her. "Gray called you she. Are you girl or boy?"

"Girl, and I regret it. I would like to join the war band like Gray and Bain," I said.

"Yes, well, you need a woman to look after you at present."

"To be sure," Dugald said. "That's why you won't do. I would rather share house room with a wolf pack." Then he remembered. "Oh, good God, I do."

Mother and Black Leg were striding along at my side.

When the one-eyed woman came to our hut, she exclaimed at the disorder and filth. Mother and Black Leg gnawed bones on the hearth and none of us were particular about table manners. But first Dugald and Maeniel put her on a bed. She looked ready to fight when they did that, but Dugald, still shivering, said, "My God, woman. I am burnt to the socket, and—" he gestured at Maeniel "—he is not human."

Maeniel put off his weapons, went wolf, and settled down at the fire. She laughed when she saw him do it.

"That's a trick I've never seen," she said.

Dugald poulticed her eye so that it took away the pain, then gave her something to drink that he said quiets the soul. She told us her name was Kyra.

Our house was built after the old manner and it was part of the currents of the world. It was round with wooden uprights and three courses of dry stone walling between them. Flexible canes were lashed to the uprights and formed a skeleton for the dome. This was covered with boiled cowhide and then a layer of green turf. More turf was piled against the walls to keep out the storm winds. So it seemed to rise, a green mound near the sea. It was warmed and lighted by a hearth in the center. The chimney—we knew of no such things then—was a smoke hole in the roof. A lattice that could be moved aside covered the hole.

I woke deep in the night to hear Kyra weeping. She lay beside me. There were only two beds in the room. Dugald had the other. The wolves slept near the hearth in the center. Dugald slept as one drugged. The wolves were also quiet, curled tails covering their noses. The Gray Watcher had slung the head above the hearth and slightly to one side, so it could begin to cure in the smoke. It hung by its long, dark hair, and as I watched, half asleep, the face seemed to take on the lineaments of life. The eyes opened and stared at me malevolently. The skin was no longer sallow and the cheeks sunken. It seemed as though blood flowed in the veins and the heart still beat.

"Doesn't weeping hurt your eye?" I asked Kyra.

"Yes," she said, "but the pain in my heart is so much worse than any pain my body could endure that it doesn't seem to matter."

I was a child and my imagination couldn't bridge the gap between my state and hers, but I wanted to give her something that would allow her some peace. "It's cold," I said. "The fire is low."

"Is it? I thought it was only my grief that chilled me. In a moment I will rise and build it up. I can't expect to live among you, whatever you and your people may be, without making proper recompense."

I was yet young, but I didn't want one who had suffered so much to feel she must be my servant. "No," I answered. "That will be my task. Tell me, the one whose head hangs over the hearth—what was his name?"

She answered me after the old fashion. "Once I had a man and a son and a child at the breast."

I glanced at her and saw the front of the rags she was wearing were wet and stiff with milk from her nipples. It was leaking out with no child to take it.

"Now I have no man, no son, and no baby. Its name was Cymry."

"Cymry," I said, trying the name on my tongue. The eyes blinked. On the head, the mouth moved. "Cymry," I said. "Cymry, build up the fire."

The flames leaped high, filling the room with light and warmth.

Kyra laughed. "So there is truth in the old tales."

"So it would seem," I answered.

The fire was dying down again, but there was plenty of fuel on the hearth. It made a pleasant blaze. The head was quiet and death took it.

"He is paid out for the things he did," I said. "You may rest easy."

But she was already sleeping.

Things went well after that. This surprised a lot of people, because we were all farmers, and farmers never think they will prosper. Or possibly they don't care to attract the anger of the gods by too much complacency.

Kyra quietly improved the house, finding hides for the floor and strewing rushes. As soon as she could begin to weave, she set up the sort of warp-weighed loom under the trees that our women have used since . . .

since . . . who knows how long—before they sailed south and traded with the people who became the Greeks at a place called Troy. She washed and cooked better than the two men. Much better. I liked her food. But we quarreled when she tried to make me dress as a girl.

"You are one, you know," she told me, "and will have to act like one. The priests say it is an abomination not to."

I spat like an angry cat. "And what did being a woman get you?" I asked. When she stood silent, then turned and walked away, I knew I had hurt her, and that was the first time I'd hurt the feelings of any human being. I was unhappy and it made me sad, so I ran after her, trying to say I was sorry. At first she wouldn't listen to me or talk, then I saw she was crying and I felt worse. But at last she stopped, sat, and buried her face in the old dress she wore, in terrible sorrow. She was silent, and we both sat in a little patch of cedar trees high on a cliff and watched the play of light and shadow on the sea. Black Leg, Mother, and I sat beside her, and a time or two, Mother thrust her nose into Kyra's hand as though offering her comfort.

The morning fog had lifted, and the clouds were rushing by, white and glowing at the tops, dark at the bottom, the color of the Gray Watcher's coat in winter. Far out to sea, it was raining. I saw the long, trailing veils of the storm darkening the horizon like misty smudges in the distance, and sometimes when the sun shone into the storm shadow, I saw the double arch of a rainbow leaping from the sea to the clouds.

She sat quiet, arms around her knees, looking out into the distance. "You are right. Being a woman didn't get me much of anything. When they had killed all I ever loved, I fought them because I hoped they would kill me also. That was when he gouged out my eye, saying it would make me more compliant, and he was right. The pain was dreadful. Rather than let them blind me, I behaved the way the other women did, doing what I was told, even seeming to welcome their embraces. He was so sure I was tamed, he left me untied. It was I who freed the others.

"They wouldn't even let us bury the dead. I hope . . . some must have gotten away . . . I hope they performed the rites. I was told they cannot sleep unless the bones are first burned, then reduced to a powder, and given to the wind. Their spirits are unquiet and will walk. The man and my son were old enough to make the journey, but the baby . . . he can't be old enough to find his way alone."

She was silent for a space and didn't talk.

"You hear him at night?" I asked. "Don't you? And then you awaken and wonder if he is lost in darkness."

She nodded.

"I will ask Cymry," I told her.

She shivered.

"He is dead and knows where the dead go," I continued.

"No," she said. "I wouldn't want him near my child. Best to let it lie, little one." And then she kissed me on the top of the head.

"I will dress like a girl if you want me to," I said.

A strong gust of wind from the sea made the cedars around us rustle, as though the thick limbs had life, and stirred the strong scent of the wood.

"No," she said, "but you must learn how to prettify yourself and prance and simper and bat your eyelashes as though you want to catch a lover."

"Like Issa," I said, speaking of the chief's daughter.

She had become worse since Bain moved into the chief's house after the fight. She spent all her time primping, seeking out pools of water in which to admire her reflection. If another girl so much as walked near him, she stopped speaking to her and looked daggers every time they met. When a trade ship stopped at the cove, she threw tantrums until her father bought her a bolt of linen cloth she and her mother could dye for a new dress, and an amber necklace with a silver cross. She wouldn't do any washing at the stream or scrub pots any longer for fear she would ruin her hands and break her nails.

Kyra began laughing. "Oh, no, not that bad," she said. "But there are many things women do that you should learn for your own sake: cooking, weaving, knitting, sewing, and how to make the most of your looks. It can be important. You never know where the currents of life will carry you."

I nodded. "Whatever you have to teach me, I will learn," I said. "I cannot promise you I will apply the lessons, but I won't disregard them either."

She put her arm over my shoulders, and the four of us sat together companionably. I heard Mother sigh as she rested her head in Kyra's lap, and Black Leg went to sleep at my side.

"I am happy I have come among you," she said. "I can't help but miss those I have lost, but you have helped heal my heart. You are deep-minded for one so young, and those two guardians of yours should be told it's time to begin your education."

And that's what I did for the next few years: learn from all of them.

Dugald gave up trying to make me into a Roman, but he did make me study Latin and Greek and read such books as he could obtain. We would quarrel, because I wanted to learn magic and he refused to teach me, saying he would rather purge these things from our people, and especially from our leaders. He told me I would marry a king, and I laughed at him. But I was learning about magic without his help.

Gray married Anna and began to help her father at the forge. Every winter we would meet secretly after the turning of the year, take the road, and go up to the mountains. Only the three of us—Kyra, Gray, and me, four if you count Cymry, the head. We would go high, where the rocks were sheathed in ice and a thin skin of snow covered the ground.

Cymry had cured well. We soaked him in cedar oil and the skin didn't rot but drew tight on the bones. His lips shrunk so his teeth showed, and even his eyes were intact. They were cloudy and sunken, but they peered through half-closed lids, and you could tell his soul was still present. The smoke from the fire had darkened his skin, and there was a stubble of beard on his cheeks.

It grows, Gray told me, after death, often for some time.

We killed a deer, dug a pit, lined it with stones, then lit a fire and heated the stones. When they were hot, we placed cedar branches on them, put the deer carcass on top, covered it with more branches and then a green hide weighed down with stones. We hung Cymry from a tree branch where he could watch us and then sat and talked while the meat cooked.

Kyra was one of the old ones. They have a name, but I will not tell it. Like Cymry's name, it is a thing of power, and one who knows it has some ability to do them harm. They were my friends; my first friends, I think, but for Dugald and the Gray Watcher, and by their learning made me what I am.

Besides, they should always have a place here. They have been part of this land for so long that compared to them the Britons are children and the Romans squalling infants. Kyra taught me their language and their lore. Once, you see, there was no ocean here, and all of this Ireland, Britain, and France was dry land. The world was very cold, and all the water that now covers the land was ice, and all of this belonged to her people. There were no farms, no cattle or sheep. None at least that lived with men. The animals were all wild, and Kyra's people hunted them in the shadow of the glaciers.

The whole world was forest, in some places so thick that no group of humans could force a passage between the trees. The oaks were gigantic; the ash towering pillars gray and gold in autumn, in winter bare as the pillars of a stately hall. The waters were choked with willows, and on the mountain-sides pale birch trees glowed against the bracken and dark stone. The thick-trunked oaks and the brown hazel dropped nuts so thick every footstep beneath them cracked. And the women of Kyra's people harvested the hazelnut and acorn to make an unleavened bread soft as the feathers on a young bird and sweet as an autumn sloe. They knew no cloth and wore the pelts of the beasts they hunted, but were, between the riches of the rivers and forest, all healthy and well fed. They had no need of war bands, kings, or lords. When they had a dispute or problems to solve, they called on those among them who could travel to the other world. Seers who could find a vi-sion and place their feet on the right path.

"Dugald says stories of the other world are but dreams and the wild imaginings of poets," I told them.

Kyra looked at me. She was huddled in her furs, sitting on a log, pok-ing at the fire with a stick. Gray was working the deer hide with a stone scraper, cleaning it so it could be tanned. He chuckled.

"Don't laugh, fool," she said. "The journey is real and so is the risk. Some don't return. But in a way, he's right. Many who undertake the journey only glimpse the borderlands, but some go beyond them and leave this world and travel into another. It can be done and the more fool he for denying it, because he is one of the ones who has made his way into the passage. But—and I can hear it in his voice—he grew afraid and he turned back. Now he wants to deny the knowledge to you."

Good smells were beginning to rise from the stone-lined pit where the meat was roasting.

"Do you think . . . ?" I asked.

"No," Gray and Kyra said together. "It hasn't been enough time. Children are always impatient. The meat is not done."

"Kyra, are you sure you should be telling her these things? And I cannot believe she is of your people," Gray said.

Kyra snorted and fixed him with a cold stare from her one good eye.

"But," he continued, arguing, "telling the child she is royal, Kyra, and talented in a way that bodes no good for her future—"

"If you don't believe there is something strange about her, then what are you doing here, Gray?"

"Yes," he said, and looked away from her into the snowy woods. "Yes," he repeated. "When she came to tell us about the ship she saw, that fool Bain tried to ignore her, but she wouldn't be ignored or overlooked. She forced him to pay attention to her. But letting her think she is royal . . ."

"I *am* royal," I said.

"Who?" he asked.

Both he and Kyra were staring at me intently.

"Dugald and the Gray Watcher don't want me to say." I spoke with my eyes on the ground. "I gave them my promise." Then I looked up. The eyes on the head were staring into mine, the hate burning in them.

Gray followed my gaze and jerked as though he'd been pinched. "God," he whispered and made the sign of the cross. I glanced at him, drawn almost involuntarily by his outcry.

When I looked back, the head was—much as usual—ghastly but dead. Kyra laughed.

Gray still looked frightened. "For a moment I thought . . . that thing almost seemed as though it were alive."

"Yes," Kyra said. "Now, let us speak of other things."

And so we did. She had already begun to teach me the songs and tales her people tell about the sky. How to know the time, day, and season by the movements of the sun, moon, and stars. The meaning of the constellations—the warrior, the fish, the dragon, the twins, the bull, the lion, and many more. Each had its own song and story. They were long and the poetry was very beautiful. Easy for me to remember. There were two calendars—one for men by the sun, another for women by the moon—and the wise learned to reckon time by both. Day belonged to men, night to women; but sunset and dawn belonged to both and were more powerful than either day or night.

That was why we questioned Cymry at dusk.

At length, the meat was ready, and we feasted together. By the time we were finished eating, the snow was blue and the sun a scarlet ball on the horizon.

Dugald was at the chief's hall feasting, and Issa had told me that they were going to surprise him with a woman. Since they found out that he was a druid taught, the townspeople had made much of him by bringing him presents and inviting him to feasts in their homes. Of course, in return they constantly worried him with their disputes, marital problems, illnesses, and injuries. He was asked to tell the future for them and their children and even to bless cattle, sheep, goats, pigs, boars, and fishing tackle. He got very little peace once they found he could do magic.

They came demanding love potions, fertility potions, poisons, philters, and things that were supposed to guarantee wedded bliss. Let any creature for miles around get into difficulties during childbearing and poor Dugald would be summoned, even if it was the dead of winter or the middle of the night. But Dugald seemed to thrive on the attention, especially that of women—the young women. That meant he stayed out of my hair and let Kyra and the Gray Watcher run our lives.

That satisfied me. Kyra taught me history. Not as the Romans knew it, the story of wars and kings, but about the journey of humankind and how we won out over both gods and beasts and now ruled over both of them. In skill we bested the animals, in magic the gods. All but for the veiled She who is fate, and even the Romans bent the knee before her.

When the sun was nothing but a red glow on the horizon, we sacrificed to Cymry. Pouring red wine and oil over his head, I saw him smack his lips, and his eyes, clouded with death, seemed clouded now with drunkenness. Gray rolled his eyes and backed up behind the log we'd been sitting on. He wouldn't look at Cymry at all. Kyra laughed in the same brittle fashion she had the night when his eyes first opened and he looked at us. Then she took a large piece of deer meat and some of the liver she'd been saving and threw it into the fire.

It was a lot of moisture, and the flames darkened for a moment. And I saw the twin moons of the predator's eyes glowing from beyond the fire, and I knew the Gray Watcher hadn't been fooled by the story we had given Dugald and he was here. Clouds of smoke came up from the coals and surrounded the head hanging from the tree branch near the fire.

The eyes opened, and I looked again at the same hatred I'd seen when they first opened, but now he seemed dazed with the drink and food Kyra had given him. He moaned and said, "I taste the pleasures of the flesh again."

"Mary, Mother of Christ!" Gray cried, and then screamed as his knife in a sheath at his belt went red, then white. It had heated and begun to burn him. He tore the sheath from his body and threw it into the darkness.

"I warned you," Kyra snapped, "to not have any iron on your body."

"I know. I forgot," he said. "I'm sorry."

"Cymry," I said. "Will we be attacked next year by anyone? Not just pirates?"

The mouth worked as though chewing. "Give me more wine," it said.

"No," Kyra said. "I give you nothing. Make an answer or I'll put you in the fire."

"I will give you more, but answer me first," I told him.

The head gave a wailing cry that made Gray shudder and cross himself again. Kyra threw a cup of something into the fire, and the flames roared up around the head. Kyra gave a snort of glee at the obvious fear in its face.

"No, no, you will not be attacked by anyone."

"You lie," Kyra said viciously, throwing some more of whatever she had in the cup on the logs.

"No, no, no," the head shrieked. "I do not lie. I cannot lie."

Flame and smoke boiled up from the logs, nearly engulfing the head.

"It's true," I said. "He cannot lie. Not to you or to me."

"Tell me," Gray said, and he shocked me because he had seemed so afraid of the magic. "Tell me, is the fair child royal?"

The wind from the sea blew away the smoke, and I saw the head wearing a human visage in the flickering firelight. It released another throbbing moan.

"Ahhh, god, ahhh, god, would that I could live again."

"And what would you do then, pig? Make misery and sorrow for each life you touched again?" Kyra asked. "Answer the question."

"No, no, I swear I would not."

"Be still," I told it. "Serve me well, and one day I will release you so you may be born again. Now, answer. Am I royal?"

"No. More than royal, worse than royal, better than royal. Do you think just anyone can enslave me? Do you think I would serve just anyone? Do you think I could be compelled to serve just anyone?"

"Go," I said, "from whence you came and do not return until I summon you."

"Nooooo."

The cry was a wail of anguish, but it ended in silence. The thing was dead, returned to its former semblance, skin drawn tight over the bones, grinning teeth, and sunken, slitted eyes.

"What a question," Kyra said to Gray. "Is she royal? Certainly. The power of the first queens is in her. Besides, what told you to give her the head?"

"I don't know," Gray muttered. "I have never known. But do you think I like the life of a servant in the smith's house while Bain, the big mouth, flaunts his *royal* marriage to a chief's daughter? Anna's father is a strong, young man, not yet thirty-five. The bastard will live to grow old while I do all the heavy work at the forge."

"Be patient," I said. "The answer might be no this year, but soon enough it will be yes. Besides, it's a better life than the war band. Bide your time. I have much to learn."

Kyra stroked my hair. "You are yet a child. Sometimes I forget."

The Gray Watcher appeared on the other side of the fire. He unslung the head from the tree branch and replaced it in the bag. He was a man dressed for the cold in the same old clothes he usually wore: tunic, mantle, cross-gartered leggings, and boots.

"You lied to Dugald," he told me as he threw the bag over his shoulder.

"Dugald is a fool," Kyra said.

"No," the Gray Watcher said. "Dugald is not a fool. I think he is wrong about many things, but he is not a fool. And you" —he stared at me—"have started down a very dangerous path, one that might well bring you to ruin."

"Down into the mud or up among the stars," I answered. "I would rather chance the first in return for the opportunity to gain the second."

"And your companions?" he asked. "A vengeful woman and an ambitious man."

"You who are not always human want to search among us for noble motives," I answered. "Even a wolf would know better. I find help where I can. I need them. Teach me how to fight. No one is better at it than you, and make Dugald teach me magic. I will need to know it. Tell him either he teaches me or I venture forward on my own."

She was a child and a seven-year-old child at that, Maeniel thought as they walked back to the dwelling. Dugald had returned from the chief's house stinking of women and perfume, and he was waiting near the door. The row started right away when he heard what the child had been doing. He stomped around the house—now it had become a house—the walls brightened by Kyra's weavings and the dark pine posts Gray had carved that propped up the roof with entwined birds and beasts. At the bottom a fish leaped, caught in an eagle's talons. The big spotted cat took the eagle, and the leaping cat was tangled with the wolf; the dragon above took the stag, and the antlers spread to make the sinuous shape of the tree branches that upheld the roof. Around the walls he had made benches balanced on raven wings, and the beds were salmon legged, and they leaped among wheat and barley stalks for luck. The seal protected the door lintel, and a man's face looked from its belly.

Living among Kyra's weavings were the symbols of all the great houses of heaven: the salmon, the warrior, the queen in her chair, the seal, and—proudest of all—the dragon and the comb.

"I won't have it," Dugald shouted. He pointed at Kyra. "I won't have you undermining my fosterling's education by teaching her black magic. I'll—" He waved a finger in the air. "I'll . . . I'll . . ."

He couldn't seem to settle on what he would do. Maeniel chuckled. He shouldn't have.

"I'll have you sold."

The threat was a terrible one and quite real. Kyra had no kin to take her in, and she wouldn't do as the other women had and marry. You must understand, women are always in demand. Very valuable as wives and slaves, they have many skills—and these were women of the Painted People who turned their skins into wonderful pictures with woad, carmine, red ocher, and wood ash. I had seen Kyra's, though most of them were covered by her clothes. Vines and butterflies were around her wrists and ankles, flowers covered her breasts and belly. Spiderwebs moved wonderfully on the backs of her hands. But since she had come to us, she painted an adder around her breast and over her heart. She dyed it with something that made it look like blood and fire along its scales, and the shape of the serpent itself was dead—thick and black like the last smoke of a dying candle. When she took a deep breath, the head on her ribs opened its mouth and the fangs showed as if ready to bite. It lay among the flowers she said were painted when she was given in marriage. Not just painted, but made permanent with needles and a knife.

The ones who still had ideas of going back had hired themselves out for only a year. Others made more permanent arrangements, becoming the second and third wives of prosperous men. All had been greedily sought. All were skilled cooks and cloth workers; combers of sheep; wool spinners, dyers, and weavers. In some ways we were very lucky in Kyra. She was one of the best of them. And many women came offering her gifts in return for patterns, stitches, and other technical advice. She was one of the few who knew how to weave nettles.

At the threat, Kyra went for her knife. Maeniel caught her wrist in his hand and said, "Stop. He will do nothing." His pronouncement was backed up by growls from both Mother and Black Leg.

"If I ask Dunnel," Dugald shouted furiously, "he will."

"Perhaps he will," Maeniel said quietly. "But you won't ask."

I threw my arms around Kyra's waist. Dunnel was the chief, and he had an extravagant admiration for Dugald. "Don't let him!" I said to Maeniel.

"Hush!" he said, ruffling my hair. "Kyra, put that knife up. You have a home with me for the rest of your life. Dugald, I will turn you out should you begin any such nonsense."

"You!" He pointed at Maeniel. "You will turn *me* out?"

Dugald was in a fine fury.

"I will put a curse of wasting on you. I will put a curse of rotting on you. I will put a curse of softness on you," Dugald said.

"No, you won't," Maeniel said. "It's been tried and they don't work."

"Softness?" I asked. "Wasting and rotting I can understand, but—"

"Never mind!"

I knew it had something to do with sex, but they wouldn't tell me.

"Dugald, you lead a very soft life. I hunt for you and trade what I get for such supplies as we need. Kyra cultivates flax, combs sheep, dyes, and weaves, and is, moreover, an excellent cook. All you need do is teach . . ." He gazed at me—and he told me later my hair was a nimbus of light around my face in the glow from the wax lights and the fires, so he gave me my name, Guinevere. "All you need to do is teach the small fair one, because that is what she is—Guinevere, the fair one. And now, as to the black magic, she taught Kyra, not the other way around."

Dugald was silent then.

You must understand, my name was not written down. Those who say and sometimes write it use what form they care to. So the spellings sometimes differ greatly. So much that it might seem as though I had many different names; but in reality, I still have only one. And, like all true names, it was a word of power. But of this I will say no more, since

Dugald, I think, was partly right. There are many things that can't be written down, but others that should not be written down, and the use of my name is one of them.

So, as said when I began to describe my life, we prospered.

We were not bothered by land or sea. Maybe the fate of Cymry and his crew was famed far and wide, spread by the ever-wagging tongues of those who love such news, the traveling storytellers. Because they are sometimes drawn to a wealthy steading, you must understand these are not the real bards who sit at the tables of kings and powerful chieftains. Their songs and satires are rewarded with gold and silver; and the best of their work becomes immortal, part of what every master poet must learn during his apprenticeship and also what nobles must study as part of their training for rule. The noble need not have them by heart as a bard must, but he or she needs to be acquainted with them, knowledgeable enough to know what songs to ask for when one of the great masters visits his palace.

These things have a darker use, also. The king or chieftain must also know what satire to choose when he wishes to hold his enemy up to ridicule and scorn before his whole court that he may enrage the man or woman so they will succumb to fury and lose control of their tempers and forget good sense. A clever assault on a man's honor and dignity will draw him into folly. No, these storytellers are much poorer folk. They cannot look to any great patron for maintenance but, fiddle-footed, must wander from place to place, since more than one night's lodging would strain the resources of the more humble folk who form their audience.

Since Dugald was a man of importance, we were frequent guests at the chief's hall, and we heard many such itinerants who came to speak of wonders such as gods and dragons, and who spiced their stock of stories with gossip about the doings of the great and powerful kings and queens of other lands and places. And they added to the fund of knowledge any new and notable events that transpired even in out-of-the-way places like ours. One such notable event was the destruction of a notorious pirate like Cymry at the hands of a humble war band of boys and various folk of a small village. So, though I didn't know it, my fame and that of Bain and Gray began to spread, and a reputation for the place where we dwelt as an abode of mighty magic reached the minds of many we didn't know and never would know. And far and wide the storytellers sang in praise of our achievements.

When you come to think of it—and I didn't then—a thing both good and bad. But the upshot of it was that for the next few years while I attained my growth, we weren't bothered. And I had time to learn to fight from Lord Maeniel; Dugald taught me of real dragons and how to rule. And in between times, I ran wild along the shore with Mother, Black Leg, and Kyra.

Ah, how Kyra loved a story. She used her visits to the chief's hall to add more and more of them to the library of her mind, until I was sure she had more skill than any of the wanderers who stopped to visit us. And, indeed, some came to sit at our hearth and listen and drink in her fund of glorious tales.

Every winter at the turning of the year, we carried Cymry up into the mountains to ask him if we faced raids this year, and each winter the answer he gave was no. This gave me the most precious gift of all, time to grow. So we lived in bliss and didn't know it.

In the summer we hunted deer, rabbits, and even bear and big cats. Maeniel would take us out, with Dugald bringing up the rear, grumbling about his joints and bones. Mother and Black Leg took point, and whatever they flushed, we followed, fleeting along with them, javelin in hand. Deer, elk, and even the powerful and dangerous aurochs fell to us.

I ran with the wolves until I could run down a hare, and I can still go for miles even after a life of strife, labor, battle, and childbearing. I thought nothing of accompanying Maeniel, Mother, and Black Leg high into the wilderness of mountains to bring back a massive elk or even a wild bull. At other times we fished, working the stormy waters that ebbed and flowed along our rugged, rocky coast.

The shore here is not some peaceful, sandy refuge, but a cruel bulwark against fierce ocean; and its denizens, the magnificent and deadly dragons, were the most dangerous and most admired and most beautiful inhabitants. Most of the time we fished the rivers, streams, and tide pools; and some nights we went to the high cliffs and rocks of what the northern people call fjords. The coast was fissured with them, and some couldn't be gotten into on foot. Only a boat launched from nearby would bring us to these most isolated beaches. They offer bountiful fishing by night because the large fish from the ocean often drove small fish—herring and mackerel—into the shallows in order to trap them. We were able to take ling, dogfish, sole, and even sometimes the basking shark, much prized for the oil in its liver.

I loved the sea and tried to persuade the Gray Watcher to sail our light, skin-covered boat out of sight of land, telling him Kyra taught me to read direction in the stars. He always refused. She is too changeable, that sea, he said. Not like the smiling sapphire water that ringed the coasts of Gaul and Italy, where the summer sun warmed both beach and surf and the water was as some clear gem and could be looked through like fine Roman glass.

No, this sea was green, gray, and black; and even at high summer a treacherous fog lay on the water like smoke. Any wind or disturbance raised high waves, seven to ten feet even, in the fjords. More than once our curragh was swamped, and we had to ride it in to shore upside down, paddling with our hands and feet.

One afternoon we were fishing alone, just the two of us; we had come here to collect samphire for Kyra. She liked to pickle it so we could have it with our meat in winter. Maeniel liked it. He liked all vegetable foods. It seemed odd to me. Black Leg followed him in taste, but Mother wouldn't even look at it.

The fjord angled off into a sheltered cove, where samphire grew in thick mats that rimmed the shore. We collected quite a lot, and then the Gray Watcher and I went fishing.

Bad decision. A squall came up while we were taking mullet with a cast net; and in a few minutes a wall of icy rain hit, accompanied by ten-foot waves. The rain was thick, gray, and blinding. It was the darkest thing I've ever seen by day, and for once I understood the Gray Watcher's fear of the sea. The rain was in our faces, and we fought to turn the curragh around and get to shore. But we found ourselves spinning, because the water falling from the sky was so dense that the beach was turned into a shadow, only half seen through the rain.

I was a thin child, carrying little fat. In a very few moments, I was freezing cold and soaked to the skin by rain and the sea breaking over the sides, and I knew why the ocean takes and keeps so many. I understand I was only short minutes from death, and even the Gray Watcher, strong as he was—more than humanly strong—would not last until sunset in the freezing rain and cold.

Then the waves struck. The curragh was lifted high into the air, and I saw the cliffs above—silver granite spotted with red and orange lichen glowing and shining in the last pale light. Then we went down, and the wave we rode troughed out and another lifted high above us like green glass pitted by the wind-driven rain. Then it crashed down, the flimsy hide boat disintegrated, and we were thrust down into the sudden silence below the surface.

The turbulent water was like thick fog. My dazed mind wondered at it. I might have breathed and drowned, but instinct closed my mouth and nose. Yet, I was sure I would die when I realized where I was. The cold wasn't chill any longer, but numbness; and I felt life, like water in a broken cup, running out of me into the shadowed underwater silence. Then my head broke the surface and the world was a chaos of screaming wind and roaring surf. I used my second of time to get as much air as I could into my lungs. Then I went down again, my knees banging against the shingle.

I was in the shallows. I began to struggle as hard as I could; and for one horrible, eternal instant, the riptide pulled me back. But then I felt something knot in the back of my leather shirt. The Gray Watcher had me, and seconds later we were both crawling out of reach of the pounding waves as the rain lashed us with whips of raw silver through the rising fog.

Cold. God, it was cold! Never have I felt so cold, before or since. I lay limp, past shivering, beside a boulder, while the Gray Watcher covered me with a cowhide we carried with us on all our journeys. The cows from the mountains are like sheep and have long, thick hair on their bodies. Nowhere else, the Gray Watcher told me, are such cows seen. This time the hide didn't help much. I was still so cold I was groggy with it, barely able to think.

Maeniel went wolf and, warmed by his pelt, began to collect driftwood as quickly as possible. But I could tell both of us had been soaked, and he was beginning to falter, slowing as he piled the wood next to me.

Make fire. I pulled a branch under the cowhide and scrabbled my fingers through the pebbles at my feet. One sliced my fingers, and I knew I'd found flint. I smacked it against a cobble and sparks flew. But the wood was too wet, and the wind too fierce. The sparks burned my fingers, and one landed on the back of my hand.

My fire, I thought, rage burning in my brain. Oh, God, oh, God, the pain, as flame leaped from the back of my hand and raced down to the tips of my fingers. My fist closed around the wood, and it leaped into flame, and the Gray Watcher stopped and wondered as I thrust the flaming branch into the pile of driftwood and it became a pyre. Then I was screaming, holding my burnt hand in the rain to soothe it, and fire-charred lines ran from the center of the back of my hand, one out to each fingertip. They healed in days, but left scars. Only very faint scars, but I bear them still. Then it was all that the two of us could do to keep the fire going until the squall passed. We drew the cowhide over our heads and sat with the fire between us, not caring about the smoke, until we were both warm and dry.

I went to sleep, my back against the boulder. The Gray Watcher had flung the cowhide over the two boulders and created a sheltered spot between them. As wolf, he was sleeping on the other side of the fire. When I woke, it was at the moment of power between first light and sunrise. The light was bright, and fog filled the fjord. The high cliffs surrounding it were only shadows in the drifting mist. It lay like a thick blanket on the water.

The dragon lifted his head above the fog. I knew it was he at once, though I had never seen one before, because, though his body was gray— gray as polished silver—he had a red comb above his head that ran down between his eyes, rather like a horse's mane. Now it lay limp to one side of his neck, as a horse's mane will. There was another loose fold of skin beneath the neck, red, but a darker red than the one on top.

He snorted. I saw his nostrils close, rather like those of a porpoise or whale. He drew in deep breaths of air; and the simple act of breathing the cool, moist air seemed to please him, because his comb lifted slightly and briefly and filled with blood for a second and the throat pouch smoothed. But then, since he was moved by neither fury nor lust, both effects faded quickly.

He was so silent, the Gray Watcher still slept.

I rose and walked toward where the waves slapped quietly at the rocky shore and confronted him. I do not think either one of us was afraid. He was too magical a beast, too beautiful, to frighten me, and I was too small, too harmless, to frighten him.

Even though our boat had sunk, a lot of our catch had washed ashore. The Gray Watcher had piled the mullet on the beach above the tide line. The dragon was a guest, so I bethought me of my duties as a hostess. I went and got one and placed it in the shallows, where it washed back and forth in the gentle, early morning waves. But he didn't take it, only bent his long neck down, looking like some magnificent swan, and touched it with his nose, pushing it back up on the beach.

"No?" I asked. My voice sounded very loud to me in the early morning stillness.

He made a gentle blowing noise through his nostrils, as if to say, yes, no, I don't care for these things.

"Well," I said. "We have some samphire." We had two big sacks, in fact.

I offered him some. He took it from my hand—very gently, the way a horse takes an apple but careful of the fingers. I brought the sacks down and emptied them at the shore and watched while he ate his fill.

The light grew brighter and brighter. The mist began to burn away. The tall, frowning cliffs that surrounded the fjord began to show wet but clearly seen through the blowing vapor. Then the dragon lowered his head and butted me lightly in the chest. *He likes samphire,* I thought. *He doesn't care for fish. He would not want to eat me.* So I placed my hand on his forehead just at the frill. I touched it, and the world vanished around me, and I spoke to the dragon.

Did I say the sea here was gray, green, and black? No, I was wrong. Yes, those colors were there, but also many others: red, sometimes like blood, sometimes like the fine enamel work of a polished gem or the red-yellows and oranges that dance and dazzle in a fire's ever-changing hues. Then there is green, the clouded emerald, bearing secrets, light and fair as masses of drifting sea grass on the water, or clear, shading away into blue where the sea meets shore. But blue, blue, what do we know of blue?

The pure arch of summer sky over the ocean or the blues as light is lost, first transparent, then translucent, finally shading into shadow as the surrounding beasts reach the deeps.

I was wrong. Sometimes he did eat fish, and he and his companions, speaking in song, pursued them through the vast canyons and drowned mountains beneath the sea.

Oh, the dragon song of love and battle, hunger and grief, loss, desire, and the blazing instant of fulfillment echoed in this everlasting symphony that no human mind has ever comprehended. No human ear has ever heard. They all sing, you know—the porpoise, the whale, even the shrimp click to call for love.

These and many more things he told me in the eternal, unspeaking instant when our minds were joined. Then he pulled away—not I—and turned, swam through the receding fog back into this kingdom, the open ocean. I sat on the shingle, weeping without knowing why.

CHAPTER FOUR

HEN I WAS THIRTEEN, CYMRY'S ANSWER changed.

It had been a hard winter. A hard year, now that I think about it. We had a long, dry spring, unusual in this part of the world, and then just as the crops were well stunted by the drought, it rained buckets, drowning them. Making a living from the soil can be hell. How those in Roman territory made it, I cannot think. Maeniel said they often didn't, selling their children into slavery, starving, and finally having to flee their homes to escape the tax collectors. They were simply overburdened by the cost of legions and a government that did less and less every year, since it was controlled by the large landowners, who paid no taxes at all and cared nothing for farmers who had small freeholds.

He and Dugald argued constantly about this. Maeniel said that the road to Rome was the road to ruin, and Dugald said that they were the culmination of thousands of years of civilization, beginning in the east and spreading westward, carried by Kyra's folk who built the great chamber tombs in Gaul Armorica and Ireland. When I and Kyra complained and Mother covered her ears with her paws and Black Leg whined and stalked out of the house, they both turned on me and the rest, lecturing me about how I must learn about politics because one day I would be queen.

I said, "Ha! What would I rule over here in this quiet corner of the world?" Besides, I liked things just fine as they were. Dugald would hush me and say wait. Things were more peaceful now to the south. The trade ships were sailing—one had made port close by—and the crews brought news to us when anything made a loud noise in the world. All the talk was about the Pendragon's son being reared by Merlin. He would, they said, become high king, and even the Saxons supported him.

I went down to the harbor near the headland where the battle had been fought, and we climbed aboard the ship to see the jewelry and spices laid out on the deck for sale. Sometimes there were books, paper, and writing materials. When Dugald found these things, he bought them. I never asked after the jewelry or even the weapons.

Gray made me a sax, the single-edged blade the Frisians carry. It was about ten inches long, forged all of a piece, tang and blade together. The hilt was wrapped first with wire and then leather. I'd had my own spear since I was ten. The Gray Watcher had lately given me a beautiful compound bow that, as he said, was similar to the ones carried by Roman cavalry men. So I felt no need for any other weapons.

On this ship I saw no books. There were many people aboard. Issa was nagging her father and Bain for another necklace, this one gold. Gray was present, haggling with the captain over some scrap iron in a sack. Things were getting pretty bloody, because Gray was determined he was not going to pay the man's price and the captain was determined he was.

A young man, one of the crew, spoke to me. "Not interested in any of the jewelry?" he asked with seeming casualness.

I laughed. "I can't afford it," I told him. "I have no money. I'm just here with Kyra." She was also haggling with a withered-looking merchant, who had a dark gray beard and was becoming very dramatic.

"The woman with one eye?"

"Yes."

"She your mother?"

"No. My mother is long dead."

"I didn't think so. She is so dark, and you are very, very fair. So blond is your hair, it is almost white. I haven't seen someone so blond since I left my country. Most of the people here are dark, and if they aren't dark, they're red. But you, you're beautiful."

"Thank you."

He took my hand, drawing me away from the crowd around the goods set out for sale on the ship's deck. "Would you care to walk with me up into the rocks?"

He gestured at the headland against which the shallow-draft ship was moored. The ground was very broken there, flat clearings, then giant boulders. In a few steps you would be hidden from the folk on the ship, wandering in a maze with small clearings ablaze with green grass and wildflowers and barren spots covered with sun-warmed stone. He was still holding my hand. I looked into his eyes. They were gray-blue and his hair was a dark honey blond.

But I wondered what the reason was for his strange scrutiny and why he would want me to go off alone with him. Uneasy, I tried to pull my hand from his. He wouldn't let go.

"No," I said. "I don't think I want to—"

"Why not? Am I ugly?"

"No." I was conscious that he still had my hand. "You are quite pleasant to look upon."

"Then see." He pointed to a necklace of garnet and amber. "If you walk out with me, I'll give you that. It will look beautiful on someone with your coloring, so blond and fair skinned. I'll get it now and we can take it along with us. Let me show you how the red stones and butter amber will glow against that milky skin of yours. Come with me."

He was still holding my hand and made as if to put his other arm around my waist. I snatched my hand away and backed up. "Why would you want me to go with you and offer me presents?"

"Yes! Why indeed?"

The voice was the Gray Watcher's, and he was standing behind the young man, looking down at me over his head. The young man turned and found himself looking at the Gray Watcher's chest. In all the years I had lived with Dugald and the Gray Watcher, I had never seen him really angry. Not even during the battle with the pirates. But I sensed that he was angry now. The fair boy was one inch from dead. That was just his distance from Maeniel.

"He did no harm," I said.

"Not for want of trying," Maeniel said. "She is virgin and still a child. Now get out of my sight before I snap your neck like a rabbit's."

The boy left, easing away with remarkable quickness.

"What did he do?" I asked, wide-eyed at Maeniel's fury.

"You really don't understand, do you?"

"Oh," I gasped. And then, of course, I did. First I blushed and then I began to laugh.

The tension went out of Maeniel's body. He wound up buying me the garnet-and-amber necklace. I didn't know he had such a thing as money, but he did.

Later we stopped at the chief's hall. He wasn't there, but Issa greeted us respectfully. She was now head of the household, being married to Bain, her mother having died in the last year. Her father seemed to have aged greatly. She was her father's only surviving child, which explained Bain's deep interest in her when she was only a young girl.

She offered us wine and mead, but as was proper on a casual visit, we took only beer. Others were in the hall. The Romans say we have no seats but sit on the floor, but this isn't true. We have benches and low tables arranged around the fire pit, and since wood carving has become a high art among us, these are often very beautiful, cherished heirlooms. So they were in Dunnel's hall, fragrant cedar and the stone-hard pine that grows in the mountains battered by wind from the sea. These were twined with sea life. Seal, whale, porpoise, dulse, samphire, sloke, and sea spinach mingled with the beasts and long-necked dragons; eels, mackerel, and hake were braided together with the knots of eternal renewal.

The hall was a beautiful place with the fire blazing brightly on the central hearth. Its glow was thrown back by the jewel-like colors of the many wall hangings tracing the ancestral accomplishments of both town and family, flaming in the deep polish of the old oiled wood of its furniture. I sat where a proper girl should sit, among her male kin. Quite a few people were here visiting, to take advantage of the trade ship's stop. But we were all surprised when the young man who had propositioned me on the ship appeared before us.

"My name is Farry," he said, "and I am the son of the captain, Cuan. The request I made of the young lady here was an honorable one. The jewels were valuable and a seafaring man is not in a position to marry."

Maeniel's face didn't change. "Then it should have been made in Kyra's presence," he said.

"Yes," Farry said, "but I was in a hurry and I was afraid some other might snare her. And I didn't know she was a noble. She dresses so . . . so . . . plainly. The jewels were mine to dispose of and I would have made good the gift. But that's not why I come here today."

"What is it then that you want?" the Gray Watcher asked. "She is not for you, however much you offer. She is too young as yet, and most noble."

"I know. I know," Farry said. "Her line has numbered many kings and queens, and that is why she is in danger. Lord Merlin still hunts her, and there is a price on her head. I was told this by one of my crew, who said I should try to snare her and carry her off to Cornwall, where she would command a huge sum from the chief druid and other British princes. She is a great prize, and I can see why. That was the reason I took her hand and behaved foolishly, but I am here to say I had no bad intent."

Maeniel was about to answer, but I placed my hand on his and spoke to Farry. "I thank you for the compliment of your esteem and admiration, and I value your friendship. I thank you for your warning. I had not thought the memories of my mother's influence still lingered and had believed myself all but forgotten." Then I rose and took his hand.

He looked at me for a long time, as though sealing me in his mind that he might remember my face. "I wish," he said, then gave a little laugh. "I don't know what I wish. That you were less or I were more, perhaps. Yes, just possibly that's it. The jewels do look beautiful on you. I wish I had had the pleasure of making a gift of them to you. Good-bye."

Then he turned and walked away, and I gazed after him in sorrow.

"Don't look so, girl. He's the first to fall at your feet; he will not be the last. A more disturbing thing is what he had to say," the Gray Watcher said.

"Yes," Dugald said. "I had hoped the hue and cry had been forgotten or Merlin believed she was lost or had died in my care."

"No," the Gray Watcher said. "His kind don't forget things. Not things of her sort. And, make no mistake, when the ship makes its way back to the kingdoms below the Roman wall, someone—this Farry even or his father or his shipmates—will bring word to the British druid that this child has grown into a woman and that she is dangerously beautiful and intelligent."

"What should we do?"

"I cannot think any here would betray us," I said.

"No?" Dugald answered. "Then you have a better opinion of most people than I have."

Mother and Black Leg were at my side. I could see they and Maeniel and Kyra agreed with Dugald.

"Then what should I do?" I asked.

"You? You do nothing," Maeniel said. "It is what we will all do. We are a family. I swore I would never let myself be drawn into the human struggle again, but here I am."

"I think we should go home by another than our usual route. Some of the rest of the ship's crew may be harboring foolish ideas about earning a pile of gold from this Merlin," Kyra said. "When the ship is gone, nothing will happen for a time. Soon it will be autumn and we must question Cymry."

We took Kyra's advice, and the Gray Watcher turned wolf and led us by a route only he knew back to our steading.

The ship brought illness with it. We didn't know it at the time, but not long after they left, sickness spread through the village. As usual it took the oldest and youngest first. Dugald came down with it and was affected badly, as was Issa's first child, who died. I had only a mild case, since I was usually healthy; and, of course, the Gray Watcher and his son Black Leg never got any illness. But Mother fell ill then, not with whatever afflicted the humans, but with a congestion of the lungs. The Gray Watcher and Black Leg left to hunt, since the crops were poor this year. Not only our house but also the rest of the village was in need of meat.

Kyra, who is never sick either, remained home with me to care for Dugald and Mother.

I made a bed of soft grass for Mother near the fire and slept beside her with my arms around her. Kyra made medicine. She would not tell Dugald what was in it, and he swore at her when she tried to pour it down his throat.

"Woman, I will send you boils and the flux if you don't leave me alone!" he yelled as he lay shivering in his blankets.

"Be quiet, you old fool, and drink this. It will break your fever."

"Fever. Fever. I have no fever!" Dugald yelled. "You left the door open. I'm just cold."

"A plague on you for a two-legged jackass," Kyra screamed. "If I ever saw a case of the ague, it's the one you have now. Shut up and drink before I hold your nose and pour it down your throat."

"She will, too," I said from my place beside Mother near the fire. "And I'll help her. You know her remedies always make you better."

"If I heave till my toenails come up, it will be all you women's fault!" he screamed.

"You won't. Now, dammit, drink," she told him.

He did, swallowing the contents of the bowl in one draught. Then Kyra wrapped him in woolens. He began to perspire, and in no little time his fever was broken. Then she came over to check Mother.

"How is she?" Kyra asked.

"Not good," I said. "I can hear her breathe." And I could. The empty and fill of her lungs made a gurgling, rasping sound.

Kyra knelt down and put her ear against Mother's ribs. "I cannot think what else to do," she told me. "I dosed her with the same drugs I did Dugald, but her tribe doesn't perspire the way humans do, and her nose is dry and hot. Besides," Kyra said and made the sign of the cross, "I think she is much sicker than Dugald."

Mother opened her eyes and looked at me. "I am old," she said. "Old for one of my kind. You have been a good daughter to me. She has been a good friend. Tell her to go to sleep. Her potion took away the pain in my chest. In the morning, I will be better."

I told Kyra what Mother said. She nodded, then dipped a small bowl of stew from a pot on the hearth and gave it to me with some bread. The oatcake that is cooked on a griddle or flat stone near an open fire is hard but softens when it is dipped in broth. She got some for herself and offered Mother some, but Mother refused it and placed her head on my lap and slept.

Dugald snored on his bed against the wall.

I didn't realize I was weeping until I tasted the tears on the bread. Kyra brushed the tears from my cheeks.

"I'm afraid. I'm afraid for Mother. I cannot remember when she has not been near me. I remember her better than my human mother, and her teat in my mouth with its warm flow was my first comfort."

"You have led a strange life for a woman, but I cannot think it has done you any harm," Kyra said. "And, yes, I would rather offer you the comfort of kindly lies, but I know you would see through them. I believe you are very right to be afraid for Mother. She is old, after the fashion of wolves, and I have no recipes for healing her. I wish I could do more, but perhaps she is the best judge of her state, and she will be better in the morning." Then she kissed me on the forehead and went to bed.

I finished eating, lay down beside Mother, and closed my eyes. The next memory I have is of white roses, the smell of them and the feel of petals with my fingers. I was walking among bushes filled with them. Each plant had long, trailing canes that rose from the top and fell away toward the ground; and each long branch was covered with white roses, pale without any trace of color, not even at the heart. The stamens and pistils were as white as the petals.

The air around me was thick with mist, and I could see no more than a few feet in any direction. *These are the roses of fairy tales, and this is no dream*, I thought. And when I looked down at my feet treading the white petals into dewy emerald grass, I knew it was no dream. And then a mound twined with white roses was before me and an opening that was a door to darkness.

I knew there was danger should I meet anyone, but I entered and found myself in a forest at night. I remembered Maeniel telling me about

86

it, about trees, giants so wide the arms of many men outstretched could not span them and so tall they seemed to have caught the stars like flowers in their branches. It was a pathless forest, floored with ferns, and they were soft under my feet. I walked toward a waterfall that fell from a cliff even higher than the trees. In the darkness the water was silvered, glowing as though illuminated from within. It fell foaming into a basin, where it sparkled with a glow that reminded me of the star blaze of the sky on a mountain night, where the eye looks into diffuse clouds of distant light.

I came close to the basin and looked into the light that was sparkling, dancing, foaming, leaping in endless, ever-changing patterns, flowing into a lower basin, then into a stream, where it lost itself among the trees. Abruptly, I was back in our home, and Mother was no longer beside me. I lifted my head and saw she was standing in the door.

"I came to say good-bye."

"No, Mother," I said as I sat up. "No."

"I don't fear death," she said. "None of us do. It is God's gift to us. We don't really ever even think about it. Not the way you do. I look forward to plunging into the stream, being carried on by the rapids out toward the shore and into the weir of stars of the eternal sea."

Then I found myself back in the forest at the pool of light with Mother. She looked up at me. "I will always come when you need me," she said. "As long as life lasts."

She lowered her muzzle to the pool of stars, drank, and vanished.

I found myself back in our home. I still held her, but she was cold in my arms.

We made a pyre for her on a headland, one of those empty ones made only of windswept rock. Not everyone receives a pyre. Some are abandoned to the birds and the sea eagles, who clean the bones that they may be burned or returned to the houses to be kept and buried near the sleeping places. There are many different stories. The Christians say they must be buried to lie in the ground so they can find all their parts on the last day. Dugald was somewhat of this opinion. But Kyra, Maeniel, Black Leg, and I believed in doing it the old way, setting the spirit free to wander the stars and look for a new home. Besides, Maeniel pointed out, Mother was a wolf and maybe she didn't want to go to a place where there were humans. I could understand that—we humans have a bad history with each other and a worse one with animals.

Others want to bring the bones back so that the spirits can guard the hearth and return to a woman's womb, so they won't go somewhere strange and join another family but be with their own people. And, considering the way some children become small copies of their parents, I can believe this works. Empirically speaking, of course. This is what Maeniel calls such conclusions—empirical—or as derived from observation. Wolf or not, I can believe he has a better education than Dugald. But we must do honor to Mother's spirit and to her accomplishment—me! Because Maeniel, Black Leg, and Dugald all believe I would have died had not Mother been willing to give me her milk and for no short time. A wolf pup would have been far less of a trial.

Black Leg came in as we were making the body ready for the pyre. I wrapped Mother in a clean, undyed linen cloth and scented the bundle with juniper, cedar, and rose. Black Leg was wearing pants and carried a roe deer over his shoulder, and he said to the rest of us, "I am now a man. I remained in the other shape for her comfort and ease, but she told me I would be free to choose my state when she died."

Maeniel went over and kissed him on the forehead. They smiled at one another. Kyra wept. Then she kissed Black Leg, and so did I. He looked at me strangely when I did. Maeniel frowned, then put his hand on his son's shoulder. "She's your sister," he said.

"I know," Black Leg answered, but his look was still intense.

Dugald threw up his hands. "I cannot believe this," he said.

"I can," Kyra told him. "Shut up. Don't give either one of them ideas."

Both Black Leg and I felt something for each other, but at that point we weren't sure about it. He was younger than I was by some two years. He was not yet a man. Kyra fixed an old shirt of Maeniel's for him, taking it in in places so he could wear it.

There is a lot to a funeral. First, we must each bathe. Since it was almost winter, we put up the bathhouse. It's a sort of shed where you build a fire and heat rocks. People bathe two different ways. One is to throw water on the heated rocks and sit in the steam, the other is to put the hot rocks into a basin full of water to heat the water, and scrub yourself with nettle soap. I like to just sit in the steam, but Kyra made me bathe with water. Then she turned me around and washed my back.

"He loves you," she said. "You don't know it and I'm not sure he does either."

"He's my brother," I said.

"No, he's not," she answered. "He is the son of a wolf and a half human."

"I could do worse," I said. "Since we met Maeniel, we have never gone hungry."

"Yes, we are as prosperous as many who live on fine, strong farms," she agreed. "That fool Dugald keeps talking about you as royalty and says you are destined for a king."

"I have heard of kings," I told her. "I have read of kings, but I have never seen one, and I have begun to think Dugald is touched in the head. Why would a king marry me? The merchant's son aboard the boat seemed to believe I should consider myself lucky to be offered a nice present for lying with him."

Kyra slapped my shoulder a little harder than she had to—just to get my attention. "I'm finished here," she said, then handed me the bucket and dipper. "Rinse yourself off. What do you know of men lying with women?"

I shrugged, rinsed, and began to towel myself dry. "Last summer Black Leg and I invented a fine game. You know how couples sneak away to be by themselves in the rocks, the woods, or even the hayricks? Well, we would creep up on them and yell."

"Merciful God," Kyra said. "It's a miracle you weren't killed. Some of those men—"

"The women weren't sweet about it, either," I said. "Once or twice they got me with a rock. Remember when I told you I fell?"

"Heavens," Kyra said.

I shrugged. "I'm nearly as fast as Black Leg. She was just lucky."

"Lucky? A finger-long cut over your ear," Kyra snapped. "I *thought* you were lying at the time. You are nearly as quick and well balanced as the wolves and you never fall. Nice to know I was right."

I shrugged again. I was settling my loincloth and reaching for my *strophium* to bind up my breasts. "At any rate, I know what the procedure is. Both Black Leg and I know how to do it. Do I have to wear this?"

"Yes-s-s-s." It was a hiss. "Absolutely. Now—and never go out without it again. You and that hellion brother of yours are much closer to being grown than I thought."

Kyra went out and brought back a beautiful white blouse and another new pair of deerskin britches. I put on the garnet-and-amber necklace and combed out my hair. Kyra pushed me back to arm's length and looked at me. Her one eye was sad and her expression somber.

"You are very lovely now and soon you will be beautiful. And not in an ordinary way. Youth is always beautiful, but you are like some creatures of fairy born to bring ill to mortals. Only trouble can follow such gifts."

I laughed. "I am a dowerless girl. Dugald says I bear a great name, but who marries a name? Kyra, don't be foolish."

Then I kissed her, and we went to do our sad duty. We had built the pyre of cedar, ash, and oak. Since she had been more than wolf, we resolved to send Mother's soul into the wind at twilight. We waited until the sun was on the western horizon.

Maeniel covered Mother's head, and I kissed her between the ears on the top of her head, the way I always did. Black Leg, in buckskins, kissed her the same way. We must have been a strange sight on the lonely headland. The sea below crashed and thundered as the tide began to go out. The wind was a high, shrill keening, and we stood together, the four of us, after I placed Mother's mortal shell on the pyre. We held hands and said good-bye.

Dugald *didn't* make his usual weak remarks about heathens. We soaked some hanks of wool in oil and wine, pushed them among the logs, then we kindled a small fire and tried to light the pyre. She made a small bundle on top of the big pile of wood where we had curled her nose to tail as she usually slept. But try as we might, we couldn't get the wood to burn. The sun slipped below the horizon, its glow kicking long legs out over the water. With the approaching darkness, the wind picked up and began to flail us with spray from the surf.

And then I understood.

I'm not sure how I understand these things. Dugald has all sorts of explanations, but they raise more questions than they answer for me. I simply knew. I walked out on the headland and put my hand on Mother's body, a cold lump under the linen.

"It's all right," I said. "I'll call if I need you. Go! Find your peace."

The fire leaped from my hand to the wood, as it had the day on the beach when the cold almost killed Gray Watcher and me. The fire burned far more brightly and fiercely than the amount of oil and wine we had included among the wood could explain. White hot, the flames roared through the logs until the heat drove us back far from the headland. The flames consumed the she-wolf and blazed with fierce intensity as the roaring, exploding sheets of fire took my mother's soul to the stars.

CHAPTER FIVE

HERE IS MAGIC. THE FEW THINGS I HAD learned were really only tricks. I found out when I encountered the real thing. We questioned Cymry again at the turning of the year. As always, I asked if we would face raids that year. He said yes, but then would say no more. Kyra, as usual, tormented and threatened him. He wept and begged for more wine, oil, and meat. So I gave it to him, but either he didn't know or wouldn't tell us anything more. My own feeling was that he didn't know. The world is a complex place, and any other world would be, also.

Winter was upon us, and it would be a hard one. The rain and cold in the late summer had killed the wheat crop and a lot of the barley. Rye and oats were all that was left. I went out with the other women to collect acorns and hazelnuts, and we got quite a few baskets of those. The meal would be ground and added to flour for bread.

I was working with the other women when the Gray Watcher came to call me. We had spread the hazelnuts and acorns out on the threshing floor. We were drying them. Put them away wet and they become moldy. The old people, the first people, lived on them. One way to make sure you had plenty of food was to allow both oak and hazel trees to become widespread, so they broadcast the seed in any area where it looked as though it would grow well. We had no problem in collecting a lot of both. Storage and processing were the difficulty.

This was the reason the chief was important. That's a leap. Maeniel called it a route to power. He served the community by maintaining an area of dry storage under his house and by defending a large amount of common land where stock could be grazed by each family. He saw to the forest also, where our pigs foraged. They got most of the available hazelnuts and acorns on level ground. So I and the rest of the women had been climbing around the rocks for several weeks, collecting the surplus. It reposed in big baskets on the threshing floor. They had to be turned every day to ensure they were dry before they were placed in the basement of the chief's house.

One thing knocks against another, like a wave brought into being by an offshore storm that ends by crashing into a beach a dozen miles away in the sunshine. If the wheat and barley crops both failed, we would not have enough food to overwinter the stock, the sheep and cattle that provided both milk and meat for the summer. Yes, we could collect acorns and hazelnuts as we had, but if we took too many of them from the forest, then the pigs would not do well, and they are a staple in winter. But we women could collect acorns and nuts from the rocks where the pigs can't forage, and the men could fish and bring in cod from the deep, cold water off the coast.

Neither task is easy. Both are arduous and can be very dangerous. Issa was in bed with a badly twisted ankle. All the more dangerous because she was due to deliver her second child in a few weeks. The rest of us were weary from toiling over the water-soaked nuts. The ones collected from the rocks were apt to be more tainted by damp than the ones in the forest.

The men who must fish had to take out the old pirate boat, since it was the only one we owned that could be trusted in deep water. It took ten men to row it—at least ten men—and they would be hard put to control her. Maeniel was among the crew. The chief wouldn't risk more than twelve men on her, because we all knew that, should she go down in a storm, the icy water would claim her crew in a few minutes. Only a little over a hundred people lived in our hamlet. Twelve men would be a disastrous loss, and twelve young men at that. The grieving would never be done. The loss of so many sons, husbands, fathers, and brothers might destroy us. The women might leave, never to return.

It has happened.

They look around at houses, fields, woodlands, and shore and say, "We are accursed. Let us go. Women are always in demand. I will not want to look on sea or shore that has taken my life, my love."

We have, you know, four fairs. The women offer themselves to the king or queen as the case may be. The king makes a loud noise among the people and says, "We have women here for the taking; who needs a wife? Hire them for a year. See if you suit. Yes, some have children at their skirts. All the better. You will know they can breed well. Come and look, tender your offer to me. I will hold the cash till we see if both of you will make it permanent or not."

I had a mind to do this myself when I became a woman. That way you get a good look at him and can name your own price. Dugald, Maeniel, Kyra, and I had a terrible blowup about it. They wanted to marry me off, as propertied women are by their king. I was against this, royal or not. I had no wish to be bestowed in a place not of my choosing, with a man who possibly only wanted me because his kin told him it would be to his advantage to be with me.

Then Dugald flew into a rage, a terrible rage. He broke all the cooking pots without even touching them, stirred the fire to such a roar that it nearly consumed the roof, and even awakened Cymry from his tranced place among the dead. He began to scream. Kyra, Maeniel, and Black Leg ran. He told Maeniel—before he ran—that this is what came of teaching a woman to be independent and know her own mind. That she would set her face against both wisdom and the wise, and that the auguries had foretold that I would wed a king.

I stomped my foot and said, "Fine! Who can escape her fate? But if I am to wed this king, then where is he? If I am to take him to my heart late in life, then I am not minded to wait so long, but will have others before him."

"No," Dugald screeched. The fire began charring the roof beams. It

94

blazed so high, fanned by his magic wrath. "No," he repeated. I would have none before this king, and for Black Leg to get that look out of his eye. Or he would use his powers to drive him away so that he must go run with his brothers who led lowland packs. Then I stormed out weeping, following the rest.

But both Maeniel and Kyra made me promise to humor Dugald for at least another two years. A few days after that, when I and the other women had begun gathering the hazelnuts and acorns, Magetsky, the raven, returned. She lived with us off and on when she hadn't taken up with a mate. Maeniel said she was the only bird he knew that was a tramp. Love 'em and leave 'em.

I had no idea what he meant, but let me tell you, Magetsky didn't improve Dugald's temper one bit. She'd picked up a few new tricks. Her old ones were bad enough: squirting shit on your clothes when you were bathing or pinching the tender area between forefinger and thumb if you didn't let her share your dinner. But now she had learned to make a sound like a cow fart, and she liked to perch in the rafters while we were eating and do this. And while flying, she had perfected her ability to aim her ordure—that is the polite word—at anyone walking below.

One evening at dusk, she nailed Dugald. Splat! Right on the top of his head. Kyra and I laughed until we were sore. But Dugald called up a really bad curse, placed it on an arrow, and sent it winging after her. We didn't see her for a few days, and Dugald walked around with a satisfied smirk on his face. But then she returned, looking bedraggled. She said it had taken her a day and a night to outfly the curse, then a storm had blown her to Ireland. The weather was deteriorating, and she had the very devil of a time getting back. She complained of Dugald to Maeniel, but he told her she deserved what she got and to think twice about using Dugald for target practice anymore.

None of us gave it a second thought. I because I was a child and children think they know everything. Maeniel didn't because, though he is magic, he doesn't understand much about it. Kyra did worry, but she was working hard with the other women and didn't confide her fears to me. But some sentinel saw the effects of Dugald's magic and passed the word to others, who had been waiting for a long time.

The dead ride hard.

Maeniel and Black Leg came by. Maeniel handed me my bow.

"Hunt," he said. "We will be gone a few days. You, Black Leg, drive the deer toward her."

"I thought you were both going," I said.

"No," he told me. "The chief won't risk more than one man from any family. What would Dugald and you do were you left alone? I know you believe you're grown, but I worry about you nonetheless."

So I turned our nuts into the rest of the baskets, and Black Leg and I set out to hunt.

"So why can't you stay home and marry me?" he asked once we were out of earshot of the other women.

"You are my brother," I said.

"No, we are not blood relatives," he said. "Maeniel and I have fostered you, but we are not kin."

This was true.

"The church frowns on it," I said.

"And since when have you ever given a damn for those mad monks living on the islands off the coast? If we followed their teaching, we would have died out years ago. Or, I should have said, you would have died out years ago. I am but a humble wolf. But you humans are a plague upon the earth."

I began laughing.

He pushed me, and it only made me laugh the more. "I don't know if I want to lie down under any man and wiggle and moan the way those silly girls do."

"Well, you won't have to," he said, "because I don't want to lie on top of any knobby-boned woman and make her wiggle and moan. Not any woman, least of all you. I'd rather go into the forest and throw myself atop a deadfall tree. I don't know why they want to do it anyway, and, besides, you have more sharp edges than a sack of firewood."

I picked up a stone, threw it at him, and raised a knot on his ribs. Then ran. I said I could outrun even the wind. He chased me to the top of the hill and down the other side into the valley. He was stubborn about it, though. He wouldn't turn wolf. If he had, he might have caught me, but he remained human, and so by the time he ran me down, though I was breathing hard, he was completely winded.

It was late afternoon by then, and we were near a lake where the deer came down to drink at dusk. We sat down on a rock to talk and wait for evening. He was still on the same subject.

"No, really, why can't I marry you?"

"You're younger."

"Only by two years. It won't be long before that won't matter. I love you," he said seriously. "I don't want you to go marry some old king."

"I'm not marrying any king. Dugald is stuffed with foolishness. Losing his place at the queen's court turned his brain."

"How many kings do you see hereabouts? Fool! The closest thing to it here is a chief, and he's ancient. Oh yes, forty is to thirteen. And all he has is that prissy Issa, who is married to Bain, and he beats her. He took a swing at her when she caught him with the serving girl the last time she was pregnant," Black Leg said. "I wouldn't try to beat you if you married me."

I was sitting cross-legged on a sun-warmed boulder. "That's because you're too tired when you finally catch up to me," I said.

"No." His face grew serious. "I love you. I don't want things to change. No, I wouldn't harm you if I weren't tired. We, the gray people like Maeniel and I, aren't dangerous in love. We could keep you fed even if all the wheat, oats, and barley died of the cold. I could kill every day and not just when the chief wants to make feast in the hall. He kept us fed when we didn't think about men and women at all. When we lived in the mountains alone with the pack."

He leaned against the boulder and looked up at me, and I saw he was serious. Then I became serious, too.

"You're right," I said. "I don't want to sell myself to some man either, but I don't know if I have a choice."

"You do have a choice—me." He stretched out his hand toward me, and I took it. "See how easy it is to make the pledge?" he said.

I pulled my hand away and looked out toward a standing stone that overlooked the sea. They called it the Beltane Stone. It is the festival of desire—on the first of May, when summer is established and men go to the assemblies to present themselves to the king, and the girls without land or other property hire themselves out looking for a permanent arrangement.

As I said, women were always in demand. There were never enough of us to go around. A strong, skilled, handsome woman could do well for herself, especially if it was her first outing and she was fair. No powerful man would want me as a first wife, but I might become a third or fourth wife of a strong lord or the successful leader of a war band. Such always wanted more women. There is no great wealth without many women. A man needs women to till his fields, spin, weave, gather wool, and tend to his dairying, not to mention to care for the children he has fostered on them. He gives the women the means to wealth—land, sheep, cattle; she spins and weaves the wool, churns the butter, makes cheese, and grinds the grain for porridge. She may claim her share for the work she contributes and her skills.

A minute later I saw movement in the heather and brush on the hillside. "Someone is here, besides us, I mean," I whispered softly.

Black Leg immediately crouched down. I remained where I was, knowing I must have been seen. At heart Black Leg was a wolf, and wolves need no lessons in furtiveness. A few seconds later, I heard footsteps and Gray came into view on the path.

"What are you doing here, Guynifar?" he asked. "And alone?"

"She is not alone," Black Leg said as he rose to stand beside the boulder.

Gray jumped. "So I see."

"Yes, and if you meant her any ill will, you would not have seen me till my knife was in you."

"Terribly suspicious people you are—Dugald's family," Gray said.

"Yes," I answered. "And you have reason to be glad."

"True," he said. "But what are you doing?"

"When the sun is closer to the horizon, we will hunt," I said. "The chief is giving a feast tonight for the families of the men who man the boat. We hope to get a deer, maybe two."

Gray nodded. "I have rabbit snares here."

"We were passing the time until twilight talking," Black Leg said. "Talking of marriage."

Gray chuckled. "I had thought you both too young to worry over that."

"No," I said. "Though we cannot understand what all the wiggling and squirming is about."

Gray did laugh at that. Laughed till he had to sit down and wipe his eyes. "Yes, yes, I know. Being a friend of your family, I have heard the angry complaints of some of the couples you managed to surprise last year."

"What did they want?"

"They felt you both needed a good spanking."

Both Black Leg and I were indignant about that and expressed it. Gray shook his head.

"No, I fear all your guardians, Dugald and the Gray Watcher, are downright dangerous, and I can't say I would court Kyra's enmity either. No, I told them they brought it on themselves. Either behave better or hide better, I said to them, but I promised to speak to the Gray Watcher if your mischief continued. But then the weather turned nasty and—"

"Why do they do that?" I asked. "And why do they hide when they do it? Are they ashamed? And if so, what have they to be ashamed of and—"

"Stop—stop—stop!" Gray cried. He was laughing so hard he had to lean against the boulder I was sitting on.

Black Leg looked disgusted at the foolishness of both adults and humans.

"Oh, God, you are children," Gray said. "And the only proper answer is that in the fullness of time, you will learn all the answers to your questions and many more you haven't even thought of. But for right now, be content to wait. Wishing never made the tide rise or a pot boil. Only time can bring certain things about, and, lucky for the two of you, time is something you both have."

Black Leg and I looked at each other.

"Well," he said, "we weren't talking about that anyway. She wants to go sell herself at the Beltane fair. I think she should stay home and marry me. We are not blood relatives, but she has been fostered among us. I am almost as good a hunter as the Gray Watcher. I can provide for her."

"I don't doubt that," Gray said. "No, I don't doubt that at all. No other family could send out two children and even hope to have them bring home a deer by nightfall. All of your people are a skilled lot, but strange, very strange," he said.

Again, we were both indignant. "Strange?" I asked. "How strange?"

Gray met my eyes for a second, then looked away at the lake in the bottom of the valley. "No, don't go to the Beltane fair. Not this year or even the next or the one after that. Many men would look upon you with desire not caused by your skills. Many would offer for you, but you are best bestowed with your family. And if you must marry, take Black Leg. He best understands you."

"It's getting late," Black Leg said.

"And I," Gray said, "must check my snares while there is still light."

Black Leg vanished into the brush. I went and collected his clothes and folded them behind the rock, then picked up the bow.

"He will check for you," I told him.

He shook his head. "Yes, I know. Is he hungry?"

I shrugged. "I don't know, but if he were, he wouldn't eat what belonged to you."

Gray folded his arms and looked out over the forested margins of the little lake.

"In a minute or two," I explained, "he will be back behind the rock."

Gray waited patiently. In a few minutes four hares and Black Leg appeared behind the rock. Gray went down on one knee and began to clean, skin, and gut the hares. I sat quiet, completely still. The sun was just touching the horizon when I could tell from small movements that Black Leg was positioning himself in the low brush at the lakeshore.

"Be still now," I told Gray. "He's in position."

Gray finished with the hares. He stood. "Where is he?"

"In that little patch of willows that runs right down into the water," I whispered.

"How can you tell?"

"I don't know how I tell. I just know," I whispered back. "Now, be quiet. Maeniel gets angry if I lose arrows."

Half the sun went behind the small crag on the other side of the lake.

The valley and the lake margins lay now in deep shadow. The air was cool, and it was very quiet here. No bird or animal made any sound. I saw shadows move on the margin of the lake on the other side. They were here. I found myself kneeling, bow in hand, watching.

The sun sank lower. As it did, it moved from behind the crag and lighted the narrow end of the valley where the lake turned into a falls that rushed through a rocky bed down to the sea. The dying sun passed out from behind the crag on its journey toward the horizon and illuminated that end of the valley with a shaft of brilliant orange light. I was conscious the bow was in my hand, the arrow nocked.

Black Leg made his rush. The deer fled along the lake margin in the shallows, splashing through the water and into the light. The first was a pregnant doe. She is sacred and may not be brought down. The second, a young stag with a fair rack. Tough! Cook him for two days and he would not be done. The third, another doe with a fawn, but the fourth, a yearling spike buck, good eating. The arrow was gone before I had time to will it.

The yearling made one more leap. For a second I thought I'd missed. Then he died, going down into the water and sending a fan of spray with his sliding body.

"Looks as though it will be only one," I said when I jumped down from the rock. "Black Leg should have waited until there were more to choose from. A few minutes and we might have had two," I grouched.

"Be content," Gray said. "I don't know of a half dozen who could do so well and none are eleven- or thirteen-year-olds."

"Help us get the carcass to the chief's hall and we will give you the heart, brain, and liver," I said.

Gray answered, "Done," and we started walking to the other side of the lake. I carried Black Leg's clothes. Gray slung the hares in a tree. I carried my bow on my back. Black Leg was sitting on shore when we reached the other side.

Gray waded in and pulled the dead deer out of the water. The boar almost got him. It was as if the beast had been waiting. Black Leg, still a wolf, went for him, and the boar turned as though sensing that Gray, in up to his hips, was too far away, and with one vicious slash of his tusks, tried to disembowel him. The beast failed but he opened a ragged wound on Black Leg's side.

God, I remember thinking. *God in Heaven, we'd come out without spears.* I had to protect Black Leg. I snatched up a stone, and a second later it smacked into the boar's snout. I had never seen a boar before. That's a strange thing to say, since the boar hunt is the sacred testing ground of the young men in the war band, but for this reason they are scarce and not often seen. But all those I had ever seen were dead and strapped to poles, ready for the initiation feast of some young warrior. Even dead they were frightening. The open mouth with its long, yellow fangs that can tear even a strong man's arm or leg off; the tusks at either side of the leathery snout built to disembowel the boar's opponent should he question his right to the sow's favors. Disembowel, that is, as in rip out your guts. Disembowel. And they can do it in a half second to a dog, man, woman, wolf, or even a tame pig.

We were all moving fast now and hoping the pig wasn't faster. A spear is the only way to deal with the boar's madness. A long, strong spear, with a crosspiece to keep the boar from walking right up to kill you, even when you have the spade-shaped blade in his body at the heart.

I held a bow and brought only four arrows.

"The sea!" Gray shouted. "The sea. He won't follow us into the surf."

We all jumped into the lake. The water was not deep, but not shallow enough for the pig to get at us. In less than a minute, we were at the falls and that was dangerous, not that they were high, but because the footing was slippery.

Black Leg's paws scrabbled on the wet, mossy rocks, and he went over, dragged down among the rapids by the current. Gray abandoned himself and dove, letting the current take him. I tried to keep my footing and paid the price. I slipped and fell hard. Then I was pulled down in the narrows, where the stream ran between big rocks. My body crashed against one of them, and it drove the air out of my lungs. I breathed water and came up retching. The only thing that saved us was that after only a very short distance, the stream reached the sea, and we found ourselves wading in surf.

The boar, racing along the stream bank, was right behind us, those sharp, cloven hooves of his throwing sand as he charged along. It was brighter here, because the sun wasn't behind the rocky hills. We fled along the margin of the ocean, running in the sand at the foot of high cliffs.

I could see that, not more than a mile away, ahead of us, the beach ran out. A spill of rock from the frowning cliff above sloped down, black and ominous into the water. Black Leg, on four legs and faster than Gray and I, ran ahead, but I could see blood streaming from his flank into the water. I don't remember screaming, but I must have, because Gray snatched me up and plunged into the sea. When we turned, the boar stood in the shallows watching us, eyes glowing in the sunset light streaming from behind us. Gray had me by the scruff of the neck. I understood why when a wave broke over my head, and he lifted me out of the water.

He was only in up to his waist, but I was in up to my neck.

"The bow!" he shouted.

I was still holding the bow in my right hand. "No use," I answered. That's why I tried to walk down the falls. The bowstring is braided sinew. Once it's been in the water, it won't work till it dries.

He nodded. "Can you ride the waves?" he asked, and gave my body a light shake.

"Yes," I told him.

He let go of me and struggled off to his left. Another wave hit, and it didn't break but lifted me slightly. I went up with it and came down a little closer to the beach.

The boar locked eyes with me. *Death.* I heard the word as if it had been spoken. *Death.* Pig, *your* death, you mean, I thought back at it.

Another wave. It moved me both closer and to my right, away from Gray. The sun was at the edge of the water by now, a dazzle I could feel as well as see from the corner of my eye. The heat burned at my back. The water was cold. It would suck the warmth out of my body soon, leave me limp and not even able to think clearly. In no little time the sun would be gone. Death! The pig held my eyes. I wondered what Gray was doing, but didn't dare look. Somehow, I was holding the pig's attention.

Another wave, this time higher, a massive swell. When I came down,

I was in only up to my waist. I was face-to-face with the pig. I could see the blood on his tusk where he'd slashed Black Leg. He was waiting. One more wave and he'd have me. Where was Gray?

I pushed hard with my feet, jumping back into the waves. Gray brought the club he'd improvised from a big piece of driftwood down hard on the pig's head.

It went right through.

Gray screamed, and, throwing aside the club, turned once more toward the water. But a second later, he was down, the pig's tusk in his ankle. He screamed again. I ran toward him. This was no natural beast, and I did have fire in my right hand.

Black Leg came out of nowhere and lunged at the pig's haunch. His teeth went in; my hand was on its shoulder. There was a terrible stench in the air, and I knew it felt my touch.

Gray picked himself up. Black Leg let go, and the three of us bolted toward the rocks ahead. We reached them just as the sun's last rays painted a mirrored road over the water. We climbed frantically. It was getting dark.

"What is that thing?" Gray cried.

I was shivering violently. "I don't know, but we have to build a fire, and do it right now before it gets dark! It may take another shape at night."

Black Leg could climb better as a human. I could hear his teeth chattering. Gray pulled off his shirt and threw it over Black Leg's head. I looked down and nearly fell from fright. We were high, high above the beach. I looked up and saw we could get no higher. The cliff towered over our heads, stretching out over the water. We had reached a place hollowed out by wind and rain beneath the top, a shallow grotto. We were trapped.

Fire, I thought. "Fire." I found I was speaking aloud.

"Fire."

The rockfall was laced with driftwood, blown up by the waves driven by wild storms during the spring and summer.

"Fire!" I screamed.

"Fire, well and good," Gray shouted. "How will we light it?"

"You'll see. Get some wood." The sun was only a red glow on the horizon, the clouds an iridescent purple and black. "Hurry," I commanded.

Something was climbing the rocks. I couldn't see what it was and didn't want to. *I'm not ready yet*, I thought. *Not ready to die*. Why was I so cold?

Black Leg crawled toward the curved wall at the back of the grotto and huddled against it, shivering. Gray piled wood at my feet. He, too, saw something that was not a boar climbing toward us. Frantic with fear, he was snatching up every bit of fuel he could see.

I thrust my whole arm into the pile. The answering curtain of flame singed my hair and burned off my eyelashes. I only got the lids closed just in time to keep the fire from searing my eyeballs.

"God!" Gray shouted. It didn't sound like a curse but a prayer.

The rest of the driftwood went up with a rush, casting its light down the rockfall to the beach. Whatever had been climbing, fled, wailing.

"How did you do that?" Gray asked.

"I don't know," I moaned. "I've been able to do it since I was about nine. Please, please be quiet. Let me get warm."

I crawled up next to Black Leg and threw my arms around him. Gray crawled around, finding more wood and throwing it on the fire. At last he tried to rest, leaning back against the curved stone wall.

At length I stopped shivering. Black Leg and I got warm. He had lost his clothes, but Gray's shirt was long enough to cover him to his knees.

"So, you want to marry her?" Gray said, and laughed. He looked at Black Leg. "You may be the only suitable candidate. I'm very glad you can do that, Guynifar, but I think most husbands might find it disconcerting if you snapped your fingers to light the fire when you cooked breakfast."

I studied Gray's ankle in the firelight. It was badly mangled.

"Not fair," he gasped. "I couldn't hurt it, but it could carve me like a chunk of soft wood."

Time stopped. That's the only way I can describe it. *Fire is in my right hand*, I thought. *What is in my left? It's not long, I will be a woman, but as yet there is no blood.*

Then I remembered Mother drinking from the pool of stars at the

105

foot of the falls. The dream place. When I told Maeniel about it, that's what I called it, the dream place. He'd shaken his head and said, "No, it's not a dream. I've been there once—no, twice."

I asked him where it was and how would I get there and back, but he said he didn't know. He'd never seen a map. Then he smiled strangely. "It has something to do with the boundary," he said. Boundaries are always important—the sea and the shore, the river and its margins, day and night, life and death. "Yes," he had repeated, "life and death." He said he'd never been there, to that place, unless death had been involved, whether it was his own or someone else's. I was there.

The spray from the glowing waterfall was on my lips. It was day, but in the deep gloom of the summer forest the waterfall was like a column of light. Sun struck from within as though the light were not shining on the water but from it, not blue but a drench of sparkles and pale, pale gold. I was there; I could smell the air, clean, so clean it held only the scent of the trees and grass. Clear and pure as a draft of water from a well tapped for the first time. *It is the sea,* I thought. *Spray from the sea pounding the rocks below.*

The world transformed itself again. I was in the clear sun-shot brilliance of the ocean, kissed by the sun. Rising. Rising, the water becoming more and more transparent as I rose from the depths. Up, up, up like a porpoise leaping. Oh, the joy of it. Up into the light.

Then I was in the grotto with Black Leg and Gray. My hand was on Gray's ankle, and it was whole once more. There was no sign the boar had ever touched it.

Maeniel was standing on the shore with Kyra. They were cleaning ling. Or rather, he was cleaning the fish. Kyra was boning them, rubbing them with sea salt, and hanging them on a drying rack. The chief was present to be sure the count was fair and the salt cod would be distributed equitably. The men who took the boat out got half, their pick of the fish. The rest of the people took the other half.

It was warm. The sun was shining and everyone hoped this would continue until the fish were dry. If it didn't, they would need to smoke them. Smoked fish tasted better and were more tender, but smoking was more work and took a lot of fuel. The women who would collect the wood were already weary from having scrabbled among the rocks for the acorns and hazelnuts.

Dugald was dressed in a robe Maeniel had never seen. It was a caftan, dyed brown and woven with black ogam symbols at the neck and hem and bordering the long, flowing sleeves. Maeniel, who could read the sticklike ogam, saw that these were blessings intended to protect the wearer. The blessings of Christ, his mother, and the whole heavenly choir were invoked. What was written on the hem made Maeniel smile.

The "heroes" weren't neglected, either. Ah yes, the "heroes," who would never be forgotten. Emissaries from Rome had a tendency to frown at the cult of the heroes, and it was rumored that a few who became abusive had been subjected to the test of the sea. Maeniel wasn't sure how this was handled, but the ocean was dark, cold, and very deep, and the people doing the testing could make sure one either passed or failed. So most of the legates were discreet. One might be glad these wild people called themselves Christians, even if a few additional beliefs snuck in under the blanket. It did trouble him that Dugald had been invoking magic, as the clothing indicated. What could be wrong?

Dugald reached him. Seeing how he was dressed, others made room for him quickly. Maeniel drove his knife into the section of oak trunk that he was using as a table and turned toward him.

"She is gone. She, Black Leg, and Gray. Gray's wife told me he has rabbit snares near the lake. When he didn't return last night, she came to me and asked if Black Leg and Guinevere had seen him. I told her no, I hadn't seen them and you told me you sent them hunting near the lake before you left on the boat. I have been searching since, in my own way. They are not near. I would have found them." His face was sick and sunken, filled with fear.

"Old man, old man, what have you done?" Kyra spat. "You are hollow-bellied and mad-eyed with guilt."

"It's true," Dugald whispered. "I am. The bird, that thrice-cursed bird, that's the cause of it all."

Maeniel snapped his fingers hard. Magetsky left off feeding on fish guts with the other ravens and flew to the stump, landing next to Mae-niel's knife. She gave a strident *kugh* and made kissy noises at Dugald, as if to tell him she was none the worse for her adventures.

"I put a curse on her," Dugald said. "She made me so angry, I called a black wind and launched the devil's arrow at her. I have not engaged in such noisy sorcery in many years. I'm afraid I may have awakened some-thing, perhaps something terrible."

"She wouldn't be easy to take," Maeniel said. "She is innocent, and that's why I called down protection for her from the Lords and Ladies of the sunlit heavens. She is Guinevere, one filled with light."

He turned to Magetsky and addressed her in angry Second Raven. She fixed one onyx eye on him and made a sound like water bubbling out of a jug or possibly someone's gut in the throws of diarrhea. Maeniel made a sound like an angry wolf, so low a rumbling that it was almost below the range of human hearing. Kyra and Dugald knew she could probably hear it better, but even to human ears it carried a heavy freight of dark men-ace. Magetsky wasted no more time. She flew off toward the valley.

"She will begin her search. She can go places even I cannot."

"What's wrong with you?" Kyra upbraided Dugald. "I thought you had forsworn magic?"

"I had, woman, I had. But that bird so filled me with fury that I lost my temper. My foot slipped. It's been so long. We have been hidden here, and comfortably so, that I didn't think—oh, Christ—I am ridden with guilt and terror. The magic of the ancients was nothing but a curse. It de-livered us into the hands of the Romans. Now it sells our souls and bodies to the Saxons in the form of Merlin. Relying on it cut down Bodiccia and my order, the thinkers and dreamers on the isle of Mona. What have I, in my stupid anger, done?"

He shook his fist in Maeniel's face. "There are people . . . who . . . who . . . call on the . . . the 'heroes' and they are answered. She is one, such a one. By birth, by breeding, by nature, such a one, and I have taught her nothing of what she needs to know to protect herself."

"Why? I thought after she warned us about the ship and compelled Cymry to speak, you promised you would make her your pupil," Kyra shouted.

"Keep your voice down," Maeniel snapped. "See how people are looking at us? Things are difficult enough here. Think how quickly the tale of a sorcerer's ill wish might spread. And, Dugald, you are no help, appearing in that robe today. Magic made me a man," Maeniel said.

Dugald snorted. Maeniel looked at him through his eyelashes. Dugald's return glance was a challenge.

"It was spring," Maeniel said. "The older women brought the younger ones to the grove. Some wept, some didn't. They knew they were to be sacrifices. The old women made sure they were all fit."

"All virgin," Kyra said.

Maeniel nodded. "They gave the women drink. Some finished what was in the golden bowls, some didn't. One bowl lay on the grass in the shadow of the trees. The girls danced around the fire. That was what drew me in the first place. The heavy scent of smoke and perfumes rising from the fire. It was intoxicating. But by then, I drank in the powerful fragrance given off by their naked bodies. The priestesses watched the moon rise.

"Honey mead was in the bowl. All—even the beast, even the wolf— love sweetness. I drank. The bowl held other things besides mead. The madness of springtime took me, and then I looked up. She walked toward me, and though she seemed solid as you, not one blade of grass bent beneath her feet. She was not just beautiful; there was nothing about her that was not beautiful. I cannot say if she was clothed or naked. She wore her loveliness like a garment of light.

"I knew her. We all know her. We are her people, and when she journeys on the earth, we protect her. So it was when she was Leto and carried her son filled with light to the navel of the world at Delphi. We traveled with her and hunted for her until she, with a sad travail, gave birth to the son of the stars. When I saw her walk toward me, I was filled with an astonished joy.

" 'Flee,' she said, 'or yield up your surrender, wolf.' I yielded up my soul, oh, so gladly. Oh, so gladly. She touched my forehead. I might have turned away, turned and run away and not let her fingers rest on my head. She would not have pursued me. She pursues no one. But I was still and let her make of me what she would. And then her hand fell back. I knelt before her on the grass as a man. She smiled and became even more beautiful.

'Why, you are fair,' she said. 'You are my Niall.' For I was dark, my hair curled around my face."

"She is madness," Dugald said. "She is an agony of madness."

"Yes," Maeniel said, "and in her dreams we see all of our desires." He stuck the knife in the oak trunk.

"Magic is not good in war. It betrayed Bodiccia; it betrayed them at the isle of Mona."

"Nonsense," Maeniel said. "One flaw of your people is that they will quarrel with each other simply to entertain themselves on a rainy evening. The other is a strength and a weakness. They have a breadth of vision that sees the splendors of this world and the one beyond. But that very breadth of vision causes disorganization. And I tell you, war is not valor, courage, or even dark things like anger, rage, or killing. War is organization—and the discipline that goes with a high level of organization. The Romans understood this, and to them everything others find precious, lovable, joyous, interesting, admirable was simply a heathcomb to be offered on the altar of the gods of war. They had the victory of this understanding, and they also bore the everlasting oblivion of its final, inexorable defeat.

"If Bodiccia, Guinevere's great ancestress, fell, it was not because of her magic but because she didn't have enough time to put together an organization strong enough to defeat her enemies. We will—you, I, Kyra—give this girl time!" Maeniel pulled the knife out of the wood, then stabbed it down again to the hilt. He turned and a moment later he was in the trees near the beach, then he was gone.

We woke to a gray morning. Fog covered the sea and the fire we'd built on the rocks was burned to coals. Black Leg's head was on my lap, and Gray was stretched out with his face and arms near the fire, as though he'd fallen asleep tending it—as he must have. I couldn't see the boar, because I couldn't see the beach, but I could hear his snuffling near the rocks. I lay and watched the sun grow brighter as it tried to burn through the mist.

"What will we do?" Black Leg asked.

Gray awakened just then and looked up at me. He rolled to his side and glanced down at his ankle. Only a few red marks remained of his injuries. His narrowed eyes returned to me. "How did you do that?"

"I was hoping you wouldn't ask, because I don't know," I said.

He nodded. Then he sat up. I still had the bow and three arrows, but Black Leg's clothes were all gone. He was barefoot and wearing only Gray's shirt. I'd lost my shoes sometime during the flight along the beach. I still had my other clothes. Gray had only his britches and was barefoot.

"A fine bunch we are," he said. "I'm cold and would do murder for a drink of water, and the pair of you are as ragged as any I have ever seen. What is that creature? I spent the night, most of it, shoving every piece of driftwood I could find into the fire in mortal terror that *something* in the dark might find a way to climb up here."

"Maeniel—Father, that is—says such things are more powerful at night," Black Leg spoke fearfully.

I had unstrung the bow and placed the string in its leather pouch under my shirt. It felt dry now. "When the fog clears, I might try to kill it," I said.

"You sure you can do that?" Black Leg asked.

"No," I said. "I'm not, but I have no better ideas." My neck was stiff and my shoulder was in a cramp. I wasn't feeling good-tempered.

"I do," Black Leg said. "I smell green."

I said, "Yes," hopefully.

Gray pawed at his hair. "How do you smell green?"

"He means," I told him, "there is an opening in these rocks into—I don't know—a glade, some way out."

Following his nose, Black Leg began to crawl around the big boulder that blocked our way up. The passage we found was choked with driftwood, deadfalls, living brush, and blackberry and wild rose canes, coils and coils of them. Some of the vines were thicker around than my wrist. It led into a streambed with a trickle of water in the center. We all sighed with pleasure and relief when we lay on the stones in the stream and drank. For a time it seemed we couldn't get enough. I looked past the high banks and saw a forest—pine, oak, ash—clustered at the stream, willow turning green, yellow, and every mixture of color between, in the morning sun.

We had to follow the stream a good way. It was deeply cut. The tree branches were laced together above us, and the thorny briar and rose vines twined among the willows that clustered in the cut blocked any escape into the forest. They did have a few berries on them, and even rose hips, and we were so famished we gathered and ate them. The wild roses were everywhere. The air near the stream was heavy with the perfume, though there were no flowers to be seen.

"I don't like this," Black Leg said when we had been walking for a time.

"Nor do I," Gray said apprehensively. "We must have come a long way in the evening, running from the boar, because I have hunted over most of this land all my life and I remember nothing like this place."

"And the roses," I said. "They are all around us."

The stream broadened, the banks getting lower and lower. We came to a lake surrounded by forest. A path, not a very well-marked one, ran along the margins. We were very hungry now and very tired, so we turned onto it. On one side the lake spread out. How far, I couldn't see, because a fog bank drifted across the water. Beyond it I saw mountain peaks rising out of a low-rolling mist, bright, fair as gauze drapery in the new sun. The black dragon lifted its head above the water.

I heard Gray gasp.

Black Leg, feeling threatened, went wolf. I was attracted. I didn't think it would hurt me. After all, the first one hadn't. On one side, the trail ran close to the water along a black rocky scarp that projected into the lake.

"Stop!" Gray cried, because if I took that path, I would be trapped between the rock and the water.

But then I knew the dragon would want to feel secure, too, and it wouldn't come into the shallows among the trees and water lilies where Gray and Black Leg were standing. I wanted to see it more clearly, because I had never seen a black-skinned one before. When I entered the path, it swam toward me, rather the way a swan would—seeming to glide—pushed along by flippers on the squat body until it was close to shore. Then the head looked down at me.

At first I thought it looked like a snake, but then decided it didn't, because no snake ever had eyes like that. They were large and glowed like magnificent black opals, taking up most of the face. The skin looked not like plates or scales but silk, shining black, soft silk. This one was not vegetarian, because I could see dark fangs projecting down from the mouth and curving as they rested on the outside of the lower jaw. In addition, it had two long whiskers, one on each side, extending from its nose just below the nostrils. They were like the nostrils of the first dragon I'd seen in that they could be closed when the creature dove into deep water. Its neck bent like a swan's as it studied me.

For a time we were very still. I looked beyond the dragon at the lake and basked in its beauty. The water was very still, only a light breeze ruffled the surface. In the distance the moving mist draped the shoreline and the rocky promontories that thrust out into the still water. In other places I could see trees that extended down to the shore; and in yet others I saw wetlands where water lilies, sedges, reeds, cattails, and white and yellow cress were clustered in shallows that must have extended for many miles. The broad, still surface reflected the tranquil, cloud-filled sky.

I drew a breath. Even the air was filled with loveliness and peace. "Of all the fair places I have ever seen, this is the best," I whispered.

"Yes," the dragon agreed. "It is, and it is a very rich place, also, filled with fish, frogs, snakes, birds, herons, kingfishers, ducks, geese. And the woods on its margins have deer, elk, hare, rabbits, grouse, and pheasant, not to mention many doves and even quail. But I am prolix, and yet I have not told you a tithe of the wonders and beauties to be found here."

The yellow iris was springing up from the rocks at my feet, sharp, leafy spears with flowers the color of sunrise. "Do you mean me harm?" I asked.

"No, how would I harm you? I am a hunter of the great abyss. The creatures there are mostly small; squid, jellyfish."

And then I saw its prey, grotesque fish that swam in darkness and carried lights on their bodies like jewels. They swam through the trenches of ocean, being very little more than stomachs, lures, and eyes. Herds of shrimp moved up and down according to the cycles of the sun, bodies transparent as fine crystal, sleeping in the depths by day, rising to the surface at night to spread their starlike lights across the waves, be fed on, and breed.

Jellyfish wandered among drowned mountains like phosphorescent bells, tentacles drifting sometimes for miles into the darkness. Huge schools of squid feeding on the drifting detritus of life were able to fly by, shooting water through their bodies and leaping from wave top to wave top when the dragons pursued them. But, best of all, deep fissures in the depths flared from beneath the earth's mantle, warming and lighting the frigid darkness of the deepest sea.

The warmth of earth's crust fed whole colonies of tube worms and anemones, splendored star bursts of color, oddly living where no light ever shines. Many different fish and crustaceans—shrimp and crabs that danced on stilts, starfish with arms like snakes, and a dozen different kinds of shellfish—clustered at the vents. All living, loving, dying in a world without light or sound on the edge of a universe of darkness.

"I dove to the deep," the dragon said. "And I remained too long. I tried to help another of my kind, trapped by a mud slide in a cave in a canyon that has not seen the light since the first torrents of rain fell and made seas of earth. I loved this one. I failed. We failed. I have rested and filled my eyes with light to ease my almost mortal grief. So, you see, even if I would—which I would not—I could do you no harm. But, have a care. Others here might not be so willing to allow you to pass."

With that the dragon turned and swam out toward deeper water, and then was gone. Gray and Black Leg joined me on the path.

"It spoke to me," I said, "and told me of its origins and its life."

"Some teeth on that thing," Gray said. "I have never seen a black one."

"It lives deep and feeds on squid and strange fish," I told Gray. "It warned me."

"I need no warning about this place," Gray answered.

"It is very beautiful here," Black Leg said. "I would not mind if we stayed. Wolves are not ambitious the way men are. So long as we have game, who cares?"

I heard a snort.

"No!" I cried, because I knew what it was before I looked. The boar.

Again, we all ran.

CHAPTER SIX

E FLEW PAST THE ROCK. I WAS DISGUSTED. I doubled back. The big boulder next to the lake was steep and had trees on top. I ran up the side. A big willow on top had roots and branches that hung over the lake. The trunk rose at an angle. I was barefoot and small. I ran up the trunk like a squirrel.

Gray and Black Leg took refuge in a nearby tree, an oak with low branches. I had my bow and still had three arrows. The string was in its pouch inside my shirt. When I was safely in the tree, I lost no time in stringing the bow. I could hear the boar snuffling and panting, trying to find a way up the rock into the trees. I knew the rock wasn't as steep as the pile we'd climbed last night and he probably could.

"Hs-s-s-t, make noise," I said to the others.

Just then the boar made it. Black Leg let out a howl. He can do it when he's human, too. The boar arrived at the foot of the tree he and Gray were in. It paused, swung its head back and forth as though puzzled, snorting and pawing the ground. I studied the thing and took aim at one of the beast's little eyes and let fly.

I was right on target. The boar staggered and gave a grunting squall of pain, then staggered away, its back to me, shaking its head and giving almost human moans. I heard a cheer from Gray and Black Leg.

"You got it. You got it."

The wind hit then, so hard it nearly dumped me out of the tree. The day had been warm, sunny, and bright; but this wind was cold, like an icy frost that precedes a storm. Above, the sky darkened. I saw that the mist in the distance had moved closer to shore and was drowning the light. As I watched, the boar went down, blood streaming from its nostrils and mouth.

"It's dying," Gray said.

But Black Leg was looking up at the sky. He made the sign of the cross, and I knew we were both afraid. This was no natural beast. I could not think it was dead, and I was right. It wasn't.

The wind blew hard again and the dust rose. And the boar was gone. A warrior stood where he had been. He was wearing only a skin tied at the waist with a thong. He was dead, and his head had been taken, but it had been sewn back on with coarse sinew. There was a hole in his chest where the sword went in. It, too, was sewn shut with sinew.

He looked at me. "Will you come down, or shall I fetch you?" he asked.

The mist glided in among the trees, and it seemed so dark now as to be late in the evening of a gloomy day. The air smelled wet.

"I don't think I could bear your hands on my body," I said. "I will come down."

He turned toward Black Leg and Gray. "I have no orders about you. I don't want you. Go."

"No!" they both shouted.

"Yes," I said. "Get Maeniel."

"I don't know if even he can come here," Black Leg said.

"I'm betting he can," I answered, "but he won't unless you fetch him—go!"

"Yes," Gray said, and shoved Black Leg away. "I will bear my lady company. Do as she says, get Maeniel."

By now we were both on the ground. I climbed out of the tree, but when the dead man moved toward me, I eased back. "Don't touch me," I said. "I have some little power, and if you touch me, I will fight. I don't know if I can hurt you, but I will try."

He was very big and dark. He wore the torc below the seam where his head had been sewn back on. He was the largest man I had ever seen, and I also saw he had a sword. He wore it slung on his back in the old-fashioned way. Even Gray looked small near him.

Gray asked Black Leg, "Give me back my shirt."

Black Leg went wolf and ducked out of Gray's shirt. He shook it out.

"Don't make flea jokes," I said.

Black Leg was still there, ears laid back, studying the warrior.

"Trust me," Gray said. "Flea jokes are the farthest thing from my mind."

"Kyra makes them and Maeniel ignores them, but Black Leg gets mad," I explained.

The dead man turned and extended his arm, pointed his finger down the path away from the lake, and said, "March."

Gray and I marched.

The dead man followed. The road led downward, away from the water and light. The wood here was gloomy, filled with ancient oaks, and mist hung like wraiths in the shadow of the spreading branches and kept out the sun. We found our way through the trees with difficulty, because the big, gnarled roots invaded the narrow path. There was no leaving it, because dark water stood in the hollows between the roots. Serpents moved in the water. Both Gray and I were afraid of them. The path wound this way and that between the trees, and we despaired of ever finding our way back, even should we win our freedom.

Yet there was life in this woods. The trees, thick-barked and black as they were, wore clusters of oak leaves that shone wetly like dark jade carvings in the murky light the fog let in. Beyond the path, I could hear birds among the branches. They were small finches of gray and green, no bigger than my thumb. Here and there I heard the wild pigs snuffling as they searched for the big acorns the trees dropped. The acorns were big, long, and fair, with brown coverings and deep, well-sealed cups.

I paused to watch one of the tiny birds investigate the meat of one that lay crushed on the path. I felt, rather than saw, the dead man come up behind me. I jumped forward. The bird flew. I turned and looked up at him. He was very close, and I could clearly see the death wound in his chest sewn shut and the other where his neck had been severed to take his head. It was as though I could feel the chill he radiated freezing me.

"Do not despise me, fair one," he said. "This taking is by no will of mine. I am but a messenger, an emissary, sent by the Lord of the Dead. I was long ago dedicated to his service. It would not have been my choice to be a man of Dis."

My hair was braided and pinned up at my neck. I brushed it and felt the moisture of the fog that drenched it. "How did you die?" I asked, looking up at his bloodless face.

"Long and long and long ago, my people came here. Before cairns and barrows, houses, cattle, forts, and kings. We looked upon it and knew it would be ours. It was new and the gods danced in the night sky with draperies of light."

The aurora, the northern lights, I thought.

"Nothing is without price, and the lot fell on me. I was sufficient, they thought. A finer warrior, a greater hunter never lived. You would not give the gods less than the best. So they dug a pit, for I must die three times. Then I was set head down in the pit. When I was in the pit, I admit I was weak. I struggled to breathe. Then they pulled me out. I looked on light for the last time—I never knew how precious it was, for I was vain of my accomplishments—then the spear went through my heart. I dimly felt them take my head. From that time on, I served the Lord of the Dead."

His tale filled me with sadness. I turned away with tears in my eyes. I could not despise him. No.

The path and its difficulty continued until we reached a tree on a low hummock. It was lightning-blasted long ago, only half alive. The other half was hung with the heads of men.

The servant of Dis carried food. Dead limbs littered the ground.

"We must rest," I told our guide. "We have come a long way and are weary."

At the base of the tree, flat stones formed a ring around a place that seemed a hearth. I stirred the ashes with my toe. "Fire?" I asked our guide.

"Passersby come here to the wildwood. Some light fires," he said. Then he went to a hollow log, pulled out coarse meal and a bottle of oil.

It was cold here. The wind from snow-covered peaks beyond the lake brushed the hilltop. Looking behind, I could see the lake in the distance, and in places the sun shone on it. Below, the forest was filled with white fog, green leaves, and dark water. To one side, far, very far away, I saw sun and a shining city. Flying buttresses supporting slender towers climbed into the clouds of red, purple, violet, pink, yellow, all with edges shining in the city's light. The green hills near the city were covered in long grass that seemed to dance with the winds of summer.

"What is that?" I asked our guide.

"The timeless place," he said. "The heart of light. But we cannot go there. Lady, you are for the dark."

And, indeed, ahead of us I saw smoke and thick black clouds with lightning among them, long writhing flashes twisted like serpents of brilliance.

"Let us make a fire here before the rain comes upon us," I said. "If you have flour and oil, I can make bread."

Gray collected some deadfalls; they littered the ground, fallen from the shattered oak. The dead half of the tree bore its evil fruit. They swung by the hair from its boughs, bleached white by wind and rain. They had the look of men long dead—withered skin, empty sockets that once held eyes and many teeth. When Gray was finished collecting the wood, I seized one long, twisted branch in my hand, and it burst into a blossom of fire.

The warrior stepped back with an exclamation, but most strange were the heads. I heard whispers. They sounded like a room full of people who have seen a wonder and speak of it in low tones among themselves.

"What is this place?" I asked our guide. The fire was blazing now.

"These are those who can go to neither the dark nor the light. These are the false. False to their friends, to those they loved, to all those who did them good, who loved them, who deserved kinder treatment at their hands. Those they betrayed, to the ruin of both body and soul. No one will accept them—neither heaven nor hell, paradise nor desolation, light nor dark, will let them in. Here they remain."

I knelt and turned my eyes away from them, kneaded the bread and cooked it on a flat rock heated by the fire. Gray and I were ravenous, and we ate every scrap, though it was poor stuff—the flour brown with weevils working in it. They speckled the bread like caraway seeds.

Our captor, guide—who knows what he was—tasted a bit, only a bit, that I gave him. Then I asked him to remember the sun. He almost smiled, and I took his hand with both of mine. I remembered what I had thought about last night when I'd healed Gray. We were kneeling in a circle around the dying fire. The wind was blowing, and it was very quiet. All I could hear was its low keening in my ears. I dreamed of forests, endless forests—pine, spruce, fir, drifted deep in snow, white, shining, pale as spindrift blown from the tops of waves. Of people wearing skins, who hunted through the forest, laughing.

I knelt, looking across the fire at a girl. She was as fair as I am fair; it was clear she loved laughter and life. There was a vast sense of primal innocence and peace. Then it ended.

He was dead, and I didn't expect him to change, but he did; and I wondered what I might have done, because, though he looked the same, there was life in the eyes when they looked into mine when there had been none before. I wasn't sure if that was a good thing or not. Then we bowed our heads and prayed for a short time. Gray and I made the sign of the cross. We rose and left the tree with its sad, evil fruit and walked on into the darkness.

When we reached the plain, I could smell the fires. The smoke was borne toward us over a wasteland of stone, cold in spite of the flames rising from the fissure in the rock. Both Gray and I were barefoot. I had accepted it now. We—no—I had been summoned to the darkness by the Lord of the Dead. I cannot think why Gray had accompanied me but that he felt close. We had always been friends, but Maeniel and Dugald had warned me. Death is the fate not just of our kind, but of all living things. Maeniel told me once that a very wise woman told him that if we did not die, we could not live. I have been overjoyed to live. Everything has its price. It was very strange that a boar should come to me, come to summon me. They are the messengers to kings. I am not much. Bodiccia's line caused it, though; it is an important family, nurtured through the centuries by the noble houses of Ireland.

If death be the last thing I do, why, I pray the gods and heroes of my people that I try to do it as well as I have done more pleasant things. So Gray and I hobbled on, but when our guide saw we were suffering, he stopped and improvised shoes from the hide he wore. It was, he told me, the skin of the aurochs, the great bull of the woods, he wore.

They were crude footwear, made after the manner of ours. The hide is cut to the measure of the foot, a little larger, then holes are cut in the sides to hold the thong that is attached to the ankle and leg. After this, we walked more comfortably. We went hand in hand now. Gray held mine in his. Fire and ice, that was all around us now. Cold, ink-black stone with fissures through which flames leaped, heating the nearby air. As we drew away, we felt again the cold wind that swept across the wasteland.

The sky was thickly clouded; the fires reflected their light against the clouds. When we topped a rise, I saw the hall of Dis. Three rings of fire and in the center a throne overlooking the central pyre.

"I must go first," our guide told me. "The bridges are unseen."

The throne of Dis is the meaning of the maze. We walked around the first ring till our guide told us to stop. Then he crossed; the bridge was only a shadow over the flames. I followed, my feet feeling their way because I could see nothing. Once the fire roared up around me, the flames licking my arms and legs.

I closed my eyes and stood fast. I whispered—yes, Dugald had taught me some things—"A compact with thee, Fire. Fire, do not harm me." And it didn't, neither did it burn my clothes. I was mindful of Gray. "A compact with thee, Fire," I whispered. "Do not harm my friend." Then I added, "Please," because it doesn't do to be insolent with the elements.

The fire didn't harm Gray, but it did burn some of his clothing. His trousers were handwoven wool. They smoldered. His shirt was linen, and it was left in ruins.

Our guide nodded. "She witched you," he said.

Gray was very pale, but only said, "Lead on."

"We must walk," our guide said. "He—" he inclined his head toward a distant figure on the throne in the center "—changes their position from time to time."

"What if he changes them while we are in transit?" I asked.

"That," said Gray, "is really a fool's question. Enough already. If I think on it too much, I will be useless. Don't answer."

"You are brave, both very brave. Most of those I have conducted hither were gibbering with terror by now," our guide said.

"Well, we are, but trying to put the best face on it," I said.

"Pert," Gray said. "No matter what the circumstances, ever pert."

Our guide responded with only a smile. Gray seemed to find it rather ghastly, because he looked quickly away. But I returned it with a smile of my own. It took an effort to surmount my terrors, but I did.

"Talorcan is my name," our guide told me. "It is a word of power. Summon me if you will as boar or a ghost. I am a mighty man. For this is my payment for my sacrifice. I feel the steel in my heart when it is spoken."

We had reached the second bridge. The fire no longer made trial of our courage. We crossed easily and had no difficulty with the third, and then we stood before the dreaded Lord of the Dead. Gray went to one knee before the father of nightmares, but I stood my ground.

"You have no right to conduct us here. We are yet living," I said, "and you have no power over us."

You see, up to then I had not thought my ancestry a real thing. Bodiccia. What folly; I am a poor girl. I hunt, cook, clean, tend fields and our garden, and learn spinning, weaving, and dyeing at Kyra's feet. And I shall make the best bargain I can with some lordling and do all those same things in his household. And in addition, I will share his bed and bear his children. This is the lot of an ordinary woman, and if he be loving and generous, and I industrious and honest, it is not a bad one.

But now I understood, to my sorrow, that Dugald had been right. I am no ordinary woman, and born to a different fate. I would not go whimpering. The thing on the throne chose to be amused by me, not offended, and it laughed. Even its laughter was a horror. The flames from the pit at its feet leaped and writhed around it. They were like serpents, these flames, and they coiled, uncoiled, twisted, hissed, and tried to bite. One leaped at my foot above the spot where the laces held my shoe. I felt the fangs press at my skin, but then they dissolved, sparking away into nothingness.

The throne it sat on was an evil sort of thing, a mockery of the garden of life, of an apple tree. The throne itself was made of steel, with leaves of emerald, flowers of bone, and apples of ruby. The fire which would have destroyed any ordinary fruit left them unharmed. Besides the apples the tree was also hung with the fruits of both victory and defeat: the heads of men. They were living yet and joined their master, the king of the dead, in laughter.

The face of the creature on the throne changed sickeningly. Now covered with blood; now withered, wasted by disease and pain; now bloated by drowning or twisted by torture. He was all death and all death was met in him; and I felt very small, a sparrow in the talons of a hawk, and I understood what it meant to despair.

One of the heads spoke loudly enough for me to hear. "Hs-s-s-t, my lord." And death inclined his face to it, where it hung among the leaves and fruit on an iron bough.

They spoke together in low voices.

Then the Lord of the Dead laughed again. "That should do nicely," he said. One shadow hand pointed to a place on the right of the throne, at the edge of the pit. Then he directed Gray to the left, so we stood facing each other over the fire.

"Hear now my ruling, my *geas*, and you—each and both—must accept it. She will be your second wife, Gray, and you will lie with her here before my throne. And you, Gwenifyr, will serve him all the remainder of your days, until I welcome you both into my realm forever. You—each and both—will have none but each other now and for whatever lifetimes you have to come."

It was a dreadful curse. We would be bound to each other for all time. Slaves through the years, living out stunted lives together. If we tried to escape, the *geas* would bring us to death, and from death we would return to live again, only to be condemned to the same ghastly fate as before, world without end.

Then Gray showed what he was made of. I was in tears. Yes, truly I was, because, you see, I only half comprehended the sheer awfulness of it. But Gray met the face of nothingness, and he said, "No."

The sound was like a crack of the lash; and indeed, a whip of fire encircled Gray's body. When it faded, he was both burned and bleeding in a dozen places. He staggered to his knees, sobbing and crying out with pain. The fire lash cracked again. Gray screamed and screamed, in a way that made even Talorcan cringe, until Gray lay facedown in a pool of blood.

I watched as he struggled to his knees. I saw what remained of his clothing was drenched with blood, and one eye was gone, sucked out by the lash.

I screamed, and for a moment I felt myself surrender to the horror I felt. "No! No! Stop! I'll do whatever you want, only don't hurt him anymore."

"See." Death laughed again. "See, little one, how easily you break? Now." He gestured toward Gray. "Come around to the front of my throne and consummate your marriage."

"Yes," Gray said. "It is no shame, dread lord, to be destroyed by another's pain, for that, I have observed, is what causes most of us the worst suffering. But I am not dismayed by my own. Dear to me, oh, so dear to me, is the fragile envelope of flesh I wear. But even fairer is my honor!"

And so saying, he plunged forward and down into the fire.

I remember thinking, *Yes, he's right. That's the best way.* But the time of thought is nothing, and I followed.

Gray felt the fall. At first it seemed the fangs of a hundred serpents tore at his flesh. He was unable to imagine a fire pit with no bottom, but this was one. As he drove down through the fire snakes, they tried to seize him, but failed. He saw darkness rushing at him. He knew she had pitched herself over the edge behind him, but then she was a worthy descendant of ancient queens. So he knew death was not far away. He had a second to mourn his loss, but when he slammed into the darkness, he found it water. Why? Then he thought, surprised, *I will drown.*

But he didn't. He wasn't sure how long he held his breath, but he was swept along by a current that sucked him down and down. Then he broke the surface and felt air on his skin. So, not knowing what else to do, he breathed. He seemed to spend an eternity in darkness, but at last it was as if something spat him out.

He saw the water was green and filled with silver shapes. Fish? No, dolphins. He struggled toward the light. His head cleared the surface, and above he saw spires of clouds glowing in the late afternoon sun. One of the dolphins nudged him forward, and he saw a line of cliffs in the distance. He struggled. The salt water stung his body in a thousand places. He could see from only one eye, and he knew the Lord of the Dead had maimed him, but he was a kind that does not willingly die. He began, pain or not, to swim toward the shore.

Something strange loomed before him. He reached out to push it away and felt wood. A large, heavy piece of tree swept out to sea by a storm. He embraced it with more fervor than he ever embraced a woman. The tide was at the flood. He rode it to shore. He found himself beached in a cove on the very strand along which they had fled the boar. Above the tide line, the tracks belonging to the three of them marked the sand. The boar had left no tracks, but then all things considered, this wasn't surprising.

Thirst tortured him, and a multitude of wounds, scoured by sand and salt water. All he wanted to do was lie still and be left alone. So he lay for a long time, trying to gather strength to rise and search for water. It was his greatest need. He heard a rush of wings and saw a raven land next to him. He recognized the bird. It had a lot of pinfeathers. She had lost quite a bit of her plumage after Dugald chased her off to Ireland, and it was growing back.

She squawked, "Gray."

"In the flesh," he croaked back. "You illegitimate, louse-ridden, misbegotten terror of a bird. You leave my good eye alone, or I'll see you in the stew pot—"

"I believe he is alive," someone said.

When he looked up, Dugald and Maeniel were standing over him.

"For once she is innocent," Maeniel said. "She saw you and led us to you."

Dugald gave him some water. "Where have you been and where is Guinevere?"

Gray gulped the water. "Telling you that would take more strength than I have now. We were taken to the house of the dead, and she departed in the same manner and in the same direction as I did. I hope she can swim."

"She can," Maeniel said, "and she swims well. I know. I taught her."

"Good," Gray said. "I landed in the sea some little way off the coast. A floating log brought me in. Lift me up and I will show you. I'm half blind. I can't see from here. Is my eye gone?"

Dugald examined him closely. "No, the side of your face is swollen and there is a cut on the eyelid. I am not the Lord Christ, but I can help." He rested his hand on the side of Gray's face, and some healing was done. The swelling went down a little.

When Gray realized he had two good eyes, he fainted.

Dugald drew back. "I see we will get no more from him."

Maeniel was pointing out to sea. "Look, Dugald, the dragons. I never saw so many—not in one place before."

Dugald rose and placed Gray's head gently down on the sand. "You evil bird." He addressed Magetsky. "Stay away from his hurts."

She soared and aimed a squirt at him, but didn't quite dare hit him. It landed on the sand nearby.

Maeniel laughed. "She won't be wanting another journey to Ireland."

Then Dugald looked where Maeniel pointed out to sea. "At least twenty, maybe more. I didn't know she was friends with them. You didn't tell me they had met."

"Yes, once," Maeniel said. "When she was much younger. Once. I couldn't see the harm in it."

"No, no!" Dugald cried, wringing his hands. "No. They have her. There would not be so many otherwise. They have taken her. She is among them." He tore at his beard. "No!"

"Old man," Maeniel said, "you frighten me. What will they do with her? She's like my daughter. I had thought she might take my son. She could come with us. Live free."

"I cannot think," Dugald cried. "And they are strange cattle—"

"Cattle?" Maeniel said. "If there is one thing they are not, it's cattle."

"I don't know," Dugald cried again, sinking to his knees beside Gray on the sand. "She was not to meet the dragons. And now I do not know."

CHAPTER SEVEN

HE SURFACED AMONG THE DRAGONS, AND there was no question of letting her go back to shore. One of the giants, a silver-maned beauty, simply came up under her, and she found herself seated on his back. A chorus of voices sounded in her mind as they greeted her with relief, joy, pleasure, and some indignation. It was hard to get a word in edgewise.

"My friends," she said, pointing to the shore.

"No," the voice of the one she rode told her. "Your guardians have become careless. You were nearly lost to us. It never occurred to anyone that even Lord Dis would want Merlin in his debt. Only your courage and the man's saved you both from lifetimes of pain."

"I cannot think a man like Gray would have been a fate worse than death!" I was angry because I had never loved him so much than in that final moment before the dark lord. I had known him a brave man from the first when he, not Bain, the leader, led the war band down to the pirates.

"No, they cannot protect you. You will not leave us for the present."

"Then tell me if he is alive, as I am."

"He is, and on the beach with your friends. They will care for him."

"I hope so," I said, looking back.

I could see a few figures clustered on the sand in the distance before we sailed into a fog bank and the wild cliffs and shingle shores of my home were lost to view. It was then that I realized how tired, sore, and drained I was. I threw my arms around the dragon's neck and rested my head against the slightly rough skin.

In the natural world it was evening, and my depleted body had no defense against the coming night's cold. "I wish you would let me go ashore," I said. "I could make a fire and get warm, and I'm so hungry."

"Presently!" was the terse reply.

I could hear them talking about me among themselves, and they, too, were worried about where to take me—at least for this evening.

"I suggest we try to make the gates." This was from Silver Mane, the one I was riding.

"No." The voice was female and rather warm and low in tone. "There's a squall out to sea, and while I don't think it will move inshore, we are headed for some high, rough waves. We might not make the gates much before midnight. She's a land creature and not equipped to defend herself against the cold night air."

"What do the dolphins say?" another one of the pod questioned.

Music danced across my mind, and I saw rising waves with deep troughs, purple, green, and black in the failing light.

"I vote for the island," the female voice said.

"I don't like it," Silver Mane said. "On that island something remains. They were powerful in their day."

"But would have nothing to do with Dis, I'll bet," the female voice contributed.

"That's true," Silver Mane agreed. "Tomorrow we can swim to the gates and take her to a place of real comfort."

"Listen," one of the other dragons commanded. "Listen. One of the great blue whales is singing."

And again music floated into my mind. It told of a land frozen summer and winter alike. Of bergs drifting, glittering like diamonds in an all-too-brief sunlight; of bears white as the snow packs over which they hunted; birds that didn't fly but swam, insulated by their feathers in an almost frozen sea; of shrimp so thick the water was almost a soup. This is the harshest, yet richest, ocean of the world. Then the song ended with a vision of the sunset far out to sea, with rills of light on the water.

"Is it not lovely?" the female voice asked.

It took me a moment to realize she was speaking to me. "Yes," I answered. "Do they all sing? All the sea creatures?"

"Yes," she said. "And all have different songs. We, the dragons as you call us, have our own. You are very tired, little one. Hold on to my husband tight, and we will take you to our island. It belongs only to us and the birds now. The most recent inhabitant was a hermit from the great foundation of Iona. He sought the love of God, union with the love of God, and we think he found it. Then he returned home to his brethren, there to die, be buried, because if he was one with God, he was one with them also, and he wished to take joy in their faces before he set out on his last voyage alone."

Then I heard the cries of seabirds, and a shadow loomed up through the fog. The dragon, Silver Mane, came on land, moving up the beach using his flippers the way a turtle would. The wind from the sea blew away some of the fog; and beyond the beach, in a grove of white birches, I saw the beehive hut of the anchorite. It was half buried in the new blooming gorse bushes, and the yellow flowers were sun-gold against the grayness.

He had kept a garden near the hut, and while the vegetables were gone, the wild rose, grown for its hips, stretched over the top of the stone hut, and sage and rosemary bloomed near the door. Briar vines were twined among the birch trunks and were covered with flowers as the night sky is sprinkled with stars.

"Nothing larger than a bird lives on this island. Here you may sleep in peace," Silver Mane said. He moved rather well, I thought, on land, but it was obvious he didn't care for it, because he went back to the water as quickly as he could.

The first order of business was to build a fire. The beach was filled with driftwood, and there were many deadfalls among the trees.

As you know, I have no problem lighting a fire. Then I took a torch and investigated the hut.

It had a bed of sorts, with an animal-hide webbing, and there was a package in a cowhide pouch near the bed. I opened it and found a fine, soft gray blanket. There were two stone crocks against one wall. They had tight-fitting lids, and one still held salt, the other honey, now hard and crystallized. The blanket I placed on the webbing. There was enough to cover the webbing, then turn to cover me.

"How is this possible?" I asked the dragons, because I could hear them off the beach in the water, speaking in low voices to each other.

"He made it of thistle fiber," she said. "It is some of the strongest and longest wearing of fibers in nature, but it takes a long time to gather, and still longer to weave. Immersed as he was in the love of God and the beauty of the world, the holy man cared nothing for time and had the patience to weave the silk of spiders and decorate it with the scales of a butterfly's wing. He left it here, since he would not need it any longer, so that if some troubled wanderer found it, it would serve to warm him as it warmed its maker long ago."

It was dark by then. The dragons tossed a big fish ashore. I made a cutting stone, cleaned the fish, then cooked it on heated stones in the pit near the fire and fell to. I ate every scrap. I had in my whole life never been so hungry. Then I finished another one, this one wrapped in seaweed and seasoned with both salt and the crystals of honey.

I don't remember repairing to the bed in the hut and wrapping myself in the blanket, but I must have, because I woke in the night hearing voices but not understanding what they were saying. For a moment, I was confused. Then I remembered the dragons. I must be overhearing the sounds of the conversation as they fished among the waves. So I slept again.

When I awakened, I lay quiet, looking at the gray light through the door of the hut. The blanket was warm and had a good smell of dried herbs about it—rosemary, sage, and something more elusive, lavender. Kyra had been keen to teach me herb lore, and I learned about it, as well as cooking, from her. The Gray Watcher taught me to hunt with the stone knife I had made to clean the fish last night. I thought I'd been lucky in my friends and companions. They had taught me to make my way anywhere.

Are you awake?

The query was in my mind. "Yes," I said. Then I rose and folded the blanket, replacing it in its cowhide pouch.

I was thirsty. Last night it hadn't bothered me. There was moisture in the fish, and I had swallowed more water than I wanted while being swept down the underground river from the halls of Dis. But now I felt thirst, and I wondered if there was fresh water on the island. I asked, because I found if I didn't project my thought, the dragons wouldn't hear me.

"There is a terrible storm rising," Silver Mane said.

I hurried out of the hut and saw the sun rising in a sea of flame.

Then his wife's voice joined his. "We must swim out to sea. To remain this close to shore could well mean our deaths. We could be dashed against the rocks and killed."

I dithered a moment. The danger was great. Summer storms can be fierce. If I journeyed with the dragons, I might be swept from my perch on Silver Mane's back. And drowned. They would be hard put to save themselves in the towering seas, but this island might not be safe either. By day I could see that it was saddle-shaped, narrow and low in the middle, but with high, rocky cliffs on either end. The monk had located his hut a little above the lowest portion, to one side of the center, where trees and shrubs grew. But at the lowest point in the center, I could clearly see a rocky, sandy trench, overgrown with salt-loving plants—samphire, and thorny yellow-flowered herb—interspersed with wild sea grass, whose heads bowed to the wind now beginning to gust wildly. Another copse of birch and willow clothed the rocks that rose steeply to the cliff.

"If you will come with us into the maelstrom, come now," Silver Mane commanded.

"This is a killer storm," his wife said. "The whales are in it, and they sounded to escape the fierce blast. It is no natural storm. This Merlin hunts you, and he will throw all his power against you, wherever you are."

"Then flee," I said. "I am a land creature. I can shelter in the rocks up there."

"Are you sure?" Silver Mane asked.

"Yes."

I dashed back to the hut to pick up the hide pouch with the blanket.

"Whatever you both do," Silver Mane's wife said, "do it quickly."

131

The rising sun had been extinguished by sooty thunderheads on the horizon, and waves began to pound the beach hard. When I ran back out into the open, the two dragons were already swimming away.

Which end of the island? I looked to one side. The cliff seemed almost sheer. On the other side, a gradual slope led up the cliff. I turned to go that way and saw Mother. I stopped, gasped, and my eyes teared. She seemed to rise out of the sea itself.

A gray wave lifted, arched; and the form at the top curled into a wolf's head, back, and shoulder. She sprang clear of the breaking sea, falling water melting into paws, then a plumed tail, and ran toward me. I saw the direction in the lines of her body. This way, and she led me to the steeper cliff. I followed without question, through a giant rock garden where wildflowers grew in mad profusion, their colors burning against the pervasive grayness of granite and the rising storm. Hawthorn, purple vetch, blue cornflowers, yellow cowslip, and marsh marigold.

Mother bounded from rock to rock over what seemed an enchanted carpet, until she reached the cliff. And here there was a stair. I was afraid and the wind was already battering me, but I could see human hands had chipped out this stair, even though the heavy spring growth seemed ready to choke it. Pliant willows and hawthorn canes were rooted between the stones and covered with starlike flowers; rowan and holly with its thorny green leaves were dug down into it on either side, and brambles coiled across the inner face of the risers.

The steps were deeply worn by the passage of many feet; the hollows filled with moss and lichen. *How long?* I was able to think as I followed Mother up and up, until we reached a well at the top. The well looked as though some mighty force had tried to blast it into ruins. I could see the wall of rock. Behind and around the rock was blackened, burned by the fury of the assault. It was clear that in some places the stones themselves had melted in the heat directed at them. I knew no force more powerful than lightning or more dangerous than fire, so I wondered what it might have been. Then I reached the well curb itself. It was made of volcanic glass of the kind you see on the vitrified forts and flints created in volcanic earthly fires, yet the water still ran.

All this must have happened long ago. How long ago I couldn't begin to imagine, because the detritus of the attack was deeply stained, pitted by the erosion of centuries, dotted with lichen, gray-green and gold, and thick with the wiry stems and lacy fronds of bracken and the clear emerald velvet of moss. The water trickled in a steady stream from the shattered cliff face and fell down, down, below the well curb into darkness, where I heard the steady plunk of the stream where it vanished into the rocks.

On the other side of the well, a tree trunk poked up through a crack in the stone. Or perhaps the tree made the crack, because it was very old and the marble and granite stones through which it grew were pushed back by the strong, twisted roots that erupted through them. The wind was no longer gusting. It was blowing a gale now; and as I looked out to sea, I saw the sunrise, purple, red, and gold, leaping like a conflagration among the soot-stained clouds of the rising storm. I suppose I was afraid, but now I cannot remember the fear, only the beauty and the exultation, and I did not have to be told this was a place of magic.

Mother had paused on the other side of the broken well curb. "Drink," she said.

I leaned over the well, the darkness below, and pressed my lips to the mossy trickle of water that ran down into the well. I will never forget the taste of that water. Only a few drops completely satisfied my thirst, and I felt I had been given the fairest beverage I had ever had. The water tasted of morning, of the few moments between the glow on the horizon and sunrise. And of the violet light of evening when weariness and a sense of accomplishment fill the soul. Of summer, when the smell of new-mown hay is heavy on the wind, and of winter midnights, when the air is still and the stars are a fountain of light.

The wind had, it seemed, ceased to blow, and I knew I stood outside time. And then I saw her.

She is the Flower Bride. The tree clinging to the cliff on the other side of the well was a quince, and she seemed—no, was—formed of the flowers. Blue eyes the color of the martin's breast; long dark hair, brown as the quince's bark; and skin pale, creamy-white, and brushed with the merest hint of flame like the flowers. Mother sat at her feet, and one hand rested on Mother's head. She looked at me with the detached assurance of an immortal gazing at one of the creatures of time. I tore my eyes away from her face and looked down into Mother's. I felt her love.

"Up," she told me.

I saw another stair, this one choked with winter-burned blackberry vines and barren gorse bushes. It led to a shelter in an overhang at the top of the cliff.

"I don't know if I can get through," I said.

Mother grinned—as much as a wolf can grin—tongue lolling, eyes sparkling. "Burn your way through," she said. "No fire of yours can harm anything of hers."

The Flower Bride smiled.

Then the wind was a shriek in my ears, and both Mother and the guardian of the well were gone. Then I knew why they had come. Merlin's use of Dis involved the kind of favors the powerful do for one another. You scratch my back, I'll scratch yours. But this time Merlin had laid it on the line, and if he failed to destroy me, the spell he used to call the storm would rebound on him.

Fire poured from my fingers into the dead wood that blocked the stair. It roared to life even though it was beginning to rain now. As the savage wind drove the outlying rain bands, they struck like whips lashing the island. In a flash the dead vines were a blazing mass, and then they were carried away by the blast, the first cold downdraft of the squall line moving in.

I ran up, sometimes having to stop and cling to the stubs of bracken and briar the fire hadn't touched as the wind tore at me, trying to fling me off the stair into the roaring sea below. Then I was at the top, under the overhang, the rain beginning to teem down. The approaching storm was a giant mass of cloud robed in gray veils of rain, ready to slam into the island. There was a hole in the rock wall at the overhang, and I went in like a snake, landing in a little cave carved by the wind and rain. It was no more than a hollow in the rock.

I pulled the blanket out of its pouch, wrapped it around myself, and watched the storm rage. There was light in the cave, and I saw it came from a small hole in the roof, worn by ages of wind and rain. A vine—it must be getting enough light—covered one wall. Though the storm was at its height, no rain came in that way, and the cave was dry. Lightning flashed blindingly, dancing, it seemed, over the whole island. I rose and hurried away from the opening and pressed my back against the wall. I felt a shock. The air crackled with electricity. He was seeking me, even here.

The scars on my fire hand flared green in the room, and I felt pain drawing my fingers into a claw. And I knew he was feeling for me. I edged away, my back against the wall, and the glow on my hand lessened. I felt the power extend itself toward me. I moved farther toward the vine and wall it clung to. Again the glow in my hand lessened, but by now I was under the light well, wedged into a corner next to the vine. The lightning flashed again, accompanied by an explosion of thunder so violent the walls shook. Outside, even over the roar of wind and rain, I heard the wild screams of the seabirds as lightning scorched the rock. My fire hand twisted and thrummed as though it had a life of its own. Fear and pain were a mix in my mind and body, the pain in my hand now so intense that it made me dizzy and nauseated. I staggered forward, and the pain grew less. I moved forward another pace, and the pain eased. I felt numb with relief. Again it struck, and I eased forward.

Then I rasped, "What is happening?" He was trying to force me into the rain, and when I was clear of the doorway, the lightning would fry me where I stood.

The fear of death is a wonderful and terrible thing. It sent me fleeing back to the wall, under the light well, near the vine. The pain struck again, and I understood my choices, because the palm of my fire hand was purple and the purple shaded away to blackness at the nails. My hand was dying. I had seen gangrene in the foot of a girl who had broken her ankle in the rocks while playing along the shore. The bone came out through the skin. The foot mortified, then died. Dugald and the chief took the leg with an ax. Dugald said it was the only way to save her life, and I knew I might have to take an ax to my right hand. I turned my face away, knowing that hand or no hand, I would not yield.

Pain lashed at me again. This time I was sick all over the floor. The room darkened around me. *You haven't time, bastard,* I thought, *to kill me. I don't know if you can kill my fire hand, but it won't matter. I will—not—give—up.* Then I was sick again.

By then the storm was dying away. The lightning stopped and the rain came straight down, splashing on the opening I'd crawled through. I crouched down into a squat, thankful the pain had ended, cradling my right hand in my left while life crept back slowly into the fingers. Only knowing I had won and wondering what the cost would be to me and my attacker. At last I moved away from the spot where I'd vomited, crossed my legs, and sat with my back to the wall and closed my eyes. Color was coming back into my hand, and the fingers, while still purple, were no longer black.

The staggering relief from intense pain and the soothing sound of the rain must have caused me to drift off to sleep.

"Remarkable," a voice said. It was masculine.

"She has great courage," a woman's voice agreed. "I hope it is not wasted in one of their futile struggles. They are prone to folly."

"They? They? And what are we?"

I woke then, frightened. My arm banged into the vine, and it stung me. Not badly, just so I moved away from it. The rain was ending and the light was better. I looked at the vine and found staring into my eyes the holes of a blackened skull.

I slithered all the way across the room, until I was squatting near the opening. My arm gave me a pang. I looked down at it and saw the palm was pink, while the fingers were still pale and felt cold. I could move them well, and they looked to be returning to normal. Then I studied the wall the vine covered. I couldn't be sure, but there were at least a dozen of them. Skulls, I mean. In some places the vine grew very thickly, hiding anything behind it, but in others I could see empty eye holes and teeth, and here and there a glint of metal.

"Oh, how delicious, my dear," the voice said. "She has discovered us. I do so enjoy the look of consternation on their faces."

"Be quiet, Jetembo!" the man's voice broke in. "I can't, never could, delight in frightening children, and that's what this one is—a child. Now, go away," he addressed me. "We know you took shelter from the storm. It is ending. Leave. We and this place have nothing to do with you. Nothing to do with anything now—not really." He sounded almost wistful.

"Wait a minute!" The voice belonged to still a third woman. "I saw something rather unusual, Pome. I saw this child, as you call her, repel a magical attack of great viciousness. Someone, something in this miserable asshole corner of the universe, tried with great determination to kill her. I want to know more. This is the first interesting thing that's happened in several thousand years, and you want to send her away?"

"Merlin—chief druid of Britain—he wants me dead. This is the second attempt. He almost got me, and if you're friends of his . . ." I began to edge closer to the cave mouth.

"We are not," the woman's voice said. "Frankly, we wouldn't bother with a slippery little backwoods practitioner like—like the Merlin."

"The Merlin?" I asked, surprised.

"Yes. The Merlin. It's a post, an appointive one, I believe."

"Appointive?" I asked.

"As opposed to hereditary," she answered.

"I wouldn't mind knowing a few things myself," I said mildly.

"This is forbidden," the one called Pome stated flatly.

"Don't be a fool," the woman's voice replied. "Mountain ranges have become hills since we came here, since we were put here—jungles, deserts, and land masses covered by seas. What does it matter what we say or to whom?"

Pome sighed. "I suppose you're right."

"True, my dear," the other woman, the first who had spoken, said. "But they are terribly dull conversationalists."

"Then go visit the dream, Jetembo. But don't interfere. Now, tell me about your problem."

So I did, describing everything from the first—how I had been driven into the underworld by the boar, my friends, and my life. By this time the rain had subsided into a mist. And I finished my tale by asking a question of my own. "Who are you and what's your name? I know that of your two friends, but I don't know yours."

"We are—" She hesitated, then said, "slaves. That is the closest word to it in your tongue. We were left here by our captors to guard . . . something important. Our lives depended on our doing a good job, but like many slaves have over the centuries, we revolted against our masters."

"Our punishment was to be entombed here—not living and unable to die," the one called Jetembo snapped. She sounded as though even after so long she didn't like to be reminded.

"The vine?" I asked.

"Oh, heavens," Pome said. "I'd forgotten about children. They want to know everything. A plantavant," she said. "It's a plant with rudimentary consciousness, like an animal. It both imprisons and protects us. Don't touch it, or it will hurt you."

"I think it already did," I said.

"Yes, but it can do much worse than just cause a little skin irritation. Don't bother it again." This was the answer given me by the first woman who spoke. "Now, as to your problem, I can give you only a little help, and that is advice. But it is probably fairly good, since I once was an adviser to rulers, kings, emperors, whatever you might call them. I myself devised the plan that brought me here."

"A foolish boast," Jetembo said.

"But not a vain one," Pome said sternly. "The advice is fairly simple," she continued. "You may not draw back now, but must—*must*—go forward; otherwise, you will die. Your enemy is determined to see you dead. The only way you and those you love can survive is to go forward."

"He includes even those I love in his fury?" I asked.

"Yes," was her reply. "I felt the implacable hatred in his magic when he struck at you. He has failed, and that weakens a sorcerer, so you have some time. Where are these dragons taking you?"

"I'm not sure," I answered, bewildered.

"Well, then, find a place and time on the shore when the wind is out to sea, and call me. I will respond. My name is Lais. Now go—for you are not allowed to remain here after the rain, and it is ending."

"I salute you, protectress of your people," I said. "All honor to you and many thanks for shelter."

Then I turned and left. Indeed, she was right, for the clouds were breaking up, the remaining rain only a fine mist in the air. I hurried down the stair to the well. I paused again to sip the wonderful water, and then remembered I'd left the blanket up in the cave. But when I turned to look back, the stair was gone and only a few broken marble steps remained halfway up.

And then I did flee, running hard until I reached the beach, where I found the dragons in the shallows, waiting.

They delivered me to Tintigal at midnight, to the quay on which I was sure the Gray Watcher must have first set foot in Britain. The queen, Uther's wife, Igrane, waited with her women, all wrapped in dark mantles against the cold. The dragons would not swim into the pool of torchlight surrounding them. As they told me during the journey, no other living creature is at peace with men. We have attained great power, and we use and abuse it in a casual manner. Knowing no laws but our own, we are a scourge to all the other great kingdoms of life. They might feel a friend-ship with me, but not with others of my kind.

So I landed alone and began to walk toward the people waiting in the pool of torchlight. I was very tired and wanted nothing so much as a bath and my bed. The dragons told me Igrane and her ladies would receive me. I thought, with great longing, of Kyra and my friends Dugald and the Gray Watcher. I would have preferred to be with them or in the sweat-house with Kyra.

Fog lay on the water, and indeed the dragons had stood out to sea, waiting for it to thicken before they would approach Tintigal.

"Well, where is she?" I heard an arrogant voice demand.

My whole body stiffened. I knew, but didn't know how I knew, the voice belonged to Merlin. He—here? I couldn't help but be frightened but at the same time curious about the man who hated and hunted me al-most from the day of my birth. Then I heard Igrane's rather tart reply.

"You know they are afraid of you and your bowmen and won't come near the lights."

"Dragons," Merlin's voice spat. "Am I to be persuaded of the exis-tence of dragons, or is this simply one more deception in a long series of your deceptions?"

Ah, well, I must make my entrance sometime. Why not now? I thought.

"The dragons have come and gone," I said, stepping into the light. "They brought me. I am Guynifar."

They were gathered in a semicircle around the torchbearers, Igrane at

139

one end. She reminded me of some dark pillar, wrapped as she was in her mantle with a veil covering her head, only her pale face visible. Merlin stood at the other end of the crescent. He was as dark as the Gray Watcher had described him to me and looked only a bit older than the very young man who had engineered Vortigen's death. One cheek was deeply scarred. You see, Dugald, after the manner of druids, had told the Gray Watcher the truth as far as it went when he told him magic was stronger in the young—but what he didn't tell him was that a powerful practitioner can use his power to prolong his youth. And Merlin looked as though he were only perhaps thirty, and I knew Vortigen died nearly seventy years ago.

Our glances—Merlin's and mine—crossed like drawn swords. Almost, you could hear the clash of naked steel. I was surprised at my own boldness, but then I remembered Lais's words. I had mulled them over on the rest of the journey. I was in a fight, and from this battle there would be no backing away.

In fact, for a moment he seemed intimidated. Then he spoke. His acid words were not intended for my ears alone.

"Look at that, a peasant—not much, is she? Well." He turned to a young man at his side. "This is what they want to marry you to, a woman of the lowest sort. Christ, I wouldn't hire her to sweep out your chamber. Not," he said, and grinned, "that she might not be useful for entertaining my men."

He turned to them, and I saw he was surrounded by men-at-arms. They began laughing. The laughter sounded as if it might be a bit forced, but I was too insulted to take much notice. I knew my cheeks burned, not with embarrassment but with fury. I wanted to hurt that man, but then I came to the belated realization that he was not important—nor was even Igrane. The only important one was the stripling at his side, and I knew it must be Arthur. Arthur, who would inherit the seat of a high king. Arthur, the descendant of a man who wore the purple and commanded the greatest empire ever known.

Our eyes met, and in the silence I heard the slap of waves against the stone quay, the hiss of torches, and above them the sound of the wind, that eternal and unending sea wind that purifies the shore. It flattened the admittedly ragged clothing I wore against my body.

"Don't speak so," he said quietly to Merlin, "to a child and a virgin. Don't make her hate you on your first encounter."

Then he stepped away from both Merlin and his mother, and I saw he was now and always would be his own man. No puppet this, dancing to the tune others played.

"I came here," he said, "expecting to be disappointed, but I find I am not. You are as beautiful as the morning star, and your eyes hold the fierce pride and beauty of a sea eagle. I cannot know what marriage I may be called upon to make, but to the extent I am free to follow my own inclinations, I will certainly make you an offer. We might not ever know full marriage, but it would be an honorable arrangement."

He was referring to the fact that most chieftains of his rank take— sometimes must take—more than one woman, and also that men in some professions find it both inconvenient and sometimes impossible to marry in the conventional sense. So, rather than let the woman fall into poverty and disgrace and her children with her, they make other, quite legal and acceptable, arrangements, my seafaring friend being a case in point.

I could not but admire him, for both his diplomacy and his tact. In one smooth stroke he had offered me the respect and recognition due my rank, disarmed the malice of his most important and dangerous adviser, shown courtesy toward his mother, and smoothed over what might have been a dangerous quarrel. But then, I had also been put in my place, as one who might not aspire to the highest prize—a crown.

As we climbed the stair into the fortress, Igrane asked me, "My dear, what did you ever do to dear Merlin that he has fallen into such a deep . . . snit?"

"I think I didn't die when he wanted me to," I said bitterly. I had just been both complimented and snubbed. I wasn't sure which one was more important. I was almost dropping with exhaustion.

When the women conducted me upstairs, I was hoping to get to bed, but they undressed me. I didn't like this. At home I sleep with Kyra, and we have a curtain. She wove it. The wool is gray and blue, but it has salmon on it—pink, red, and silver, as they are when they come upstream to breed. The salmon is a symbol of fertility and chastity to the Painted People, since they love only at the appointed time but then have many children.

But anyway, Kyra and I give each other privacy when we dress. Not these women. When they got my clothes off, they had to look at me and talk about what they saw.

"He's right," Igrane said. "She is a child yet." They lifted me on the bed and . . . looked! "A virgin, also."

One of them touched my cheek. She sighed. "Rose petals." Another touched my breast and laughed. "Rose hips."

I scrambled off the bed and made a break for my clothes, but Igrane caught me by the shoulders and wrapped a white linen mantle around me.

"No, you need a bath."

"I will be more than happy to take one. Now, stop pawing me," I said firmly.

Igrane pointed at my clothes. "Burn them."

"No," I shouted. "Those are my good riding pants. See, the seat is leather and the knees and ankles, too."

Igrane sniffed. "They can be laundered?"

"Yes," I said.

"The shirt?"

"Well, it is sort of—"

She tossed it aside. "The shoes?" she said. Her hand touched the laces. Then she jumped back, gazing at her fingers as though she had thrust them into a fire.

"I got them in the halls of Dis," I said. "They were a pledge of friendship and fealty. Leave them alone."

"Dis," she mused. "Dis. Merlin takes you seriously. Now I can see why." She studied the crude leather things on the floor. "Don't worry, we won't touch them. No one would want to. Now, go bathe and wash your hair."

I did, but I took my shoes with me. The bath was a Roman one, modified a little, perhaps for the climate. The spring water was heated by a hypocaust. It had a pool—marble, round and white—and the water in it was clear. Rose petals floated on the surface.

"Of all the flowers," Igrane said to me, "I love the rose best."

Igrane would. It is the goddess's flower. She became a bird and danced with the serpent wind, or some say a dragon, and conceived the cosmic egg. Then she placed it in a nest of rose petals, though how she got the roses when there was no earth for them to grow in always bothered me. I had pointed this out to Kyra, and she told me to stop criticizing or she wouldn't tell me any more stories. So I'd shut up, and Dugald and the Gray Watcher had laughed at both of us.

I was still wrapped in the mantle, so I didn't notice the chill until I took it off. The room was round, but the walls weren't solid, and the sea wind blew through them. I saw they were simply alabaster screens. Six pillars supported the pavilion roof, and each held an alabaster lamp that made the white marble of the pillars, screens, floor, and the pool shine brilliantly in its light. The only color in the room was a band of mosaic on the floor that fringed the pool. Pictured there were roses, vervain, oak—the leaf, female flower, and acorn—and the same for the ash, the rowan, the hawthorn, holly, hazel, cedar, beech, and birch. And last, the mushroom and the mistletoe. And I understood what the steps for the dance must be when I put my foot on the vervain.

The sacrifice was on the altar, ready to be poured into the trench: oil, fruit, wine, and last but not the least, a sleeping child. The thick scent of verbena filled the air in the smoke rising from the fire, ready to chase away the smell of blood.

I jerked my foot back.

Igrane was alone. Her women had departed. She was looking at me from under her long eyelashes.

"I wondered if you would feel it," she said.

"I didn't have to feel it," I said. "I saw it."

"Yes, yes, I can understand just why Merlin is afraid of you. Go around. There is an opening in the circle. It is never wise to close such a thing."

I did and sat down in the pool.

"My women will help you bathe," she said.

"No, thank you. I have been taking my own baths for some years now."

"Pert," she said.

"I was called that in the halls of Dis," I replied.

So she went away.

There was soap, heavy with myrrh, surprisingly rough. I scrubbed myself with it. She left the white mantle and a nightgown on a chair in the corner. When I rose from the pool, the sea wind struck me and the flames flickered in the alabaster lamps. The water was hot, and the cold, moist sea breeze felt good. I studied the circle and went to the cedar. I put my foot on it, and the circle of light in the pavilion fell away, and I was part of the clean wind. I breathed deep the air of freedom and thought of the Gray Watcher and found myself in our house, our steading.

It was late and the fire was banked to coals. Dugald and Kyra were asleep, but the Gray Watcher and Black Leg were curled together at the fire pit. The Gray Watcher must have felt my presence, because he opened his eyes and lifted his head. Black Leg must have felt him move and did the same. The four mirrored moons of their eyes stared up at me.

"I am well," I whispered, "and will return."

Black Leg flicked his ears forward, then back. He said, "So! We wondered." He didn't say anything about worrying, but then, you can't say that in wolf.

I said, "Love," which is not often said in wolf but means a lot when it is.

He answered, "Always."

I pulled away from the cedar and stood drenched in sorrow and cold in the night wind. Then I hurried to the chair, dressed, and went to bed.

I was surprised. I had the bed all to myself. It didn't feel right. No one ever sleeps alone by choice, but I was so tired I knew nothing after I lay down. When I woke, I found myself still alone. Someone had left a tunic and trousers on the chair. They were very fine white linen, the standard dress for all children and young adults. I slipped them on and began to explore.

The next room was filled with the sort of things one finds in the workrooms of those who are given over to natural philosophy. I know, because Dugald tended to collect them also. Books, both in scroll form and bound. A shelf of stained bottles and clay flasks; these were labeled in Greek. I knew the alphabet but couldn't read the language for the simple reason that Dugald could not obtain any books in Greek.

Dried oddities—a sealed glass box of dried bats, a four-armed starfish, dried vipers. I recoiled from these as if stung. A live black cat eyed me suspiciously, and when I addressed it in cat, its fur stood on end and it ran. The end of the room opened out onto a terrace garden, like the one the Gray Watcher described to me; and as he had said, the white roses were trained against the wall.

Against another wall was a couch. It was filled with pillows. I wasn't sure if it was really a couch or a bed. It was covered by black silk—or I thought it was black silk until I drew close to it and saw the midnight stars glowing at me through the darkness. I eased away from the couch. Near the door to the terrace stood an oval mirror. I could see myself moving through the room in its surface. It watched me. I know, because the position of its legs had changed since I'd entered the room. I could see where they had moved by traces in the dust on the stone floor.

It and I had a little dance. I would move to a position where it couldn't track my reflection, but when I looked away and then back, I would see my shape reflected there once more. Yes, I thought. *It moves. Definitely it moves.* Then I drew close and studied myself in the glass. I did notice the couch was not reflected at all. To the mirror's eye, the only thing present was a stone wall.

I shivered. No, I would not care to sit on that couch. The mirror was on a swivel in its iron frame. It had two sides, but when I reached down to try to turn it, I encountered resistance. Perhaps it didn't turn that way, so I reached for the top. Same problem.

I faced away and looked out over the sea, sparkling in the sun. From here you couldn't see the lower part of the island, only the water and small, puffy clouds floating against the horizon. Then, very quickly, I stepped around the mirror. It tried to turn and block my view, show me only the reflecting glass, but it wasn't strong enough to stop my push. When I pushed it back, then, as if accepting the situation, it remained quiet and its surface reflected only what I had seen gazing through the window—water, sunlight, drifting clouds, and sky. For a moment I was puzzled, and then thought, *Why?—yes!*

"Silver Mane," I said, and within a moment I saw the silver-crested dragon and his wife. They were following a drifting kelp bed off the coast and feeding on small fish, crabs, and squid in the kelp forest. They looked happy lazing along in the sun.

"The island," I whispered, and found myself looking upon it from the beach.

The anchorite's hut had survived, but inside I could see the bed turned on its side and a layer of clean sand on the floor; and I knew that, had I remained there at the height of the storm, I would have drowned.

"Dugald," I said, and he presented himself to me, standing in our house.

He saw me, too, and gasped. Kyra looked up. She was tending the fire. "Thank God," she said.

Dugald shook his fist at me. "Where have you got to?" he asked.

"Tintigal. I'm with Igrane. This is her mirror."

"Mirror, my withered ass," he said. "She is a sorceress, trained in all the worst sorts of black magic."

"You old fool," Kyra said. "Stop berating the child. Aren't you at least glad to see she's safe?"

He looked shamefaced. "I suppose so," he admitted grudgingly.

"I think Arthur is going to make me an offer, but it won't be marriage."

"What?" he screeched. "A lady of your rank? Don't you dare say yes, you hear me? Don't you dare."

I shrugged. "Well, at least you ought to be pleased that I'm no longer thinking of selling myself at the Beltane fair."

Dugald let out a yell, but that was all I heard, because the mirror clouded over, and I saw Igrane appear.

"You are precocious, aren't you? Found the mirror and already know how to use it."

"I'm sorry. Should I not have?"

"No," she said. "I could have sealed it off, had I feared tampering. Was that Dugald I heard grouching and complaining?"

"Yes."

"He and Merlin both are the most contentious men; but of the two, I like Dugald better. Merlin is malicious, not to mention downright dangerous." Then she came in with a tray. She brought me wine. I was not familiar with it, so I did not care for the taste. To me it was bitter, though the barley malt beer the coastal people drank to keep out the cold would probably have been a barbarous, vile mixture to her. There were other things on the tray I did approve of: fresh baked flat breads; eggs in a sauce of onions, garlic, pepper, and spices; cheese and oat porridge with milk and butter.

The divan in her study was a place to sit down. She lifted the star-covered mantle that covered it.

"A wondrous thing, that," I said.

Igrane laughed and spun the silken thing about her. She vanished. I mean, she really vanished. Not blended into the background, not made herself more difficult to notice—which was one of the glamour tricks Dugald taught me—she vanished. I stood openmouthed, staring at the place where she'd been standing only a moment before. Then she reappeared, laughing, and began to fold the scarf.

"I was demonstrating it for a friend the other night," she said. "Beautiful, isn't it? It's been in my family for . . . for . . . uncounted years. It will work for the women of my blood. A pretty toy," she said. "That's how I got Arthur. I wore it the night I went seeking Uther Pendragon."

"The story goes," I said, "that he and your husband, the Cornish king, quarreled over you and that Merlin disguised Uther as your husband, and he lay with you and got you with child, all unknowing that he was not your lawful husband."

"Oh, the great fellowship of the bards. A stinking, stupid war between two fools who should have known better, and they turn it into immortal romance. But, my dear, men don't fight over women. Never. Women simply aren't important enough. They fight over money and power."

"So Dugald says."

"Dugald is wise," she told me. "At least, in that respect he is.

"I am Cornwall," she said. "Do you know what that means?"

I did and said so.

"Good. Dugald hasn't neglected your education. When Gerlos married me, he attained the sovereignty of Cornwall, but he must—for one night at least—yield me up to the high king. He had designs on the position of high king himself and wouldn't, so I languished here—which, by the way, didn't bother me at all—while those two bulls locked horns. But the intimations that I must lie with Uther wouldn't let me rest." She paused for a moment.

"Sometimes, not often, all the oracles say the same thing. Do you know what I mean?"

I did, and nodded.

"The future is read in many ways: from the fall of sticks, the beach patterns of sea foam left by a full-moon tide, the flight of birds, the deformity of the young of domestic animals, and last, but not least, in the entrails of a man drugged with mistletoe and gutted by a bronze and gold knife. He is left to struggle in the dust and the future read in his writhings. Most oracles don't agree with each other. One says, or is interpreted to say, one thing." She shrugged. "And then another a few days later says something else. I read that to mean you're on your own. I think the gods must, at times, grow weary of being continually annoyed by boorish men and even more foolish women.

"But sometimes, in matters of great import, they all say one thing, and they say it over and over again. So it was when the spirits were consulted over whether I should lie with Uther. My duty is to my people." She frowned and seemed sad for a moment. "So I contacted Merlin. My husband found out and had me guarded—a nuisance. But he knew nothing of my mantle, so I wrapped it around myself and went to Merlin. He conducted me to Uther.

"When my husband found out, he flew into a rage, then fell into despair. He died in the next battle. Some say he didn't defend himself." Her brow furrowed. She pointed to the divan. I could see it quite well in the mirror now. It seemed the mantle hid completely whatever it covered.

"Sit down and eat your breakfast," she said. She must have noticed I was munching the bread even while we were talking. I walked over, put down the tray, and began eating.

"Nine months later, I bore a child," she said almost sadly. "Since Gerlos and I hadn't lain together in some time, there was no question about whose child it was. Uther married me and added Cornwall to his considerable possessions, along with me. But still I have never been happy with Uther. Indeed, we hardly know each other. I remain here while he occupies himself with his numerous concubines; and once I was happy with Gerlos, before he was bitten by the bug of greed and ambition. But my advisers told me the country could not stand too much more war."

I understood perfectly what she was talking about, and I understood that it was the reason I was here. You see, that is why my distinguished ancestress raised the standard of revolt among a conquered and resigned people. When the Roman came to her to claim her husband's kingdom at her lord's death, she understood it was her duty to lie with him. But when he and his men polluted her two daughters, he committed sacrilege. Not simply sacrilege, but sacrilege of the worst kind. The Roman was greedy. All he could think of was how great a man he could become if he took the Iceni gold to Rome. As it was, it cost him his life.

Folly and willful blindness overcame his judgment, for even the Romans know women bring sovereignty to a ruler and put weapons in a man's hands. As they say, a woman is a temple; and so, they must understand, it has always been so and always will.

I ate, drank the wine—for I resolved to cultivate a taste for it, since it was the mark of a noble house among the Britons—and listened politely to Igrane's instructions about how a well-brought-up girl should behave at the banquet they were having tonight to celebrate my betrothal to Arthur. You see, among them it was a foregone conclusion that I would become one of his concubines. I wondered who Uther, Igrane, and Merlin had picked out to become Arthur's wife and queen, but my acceptance of him would please the ruling families of Ireland, Dalraida, Somerset. I was marked by magic, as Igrane was.

"Most of the women among the ruling families have something of this sort," she said, indicating the scarf. "I imagine the distinguished ancestress and foundress of your line had something that simply reeked of raw power, as this does. Some treasure that helped her to succeed against the Romans."

"I wonder what it was?" I asked.

"Who knows?" Igrane answered, shaking her head. "Whatever it might have been, it was lost in the savage bloodletting surrounding her when she died, as was entirely proper, by her own hand."

I knew Arthur would be coming, so I finished my food and then hurried back to my bed to put on my shoes. Igrane gave a start when she saw them, for they were greatly changed from the battered, dark leather foot covering they had been the night before. Now they were white, soft, pliable, sporting gold trim and long laces that I wrapped on my legs to below the knee.

He remembers me, I thought, *my friend, for we became friends, the servant of Dis.* Then I saw Arthur come up the stairs. By day, he was even more handsome than he had been by torchlight. He was accompanied by two of his friends. He introduced them to me.

"This is my brother, Cai."

The boy smiled. He looked a year or two older than Arthur. He was dark, with rather fine brown hair. He had an otherworldly look, and I realized why when he took my hand—I felt the sea.

"I was fostered with his people," Arthur explained. "The quiet filled me the way a goblet is filled with wine."

Yes, the Seal people. If he were not shape-strong, he had ancestors close, ancestors who were. He reminded me of the Gray Watcher and his son Black Leg. I think at first he only meant to touch my hand, but he liked whatever energies he felt in me and carried it to his lips.

Like the Gray Watcher, honesty was a strong trait in his character, because a sadness crossed his face like a cloud shadow crossing a valley, and I knew he knew Arthur meant to deceive me. But he was too loyal to say so, and only murmured a greeting. Then he stepped away to speak with Igrane.

Then Arthur introduced Gawain, and when he took my hand, I felt myself shiver. Merlin had surrounded his young king with them. This one was not fully human, either. He was fair, as I am, and with more than human beauty. He was male, so male that maleness screamed at me, and yet . . .

I pulled my hand back from his as quickly as possible. He eyed me the way a connoisseur studies a work of art, then turned to Arthur.

"Magnificent," he said. "She will need some time to ripen, but then"—he made a very Italian gesture—"she will yield a thousand pleasures to a practiced hand."

I noticed he was dressed as a Roman. No leggings or trousers—only tunic and toga. I later learned he had been fostered in Rome. He gave Arthur a wicked grin, then turned away and joined Cai. They sat together next to Igrane's reclined figure, on a cushion near her feet.

Arthur took my hand. I was trying to hide the fact that I nearly melted when he did, so I didn't notice where we were going until we reached the garden overlooking the sea. The roses against the walls were in bloom, and the masses of herbs in separate beds, rosemary and fennel, perfumed the air. Vines I didn't recognize grew down from above and over the marble rail we leaned on. Each gust of wind shook the white roses and drenched the air around us with a mixture of fragrances that murmured wordlessly of intoxicating desire.

He was standing behind me, his right hand on my shoulder, holding my left hand with his. I was having a lot of trouble thinking at all, and I decided that was probably the idea.

"I told you I would make you an offer," he murmured into my ear.

I sighed. No problem about that. He was right; I was smitten.

"Your rank, virtue, and beauty all deserve my affection and profound respect."

I made approving noises—also not difficult.

"My mother," he purred, "owns extensive estates in Cornwall. A particularly beautiful one lies in a valley near here. It has its own villa, an ancient beauty built not long after the Romans came."

I noticed he didn't say conquest. That's what it was, and a bloody one, too.

He had me drooling. I could practically see the place. No doubt exquisite and also completely impractical, built before they understood the climate of Albion was utterly different from that of Italy. Magnificent entryway, mosaic floors, peristyle garden with an entrancing colonnade. Commodious reception rooms, heated by a hypocaust. And a bath, probably heated by the same hypocaust. Wonderful! And excruciatingly expensive to maintain.

One could sit in the peristyle on a cool spring day, smell the flowers, and convince yourself that the Pax Romana still held, stretching from Arabia to Hadrian's wall; legions stood well-organized and strong, holding back the barbarian tide. Instead of the mess we were in now with Britons, Saxons, Jutes, Franks, and for God's sake, God alone knew how many others all at one another's throats, clawing savagely for power with the one hand while with the other they raped, murdered, stole, enslaved, betrayed, and destroyed as many of their fellow humans as they possibly and profitably could.

"How much land, what kind, and how many people are there to work it?" I asked.

"Hmm," he answered. His ardor seemed somewhat diminished, but I got a crisp, clear answer.

"About ten thousand acres, heavy black soil that holds water like a jug. About four villages, not overburdened with taxes or tribute. In addition, it's on the coast and fishing rights go with the property. It has five walled gardens, three orchards—apple, cherry, and peach—a fish stew, poultry yard, and a dovecote. It needs a firmer hand than my mother's to make it really pay, but I'm betting you'll develop one. As it is, she realizes considerable revenue from it, and careful attention would probably double that."

"Cattle, sheep, goats, pasture for same, foundry and forge?" I asked.

"Cattle and sheep, yes. Goats, I don't care for. Mountain pasture with a long grazing season in summer. Foundry and forge you would have to attract, or go to the considerable expense of purchasing a smith, but the space and equipment are present."

"Tannery and—" I began.

"Enough," he said firmly, then eased away from the marble rail.

We stood facing each other, several feet apart. He looked amused and a little surprised. He had beautiful eyes, and his mouth was simply wonderful. I wanted desperately to taste those curved, smooth lips on mine, but I kept the conversation on matters mundane.

"When would I take possession of this very attractive property?"

"Immediately," he replied blandly. "This is, immediately on the signing of the marriage contract."

I nodded and pointed to myself. "And when would you take possession of this attractive property?"

This was too much for him. He began laughing. When he got his mirth under control, he answered, "Not for several years. My mother would have to pronounce you ready to be . . . a wife," he added delicately.

"My," I said. "You have my life all planned for me. All I have to do is live it."

"Yes, I suppose it must look that way to you." He sounded almost sad. "But it's not a bad life. In fact, it's a somewhat better one than most people ever achieve. Certainly a better one than living in the wilderness with a broken-down, exiled druid and his god-knows-what sort of friends and a Pictish slave."

"That hurts," I said. "I love Dugald, and the Gray Watcher is shapestrong, kind, loving, and very wise. As for Kyra, she is not a slave. Neither Dugald nor the Gray Watcher would keep a slave. Neither of them believes in it. Dugald told me once that the first, last, and best gift God gave to men and women was freedom. He lives by this precept and so do I. Besides, signing the contract may present grave difficulties. I have no kin here to look out for my interests, and I am not yet of an age to act for myself. And were I of such an age, my answer would be—"

I didn't get to finish. His hand shot out and covered my mouth. "Don't say any more." There was a steely warning in his gaze. "And whatever you do, don't say no. My mother and Merlin would take it very much amiss if you did, and they are very powerful people—both of them."

His hand moved from my lips and cupped my chin. "I beg you, don't say no. They could break you—the two of them—and it would . . ." His eyes wandered away from my face, and he looked into the distance, out over the sea. "It would," he continued, and for the first time he looked like he was sixteen, "it would not be a thing that I would enjoy seeing. No, I wouldn't like it at all."

I'll give it to him, I thought after he left. He'd managed to say what he wanted me to do without ever being explicit about it. Stall—stall! Stall for time. I did have one misgiving about him. He was too good at seeming to be on both sides of an issue, sympathizing with your plight while subtly twisting your arm to get you to fall in with whatever plan the powerful saw fit to impose on you. But here we both were, and they were determined to marry me off—and to him. I couldn't help but wonder why.

Then I remembered Igrane's tirade about the oracles, and I knew my name must have come up in them once too often. So I was here, and the simplest way to dispose of me was to plant me in the countryside like a tree. I could run an important estate, give him pleasure, and bear him children before I aged too much to be interesting. And that's how it would go, I knew. Oh, we would be deliriously happy for—what? Three years? Four? Five, even? But then the bloom would be off the rose. I would have had children by then, and that changes a woman's body—coarsens her skin, thickens her waist, weighs down her breasts. But above all, it preoccupies her, and often as not wearies her. Not to mention that he sees his place in her affections slowly grow less and less as theirs grows.

And it is not like his investment would be all in me and our family, the way a poor man's is. A chief may have as many women as he cares to, as he can afford. Quickly I would be relegated to the background. Sweet Guynifar, snug in her pretty Cornish nest with the brood growing up around her knees, while he ruled, he married for political advantage, he dallied with the fresh, soft young flesh I was sure Igrane and Merlin would procure for his amusement.

In a pig's eye!

I was thinking these things over when Igrane returned. She had accompanied Arthur and his friends back to whatever place they were lodged. As she glided up the stairs, I saw she had an expression of fixed disapproval on her face. Arthur must have confided my expressions of reluctance to her.

"I hope," she began, "you will not be difficult about this."

"Difficult?" I asked sweetly. "Why, whatever do you mean?"

I think my mimicry might have been a bit too blatant, because her eyes hardened and the lines around her mouth deepened into something approaching a scowl.

"Watch out," I taunted. "Sorceress or not, you're showing your age." I had hoped to get a rise out of her, and I succeeded almost too well.

Those slender, long-nailed fingers closed on my hair. Pain, savage and all encompassing, paralyzing, lashed me, culminating in a rush of agony in my right arm and hand. I didn't scream, or at least, I don't think I did. But I did make a mewing sound and went to my knees before her. But in the last glimpse of her face, I saw the serpent, because that is what she reminded me of—a serpent. Strong, cold, secretive, and able only too well to blend into its surroundings so you don't see it until it is too late. But my taunt pushed her into revealing herself. She knew she'd been out-maneuvered, and by a mere child, and was all the more enraged. I knew I could expect no mercy from her when the time came to—as my lord Arthur put it—to break me.

I had some powers of my own, but now was not the time to force a duel. She might not win, but even if I succeeded in escaping her, there was Merlin to consider. No, Arthur suggested the best tactic: to adopt a delaying action. All this fleeted through my mind when I landed on my knees. So I began to weep.

"Stop blubbering," she snapped. "Get up and change. God knows they want you gotten up like a goddess tonight, and I've been assigned the revolting task of grooming you for the feast. No, go bathe. And I'll call my women. I wouldn't soil my hands by touching you again."

I dried my tears as I watched her retreating back, rose, and went to the bath by the sea. I wondered who had really tried to kill me in the cave on the island. I was scrubbing my hands with the myrrh soap when something occurred to me. Something had dropped the temperature of my heart to so cold a place that I shivered in the warm sun. If she meant to rule me in this way, how did she and the dark sorcerer Merlin rule her son?

No, I thought. *No! That can't be it, just can't be.* Some things are too awful to contemplate, at least for a thirteen-year-old, and the idea of what it must be like to live day in and day out with those two devils . . . well, I pushed it out of my mind, and I wouldn't think about it any longer. Instead, I got out of the pool and delivered myself over to the maids.

They were servile, and I could see why now. A few doses of the pain Igrane liked to inflict and I'll get servile, too. They were of the immature type, who like to play with dolls up to and into adulthood. Not to collect, not to keep, not to admire, but to play with, and that's what I felt like— a doll.

They curled my hair—the stink of the irons was appalling. Mud-packed my face—yes, I did have a light tan; what would you expect, as I live and work outdoors. Rubbed a perfume into a half-dozen places on my body, then overdressed me in linen *strophium*, sleeveless shift, sleeved shift, overdress of silk, and I only just barely managed to fight off a brocade dalmatic. But I won the shoe battle, because they didn't notice mine had changed. All the while, they were talking about my mother in Latin, which they didn't think I understood. Repeating poison from Igrane's own lips about how she was far too free with the "friendship of her thighs," a nasty euphemism for promiscuity.

I didn't know, I don't remember her, not really. And if she was fond of the old ways, it may have been true. Once upon a time women were much freer than they are now. Freer in speech, behavior, and the use to which they put their bodies. A great lady could make a bastard if the day was auspicious, the man a hero, or even especially distinguished in talent or appearance. No one thought any less of her for it. In fact, she was even honored for wanting to bring a fine person into the world. But the Romans, who think women an inferior species of human beings, and the church, which Dugald says mirrors Roman attitudes in many ways, have brought these old customs into ill repute. So the serving women were not slow to slander my mother; and if they didn't know I spoke tolerable Latin, Igrane, who was monitoring my dressing with an unpleasant smile on her face, probably did know, and the conversation was probably one I was meant to overhear. But I don't think I gave her any satisfaction, because I managed to keep a stupid look on my face the entire time.

When they were finished polishing me for presentation, who should show up but Magetsky. She landed in a fluff of black feathers on the rail of the garden, strutted along it among the rosemary branches, and swore at me in First, Second, and Third Raven. I would like to have said something back at her, but I was afraid to call attention to her, lest Igrane find a way to kill her. She gave me hope that Maeniel was somewhere nearby, because I knew she wouldn't fly all this way to find me, not even for him.

But by then it was almost dark, and Igrane dragged me into the procession toward the feasting hall.

When we reached the feasting hall, I knew I was in trouble. The gathering was being held in the same glass pavilion that the Gray Watcher had described to me. It was thronged with the wealthy and powerful of the British court, both Saxons and Romano-British. You see, the two were not separate from each other. The Saxons, then as now, did the bidding of the Romano-British landowners. They held down the old people, from among whom I come, and married their daughters off to Saxon lords and granted land to the ones who maintained their position, collected their taxes and duties. They granted them lands to rule, not to work, as my people did.

This Arthur was their creature; and as soon as the contract was signed, they would regard me as one of them, also.

No, I thought. *No, and no, and no! I won't do it.*

"You see," Igrane said, and pointed at a table very near the door. "We have found a few of your male kin to witness the signing of the papers."

Oh, God, I thought, and looked and looked again. On, no, they were awful. There were three of them. The center one, to whom Igrane was pointing, was red. It isn't a fashionable color at present, but red he was, with a thick thatch of scarlet hair. His face was the beetroot color of a heavy drinker, though that wasn't much of a claim to fame in this company. Nearly every fourth man looked as though he imbibed to the point of folly.

The two on each side were worse. The one on the right was big and dark, much like a bear. Wearing a skin cap and old leather armor, very old leather armor—it was ratty and the backing shone through the breaks and weak spots. The other was long and lean, with brigand mustachios and stringy hair. He was wearing a much-rent chain mail shirt.

"We believe the one in the center to be your father." The distaste and contempt in her voice were stinging.

From where I stood, they all looked drunk, pink-faced, sleepy-eyed.

The feast had not begun yet, and many people were strolling, conversing with one another, seeing and allowing themselves to be seen. Merlin was seated in the chair at the head of the table, or rather in the center seat farthest from the door. After the Roman fashion, he wore a wreath rather than a crown. It was gold and decorated with oak leaves, acorns, and the drooping nude flowers that cover oak branches in the spring. Oak leaves, flowers, and I am sure, leaves and roots would be present, also, an enchanter's crown, a thing of awesome power. The dalmatic he flaunted over dark leggings was of silver cloth brocaded with blue oak leaves. His mantle was woven silver mail.

He was magnificent.

As was Arthur. He wore gold and scarlet, as befitted the summer king, and the figure of the dragon with scarlet wattles and crest was embroidered in red and gold on his linen dalmatic. No, not one dragon, but two in the neck twine of love or battle. They do it in both; it is a test of strength. His mantle was cloth of gold.

Igrane was introducing me around in a not very flattering way.

"Yes, we will sign the contract tonight. I think it's time he made some good connections. She is from a prominent Irish family, and we have an eye on several others."

"Just as well you snagged her now. Those oracles were raising the very devil among my people." This observation was contributed by a hard-faced, middle-aged woman. "Twice my son-in-law had to put down disturbances on the river, but we will have no more problems with them. I ordered three hundred of them on shipboard to be sold to the Greeks. I find it's best to go ahead and take the money before the ship sails and let the captain absorb the risk. A lot die in transit. He paid me two hundred aurei for the lot. The slave trade is booming. I let it be known among the peasants who work my lands that I'd just as soon take my profits out in flesh as in kind. They've been on their best behavior ever since—even the house servants."

My stomach lurched. Then I wondered what it's like to be sold, dragged away from family, friends, all the familiar things in life. Taken to almost another world—there to live life out as a possession treated no better than an animal, if as well, an exile until you die. If that were the only cruelty, it would still be bad, but most often, as Kyra had told me, it's worse. Slavers, you see, don't bother with babies, very young children, old folks, not even most adults. They don't burden themselves with such trash. Mostly they kill them. Especially if they fight, they will kill them, and Kyra's husband had fought.

So he, her son, and her baby had been killed. In my nightmares—and I am visited by many of these she-beasts from time to time—I see Kyra's breasts the way they ran milk for some months after she came to us. Her dress was sticky with it, and when she and I went down to the stream near the sea to wash, she wept and wept and wouldn't be consoled. No, I would *never* become one of these people. No, I would *never* sign that contract.

I jerked my hand away from Igrane's by timing my movement when she was deep in conversation with one of the ladies. I said, "I think I'll go visit my kin."

I thought I might as well see if they were good for anything. She looked annoyed, and I felt pain in my right hand and arm, as I had before; but this time I wouldn't yield to it and walked through it toward the table. The three men glanced at one another with amusement as I drew closer, defiance set on my face. I had expected them to look worse and worse the closer I got, but oddly, that didn't happen. The closer I got, the better looking they appeared. First, the unhealthy color of the center man's face wasn't color at all. Well, it was, but it didn't stem from ill health. He was tattooed. As I said, he was red-haired and very fair skinned; the tattoos were Celtic swirls of blue, running from his hairline down his face and neck, chest and arms. The effect was striking and oddly beautiful, and for the first time I could see the art in all its glory on a warrior.

Such decorations could inspire terror in battle and respect in other men. Something a man like him would wish. As I approached, I realized he'd begun to stare at me the same way I looked at him, with intense seriousness. The man on his left had looked lean and rather unhealthy from a distance, and I judged him some pathetic hanger-on here for food. But again, as I drew closer, the first impression faded. He was dark with fair skin, tattooed like his friend. His tattoos were gray, black, and tawny, the same outlining marks and spirals covering his face and neck and seeming to extend to his whole body. His leanness didn't seem now that of ill health but rather feline. His slightest movement was an expression of grace and power.

The third on the right was even more of a shock than the other two had been. He had seemed fat and his skin mottled with red, but on closer examination I could see what seemed fat was rather massive power. He was as strongly muscled as any man I have ever seen. His hair, skin, and beard were dark, but his tattoos were in red. Even his ears were tattooed red. This puzzled me. I paused about five feet from the table and realized that my first impression had been right. These men didn't belong here. None of them were civilized enough for this room.

Were warriors at the Irish courts really like this? Did even they show this degree of ferocity and battle hunger? I studied the red-haired man in the center.

"You say you are my kin?" I asked.

"You are not alone in having your doubts. When they said you were her daughter, I didn't believe it," he replied. Then he turned to the lean, dark one. "I told you that, did I not, Kiernan?"

Kiernan stroked his long mustache. "Yes, Mael, my dearest love, you did. Indeed you did, but I think you might be wrong. It is *her* to the life."

"Aye," Mael mused, then spoke to me. "You are thirteen, they say. I never knew her at thirteen. My loss that, indeed. God help me, I never knew her at thirty. Again my loss, my dire loss. But unless I am mistaken, and most often I will tell you I am not mistaken, girl, you are her to the life. What say you, Eoan?" He addressed the bull-like one. "Is she not like my own angel, my spirit of springtime, my adored one? To the life she is.

"Come to me, girl. Place your hand in mine. Perhaps it is that I am your father."

Eoan gave a snort of derision. "And perhaps it is that you are not, Mael. I believe there are four or five other strong fellows who are in close competition with you for the honor."

I was stricken with anger. "You mock me," I said.

"Ha!" the one called Kiernan said. "It is not you we mock, but this—" he elbowed Mael's ribs "—lout's pretensions."

"My mother's virtue—"

160

"Girl, Guynifar, is it? Your mother's great virtues have nothing to do with the matter." He grinned at Mael. "It's her taste we find questionable. But I believe if you want him for a father—" he elbowed Mael again "—you may claim him at present. Later, upon better acquaintance, you may want to change your mind."

"Be still, fools," Mael snapped. "Whatever may be found about who sired her, she is the mare's true foal. Besides, she may think you speak slightingly of her mother, who was the faithful, honest, hardworking wife of that mean, grasping brother of mine for thirty years. You see, girl, when the king died and went—" He broke off. "Where do the dead go?" he asked Kiernan.

"I cannot say," Kiernan answered, "but I think it is unimportant in this discussion. Wherever the dead go, it is not here, or should I say, they are not here. Which is all that truly matters for the purposes of your explanation."

"In any case," Mael continued, "when my brother died, Riona—your mother—needed a bit of a departure from too much respectability, so she chose me."

"You do fit that description, Mael. You are a departure from respectability, all right. That I'll believe," Eoan said.

"Come, girl," Mael said, leaning toward me. "Give me your hand."

I tightened my right hand into a fist and pressed it against my stomach. "Oh, why?" I asked. "So you can sell me to Merlin and Igrane?"

They laughed and exchanged speaking glances.

"You don't like the boy?" Mael asked. He glanced over at Arthur. Now, since the table was circular and we were near the doors, Arthur and Igrane were standing across the room from us. Even a round table has a head and foot, I realized. Arthur and Merlin were at the head in the warmest, most comfortable part of the room, while I and my relatives were at the foot, near the door, the coldest, least comfortable side of the room.

Arthur was handsome. Just the sight of him stirred strange longings in me.

"No!" I answered Mael boldly. "I like him well enough—too much, in fact. I just don't care for some of his friends."

Mael nodded.

I could feel Igrane's eyes on me. I was standing half turned, so I could look from her to Mael. The pain lashed me; it hit without warning in my right hand and forearm. It was savage. I knew I made some sound of distress and the room darkened around me. Perspiration broke out all over my face and body. I could just barely see Igrane jerk her head at me in an arrogant, summoning gesture. Come now or suffer the consequences, she seemed to say.

Mael's voice penetrated my consciousness. "Give me your hand," he said again.

Hand? What hand? I could barely breathe, the pain was so terrible. She eyed me across the distance between us with veiled, cold, malicious satisfaction, but I stood my ground; and then the pain ceased, leaving me limp, almost staggering, with relief.

No, I thought stubbornly. No, I am not signing that contract. Nor am I allowing it to be signed. I glanced back at my new "relations." They looked amused. I couldn't think why. How could they know what a battle was going on?

"It appears," Kiernan said, "that the queen wants you."

"Yes," I answered. "I believe she does, but she may be sorry when she gets me."

Then I turned on my heel and started toward the three of them. As I did, the whisper of part of a conversation between my three new relatives came to me so dimly heard that I almost couldn't be sure that the voice wasn't in my mind.

"I wouldn't miss this particular encounter for anything in the world." The speaker was Mael.

Most of the guests were seated now, and so I had to run a gauntlet of disapproving stares as I walked around the fire pit toward Merlin and Igrane. They were standing together before the high seat, with Arthur a little bit to one side. Merlin held a piece of vellum in his hand. I tried to consider my choices dispassionately. I could sign the contract, but why bother? If I did, it would look as if I were going along with their plans. I might do that and hope to slip away when one of them was distracted by other matters. That might be my best chance; but in yielding to coercion, often one compromise leads to another and then another, until you find yourself in too deep to back away.

No, if I wanted the opportunity to lead *my* life, instead of the one they planned for me, then I must take a stand now. I might well fail, but real freedom is worth almost any sacrifice, or at least so Dugald and the Gray Watcher taught me to believe; and most of all, I wanted my freedom and my life back. So thinking, I reached the part of the feasting hall where Merlin, Igrane, and Arthur stood.

Merlin asked the same thing my ostensible father had. "Give me your hand," he said.

"No," I answered.

His very handsome face flushed and then paled. He hitched up his sword belt. Then suddenly, without warning, he leaned forward, his face inches from mine. Behind him, I saw his guard, all black armor and gleaming metal, shift and surround him.

"I've had about as much of you as I care to take," he whispered.

Pain lanced through my arm. This time it was really bad. My first thought was *I'm going to ruin my dress and shift.* Perspiration broke out again all over me. My hand and arm felt like they had been thrust into a fire.

"Stop," I said hoarsely. "Stop, or I'm going to piss on myself in front of the whole room."

"Yes, stop." The voice echoing my own was Arthur's. "How in the hell is it going to look if she collapses in front of every important family in the kingdom? Stop. Now."

The words poured out in a rush. I almost lost my footing as the abrupt cessation of pain staggered me.

Arthur reached over the table and caught my arm to steady me, and went on speaking.

"Maybe the two of you aren't afraid of the taint of scandal, but I am. I won't have my name on every tongue as a torturer and murderer of children. Do you hear me? Stop!" Then he turned to me. "I told you not to say no. I warned you."

I'd gotten both my breath and my footing back. I twisted and jerked my arm out of his grasp. "They have kin of mine here to make it legal," I said. "But the answer is no. I will not become your legal concubine. No!" I spat at him.

Merlin turned to Igrane. The great sorcerer, archdruid of Britain, looked petulant. "I thought you told me you had given her enough pain to render her compliant?"

Igrane was staring at me, her face pale, lips white with fury. *They are lovers*, I thought. I don't know why it came to me then, but I knew it was so.

"I thought I had," she whispered in a voice hoarse with rage. "But I'm better at it than you are. I'll use a little glamour, dear Arthur, so they don't see . . . truly, my sweet, we will only seem to be deep in conversation, but in a very short time . . ." Her hand was rising toward me. "She will do anything I tell her to do."

"No!" I shrieked. My hand shot out as though it had a life of its own.

It snapped shut on Igrane's wrist. Her sleeve burst into flame. She twisted away from me, hissing like an infuriated serpent.

"Fire," Merlin whispered. "I'll give you fire—"

And my silk dress went up with a roar. All around us, the guests were on their feet, screaming, trying to flee. Merlin and Igrane were shadows behind a veil of flame. *Death*, I thought, and then, as I had in the halls of Dis, *A compact with thee, Fire: do not harm me.* I don't know if the incantation worked or if the dress was simply too fragile to be an instrument of Merlin's revenge, but the silk was ash in an instant, leaving me wearing the linen shift underneath, smudged but intact. My heart was filled with rage and my hand with fire. Pain—yes. Jesus God! It hurt. I thought they were still attacking me; something like coal filled my palm. I hurled it at Merlin. It struck him, I swear, like a splash in the center of his chest and spread from there out and around the dalmatic he was wearing. All that silk and metallic thread . . . too bad. In a moment he was as busy as a sorcerer can possibly be.

Igrane's sleeve was wet and smoldering now. She'd doused it with wine. She was still holding the pitcher in her hand. She whispered something and the pitcher flew at me like a sling stone. *Magic? This is magic?* I ducked.

The pain in my hand hit hard again. I felt the coal in my clenched fist. Were they doing it, or was I? Igrane had one of those elaborate hair creations so favored by Roman and Greek women. Yes, they set the standard even here. The coal spun out of my hand like an angry bee and landed smack in the middle of that rat's nest of braid, phony hair, wires, flowers, and I don't know what on top of her head. It must have been lacquered with something, because for a moment it looked as though she were wearing a five-foot sheet of fire. I think she went for another wine pitcher, but I can't say, because by then I was running. I rounded the fire pit and saw Merlin's men drawn up like a wall between me and the door.

Not a hope. I'd never get past them. But I had one weapon left, and I had no idea if it would work. I stopped running and said, "Talorcan, help me." Merlin's guard began advancing. They had their shields and spears up as they began crowding me toward the fire pit. Nothing. *Oh, well . . . I* thought.

The boar exploded out of the heart of the blaze. Logs, flaming brands, hot coals rose like a fountain into the air, showering the room and everyone in it. But by then most of the guests were under the table. But the screaming redoubled for a moment, and then absolute silence fell as everyone in the room took in what was standing at my side.

He lowered his snout and clashed his teeth with a snorting sound. Did you know pigs can talk? I didn't. But this one did. The voice was snuffling and grating. As he swung his head back and forth, studying the room, he said, "Dea-a-a-ath!"

The word rang in the silence.

Merlin's guard abruptly seemed to want to be somewhere else.

"Get out of my way," I said.

They rushed to obey. Sections of the table began crashing to the floor all around the room, as the few men with presence of mind began to try to put a shield before themselves and their women to protect them from the dreadful thing at my side. All except for the three at the table near the door—my relatives. They seemed to be in spasms over something. Then I realized they were laughing.

"Oh, how right you are, dear brother," I heard Kiernan say. " 'Tis priceless!"

"Is it now?" I asked, irritated. "You might at least stop laughing and offer me some help."

The red-haired one, Mael, vaulted the table and hurried toward me. At my side, Talorcan the boar snorted and danced, his shiny cloven hooves clicking against the polished floor. He turned toward Mael.

"Torc Trywth," Mael addressed him, "eldest servant of Dis, I mean her no harm. To you—meat, oil, and wine I will pour at my next feast that you may bask in the delights of prosperity."

"Torc Trywth?" I asked Mael, who had reached my side.

At the sound of that name, I noticed Merlin's guard duck behind the tables and hide. Not so Arthur. He vaulted the table, boar spear in hand, and took up a position in front of his mother.

"All I want to do is leave," I quavered. Then, glancing down at the boar, I said, "Please, please don't hurt anyone if they don't try to stop me. Please."

I received a deep grunt that seemed drawn from his belly, which I took for assent. He was beautiful, the boar. As beautiful in his own way as Mael was when he drew near me. Beautiful as the young summer king as he stood, spear in hand, ready to protect his guests and his mother.

Merlin stood, composed, his finery hanging in rags. His mantle was wrapped around Igrane, who was sobbing in his arms. "Bitch." His voice rang out across the room. "How dare you flout me and insult my lady?"

"You're lucky," I flared back, "that I only insulted her. I could have done worse, much worse."

He shook Igrane off, sending her spinning, and raised his right hand. I was really afraid. I had no idea how powerful he was, but from the force of the storm, I knew he must be very dangerous. And I knew little or nothing of real magic and had no idea how to counter a spell cast by a sorcerer so awesome that he was feared not only in Britain but also in Ireland and Gaul.

"Don't be a fool, man," Mael cried out beside me. "Harm her and the death pig's tusks will rip out your bowels seconds later."

But I don't think even the threat of imminent death would have stopped him. The spear Arthur was holding was sheathed in iron, and before Merlin could begin his incantation, the shaft came down with a crack across his upraised arm. Merlin roared a curse that was half rage, half cry of pain. His skin hissed and stank where the iron touched it.

"Stop," Arthur said. "No more. I am the king, and I will do what is necessary here. And you *will* obey!"

Merlin's and Arthur's eyes locked, Merlin clutching his arm. "You are the summer king," Merlin said, meaning by this that since the winter king, Uther, was still alive, he was only the heir apparent.

"He is not here," Arthur replied, "and in his absence, I am king and your lord. And yours, also, Mother. And I will say what will be done and not one bit less—or more—than I say will be accomplished."

"King," Merlin scoffed. "King."

The spear spun around in Arthur's hand and suddenly, without any warning, the tip was only inches from Merlin's throat. The blade was sharp, as only old, filed steel is sharp—and ragged to boot. The slightest movement of the young king's hand would have put it through the sorcerer's throat.

"Yes, king!" Arthur answered. "And I will be king or I will be nothing."

The two men might have been alone in the room, for all that the rest of us mattered at this moment. Merlin took in one visible and audible breath, then another.

Finally, he answered, "A word from me and you might be nothing—boy."

"Another word from you, sorcerer, and I will burn you! And should I not live long enough to do it, depend upon it, my father will," was Arthur's reply.

The two men continued standing there, eyes locked for another few seconds. It was Merlin who broke. He stepped away. Igrane, not looking all that attractive since what was left of her hair looked like a charred haystack, took hold of him and began to pull him toward the rest of the courtiers, who were now lined up three and four deep against the opposite wall of the room, so afraid were they of Torc Trywth.

But Arthur turned and strode toward us. He was magnificent, and I will never forget that in that moment, I first loved him. And I never stopped loving him. I do now and always will. No one ever brought me more sorrow or pain or joy than he did. No, nothing, not even my sons, has ever outweighed the love I feel and still feel for him. And I believe—had I known what the future held for us: all the trouble, torment, battle, and grief of our lives—I still believe that I would have yielded my heart into his keeping as I did then.

In a few seconds, he was standing before me. Mael stood at my shoulder. He chuckled when Arthur arrived.

"I hadn't thought much of you, my lord, but I do confess that was nicely done," Mael told him.

"They forced the quarrel on me," he said.

"Aye," Mael said, "but it's been a long time coming, hasn't it, my lord?"

For a moment Arthur seemed to return to the rather stiff young man I had spoken to in his mother's garden. He was very controlled, but pain moved somewhere behind his eyes, almost hidden, feared and tinged with shame, but there and very powerful nonetheless. And I knew, not as whatever I was—sorceress, witch, enchantress—but as a woman who loves, that the past was very dark for him and filled with sorrow. But I basked in the warm glow of his eyes when they met mine.

He took my hand, and I gave it to him willingly. "Go in peace," he said, "but know you are mine. Wife, concubine, leman, I will have you, one way or another."

"I am still a child," I said.

He nodded and kissed me on the forehead. Then he turned to Mael and his eyes widened in shock, as did mine.

"You don't look as you did," he said.

And, in fact, the change was amazing. He had looked impressive seated, but standing he was more so. What I had taken to be worn armor was a dalmatic of golden plates, strung together with golden chains. He wore dark leather trousers, rather like my riding pants, held up by a broad, metal belt. It could be seen clearly through the open-work dalmatic. But the wonder was his armor—and the only way we knew it was armor was that he extended his arm to the boar at that moment, and Talorcan sharpened his curling tusks against his arm. The tattoos, or what I had thought to be tattoos, covering his body leaped out at the boar's touch, becoming a blue-steel grating covering and protecting every inch of his body. They glowed, shimmering as if part of the living flesh itself. As indeed, I found out later, they were.

Mael laughed in our faces.

"Armor," Arthur said.

"My delight," Mael answered, "and that of the smith who made it. His joy of creation is joined to mine, who delights in its beauty. Now, daughter, will you give me your hand?"

I did, and he took it between his palms. He closed his eyes and spoke. "If you like, I will give you a gift, something of my own, that will protect you forever from suffering through the hand where your passion leaps out to that of the universe, so that no one can strike with evil at your life's delight as Merlin and Igrane tried to do. The worst of all sins is to use the good rooted in the human spirit against itself; and sadly, it is the most common of all cruelties visited by our kind upon each other."

"Are you really my father?" I asked.

His eyes opened, and I found them green, the sort that goes with red hair, smoky emeralds, translucent, filled with light.

"What does it matter?" he said. "Am I a creature that must fill itself with pride and vanity by looking at my face in a living glass? She—your mother—was a beauty, and she wore it as the sky wears its mantle of sun, moon, and stars. I love you for the joy I took in her sweet self alone. I need no other reason. Now, be still, for my friends have already set their feet on the path of return."

I glanced at the table where they had been sitting, and the bench was empty. I thought they must have slipped out while we were not watching. Arthur was still beside me, and he glanced about, looking for them, and seemed puzzled.

"Close your eyes," Mael said.

I did, and the wings came. Always, always there are wings, soft and dusted with bright color, like those of butterflies, wide and strong like those of an eagle poised to take flight, clear and veined as are those of lacewings and dragonflies, or soft, dark, patterned in gray, white, and black—hidden and astonishing in their complexity when seen, belonging to moths. They passed through my mind's eye, a shadowed rainbow belonging to the miracle of flight. They floated over the living, glowing green that is earth's gown. Grasses—the lords over the dunes by the sea; the rocky, unforgiving hills; the stony places caught fast in drought; and the water meadows, dreaming along rivers and streams—are loved and caressed by them, brown and green, living only in their tough-jointed roots, tall at the sea bending at the incantation of the ceaseless wind, fat with roots clasping mud and damp soil by the rivers and at the edges of ponds keeping it from being torn away even by the immortal destroyer of mountains, water.

My eyes opened and I saw the vine begin at my shoulder. The sleeve of my shirt was gone, dissolved by the nameless power in this man's hand. Coiling, spreading down my arm, speaking in the statement of design and form of my people's belief that all is one, an endlessly varied procession of beauty—joining, separating, searching, dreaming, loving—an indestructible and eternal panorama of creation that we can never, never love enough. Both spectator and participant, protector and destroyer, but above all, joined to the everlasting splendor that is it, us, and God.

The doors to the dining hall burst open as if struck by a mighty wind. I was amazed to see light beyond them. Behind me it seemed every last stick in the fire pit burst into flame. I turned, worried about both Arthur and Talorcan; but the boar, with something that almost sounded like a whoop of joy, dove into the fire pit and disappeared.

Arthur saluted him.

"Till we meet again, my heart awaits you," I said.

"Till we meet again," he answered, "you will trouble my dreams."

Then I turned and plunged into the dappled green dimness and was gone.

CHAPTER EIGHT

THE ROAD WAS A TERRIBLE PLACE. FRIGHTEN-
ing, yet beautiful. I found myself wearing the shoes in
the same shape that Torc Trywth had given them to me,
tough leather bottoms strung with thongs. I needed them.

It was day, and I knew I was on an island, because I could hear the
sea. But beyond that, I had no idea where I was. The island was wrapped
in a fog that was mixed with rain. A sea fog that was more like a cloud
come to visit earth than a gentle breath of cool moisture that blanketed
the rocky coast of Scotland. The fog was warm, moist, white, blinding,
and yet very light. The rain that swept over the island was also blood
warm when it soaked the shift I was wearing.

Ahead and above me the wind brushed away the mist and rain. I saw
the high, dark volcanic cliffs of what I took to be the mainland. I was at a
loss at how to reach it, and once the mist closed in again, I couldn't be sure
what direction to take. The footing was treacherous—slick, very green
grass mixed with lichen and tufts of moss. The surrounding bushes and
small trees were all dark, their thick stems armored with giant thorns.
Within the cages of thorns, they bore flowers.

How strange, I thought. They reminded me of roses, because some

171

were red—often dark as red velvet—others white, marked with scarlet bars. A few with the biggest flowers I have ever seen were a pure white. Stamens and pistils, usually yellow, were also white; the petals had the translucent substance of alabaster.

It was hot here, the muggy heat only a long summer in the wetlands brings. I had begun to perspire. The damp clouds drifting among the thorn bushes wet my face. I didn't see any other people, and the island felt somehow alien, as though no people lived here anywhere. I tore a strip from the hem and tied it up higher than my knees, the way we do when searching for shellfish on the sand flats. But before I could start downhill, the bird arrived.

It was a little smaller than Magetsky, Maeniel's raven, and very different from her. It had teeth. I saw them showing at the front of its beak, protruding slightly, short, sharp, needlelike teeth. It gave a cry, beginning like the sound of a saw slicing into a board, then rising until it finished in sweetness, rather like a silver bell. Its feathers were colored to match the thorn bushes around me, dull brown or black.

I felt a tingle in my right arm and hand. The tingle swept up to my shoulder. I stretched out my arm to the bird, and it hopped onto my wrist. For a moment, I wondered why I did that. I wasn't that trusting. I had seen Magetsky when she was feeling insulted or just in a bad mood go for Maeniel's eyes with that nasty black beak of hers. But he was, after all, a wolf and he would slap her right out of the air, turning her into a screeching ball of feathers and leaving her stunned and staggering on the ground, yelling insults at him for a long time. He would reply to the insults—most so obscene that I didn't understand them—by saying only, "Shut up or I will feed you to a fox. I wouldn't bother to eat you myself." Then she would fly into a tree and sulk, until some sort of food appeared and we got ready to eat. Then she forgot the quarrel entirely.

So you can see why I am not especially trusting with birds. But then his mind touched mine. No, I could not read his thoughts. They were so utterly different from mine. The dragons could speak directly to me, and I perceived their thoughts as words. But this being was . . . was . . . you grope for the expressions to describe those adventures in communication. He would have had no use for my food. Instead, he hunted dragonflies;

beetles; big, naked, brightly colored caterpillars and big, hairy, dark ones; worms; snails; lizards; snakes; and even fish, if he could get them.

He was respectable, intelligent, and had a family of his own in a niche on the cliffs. When he opened his wings, I saw the claws in the middle. I studied the big claws on his feet and those on his wings and decided he must be a wonderful climber. They were not talons like a hawk has, but soft, agile, and with blunt nails. I also learned in passing that he had been asked to do a favor for a friend. He wanted to show me the best way to the sea.

I thanked him as well as I could, and he spread his wings and tail. He had a rather long tail for a bird; and like the rest of him, it appeared nondescript until he flew, and then you were aware of how beautiful he was. When his wings opened and his tail spread as he flew, you could see the dark covering feathers were set off by scarlet, orange, and iridescent blue-green plumage. The tail gave him balance in the air, assisted him in climbing. He was incredibly swift, and between wing and claw he could cover an entire tree, taking all manner of prey in a few minutes. I know, because I watched him hunt.

"A moment, bird," I said when I felt he wanted to draw me to the shore. I tore off more of the shift and began as much as I could to gather the flowers blooming among the thorns.

The bird sawed. No trill this time. "I have business, bird business. Don't keep me waiting."

"Only a moment, bird," I said.

He did whatever birds do in place of a shrug and began to hunt. The thorny branch he was on was covered with red flowers. Caterpillars were eating them, dark caterpillars with orange spots. They were very hard to see among the wicked thorns, but he found them, and for a time he lost interest in me as he stuffed his crop. And, indeed, he was a marvel to watch, his wide, dark body accented by the rainbow colors of his primaries, his tail balancing him as he ran up the trunk and in and out among branches as he stripped the tree of its pests.

I took flowers, white ones—I wasn't sure why, only that I knew somehow they were important and powerful. The air was drenched with their fragrance, and I saw no insects troubled them. Nothing did. Even the bird avoided the pendant canes of the white thorn tree. I plucked flower after flower, and I knew the only reason I was able to reach out to them among the thorns was because of the curving green marks on my right arm. Whenever a thorn touched one, it leaped up like the blue armor had on my father and turned the sharp point.

You have seen our art. It makes some uneasy, an endless, nonrepeating design—sometimes purely abstract, a thing of circles, curves, winding and twisting, like the climbing tendrils of some eternal vine but seeming somehow to enshrine all creation from the mollusk to the star. It's mutable design, able to form itself into any shape, to represent any living thing.

So were the marks on my arm. They moved to the position I most needed them to protect my fingers as I delved among the thorns. At length, my improvised bag was full, and the bird reappeared, his crop bulging. He flashed before me, a glowing pastiche of black, brown, red, orange, and flaming green tail spread like a magnificent fan, dark above a rainbow below.

"Come."

I nodded and followed; indeed, this forest was a maze, clear paths rare. And as we moved lower and lower toward the sea, the rain went from an intermittent nuisance to an almost constant obstruction. I was soaked, my shift a dripping weight on my body, a sloppy mass, running water down my neck and back.

The bird was able to function well enough; something about his feathers reminded me of a duck. They repelled water, but I thought that even he was relieved when we reached the beach, and I saw in the ocean, hazed by rain, the dragon floating on the water just beyond the surf . . . waiting.

Igrane wept. She could not stop weeping.

Merlin was unsympathetic. He paced up and down in her chamber, raging. "You told me," he roared, "that you tried her, that she was a whimpering, sniveling brat and would—if sufficiently punished—do as she was *told*!"

"I thought she would," Igrane moaned in answer to his wrath. "I had no reason to believe otherwise. She gave me no reason. I swear to you. I tried." She became incoherent with weeping.

Arthur entered the darkened room. "It would seem you were both wrong."

Igrane glided toward him. She placed an arm around her strong son's neck and rested her head on his chest, her cheek on the silken tunic he wore. He put one arm around her, as though to comfort her, but the look he gave both her and then Merlin was opaque and unfeeling.

"It's noon," he said. "Why is the room so dark?"

Merlin gave a harsh, impatient bark of laughter. "I don't think your mother wants anyone to see her in a strong light right now."

Igrane drew in a ragged breath. "Oh, God," she whispered. "That horrible child might have killed me. She could have killed me."

Arthur eased away from Igrane. "Mother, I don't think she would have done—"

"Oh, be quiet," she said with a sort of anguished anger. "What do you know of magic?"

He eased even farther away from her, his face still. A dispassionate observer might have thought he seemed frightened. "Almost nothing," he answered.

"You couldn't protect me!" she screamed at him, then turned to Merlin. "You couldn't protect me. Why didn't either of you do anything to help me?"

Merlin made the bad mistake of laughing. A low fire burned in the hearth at the center of the room. A piece of flaming wood leaped into the air and flew right toward his face. He made an impatient gesture, and it shattered in mid-flight into a flock of glowing embers and fell to the floor.

"Mother," Arthur snapped. "You lost some hair. It will grow back."

"Hair!" she screamed. "Hair. This has nothing to do with my hair."

"He doesn't understand," Merlin said quietly. "Show him."

"No," Igrane cried. "No!"

"Show him!" Merlin's voice, while low, was one that brooked no disobedience. "Show him, or I'll leave you to your troubles and you may deal with them as best you can."

"No," she whispered. "No, I can't."

But Igrane positively scurried toward the mirror. "Look! Look!" she said to Arthur. "Look at my—my deformity, my despair."

The surface of the mirror began to glow, casting a pale, white light on Igrane's face. Very little of her hair was left, and what little remained was pure white. She was almost toothless, and her cheeks were wrinkled and sunken. In less than a day, she had gone from appearing a women of less than thirty years to the semblance of a hag rising seventy. The light in the mirror faded, and Igrane sank to her knees, sobbing.

"Now, now are you satisfied? You've humiliated me in front of my own son, and—"

"My sweet, my fair," Merlin said. He walked toward her.

"Don't mock me!" Her voice was a shrill cry of pain, but he reached down and caught her by the hand, raising her to her feet.

"Don't be a fool, Igrane." Merlin's voice was harsh but almost kind. "I have never abandoned you, and I never will. Tonight. Tonight the moon is full."

Arthur slipped out through the heavy curtains at the door. He walked through the garden that was still called Vareen's garden to the marble rail and stared out to sea. He was sixteen, and his eyes might have belonged to a sixty-year-old. A passing servant met the prince's enigmatic gaze for a moment, then quickly looked away. Arthur saw him shiver. People sometimes did when they looked into his eyes after he'd visited his mother. *Tonight,* he thought, remembering the words. *Tonight the moon is full.* Another servant approached. The summer king turned and pointedly stared into the misty distance, where the horizon met the ocean.

I have, he thought, *no magic. Merlin was right. There is a full moon tonight.* Then he heard a clatter, and a shout went up, one loud enough to be heard at the highest point of the fortress. The winter king, Uther, had arrived. He had only a small party with him, his oath men, but they were a wild and dangerous crew, worth ten times their number on any battlefield. His father's personal guard, sworn to form a wall of steel and flesh around him, no matter what the circumstances. And not to leave the battlefield alive if he fell but to die to a man, mingling their blood with his on the thirsty earth. Some men know from birth that they are expendable. Uther was one, his oath men others, and Arthur another. They fought to win. If you did not win, you did not run, either.

Arthur loved his father, even though the word stopped in his throat and would go no farther. So he went down to greet him at the quay. When Uther saw his son, he threw an arm around him and kissed him. Neither man could speak the word "love" in the presence of the other, but kinship allowed this ritual, and they both gloried in it.

"I told you not to come here alone," Uther whispered in his ear as they embraced.

"I had to. I will explain later," Arthur answered in a low voice.

Uther nodded. He trusted his golden son's judgment.

"Besides," Arthur said, "I'm not alone. Cai and Gawain are with me."

Just then Cai appeared at Arthur's side. He went gracefully to one knee before Uther. Uther raised the boy and embraced him the way he had his son. "Gawain?" he asked.

Cai and Arthur exchanged a speaking glance. "He's with a woman," Arthur said.

"*She* keeps sending them," Cai told him.

The *she* referred to was not human but rather the woman spirit of the isles Gawain's father ruled.

Uther chuckled.

"I'll give orders to prepare a feast," Arthur said. "Mother is . . . indisposed."

Uther looked delighted. "Soooo," he said. "What happened?"

"I'll tell you later," Arthur said again in a low voice.

Uther nodded. "The kitten she and Merlin tried to tame had claws."

"You knew?" Cai said. "I mean, about the girl. She is . . . called Guynifar."

"Yes," Uther answered, "and someone was wise enough to call down the people of light's protection on her. Her line is a dark one, some say. Cursed. Is she still here?"

Arthur shook his head. "No, she is gone. She escaped."

"They didn't want her to leave?" Uther asked.

"No," Arthur answered.

Uther whistled softly between his teeth. "She must have very sharp claws indeed. What do you think of her, my son?"

"I liked her very much. Mother wanted to make an arrangement with her for me. Not marriage, but she was offered a settlement of land and money."

Cai began laughing.

"I take it she declined?" Uther said.

"I'd say," Cai answered. "She burned Igrane's hair off, set Merlin himself on fire, and summoned the Torc Trywth. . . ." Uther was laughing out loud by then. "They gave her leave to depart."

"I imagine so," Uther said, wiping his eyes. "I imagine so. But my son—" he began, then he saw Arthur's face go blank. He knew the look. The boy didn't want to talk now. Oh, no. The girl's genealogy was known to him, and everyone along the coast had heard the predictions of the oracle that were spoken of even by the most backward peasants. But the women of her line—men were mere adjuncts of its supernatural women members—never boded any good for the families they married into. Yes, Riona had been the wife of a minor Irish king, one so unimportant that Uther couldn't remember his name. But the man had been much older than she was and was several years dead when Riona conceived this child.

The queen's reputation didn't include promiscuity. She would by no means lie with just anyone. There was no telling what sort of being she'd summoned and seduced to create this offspring. It was said that when Dugald saw the breeding queen, he received a blow that stretched him senseless on the floor for a half hour. Though the tale no doubt had grown in the telling, the thought that this child might become his daughter-in-law was disconcerting to Uther.

Arthur was announcing a welcome feast for his father's oath men. Cheers were ringing out all around Uther, and he was swept along up the stair toward the citadel.

The feast was turning into the sort of drunken rout Uther expected. Quarrels had erupted in Anglia among the landowners. The Saxons chose up sides and joined them. God, what a broth of mischief that had been. He had been campaigning there for the last three months. The conditions along the coast were miserable. Pirates had taken advantage of the disorder to raid the villages there, and then the inland lords started hanging those fleeing pirates. He wasn't sure if he had quelled the disturbances or if famine and plague had simply exhausted all the participants so much that they no longer had a will to murder each other. Now there was this worry. A woman of . . . no, her reputation was not dubious, rather, more frightening. Someone threw more of the green branches on the fire and a cheer rose all around him.

The room darkened as the fire sank down. The man who brought the herbs to the fire staggered back to the table. Remarkable . . . he could still walk. Uther was sure a good many of them were sunk into complete paralysis by the mead and the steam rising from the fire pit. A good third of his men were Saxons, and they were much addicted to the stuff. And they had little chance for pleasure in Anglia. They would make the absolute most of this opportunity tonight.

Hemp, they called it, and burned it in their sweat baths, especially the rosin given off by the weed and its rudimentary flowers. As far as he was concerned, it made his skin feel as if he were being attacked by a legion of insects, crawling all over his body, and it also gave him diarrhea. Since he had to remain until the last man passed out, he hoped that he wouldn't get a lethal enough dose of the nasty smoke to bring on his usual reaction. God help them, this was their idea of fun, and he wanted them to enjoy the feast. They deserved something after the last two months in hell.

He glanced over at Arthur. Apparently his son didn't enjoy drunkenness either, because he imbibed very little and spent most of dinner in close conversation with Cai. It concerned Uther that he hadn't been able to corner the boy and get the full story of what happened from him. But then, he was secretive about his own business, and Uther knew why.

God, did the boy have to pay for his sins? When Igrane's husband raised the standard of rebellion against him, he had accepted marriage as the price of her betrayal of Gerlos. Now he detested her and didn't trust her lover, Merlin, either; but, here again, with Merlin he was caught in his own trap. If the druid hadn't supported him when he succeeded his father, he didn't know if he could have persuaded the southern Romanized nobles to accept him. As it was, he had to crush Gerlos in Dumnonia and steal his wife. Christ! The smoke made him dizzy.

Then he had fostered the boy with Cai's family in his own land. Morgana lived near the sea. He'd had to take Arthur by force from Igrane in order to bring him to Morgana. He wasn't a man to strike women, but that day had been a nightmare that rode with him ever since. He was sure Merlin was responsible for that—the dreams. He had broken Igrane's nose and her jaw when he took the boy; and, no doubt, she had now a large and vicious ax to grind. So he endured the torture of his recurring nightmares stoically.

Almighty God, it had been worth it, though. Merlin still got to tutor the boy, but only under the watchful gaze of Morgana; and his sister's people had not failed him. He smiled grimly, remembering the tale told about the women of that family. Some deserters from the legions at Isca Silurum and armed brigands descended on their stronghold. They thought to have an easy time of it, since the men were away; but the women—yes, those women—made trophies of every man jack of them, and they resided now among the other heads swinging from the rafters of the hall. He had been shown a few on his last visit and the remains of the legionary equipment they carried with them.

Morgana was a priestess of the war goddess, whose name she bore. From the youngest child to the eldest grandfather or grandmother, they played at farming and worked at war. They hadn't done badly by Arthur. He'd brought the boy along with him when he went to clean out a nest of brigands at Venta Icenorum. The pirates had landed, massacred the people there, burned a villa, and were raiding among the other villas in the countryside. He and his oath men rode in to clean them out—a king's duty. He lost the advantage of surprise when one of the lookouts escaped his bowman, and they were able to muster in the pasture on the edge of the village.

He hadn't seen the dry streambed in time; it was too thick with new grass. The ground was butter-soft, and his horse went in to the fetlocks. He went flying, like a green youngster, right over the front of his saddle, somersaulted, and landed at the feet of his enemies. He found he couldn't move, and spared a thought that he hated to orphan the boy so young . . . when he saw a war horse fly over him and his fallen mount. It landed in the faces of the cutthroats charging in to take his head, and his adolescent son turned into a killing machine before his eyes.

Too close to the nearest for a clean stroke, Arthur was forced to improvise. He sliced the horse's head off. The beast fell, overbalancing the man on his back. With a twist of his blade, Arthur cut his throat. The man on his left and Arthur's right drove down with a battle ax. Arthur jerked his war horse into a rearing climb, hooves pawing at the sky, and the ax missed. Arthur drove his sword through the man's throat and out the back of his leather helm.

Even on the ground, counting his last seconds of life, Uther admired the strength of wrist and arm it took to disengage the sword and carve off the last warrior's head and arm in one scooping cut. Too many, Uther thought. The boy is a marvel, but there are too many, because more of the pirates were pressing in on all sides. But then Cai and Gawain were there, and Uther realized as heir apparent, Arthur must already have oath men of his own. Cai favored a mace, the head weighted with lead and covered with long spikes. It took the arm of a bear to swing it, but then, Cai was of the Bear order, the warrior sodality of his *tuath*; and Uther knew, true to Morgana's word, he had probably been initiated into the select group—men and women—of the Bear.

Uther had sprained his wrist, twisted his knee, knocked out two teeth, and broken one of the bones in his upper jaw; but he didn't consider himself badly hurt and was conscious when Arthur, Cai, and Gawain carried him from the field. The physician gave him opium when he had to pull the root of one of his teeth; the other was gone, leaving only a hole. Between the pain of his broken jaw and the considerable additional discomfort of having the tooth root cut out, he was still awake when the screams began. He woke Cai, who was sharing the tent with him.

"What is that?"

Cai ruffled his thick, dark hair with one hand. "The prisoners," he said. "I wanted to hang them, but Arthur saw what they had done in the village, and he gave them to the people. The people were mostly women."

On the other side of Cai's cot, Arthur was sleeping the sleep of the just. The noise didn't bother him.

The opium must have worked, because when Uther woke again at dawn he felt well enough to ride. After they mounted, they rode past the church to water their horses. The church was of the kind built with dry-stone walling in the form of a cross. It had four doors. A fresh hide was nailed to each door. The hides were human.

Uther looked up from his cup. God, that damned smoke. He could barely see, his eyes were tearing so badly. He peered over at the bench where Arthur and Cai had been sitting and saw they were gone. Better than half the men in the hall were draped over the benches or passed out on the floor.

Uther gave a sigh of satisfaction. God, he thought. *The idea of my bed waiting, warm, soft, clean, and comfortable, is sweeter than wine or women or even gold, the throne of power, any of the things I sought after so urgently in my youth.* Stiff, he pushed himself upright. A half dozen of his men—they were sober—accompanied him. He was their king and might never be left alone. They shared his chamber, guarding his sleep, and when he reached it, his bed was all he had wished for. The sound of his closest companions settling in for the night followed him into his dreams.

Sometime well before dawn, he woke, both smelling and hearing the sea. The tide was going out. He could tell from the sound of the waves. Someone was in the room.

For many years he had lived, sleeping and waking, with his hand inches from the sax Morgana had given him when he was twelve and his first beard was cut. It was a beautiful thing, sixteen inches long. The front part of the thick blade was sharpened on both sides up to the hump, which is the strong point of a sax. This thickening keeps the blade from bending or breaking, no matter what. This sharpness on both sides up to the middle allows for quick, easy penetration. Beyond the hump, the blade was sharp only on one side, sharp and saw-toothed. Painful, destructive, and difficult to pull out.

The hilt was ordinary, wire wrapped and covered with leather to offer a solid grip. The hand guard was long and narrow, light, yet offering good protection to the fingers. He kept it under his pillow, and the world always looked better when his hand closed around the hilt.

Who the hell could get past his guard? And how the hell did he do it? Uther didn't doubt for one second that the visitor was "he." Igrane hadn't come near *him* in years, and other women were admitted only by invitation; and of late, he had issued very few such invitations.

The only light in the room came from a hearth in the corner; a smoke hole above it let in brilliant moonlight. It formed a faint, silver haze around the coals. A dark figure loomed, and then the faint light of fire and ice showed him his son's face. Uther was pierced by a terrible sadness, but if Arthur wanted his life, he could have it. Is not the king's life always forfeit to the gods for victory in any case? But the boy held no weapon. He was armed, but only lightly, as if for travel or the hunt. The only thing in his hands was a small clay lamp. He was holding it in one hand and shielding it with the other.

When he felt his father's gaze touch him, Arthur smiled and placed a finger on his lips, calling for silence.

Uther found himself conspiratorially smiling back. He slid out of the bed and followed his son silently. They were out of the chamber and on the stair. Cai was waiting with dark, nondescript clothing for the king.

"If this is about a woman—"

"Sort of," Cai said. "We are spying on Merlin and Igrane."

"Amazing," Uther said. "I have never been able to find out anything about their liaison at all."

"We have an informant," Cai said.

Arthur said, "Be quiet." He knelt before Uther. For a second, Uther was puzzled, but then he realized Arthur was binding up his leggings. "We can explain on the way," he said, and then they hurried down the stair.

Arthur and Cai traveled on foot. They offered Uther a horse, but he refused it. "I was part of Morgana's family," he whispered to them. "I know her insistence on the footman's skills. I can keep up with you well enough."

He did, too, though he well knew their youth would have allowed them to move faster. They matched their pace to his, so as not to make him too uncomfortable. The only break they took was when he called a halt because he knew where they were going.

"The place," he said, "has no good reputation and, moreover, is being claimed by the sea."

"We know," Arthur answered. "Did you think they would pick a pleasant, sanctified site for their workings of black magic?"

Cai grunted in assent.

Above, the clouds were flying fast, skimming past the full moon, and the world around them was now light—almost as bright as day but for the thick, velvet shadows—now dark as the final blindness that falls over the eyes of the dying. Arthur and Cai slowed as they approached the coast.

"Will they have begun?" Arthur asked his foster brother.

"Ena says not," he answered. "They will wait till it clears. If it doesn't, they won't act. They need the moonlight."

When they reached the cove, the sky, burnished by the sea wind, was just beginning to clear. They concealed themselves on the small hill overlooking the twin headlands. Uther couldn't repress a shiver of fear when he looked down. The cove reminded him of nothing so much as a woman's spread thighs, and the spring bubbled from a capstone between them. And on the hill where they lay hidden, they might as well have sheltered between her breasts.

"There is no one here," Uther whispered. "I can't believe I left my warm bed for this nonsensical adventure."

"Oh, they are here," Cai whispered. "My lord, your nose suffers from the Saxon smoke. I can smell them."

Even by the sea near the source of the spring, the vegetation was lush. There were thick bushes, holly and white thorn, and reeds and cat-tails clustered in the damp ground. Where the ground was coated with salt water at high tide, samphire crusted the mud. As the sky cleared, something Uther had taken for a rock threw off its cloak and walked into the pooling water of the spring. It was Merlin. At first, Uther thought he was naked, but he wasn't—only bare-chested. He wore a garland of net-tles on his head and a deerskin held on at the waist with a golden belt.

"Bring them," he commanded.

Two other caped figures emerged from the shadows. Uther recognized one. She was Vivian or the Vivian, one of the Vivians given to be the chief sorcerer's "comfort." Marriage wasn't possible for him, wasn't allowed. He could not leave sons, but his desires were recognized. Hence the Vivians. She was leading someone by a chain. This figure went to its knees before Merlin.

Igrane? Uther considered.

No, for Merlin laughed at the caped figure. "What?" he asked. "Shy? And at this late date? Strip him," he said to the Vivian. She pulled away the dark mantle and revealed a young man that Uther recognized as one of Merlin's personal guards. He was trembling.

"I don't want to die," he whimpered.

"Naturally," Merlin answered almost sweetly. "No one does, but don't give way so much to fear that may be groundless. We have done this before, and you didn't die then, did you?"

"No, no," the boy whispered, "but I almost did."

Merlin laughed. "No, you never even came close."

Just then, the sea breeze began to quicken before the sunrise swept the last clouds away from the moon, and the scene was brilliantly illuminated. The man kneeling before Merlin was naked. The Vivian had been leading him by a chain fastened to a huge cock ring. It was so large that it must have made normal sexual intercourse impossible. Merlin was stroking the boy's cheek.

"I can tell you're absolutely terrified," he said. "If you don't want to take part in the rite, I can always find someone else. If you want to go home, you have but to say so. However, it will be some time before I care to call on you again."

"No, no," the boy whimpered. "No. I want—I want to feel—that—again."

"Well, then," Merlin said, "reconcile yourself to the risks and prepare to show yourself submissive to my commands. Remember, I will not accept anything less than perfect obedience."

"Yes, yes . . . my lord."

"Oh, put a bit more conviction into it," Merlin insisted.

"Yes, my lord," was the reply.

"Very well. Stretch out on the stone facing the sea. Vivian," he said to the girl, "tie him using the silk ropes, please. We wouldn't want any bruises now, would we?"

The boy was tied. Vivian took her work seriously, and twice he cried out at the tightness of the trussing.

"Oh, be quiet," Merlin said. "Otherwise, I'll give you something to whine about."

Thereafter, his victim was silent.

Then Igrane was there.

Where had she been hiding herself? Uther couldn't guess, but one moment no one else but Merlin, Vivian, and the boy were on the shore, and the next she was there, wrapped in a dark mantle. It covered all her body but her head, and he could see how much age had taken her. Her remaining hair was white, and her face was lined and wrinkled. Uther gave a gasp of surprise. He turned to Arthur and was answered by the cold, opaque look he knew so well and a strange smile.

"You knew," he mouthed.

Arthur nodded.

Merlin knelt on the rock behind his victim and began to caress the boy. He writhed in an ecstasy of pleasure. The moon was bright now, the sea gleaming like old silver. The boy began to plead for the final release. Merlin only laughed. The boy had an erection so stiff that it looked painful. The sorcerer was careful not to touch the genitals. He seemed to be waiting for something. He slapped the boy gently on the rump, then left him and walked through the pool to where his Vivian awaited him. The boy moaned in pain. Watching him, the three on the hill didn't doubt he was suffering. Uther had never seen a male so engorged. His organ looked big as a horse's.

But Merlin looked weary, as though nothing about the ceremony interested him very much. He had a preoccupied and businesslike air like that of a whore whose customer was maddened by lust but needed special handling to bring down. The boy suffered for a time, then it was obvious his desire began to ebb. Merlin took a drink from a cup the Vivian offered him, then returned to his subject.

This time the torment was worse. The boy was rendered incoherent and desperate. He was struggling so hard blood dripped from his wrists and ankles where the silk ropes bound him. This time Merlin gave a snort of satisfaction.

Cai leaned over and whispered in Uther's ear, "Look at the spring."

He did and felt his skin crawl. The water flowing from under the capstone had been a trickle, visible only as a gleaming wetness on the sand. Now it was a steady flow. Again the sorcerer took a rest and a drink, ignoring the now-violent struggles of his creature. Again he allowed some of the boy's tumescence to subside before again beginning to stroke him.

This time his subject began screaming.

The sorcerer was annoyed. None of those on the hill saw what he did, but he did something, because the screaming stopped. Then, when the sorcerer stepped away, they saw why. The end of the silk rope that held his captive was looped around his throat; and, as they watched, the sorcerer drew it tight, bending the boy's body into a bow, his heels and wrists together, touching his spine. And as he did, the jerking body spent in wave after wave of sensation that appeared as incredibly pleasurable as it must have been horribly painful.

Merlin laughed again.

And Uther knew horror, disgust, admiration at watching a process so perfectly accomplished. The boy was reduced to nothing but the wild flow of sensation the dark sorcerer wanted him to feel. The little death. What would or could be left of a human being after such an experience? The passion in the boy's body faded after who knew how many spasms. The spring was gushing like a woman in the throes of passion or struggling in childbirth. The boy's seed mingled with the bubbling water. He was done, finished. Whether he would die or not depended on Merlin.

He cut the rope tying the wrists and ankles to the boy's neck and rolled his body flat on the stomach, the boy's face above the spouting spring. After perhaps half a minute, the boy began gasping for air. After another few moments, he was able to struggle and try to break Merlin's grip on his hair. Merlin knelt on his back and held him there. When it was clear he was recovering, Merlin pushed his face into the water, then pulled it out and held his head back.

The men on the hill could hear the boy's hoarse cries and even his wildly gasping breaths.

"See," Merlin said. "You are alive. Did you know that?"

"Yes, yes," was the hoarse reply. "Let me up. Please, please let me up."

"Presently," Merlin replied calmly.

He bent the boy's head back, and the men on the hillside could see his face. Then, with one swipe of the knife he'd used to cut the ropes, he cut the boy's throat. He almost decapitated him, and the neck and trunk of the body flopped forward as the last beats of the struggling heart drove the blood out of the body and into what was now the swirling maelstrom of the stream below.

She rose from the water, smoke, and dark-clotted blood. She seized Merlin, and it was his turn to scream. She kissed the sorcerer, and Uther buried his face in his arms and pressed his body against the earth. He didn't want to think what her kisses must be like, and he certainly didn't want to see any more. She seemed made of water but clothed in the flashing lights that sparkled in the tides of winter. Her hair was made of serpents; and they coiled, falling down her neck and around her face, hissing and striking in all directions. But her face was the worst, the face of one drowned weeks ago—bloated, swollen, noseless and lipless.

He began to whisper a prayer, then to his shock found a hand clamped over his mouth.

"She is a mighty hag and will know if you speak a holy name. Be still, my lord," Cai's voice spoke.

"We must flee. Can we chance it?" Arthur whispered coolly.

"Wait," Cai whispered, "just a moment."

Suddenly the horrible apparition seemed to melt, folding into Merlin's body. Igrane began screaming as it turned to her. Now it was no longer Merlin, but a wrack of things the sea cast ashore—nets, driftwood, broken floats, lengths of twisted, rotten rope, lashings of kelp and dulse—but the snakes were still present. The hair made from them curled, coiled, and writhed, hanging down as far as the ground. Uther watched in sick horror as it embraced Igrane, the serpents striking at her body again and again.

She was borne down under it to the spring, into the shallow water near the twisted remains of the sacrifice Merlin had offered. His head lay on one side of the still-bubbling spring, his body on the other. Igrane gave a ghastly shiver, and Uther knew the thing had somehow managed to penetrate her body.

"Now," Cai whispered.

The three crawled away from their shelter as quickly as they dared, then took to their heels. Uther found only after some miles had passed that he had outrun the two younger men.

When he entered the door, the first thing she did was slap Cai's face. "You, you, filthy louse," she screeched. "I thought you'd gone and abandoned me here with her, foul witch that she is." Then she turned and saw Arthur and the king.

She went ghastly pale and fell to her knees. "Oh, my God, Christ, the saints—oh, God—I can't remember a single one. Oh, God—you rat, why did you let me say such things before her husband and son?" This last addressed to Cai.

"We didn't hear anything, did we, my son?" Uther said.

Arthur looked at him and said, "Hear what?"

Cai pulled her to her feet. "This is . . . Ena." He was holding her left wrist, and she drew her right hand back for another slap. Cai said, "No, one is all you get."

She stared back at him mutinously. "And you'll do what?" she snapped. Then she pulled her wrist free and stalked away to the other side of the room. "All right, all right, I won't hit you anymore. Besides, your mother reared a strong one. It only hurts my hand."

"Tell them about the queen, Ena," Cai prompted.

"She is young. I swear, she now looks younger than me. All her hair is back and down to her waist and—and—and I want to go home."

"Your family will give you the very devil," Cai said. "Go to my grandmother." He turned to Uther. "She's pregnant by me. The arrangement was a proper one, but she's a Saxon."

"And," Ena broke in, "they won't understand at all. They will call me a trollop."

"Go to Morgana," Cai insisted. "She will understand and care for you."

Ena stamped her foot and shouted, "What? Give myself into the keeping of one of those wild bitch women of yours that will bestride a man as quickly as a horse and master both of them?"

"Morgana will be no end pleased by that description of her," Uther contributed mildly.

Ena slapped her hand over her mouth. "Oh, God," she screeched between her fingers. "You—" This to Cai. "You, why do you let me say such things when and where I shouldn't?"

"The problem is not ordering the course of your speech. It's shutting you up in the first place," Cai said.

Arthur spoke quietly. "The Saxons don't understand our domestic arrangements, that is true, but Cai is my close friend and a tolerable match anywhere in the kingdom, Ena. Your family won't be displeased. I think you would like Morgana, and I don't believe she would be entirely displeased by your description of her."

"Especially since there's a great deal of truth in it," Uther ventured shrewdly.

Ena was weeping now. Cai crossed the room and embraced her. "Yes, come with us. We are going back there."

"The queen, how can she make herself young again?" Ena sounded desperate and frightened at the same time. "What did you see last night? What did she and Merlin do?"

Arthur, Cai, and Uther exchanged glances.

"Don't trouble yourself about it," Uther said, suddenly becoming very much the awesome winter king. "Cai, go to her quarters and help her pack. Don't leave her alone—not now, not any time until we are away from Tintigal. Far away."

"Father?" Arthur asked.

Uther put his hand on his son's shoulder.

Uther had just realized something that had been tugging at the edges of his consciousness since last night. He understood why Arthur had been allowed to enter his chamber so silently. His men were efficient guardians. No one, no one, had ever been able to creep up on him while he slept before. The only reason that Arthur had been allowed to do so was because some watcher hoped that he was sneaking in to murder his father. So a gentle, subtle spell had been cast to facilitate his actions. The fortress must be filled with Merlin's eyes and ears.

"Last night was not the end but the beginning, and I want no one that I love or who has served me well within the queen's reach after I am gone."

Ena's mouth opened.

"No, no more talk. Be quiet, girl, and do as I say. We ride within the hour."

Cai spun Ena around and marched her out of the room.

"Arthur," his father repeated, "do as I say and do it now!"

Arthur bowed, then left.

Uther was Morgana's half brother, so the blood was thinner in him, but enough of her powerful gift of prophecy was part of his nature to be able to warn him that Igrane and the dark sorcerer were planning something. Something big. The sacrifice last night told him they were ready to employ the darkest means to achieve their ends. Uther knew they must leave now, before nightfall, while those two serpents were quiescent, or they might never be able to go at all.

Arthur went to his own quarters. His rooms were spartan, and seeing them, no one would have guessed he was a king. For even if by courtesy, the winter king was supreme, the summer king was associated with him in ruling. He had brought very little with him when he came to the fortress. He had a few fine clothes, because a king must always appear in splendor to his people. Otherwise, only his weapons were present: crossbows and boar spears on the wall for hunting, another mace of the kind Cai favored—it took the arm of a bear to swing that one—and a few pikes, and two precious old swords.

He paused. For a moment, he felt a strangeness. Then understood why.

He was alone.

People were seldom alone. Men of his rank, almost never. His father's oath men were always within sight of the king, even if not always within earshot. Their lives depended on Uther's; they were sworn to fight beside him on the battlefield, to die one by one rather than allow him to be killed. And should he fall to bow or flying spear, to die to a man rather than return without him.

Cai and Gawain had vowed themselves to Arthur in a similar way when he was crowned summer king. Why weren't they here? Cai was with Ena. His father had dismissed him, but Gawain or even one of his father's oath men should have accompanied him to his rooms.

Turn tail and run, something warned!

Run!

No. He refused to be stricken with panic in his own bedroom.

But he would hurry. He would leave everything here but take the swords, one at his waist and the other, longer one, strapped to his back. He seized the belt of the shorter one to put it on.

Something stung him painfully, viciously. He jerked his hand back and looked down. The snake was injured, dying, but it still had enough life in it to strike. The fangs were embedded in the back of his hand to the gums. Arthur drew his knife. There was a chance, if the venom was not in him, he might strike upward through the roof of the serpent's mouth and rip it free, before he received a mortal dose. But even as the blade cleared the sheath, he realized this was no normal living being. A serpent is a frightening creature, but it, after all, was one of God's creatures. But not this one. It was part of her hair and pure evil, a messenger of darkness. He saw the bloody stump where it had been severed from her head.

Its venom had begun paralyzing him, but he would try to the last. He struck upward with the knife, but his arm was blocked, and he found himself looking into Merlin's eyes. There was a strange smile on the wizard's face.

Then, as he watched, Merlin, with a finger, pressed down on the serpent's head, driving the rest of the dark poison into Arthur's body.

And that was the last thing the summer king saw or knew for a very long time.

Uther and his oath men waited only long enough for Arthur and his companions to join them. Cai arrived first, escorting a still-protesting Ena.

The king left as soon as he saw them at the causeway that led to shore. A half dozen of his men always surrounded him closely. The rest followed, strung out along the road through the forest with Arthur, Gawain, and Cai bringing up the rear.

The king set a terrific pace, almost too fast for the narrow, muddy track they followed. The sky was overcast, and from time to time sprinkles of rain fell on the party.

Arthur was silent. Gawain was silent and smiling.

She must have been a particularly nice one, Cai thought.

Gawain was twenty-three and had already acknowledged four bastards. Married or not, he had the beginnings of a huge family. His father, being of the Outer Isles, was glowingly proud of his son, as was his mother. His people were given to unusual marital arrangements. But then, they were seafarers. Marriage was a nuisance to those bold people. You couldn't expect men and women who were separated for long periods of time to be as devoted as spouses that spent their entire lives together. King Lot had been married to one of his other aunts for seventeen years, but in that length of time, he doubted that the two had spent as much as a half year together.

Gawain had been conceived after his mother visited for six months on the Isle of Women, a thoroughly strange place. The high priestess, the Scathatch, had told Morguse she would conceive by the Queen of Light. She, like Dis Pater, Lord of the Dead, sometimes used other creatures to pursue her amours. And in this case, a giant sea eagle lifted Morguse to the top of a crag, and the mating took place in the air among the clouds over the open ocean.

Cai didn't know what he thought about that. When he asked his grandmother Morgana about it, she replied with a beautiful poem of a maiden brought up to the sky by such an eagle and the culmination of their desire as they soared between heaven and earth, sky and sea.

When one is high enough, one is not falling but flying, and desire dissolves every emotion but the infinitely sweet preoccupation of flesh with flesh. In the poem, the bird carried a lance of glowing rainbow light at his loins, and the woman's mad fear as they joined was transformed into ravishing ecstasy that pulsed on and on so long that the queen nigh died of the divine bird's fire consuming her flesh. She was left sated and weak on the green velvet grass near the heart spring on the Isle of Women.

Her husband was sent for at once, and he added the vigor of mortal clay to the citadel of her fire-drenched womb, and the child was drawn out of nothingness into existence. Nine months later, Gawain was born.

Women were on him like cats to catnip. They wallowed before him like lions in heat, absorbing his vitality, vigor, and virility the way the starved earth sucked up rain. Adoring him from near and far, upright and prone, day and night. He accommodated all comers with profound courtesy and deep good humor.

And there were often times when a wildly jealous Cai hated the air he breathed and the ground he walked on. But he was so amiable, kind, and good at everything he did that no one, certainly not any of his numerous amours, could stay out of temper with him long.

So he was forgiven trespasses that might have gotten other men killed on the spot. And he walked in the golden beauty of the goddess's protection.

Ena was afraid, and so broke constantly in on Cai's thoughts with querulous inquiries. "Where are we going?" "Why are we riding so fast?" "I'm not sure I can keep up." "When do we stop?" "Will we slow down?" "Why don't you answer me?"

Cai began to laugh. "Too many," he said. "Pick one."

"Oh, God, you Britons are terrible. I can never get a straight answer from you. My mother told me . . . she warned me—"

"My sweet," Cai broke in, "I can keep company with your mother, two aunts, and a cousin. They all have opinions about everything—at least to hear you tell it, they do. But aren't you afraid your own dear self will get lost in the crowd?"

This silenced Ena for a few moments, while she sorted it out. Then she began to snivel. "Now I can't talk about my family to you at all. Aren't you ashamed to be such a tyrant?"

"And yet another question," Cai said. "Let me see if I can sum it up. To Morgana. He wants to get as far from Tintigal as he can today. You can keep up. Plainly, you are doing it. We will stop soon, and we will slow down because he can't push the horses so fast for so long. I have answered you, and no, I am not ashamed."

Ena had to sort this out, also. And she was silenced for a time.

They did slow down, because as they distanced themselves from

Tintigal, the road grew worse. As they pushed deeper into the forest, mist hung heavy in the trees, blocking out the light and impairing visibility.

Cai pulled his horse in and rode knee to knee with Ena. Gawain moved up from the rear and eased beside him.

"I don't like it," he said, frowning. "This stinks of magic."

Ena was pale; she pulled her horse's reins and began to slow.

"No, Ena," Cai said. "Keep up."

"We can't go on running like this," she replied. "It's getting so I can't see anything."

And indeed, Uther's oath men ahead were slowing also. The fog grew thicker and thicker.

"What do you mean about magic?" she asked Gawain.

"We started our ride in the morning sunshine, and then murk closes in around us. It's unnatural."

"That's what magic is," Ena said. "A betrayal of our expectations— the things we depend on for our very lives. When the magic rules, fire is cold, water burns, age is youth, and youth . . ."

She had almost stopped moving. The fog was blinding, and she ceased speaking because the three heard the sound of hooves thudding behind them.

"That will be Arthur," Cai said.

"Will it?" Gawain said.

"Who else?" Ena said. Her face was pale. Her long blond hair, darkened by moisture, hung in damp rat tails on each side of her face and down her back.

"I can no longer see anything ahead of me," Cai said.

Their horses were walking now.

"I can't hear them either," Ena whispered. "We've gotten separated from the rest somehow."

The fog was a white wall around them. Trees, bushes, even the wet, oozing, muddy track they were riding along were almost hidden by the vapor.

Arthur's horse rose into view behind them, with a figure in the saddle. He was wearing the robes of the summer king, the dragon embroidered on the heavy dalmatic.

Why now, for travel? Cai thought. The royal robes might be appropriate for a banquet or an affair of state, but for riding through a dripping wood? No.

Gawain, Cai, and Ena pulled their horses onto the grassy verge. Arthur's stallion, still moving at a trot, drew level with them and began to pass.

Cai gave a sigh of relief at the two pale hands on the reins. That was all he could see. The hood of the dalmatic was up.

"My lord . . ." he said.

The figure on the stallion ignored him.

Ena was a bit ahead of Cai.

"My lord," she echoed his cry, and reached out. Her fingers brushed the sleeve of Arthur's court garb.

That was all it took.

The stallion slowed. The figure in the saddle turned toward the watching trio.

Cai felt a shock of absolute terror as he saw his friend's face with the naked, empty eye sockets of a skull.

"Arthur," he whispered.

But then it began to dissolve. Sand poured from every opening in the clothing, until at last a yellowed skull toppled from the top of a neck made of sticks to roll through the muddy puddles at their horses' feet.

Gawain leaped from his saddle. He kicked at the remains—sticks, bones, sand, dried leaves, and the ancient skull.

Cai followed, lifting Ena down from her horse.

"He's dead," she whispered, staring at the skull.

"No!" Gawain said. "No!"

When Gawain felt the world, his senses were extended beyond those of his companions. This is a gift we all share to some extent, the knowledge of where we are with respect to time, space, inanimate objects, and animate others. But his gift was heightened by his supernatural ancestry. When he approached anyone, man or woman, he could tell what they were feeling and, often as not, what they were thinking. He need only brush a woman's face with the tips of his fingers and he knew instantly how to bring her to a state of quivering ecstasy. He was similarly effective at defusing the anger and envy of men, persuading them to like him and to obey his requests and commands.

He knelt, lifted a handful of sand that had composed the limbs of the semblance and let it trickle through his fingers. The sense of wrongness was palpable. The fog surrounding them grew thicker by the moment. He felt a tendril brush his sleeve.

Real fog is moist and cool. Neither coolness nor moisture was resident in this cloud. Instead, he felt the deadly chill that is the first warning that the dead are present.

The miasmic vapor sucked the life from everything it touched. The trees were burdened with it, not refreshed as they might have been by real fog. It silvered the bark and leaves with the icy touch of midwinter hoarfrost. And he knew it would kill first the vegetation around them, then the denizens of the forest, locking them in its icy embrace until all warmth was sucked from their flesh into a frigid silence. It was already striking at the humans gathered here around the evil travesty of life, made vulnerable by grief.

Birds were his mother's creatures. Not his human mother—the other one. And he remembered how he had first seen her through the wings of a bird as it spread them to take flight between his eyes and the sun. Each feather clearly delineated, each a wondrous construction that gave the bird flight. A translucent beauty, an ordered pattern glowing with the fire of the sun shining through them.

Mother! Mother! Answer me! Help me! And she did.

"No," Gawain said. "He—it—never was alive. It was only a semblance . . . intended to fool us for a short time."

Cai turned to Ena. The expression of fixed terror on her face was in itself frightening.

"What did I do?" she whispered.

"Nothing," Gawain assured her. "Nothing. The thing would have dissolved in a short time in any event. Your touch broke the spell that held it together."

"What did I do?" Ena asked again, as though she hadn't heard him.

"Cai! Kiss her!" Gawain said.

"What?" Cai asked almost stupidly.

"Kiss her. She is in danger. The spell leaped from the semblance to her mind. The thing was . . . was . . . man-trapped. It was supposed to get one of us. Instead, it got her. Kiss her, for God's sake. If you love her, kiss her."

Cai pulled Ena's body against his and pressed his lips to hers.

He released her, feeling as though a thousand tiny insects covered his body.

"No! It's just a game with you men!" Ena screamed.

"No game, this," Cai said, lifting her into his arms and carrying her into the fog-drowned woods.

The wind was beginning to blow. He threw her onto a bank of thick bracken, just out of sight of the road.

"I want you," he snarled.

"Yes! Yes!" Ena panted. "Oh, yes! I smell the sea. Ah, God, how it pounds the rocks at midnight."

Salt water was in her mouth, blood from his lips. He'd bitten them in the ferocity of his need. The wind was blowing more and more strongly, tearing the fog around them to tatters.

Gawain, standing in the road, looking at the debris of Merlin's spell and clinging to the terrified horses' reins, listened to the cries. Both human and those of the forest; giant trees sobbing now and moaning in the blast.

He smiled, a grim smile. Cai and Ena were throwing Merlin's sorcery back in his face.

They were fiercely joined now, the forest around them crying out with passion, both its and theirs. Cai thrust his tongue almost into Ena's throat. Her loins opened as he had never felt them open before—moist, hot, flowing with need.

"In! In!" She pulled her mouth away from his to speak. "In! I want all of you. All of you."

Cai threw back his head as the overpowering spasms of his completion shook his body. He felt her nails digging into his buttocks, the slight pain driving him to even more ecstatic heights. It wrung an outcry from him more animal than human.

Then she screamed, seemingly almost scalded by her own desire. And it ended with the sun on his bare back and in her eyes as it shone through the high canopy of the forest above.

And around them, the thickets were stirred to beauty by birdsong and the summer breeze.

"He is taken," Gawain told Uther.

Uther kicked at the sand, clothes, and skull piled in the road. The three, Cai, Gawain, and Ena. With the exception of Gawain none of them would look him in the eye.

Uther's face was hard as a mountain crag.

"When?" he asked.

"Probably before we left Tintigal," was Gawain's reply. "This thing—" he gestured toward the remnants "—was likely only intended to fool us for a short time."

Ena closed her eyes. She placed her hand over the child in her belly, thinking, *I can plead pregnancy.* She glanced up at Cai's set face. *Not that it will do much good. He will likely hang the father beside both mother and child. There is a chance the two men will escape. Uther won't want to irritate his own family or break off an alliance with the king of the Outer Isles, Gawain's father, Lot.*

"I left him to go with Ena," Cai said.

Gawain's eyes closed. "I left him to dally with a woman."

"Yes," Uther said. "And I with seventy brave men at my beck and call. I let him go to his room alone. Let us not try to assign guilt."

Uther sensed relaxation in the three confronting him. They had been afraid they would face the irrational, unleashed fury of a king.

And there was fury enough in him. But he hadn't become high king of the Britons by being unable to control his emotions, and he hadn't held power so long by engaging in self-destructive savagery.

These three loved the boy as much as he did. Yes, he thought, turning away. He would love to hang, or better yet, burn or crucify someone, or even several someones. But certainly not his sister's grandson or a prince of the blood like Gawain.

As for the girl . . . God! Might as well hang his son's horse. It was standing in the road beside the remains of the semblance, looking as bewildered as the humans gathered there.

"I don't know if it's any comfort to you, my lord, but I believe we were all hoodwinked. I cannot think we were all remiss, not all at once—by accident."

Uther glanced back at Gawain.

"Sometimes," Gawain continued, "magic is most powerful when it is least seen."

Uther remembered Gerlos long ago being driven to despair by Igrane's desertion. He had used Merlin then to destroy the king of Dumnonia. Somehow Gerlos knew within the hour that Igrane lay with the Pendragon. And later, Uther had felt responsible for Gerlos's despair and suicide. Now he was certain that Merlin had sent the news of Igrane's betrayal to Gerlos.

"The last thing I should be guilty of right now is rashness or folly," Uther said. "Speak." He turned to Gawain. "You know more of magic, Hawk of May, than any of us. What is your thought?"

Gawain said, "Likely he—Arthur I mean—is not at Tintigal any longer but has been taken somewhere else. The Saxon pirates who harry our shores are in Merlin's debt—deeply in his debt. And Arthur would have been given to them to transport God knows where. If you return to Tintigal, I think you will find the causeway to the mainland held against you; and your brave oath men will die in large numbers to win admittance for you. If, indeed, they can. Merlin's personal guard will die to a man to keep you out. And likely, when they are dead, the queen and her lover will be gone also."

Uther nodded. His mind turned inward. *I should,* he thought, *do nothing, at least nothing right now.* Sometimes that was the most difficult thing to do—nothing. *I must speak with Morgana in the ancient land of the Silures—Wales, those damned Saxons called it. Typical of their arrogance, that they should name the ancient rulers of this country foreigners.*

Before the Romans, the Silures, his people, had begun to enter the larger world of cities and trade. But when the Romans came, they went back to their forests. The low mountain meadows of their land offered rich summer grazing to cattle, sheep, and horses. The valleys were drowned deep in sometimes impenetrable forests. The tribes moved among them, clearing land to plant and then, as quickly, leaving when and if the Romans made too much of a nuisance of themselves.

The Romans demanded tribute. Not knowing much about the people they had no idea how much they could demand. As a result, they got almost nothing. And the Silures themselves organized their customs in such a way as to avoid the conquest and exploitation to which the other tribes had been subjected.

How they loved threes—and every Silurian had three identities: his family, his tribe, and his, or for that matter, her, warrior society.

Hawk of May, Gawain, was one of the people of the hawk, born, as it was thought, of the union of his mother with a hawk. There were others, many others.

Arthur the Bear. Morgana—yes, Morgana—an Owl. Cai, the Seal. Most belonged to and had been initiated into more than one society. They tied what should have been a very divided people into one, since the societies cut across class, family, tribes, and were purely adoptive organizations. And they accepted both women and men.

How the church hated that, and Uther had been more than once the object of sermons by churchmen who wanted him to deprive women of the right to bear arms. But he turned his face away from the idea. He had no desire to infuriate his people; and besides, more than once the fierce women of the Silures had been the difference between victory and defeat.

He drew Gawain aside.

"How many of the lords of the wild will entertain you in their dwellings?"

"All of them," Gawain answered. "I am an oath man of the summer king. He is beloved. Morgana saw that they were all feasted."

"Wise," Uther whispered.

"None wiser," Gawain said in agreement.

"Ride on ahead and spread the word."

Gawain nodded.

"Ask that they hold themselves in readiness for my call."

Gawain nodded again.

"Caution them to do nothing without my word," Uther continued.

"But of course I will take the head of that filthy necromancer and his leman, should I happen to stumble somehow upon them . . . but I cannot think I will be so lucky. The pair will know to keep well away from me or any loyal to me."

Uther's hand closed so tightly on Gawain's shoulder that the young man, strong as he was, flinched.

"I'm sorry. Pray excuse me," he said to Gawain.

"Not at all," Gawain answered.

"As for myself," Uther told him, "I will go and speak to Morgana. I want that bastard Merlin dead! And she will know best how to accomplish that."

"My lord," Gawain said quietly to the torment he saw in Uther's eyes, "I do not think they will kill him. I don't think they would dare. When Vortigen was murdered, Merlin was sure the Saxons would prevail. But they didn't. In fact, they were forced to flee in large numbers. What they need is a high king who will accommodate them; and thanks to your artifices, Arthur is the only heir."

"How did you know that was deliberate?" Uther asked.

"Am I a fool?" Gawain whispered. "You forsook the queen's bed and have not—since Arthur was fostered with Morgana—lain with a woman who could begin to claim the high kingship for her son. Pleasant ladies all, I'm sure, but very, very low-ranking women."

Uther said, "Yes, every one of them. And I have endeavored not to get any of them with child. It is that, and that alone, that protects Arthur now. But God help the boy, it won't protect him from the kind of pain those two devils can inflict on him. And are probably inflicting now."

Again Gawain was forced to flinch by Uther's grip. "My lord," he said, "the Veneti call all along the coast to trade and get timber. Word from the lords of the wildwood might frighten the pair, if nothing else."

"I give you leave to try," Uther said. "It might help my son and make that brace of reptiles think twice before they commit the worst atrocities. Ride now, and may God go with you."

CHAPTER NINE

I WADED OUT INTO THE WATER TO CONFRONT the dragon. He was yet another kind, marked like an orca, almost blue-black on top and white beneath. His back was hard with a succession of dark plates, each with a spine, decorating him from nose to tail. His body was very slim, even slimmer than that of the black dragon's. And his fangs were prominent, even with his mouth closed. They projected from his top jaw past the lower jaw and were visible against his white underbody.

"How many kinds of you are there?" I asked.

"Possibly as many as two dozen," he answered. "Why?"

"I was just curious," I answered. "It's not an issue with you?"

"No. Why? Should it be? We are specialized for different purposes. I am a hunter and eat sharks. Red Mane, the first you met, is a plant eater almost exclusively. Deep Diver, the black one—his name is, I think, self-explanatory. Silver manes follow the drifting plant beds. I hunt and am fierce. Unlike the silver manes, I fear no storms, am a fast, strong swimmer, and travel in . . . I voyage . . . among the lost."

"Am I then lost?" I asked.

"For the moment, but I will bring you home to your kin," was his reply.

"Not to Tintigal," I said.

"No! And Igrane has a lot of explaining to do before we ever honor her with our trust again. Now get on. We have some distance to cover before nightfall."

I obeyed.

I had strapped the flowers to my waist. Their fragrance drifted around me. And indeed, this was a place of flowers. They grew here in wild profusion. The beaches were covered with them above the tide line, golden sunbursts on succulent stems.

Violet whirls hung over the edges of the cliffs on the waterways we traversed. Mounded bushes covered by white blooms clung with twisted roots to the rocky slopes leading down to the water.

Others resembled poppies, with their brilliant colors of white, red, orange, blue, and all the shades in between—cascaded from steep cliffs adorned with broken rock. The petals of these flowers were thin and soft, and since the water the dragon swam through was dotted beautifully with their petals it was clear these blooms lasted less than a day. All this I glimpsed between patches of thick fog that lay on the water the way clouds rest on air rising from earth on a warm day.

The dragon—who, by the way, was the fastest, strongest swimmer I had ever ridden—swam sometimes around the fog patches so that we basked in the warm sun; at other times he hurried through them, and I was blinded by the thick, oddly chill vapor.

"What is this place? Why are we here? How will we get home?"

The dragon snorted and made an impatient noise. "I have no answers to these questions. At least, none that make sense to me, much less to you. The natural philosophers have some theories that I cannot begin to consider discussing." This information was delivered in a suitably lofty tone. "But it is sufficient to say this is not a place and we are nowhere."

"Very enlightening," I answered.

"Ha! You think that's bad, you should hear the explanations of our natural philosophers. But we call this the realm of the clawed bird."

"Makes sense," I answered. He did have claws on his wings; teeth, too.

"Yes," the dragon said. "Yes, once he did, now he is no more. Yet we can still come here to gaze at his flowers and sip the honey made from them by the bees."

"Bees?" I said. As we emerged from a fog bank near a cliff, I saw there were indeed bees here. Bees moreover of all shapes and sizes nesting in hollows under overhangs or small caves in the cliffs overlooking the water. Some, only as large as flies, were yellow, orange, and violet and very swift. Others were black, purple, yellow, and red and large almost as my thumb.

"Don't be deceived," the dragon told me. "It's the little ones that are dangerous and will sting the hell out of you. The large black ones have another kind of protection but in return for an offering will let you drink from their combs. See them, the honeycombs?"

And I did. Some were as long as six feet, sheltered in the overhangs against the cliff face. Magnificent creations of the giant bees, colored all the shades of yellow imaginable—some so dark they were almost burgundy— running the gamut from red to brown, golden orange, dark yellow, sulfur yellow, pale yellow, and subtle greenish yellow, glowing like jewels, bright as their fostering flowers against the gray and black rock.

"The clawed bird hunts the little ones but is in a state of truce with the large black ones, and they supply him with honey for his young. But again I reiterate, don't ask too many questions here or we might be sent home. You would not care to sojourn again at Tintigal."

"No." I shuddered. "But this realm of the clawed bird, it must be somewhere."

The dragon laughed. "Only to your limited mind, and also to mine," he added with a touch of humility. "But consider the kingdom of possibility. You would say it was an enormous one, would you not? All those things that might be and all those that ever existed. Our natural philosophers believe that anything that ever struggled into existence carved out its own special niche in that kingdom. And there it will remain irrespective of time, since time does not exist there."

I rolled my eyes. "Sounds like Kyra's possible."

"Hmm?" the dragon asked.

"She tells me to wash down as far as possible and then wash possible."

" 'Possible' being a euphemism for the human reproductive area?"

"Yes," I said.

"You ought to be ashamed to play with the language like that. But then, the natural philosophers say you primates are especially gifted that way. But, I'm glad we keep our equipment inside our bodies. Enough said. I'm going to dive, so take a deep breath. And shut up. If you try to talk under water, you'll drown."

He was right. I would. You see, we weren't talking with our minds. We both made sounds. He could make sounds under water, but I couldn't. I'm certain some sort of mind contact helped us understand each other, but the specifics were verbal.

I took a deep breath and we sank. We didn't dive. I don't know how they do that, but it's very effective. I've seen snakes do the same thing. I wouldn't compare the dragons to snakes, not while they were within earshot. I wouldn't, because they consider snakes a very much lower life-form. But I have no doubt the same principle is involved.

Down here the world was blue and silent, though the water was sun-struck, and strong golden rays penetrated the depths. Down and down we went, making for an opening I could see as a dark cave in the cliff face. The kingdom of possibility—all things that ever were—had a niche there. Did that mean my mother was still somewhere within that king-dom? I had only one dim memory of her, and I wasn't sure if it was a real memory or only something Dugald told me about her later.

Her hands were cold and her face thin and pinched. She was handing me over to Dugald and saying, "She is a brave one and doesn't even cry at the icy touch of my hands."

I learned later that she was dying.

If what the dragon said was true, someday my mother and I might meet beyond the world and speak with each other. Heaven, Dugald told me about heaven. But even he isn't sure everyone goes there. In the church there are a lot of quarrels about it—who has the right to enter, who doesn't, and where they must go if they can't get in. But the king-dom of possibility sounded like a much more inclusive place. Maybe she *was* there.

Then we reached the entrance to the cave and plunged into darkness.

I closed my eyes. It's better to close your eyes if you can't see.

The whole gang of us had a big argument about it once. Kyra said it was comforting. The Gray Watcher said humans prefer an illusion of control, and Dugald says it awakens all the other senses. Black Leg said it was entirely possible they were all right and why couldn't we spend an evening eating fire-cooked venison without attempting to solve all the conundrums of the universe among ourselves. He and Mother were about done up, and he had never seen such a quarrelsome bunch in his life. And to shut up and let him eat and get some sleep.

At any rate, I closed my eyes. As I did, I felt my arm come to life and I knew it was glowing because I could see the fire even through my eyelids. But I wasn't afraid and didn't feel any great need to breathe.

When we surfaced, the air was as blustery as it had been soggy in the other place, and after the heat, the breeze was cold on my skin. I opened my eyes and saw we were off a coast, riding the swells. I saw no signs of any human dwelling. The forest came right down to the shore.

The dragon's body gave an odd tremor.

"Are we home?" I asked.

"No," he replied, and there was real fear in his voice. "We are supposed to be home, but we aren't, and I don't know why. See?" he continued. "This is Tintigal."

It was. I could only just barely recognize the shape of its rocky coast. And it, too, like everything else I could see on land, was covered by dense forest.

The sun was riding low on the western horizon and casting a strong light over the ocean, the beach, and the forest beyond. I am a she-wolf, first and foremost. Dugald formed my mind. Kyra and Maeniel taught me the skills needed to survive. But Mother left me her heart.

She lives in mine, and to a wolf is the wisdom of *first things first*.

I was but lightly clad. My dress had been burned away and what remained of my shift stopped at my knees. I was already cold and if I tried to ride the dragon all night, I would likely perish from exposure.

"I will go ashore and make a fire," I told the dragon. "If you can catch me a fish or two, it would be greatly appreciated."

"The danger," the dragon said. "Think of the danger. No one can tell what lurks in that forest."

I nodded. "But I am in greater danger from the cold once the sun sets." And I raised my right arm. "Fire is always with me, whereas you are protected from the cold by the fat under your skin. I am not. And it is imperative that I find shelter before nightfall."

He made no further objection and began swimming toward shore.

We found a sheltered cove where the wind was not so bad. I waded ashore and collected stones and made a fire pit. The driftwood I found went up with a roar and sufficient coals were left to cook the fish the dragon caught.

Then I picked the warmest spot I could, lay down, and slept.

I woke deep in the night. The world was completely dark, the only sound the wind whispering in the forest. The fire was long burned out, but the rocks were still warm. I was thirsty. I had wrapped the fish in seaweed to steam it. I had wanted the salt. My exertions were such that I craved it. But it had awakened thirst in me and the water nearby was all salt.

I waded into the sea. I had to relieve myself and wanted to leave no traces. In the morning, I would scatter the rocks from the fire pit below the tide line and brush out any marks I made on the beach. And then what? I didn't know, but I knew worrying about it right now would probably help nothing.

I waded back to the shore. My thirst grew. All up and down the coast there was darkness. No lights. That's what bothered me, I decided. Near humans there were always lights—torches, hearth fires, lanterns, candles. Even the fishermen brought light with them on the water, setting a torch in the stern of their boats when they fished at night. But here—nothing.

I was not afraid of the dark and had good night vision. But this darkness was overwhelming. I felt like I had when I traveled in the wilderness with Black Leg and Maeniel.

The wind had died down and though the water was cold, it wasn't freezing. I lay down and tried to go to sleep, but my thirst grew, tormenting me.

Finally I rose. It wouldn't help to wait. In the morning, I would be no nearer to fresh water than I was now. I would have to make the same walk along the shore in search of a place where the runoff from a brook or stream reached the sea. I might as well look now. It might even be safer. Maeniel taught me to move about in the darkness, and taught me not to carry light the way most humans do.

Even wild creatures are frightened at the dead of night; but to a creature like a wolf that can see with its ears and nose, the earth under its pall of shadow is as cozy a place as a house with a warm fire and a barred door, besides being a lot more varied and interesting.

I am not as able a night walker as Maeniel, but I can do well enough if I try.

So I set out along the beach. I walked toward the headland that was Tintigal, all the while wondering where I was and how I had been sent to this particular place. I wasn't sure but I thought I had been moved in time.

That fear made my skin crawl. I had heard tales of such enchantments from Dugald and that the druid opponents of Patrick had tried this against him and he had to fight his way back. But then I remembered something else Dugald told me: the universe has its own rules and laws. For example, if you jump from a high place, you fall. And She, the infinite mother, does not take kindly to those who violate those rules. Merlin was the one who probably sent me here and tore the fabric of the cosmos to do so. She, who does not think but is, would be trying to heal the breach, and likely I would be eventually sucked back home in the same way a branch caught on an obstruction in the current of a river is eventually pulled free to tumble along toward the call of the sea.

I knew, looking up at the cliffs visible in the ghostly light of the star blaze. There was no moon but that is when you know the universe shines with its own light—as did the coast of what had been, or would become, Dumnonia. I knew that the sea was now lower. It broke against the cliffs I could see beyond the beach. The dark forest I now skirted was submerged in my day and Tintigal an island, not the peninsula it was now.

I had to wade into deeper water. The current had driven a big pile of driftwood against the beach, just where the swelling of land that was Tintigal began. I had to wade to get around it.

I met the dragon there. He was drifting on the gentle swells of the darkened sea, his head curled over against his back like a bird sleeping. He woke when he heard me splashing about.

"Are you insane, like all the rest of your species?" he asked with some asperity.

"No, I'm very dry. I was looking for some fresh water," I told him.

He sighed deeply. "Fine—wandering about the forest at night. How will I protect you if you encounter some much larger creature that wants to eat you?"

"I am not that easily made a meal of," I told him somberly. "And, besides, if we are to travel tomorrow, I will need to find something to drink."

"I hadn't thought," he said. "Why can't you drink seawater like any normal being?"

"I don't know," I answered. "Why can't you drink fresh?"

"I can," he said, "but I find it rather flat."

"Well, I must find the runoff from a spring or a creek. If I don't, I'll be in trouble tomorrow."

He sighed again deeply and began to sniff the air. I knew the Gray Watcher could smell water, and to a limited extent I could, too. I supposed a dragon might have much the same ability.

"Damn!" he whispered. "There is a spring on that promontory." He indicated Tintigal with his head. "But you can't get to the runoff, it's under that pile of wood."

"Then there is no help for it. I must climb up through the woods."

"You can't," he snapped. "Look at that brush at the edge of the forest."

"Likely," I said, "it's only a screen. It grows thick at the edge, but once under the trees where there is but little sun, the ground will be clear."

So I plunged in and found myself right—under the trees it was very dark but the going was much easier. I had to avoid the clearings. They were thick with bracken, fern, and coiling masses of blackberry vines.

There were no paths. I followed the slope and hoped the spring would be among the rocks I could dimly see above. I did have some guidance, though, because I could smell the moisture now and the odor grew stronger the higher I climbed.

The ground grew more rocky; and the trees became less a thick, smothering darkness. The thin soil wouldn't support the tall pines and ash and oak found below.

I walked among birch, ghostly in the faint starlight, and rowan filled with pale flowers at their many crowns. Coming up from the darkness of the thick woods, I began to feel the wind again. I looked up at the stars, thinking to read them and find out how near dawn it was. And I found myself reeling. They were not my stars.

Oh, there were no big differences. Instead, they were small and rather subtle; but they were there and I was truly frightened by them, for the stars changed slowly. The Gray Watcher told me they did change, but it took many more than one human lifetime to notice the differences. And night after night we lay on the hillside and he and Kyra taught me to know them, and we marked the watches of the night by the rising and setting of the Seven Sisters and the strange, certain beauty of the pole star. Kyra taught me the tales of her people. For they knew each star pattern and had songs for each one. The salmon, the warrior, the maiden, and all the rest. And I learned the ancient wisdom that allowed Kyra's people to sail among the islands on the coast. The kingdoms of ice and snow to the north and the kingdoms of honey, wine, and oil to the south from whence came the Romans.

But as Kyra said, long ago there were no Romans, and her people sailed their hollow ships wherever they wished and traded for what they wanted. Much as the Veneti do now.

There was never a time in my life when I could not look at the heavens by day or night and, taking the seasons into account, not know where and when I was, to the hour—until now.

I was really frightened now. The sheer terror of my predicament struck me, and I felt the stone in the belly that is deep, mortal fear. But I am no fool. And, besides, I was brought up by four beings—one woman, two men, and a wolf—and none of them had any sympathy with a fit of the vapors. I found a flat rock to sit down on and put my head on my knees. And soon I was right again.

I repeated my look at the sky and found the changes were not all that profound. Besides, I had no firm appointments. If I were off a little on the time, it wouldn't matter. *Not long,* I thought, *an hour or so before morning.*

So I moved forward toward the moist odor and saw in the starlight the faint white of the falls, where the spring emptied into a pool among the broken rock. For some reason I felt uneasy and shivered. And I remembered Maeniel's warning: "Have a care when you approach water at night." He knew by experience it was a favorite spot for predators. He had, when hunting alone, often waited there himself.

I was near a hilltop and the trees stopped some distance before I reached the pool. It was a basin of broken rock. I couldn't reach the water from this side because the slope was almost a vertical drop into the pool. Not unless I wanted to take a swim, I couldn't. I saw I would have to circle the pool and go to the other side, where a strip of sandy beach allowed access to the water.

Why didn't I get up and go? Why did I find myself crouching like a mouse among the boulders?

When I tried to rise to my feet, every instinct in me screamed with alarm.

To this day, this very hour, I cannot for the life of me tell what warned me. And it was the life of me the warning saved.

Just then a small herd of deer broke cover. Their antlers were still in velvet, two spike bucks and a four-pointer.

The four-pointer, a little older and more confident, dropped his head to drink first, while his two companions looked around nervously.

I never saw where it came from. It was just there, looming up in the darkness over the four-pointer. Its talons closed on the deer's throat.

The spike bucks took flight, and I do mean flight. You have no idea how far and fast a deer can leap when it's frightened. They went into the air, then into the center of the pool. It must have been shallow, because they bounded, pushing off from the bottom, up and over the rocks where I lay concealed. One cloven hoof caught me near the right shoulder blade. I didn't feel it at the time. I found the hoof-shaped black-and-blue mark on my back the next day. And then they were gone.

All I remember at the time was being horribly afraid the thing might chase them and find me!

But no—the four-pointer seemed enough for it.

I saw the deer die; horrible panic glowed in its eyes for a second as its throat was crushed. But then the thing's jaws tore its throat out and it died.

A second later the thing was gone, vanished into the dense screen of bushes and birch that clothed the other side of the pool.

For a long time I lay there shaking. I felt no thirst, and even the icy morning air didn't seem to touch me. I just lay there, grateful to be alive. Grateful that I hadn't circled the pool and gone to the other side to get a drink before the deer got there.

Then a small miracle happened. Most take no note of it, since it happens every day. It is called dawn. Where moments before darkness reigned, I suddenly found I could see, though the world remained wrapped in gray shadow. Then slowly colors began to emerge among the gloomy shapes hiding in the shadows.

The first is brown tree trunks, branches, the scattered shapes of dead leaves that floor the forest. Then green marks out leaves, foliage clustered on the boughs, the tall stems of cattails standing stately at the pool's edge, water lily pads . . . and she was there.

I saw her by the first light, gray-green and glowing with the faint ground mist. The Flower Bride. At first I thought her only a thick growth of blackberry vines circling an ancient willow growing near the falls. Her skin was the delicate white flower petals of the spring-blooming vine, the long trailing branches of the willow her hair.

The other stood like the glowing quince tree. This one reclined as did the cruel thorny vines. And again I looked into her loving eyes.

"The pool is not defiled," I whispered.

She didn't reply. I'm not sure she could. They are woven into the warp and weft of the universe. Their time is not ours. To them each morning is the first morning. Each spring is the first and again the last the world knows. That is why no man foolish enough to love one ever survives. He is always betrayed, even if he be perchance a god. She will leave him and his heart will break in adoration and longing.

The white flower petals that were her face, neck, and breasts stirred as the first breath of morning breeze moved the fragile stems. Her eyes spoke; they rested on the ground mist coalescing in silvery wisps on a path leading away from the pool—downhill in the growing light.

Two choices. Wiggle away through the forest to my deepwater friend. Flee. Very, very tempting.

Do as the Flower Bride suggested. Challenge my fate. I was doomed to be a scullion, running about the kitchen being badgered by a cook, a lower servant in a great hall, helping prepare feasts I would never taste. Or the second or even more minor wife of a great chief. Bowing humbly to my betters and raising such children as my husband would allow me to bring up, to respect their father.

No, when I refused the curse of the Lord of the Dead and insulted the British queen in her own hall, I had chosen. And I'd best take the path.

My stomach muscles were quivering with fear, my arms and legs numb with cold. *Waiting*, I thought, *will not help matters*. At least the deer never knew what hit it. I hope if that is my fate, the same holds true for me.

Warrior's choice. Go!

I ran for the trail that led downhill in the increasing gray light. Fatigue forgotten, I flew down the path. It seemed I knew by instinct where to put my feet.

The birches at the side of the path gave way to pines, then squat, thick-bunched oaks as it curved downhill. When I came to open pasture silvered by the ground mist, I began to slow. I ventured a glance back over my shoulder and saw nothing was chasing me.

I slowed to a walk.

Ahead I saw a farmhouse. I recognized the style. It was round, the roof a thatched cone reaching almost to the ground.

But I knew no one builds such a house any longer. Its center pole was an oak, a gigantic old specimen. The branches towered over the roof, the thick leaf bundles looking like green clouds.

The thatched roof was alive, also. It was covered with low-growing soft wheat. Soft wheat is a hot, dry-country plant. It doesn't make bread flour but when mixed with water makes dumplings. The wheat was still grass colored and hadn't begun to head up. On the house roof, it was in the sun, away from the damp ground that would ruin it.

The fields were a mixed crop: oats, rye, wheat, and barley. Few farmers plant barley now. But the old people did as the poor even now in the land of the Picts, the Caledonians, do. For barley will thrive probably as well as oats when it is too wet and cold for wheat. A mixed crop will always give you something, even if it is a bad year.

To one side of the house another round building, more lightly built than the big house, did duty for cows, sheep, chickens, and geese. Pigs, then as now, were left to forage in the forest.

It had a hearth in the center, because a faint curl of pale smoke rose from the hole in the roof.

I walked in. There were really no doors; the walls were only a lattice of wattle and daub. A woman and a cow occupied the center of the room, the warmest place close to the hearth. The moment I saw her I knew who she was.

I hunkered down on my heels near the hearth. The cow was in labor and seemed close to her time. The woman was giving her water from a pail.

"Greetings and well met, my lady. I am like the cow, thirsty. Also tired, hungry, and cold."

"To be sure," the woman answered. And then without another word, she went to the cow's udder and drew a large cup of milk.

Milk straight from a cow is not usually the finest beverage. It can have a rather strong odor, but this was good—warm, sweet, and delightful. Also uncommonly thick with cream.

I drank and felt the warmth fill my body, creeping down my arms and legs to fingers and toes. When I emptied the first cup, she obligingly filled another.

Across the room the chickens and geese made soft poultry sounds as they awakened and began to pick among their straw bedding. One hen strutted toward the door.

"No, my child," the woman said. "It is too early. The hawks will be on the hunt."

The chicken turned and went back to the nest.

I emptied the cup a second time and handed it back to her. I felt much better—revived.

"You have not eaten," she said.

"No," and I was about to add, *no, thanks to you,* but I decided I'd best keep a civil tongue in my head. It's not every day one has the privilege of meeting a goddess.

But she answered me, anyway.

"Yes, you had better be on your best behavior. And no, it isn't. Besides, I was a friend to you. I sent the deer. So you are not correct. I did offer you help when you needed it."

"I can't think the buck felt much gratitude for your assistance," I said.

" 'Pert,' the devious British queen was right about that—if nothing else. You are. And I will have you know when the buck stands before me—and he has as much right to do so as you have—I will owe him a favor."

"What was that thing?" I asked.

"He, for it is a he, is the servant of a man—should I call him a man? He isn't human. But in the interest of clarity in dealing with you, I will. 'Man' is the best usage for my purposes. This man wanted, still wants, to possess the sacred spring. It has, as its guardian implies, special powers. He placed that creature there long ago."

"To protect it?" I asked.

"No!" She sounded annoyed. "It needs no protection. The Flower Bride is her own best guardian. He put the vile thing there to drive all visitors away. When the king came to perform the proper rites, he was attacked and driven away."

"The king," I said, "is the destined husband of the Flower Bride." Then, "That's wrong."

"Yes. Why do you think I'm here? He was not only driven away but also his eldest son was killed and his wife injured. A great grief has entered the hearts of my people. They shun this king and his family. They fled, leaving them here alone. They believe the land is under a curse."

I rose. I was warmer now. I went and sat on a milking stool near the hearth.

She made a gesture and the fire blazed. It warmed me.

"I can't believe," I told her, "that I am summoned here for no purpose."

She chuckled. The cow gave a bellow and the calf presented.

I started to rise.

"Don't be foolish," she said. "I am midwife to all living things." A second later the calf shot out into the straw.

The cow knew her duty. She turned and began to lick away the caul.

She wasn't disposed to worry about the afterbirth. It vanished in a puff of steam, leaving the cow to wash her offspring in peace and then nudge it toward an udder.

"You want me to kill it, don't you?" I asked.

She directed a brilliant smile at me. "Yes."

"I will need some steel," I said.

"These people are strangers to iron," she said. "They have bronze. It is, however, excellent. The axes are, at least."

"With an ax," I said, "I would never get close enough."

"Unfortunately, true," she admitted regretfully, as she stroked the cow's rump, its rather bony rump. It was clear the beast was a milk cow. It gazed at her adoringly and I noticed all the effects of calf's birth had vanished and the structures under the tail through which the calf (a she, by the way) had passed were back to their normal size and shape.

"I have," I told her, "not the slightest idea how to accomplish that feat. But if the wonder tales Kyra told me are any indication, I will think of something. I suppose I must enter your service. The tales are explicit about that, also."

"That is correct," she answered.

"A year and a day?" I asked.

"You won't be here that long," was her answer.

I mulled this over while I fixed the breakfast for the family. When we entered the hall, it was obvious the family was still abed. It was, as I have said, like the stable, round.

She opened the doors—there were four of them as is customary in a noble house, one facing in each direction. We stood together enjoying the morning breeze, looking out over the green and gold countryside.

"I'm not presentable," I said.

"You will be," was her answer. She touched my head and my hair arranged itself into a coil at my neck. Then she reached out and plucked a spiderweb from the corner of one of the doors. It became a silken snood and arranged itself over my hair.

She stepped back to contemplate the effect. "You are beautiful," she said darkly. "Just as well you won't be here long. They have another son, not to mention that the chief himself, once free of his first grief, would cast covetous eyes upon you, thinking you would make him a fine second wife."

"The dress," I said. "This thing is a rag." As indeed it was. The sleeve that once covered my right arm hung in shreds and the cloth was stained and dirty from my travels.

"Umm," she said. "Needs work."

I unwrapped the flowers from my waist. They were secure in their cloth packet.

She scented them.

"Ah, that fragrance. They are long gone from the world of living things, but they were, in their time, one of the fairest offerings of creation. Tell me, why did you gather them?"

"I don't know," I answered. "Instinct. They were wonderful, not just the looks, the fragrance. It is human, I think, when we encounter the marvelous to try to bring away some of it with us."

"A bad and good thing about your kind." She nodded.

"I did them no harm," I protested. "There were plenty of flowers."

"Yes, I can see that," she said, then touched the dress.

The torn, smudged, filthy shift vanished. I found myself wearing a soft green dress. It was simply made, two pieces of linen cloth stitched together at the shoulders and sides with holes for the arms and head. But it was fine cloth, it had a nice drape and I looked well in it. It hung to just below my knees and was cinched at the waist with a leather belt ornamented with bronze knots.

"Keep the flowers," she said. "They have many powers, not the least of which is truth."

"Truth," I said. "Truth, is it? Well, the truth is I could better use a strong spear with an iron spade blade and an iron throwing ax. Fancy clothes are well and good, but I need weapons more."

"Yes? Well, I need a powerful six-foot man covered in scale mail with a long bronze sword. Fair maidens are well and good, but this job wants more strength than you have."

"Since you can do all these wonderful things, why can't you kill this monster yourself?" I asked.

She sniffed. "It is warded against me. And flies through my weapons as if they were made of air. I could not help any of the people here when they were first attacked."

"Do they know who you are?" I asked.

"She knows," was the answer, "the wife. I said I was her sister. She has no sister. The rest accepted my story."

With its door open, the hall was cooler now. And I saw it was a proper chief's residence. Round, as I have said, with an oak, a massive tree in the center.

The hearth was near the massive oak tree but far enough away from it so that the tree was not harmed. It was on a stone platform on a stone floor.

But surrounding the center hearth was a wooden floor that extended out to stone walls that supported the conical roof. They were white-washed and, as is customary, covered with wall hangings. These were not the fiery red, bronze, black, and orange designs of the highlands, but were colored pale yellow and green shading away to blue and brown with touches of gray and even black.

"They," she said, "are of the rich farmland in the valleys, filled with trees and meadows covered by moist, dark earth. Their hearts are more quiet than yours are, less filled with strife and trouble. He must wed his Flower Bride or the land will fall to waste and ruin."

"The dragon?" I asked. "He is expecting me."

"I dealt with him. He is swimming now with a pod of gray whales, learning their songs of the ocean. At dawn—when the first light once and as it has forever transforms the water into a mirror of color and brilliance."

I was presented to the family.

The chieftain was a tall, lean, faintly blond man. His shoulder and arm had been badly slashed. His eyes were pools of sorrow. I remembered I had seen the carrion birds circling a high stone platform near the coast. His son had perished.

I bowed. "My lord," I said.

"This is Risderd," she said.

He extended his left hand. "I fear," he said, "I am not fitted to receive guests." He was on his back on the bed platform. His wife lay beside him.

"She, my Aine, is sleeping now. She was in much pain last night. I beg you, let her be for now."

"Certainly," I said very softly. "And I am no guest but have the honor of being your servant, for the present."

"A well-bred girl," he whispered to my lady.

"Indeed," she answered. "I was not mistaken in her."

The second son—he could have been no more than ten—was sleeping in the enclosure next to his parents. He had a terrible bruise on his forehead and one cheek. He was weeping.

"My brother," he said. "We slept together. I woke and reached for the spot where he lay. But he is gone."

I eased out of the portion of the house where they slept and returned to the hearth. Strange to say, I was familiar with the equipment. A quern, trivets, a stone for kneading, and a bronze pot. One difference. Kyra and I baked our bread on a hot rock. They used a clay bowl with a design in the bottom.

A clay jar with a cover held the mixture of wheat and barley. Water from the spring passed the house in the form of a brook. I found a milk jug and a crock of butter in the water, left there to keep cool.

I ground the grain, no little chore that, but the quern was a good one and the work went quickly.

I made a porridge with milk and butter as I do at home, the only difference being there was more wheat in the mixture here, this being good farmland, not like the cold, foggy, rainy climate of the highlands. I put the porridge on the coals to cook and then assayed bread making.

A pair of very small, warm, soft arms wound themselves around my neck. The little arms didn't startle or frighten me. I remembered "the lady" said there was another child. The little girl smelled like warm bread and sleep.

"Did my aunt send for you?" she asked.

"Yes," I said, "I suppose she did in a way." Then I plopped the bread down on the kneading stone, dusted the flour off my hands, turned, and embraced her.

She was a bit clingy. They get like that when frightened.

I put her in my lap and finished kneading the breakfast bread. Then I oiled the inside of a marble bowl I found near the fire, patted out a round of bread, and set it in the bowl, then placed it on the fire.

"That was careless of you," my lady said. I found she had been watching me the whole time. "You should have heated the bowl first."

"I know," I said. "The bread may stick. Kyra wouldn't have let me get away with it. But—" I hesitated for a second, then flipped the bread with my fingertips, a more difficult trick than it sounds like.

"It didn't stick," I said.

The little one was still in my lap as I sat cross-legged by the hearth.

"Hmm," my lady said. "Pert or not, I can see you are a well-brought-up girl."

"I hope so," I answered. "Kyra, Mother, and Dugald certainly did their best. But that's not the point, is it?" I said as I pulled the bread out of the bowl and tossed another piece of dough in.

"No," she answered, spooning some of the porridge I had made into a bowl. "I'm afraid you will need more than good manners and an industrious nature to handle this situation."

I flipped over the baking bread, fine, golden brown on one side. When it was done on the other, I added it to the first on the plate.

She had been crouching beside me. She rose to her feet. "I will serve the family—see if I can get them to eat a bit."

"I'm hungry, too," the child on my lap stated quietly.

"We know, dear," I said.

My lady handed me a small stoneware bowl decorated with white slip and the design of a fish on the bottom in black.

"That's mine!" the child said.

"Yes, we know that, too," I answered.

"Daddy says I have to eat down till I see the fish," she told me. "So don't put so much in that I can't get down that far." This was rather imperious.

"I won't," I promised, and ladled some porridge into the bowl and cooled it with a bit of milk. Then I patted out a smaller bread than the others and tossed it on to bake.

My lady returned. "The chief is recovering nicely. But his wife is feverish and the boy turned his face to the wall when I came in and refused food entirely. But I'm going to bring them some anyway."

"What is her name?" I asked, indicating the child.

The little girl fixed me with a look of deep disapproval. "I know my name, and I can tell it to you myself if you care to ask."

My lady laughed.

"I apologize," I said. "What is your name?"

"Treise," she answered.

"It suits you," I told her. " 'Treise' means strength."

"I know," she answered. "That's why Father gave it to me. He said I was sure about things at an early age."

I kissed her on the top of her head and seated her beside me. Then I gave her the porridge and pulled the cooked bread from the bowl. I blew on it to cool it.

She extended a hand to me. "I can do that," she said. "I won't eat it while it's too hot."

"Very well," I said. But I held it for a few moments because I didn't quite trust her.

But I was wrong. She made sure it was cool before she began to scoop the porridge out of her bowl with it.

The lady filled more bowls with the porridge and took more bread. She served the rest of the family.

When she returned, she took her own breakfast with me. We cleaned the pot I'd cooked the porridge in with bread and butter.

"There should be more people here. Servants, fosterlings, oath men. This is a noble house," I complained. "I can't do all the work here myself."

"What? Harassed already?" she said sarcastically. "Besides, that's not your job. I told you what you have to do. You are not really supposed to be their servant but their savior."

Then she rose and, taking the dishes we'd used, took them to the stream to scour them.

Their savior, I thought, and rolled my eyes. Oh fine. I didn't have the first idea what to do. My mind circled, thinking. Maeniel, Black Leg, Mother, and I had hunted large game. Horse! Yes, the Romans rode them, but often as not we ate the ponies gone wild in waste places. There were large cats, not common any longer but found here and there, that sometimes had to be killed. Lions of a sort, bear, and boar.

Only last year we had to hunt down a bear. The beast was crippled, one forepaw ruined by another hunter. It had been reduced to sheep killing but was still a formidable adversary.

These were not safe, simple, aristocratic hunts where one spent a fine day in the field, then came home to a good supper and a warm bed, but strenuous expeditions, out into the wilderness of the highlands.

Once Black Leg and I tracked a wounded deer for two days because Maeniel, our supreme hunter, drummed it into our heads that we must finish what we start and never leave a wounded animal to perish on its own.

My mind ran to traps, pits, and snares. We had taken a second bear in a pit. His taste had not run to sheep but shepherds. This seemed the best possible solution to me. A pit filled with sharpened stakes.

But that presupposed that I would be able to shadow the creature and learn something of its habits.

Maeniel had done that in the case of the killer bear. But I can't turn wolf, and while I can move almost as silently as he can, if this creature detected me, I would become its next meal. The risk was too great that I wouldn't last long enough to spring the trap.

Bad. I shook my head. Very bad.

"You are worrying," Treise said.

"How do you know?" I asked the child.

"I can see it in your face," she replied. "My father says worrying does no good at all. You should stop."

My lady was still at the stream fussing with the breakfast dishes.

"May I go outside and play?" Treise asked.

"No," I said too quickly, then realized I might alarm the child. I was frightened, but it wouldn't do to communicate my fear to Treise, at least not all of it. She should be warned to be cautious but not so frightened as to be immobilized by terror.

I had once seen a three-cornered argument between Kyra, Maeniel, and Dugald about that. "There is risk in life and she must learn to deal rationally with the fact," Maeniel had said.

Dugald was for terrifying me about certain things. Maeniel had felt there was no virtue in this approach. I'm not sure what Kyra had thought, except that she said, "A fool's paradise is still paradise. I would never have known joy had I been warned how it must end." Then she wept and we gave over arguing and tried to comfort her.

Well, there were risks enough here. But overall, I liked Maeniel's attitude the best. While I live, I will live. In the meantime, there was work to be done.

The hearth must be swept, the cooking utensils put up. She brought back the clean dishes, and they must be placed safely away in a storage niche near the fire. They were bestowed near the big tree that occupied the central space near the hearth.

I must make an offering beside the trunk—oil, bread, and wine. Sweep the wooden floor, feed the stock, air out the bedding, wash any dirty clothes. Then there was the matter of a light meal at dusk and a more heavy one later in the evening. And in addition, no small matter, figure out how to kill that damned thing.

"What will we do?" I asked her.

"I will see to the stock," she said. "And help wash the clothes. There will be milk. Can you churn and make curds?"

"Yes. Thanks to Kyra, I can do all womanly things."

"Good. You sweep the floor and water the garden." She pointed out the door to the south. A large kitchen garden sweltered in the morning sun. A few of the plants were already wilting.

"It was fenced, but what about deer?" I asked. "There is no dog."

She laughed. It was not a pleasant laugh. "There were two dogs a few weeks ago. They both disappeared."

"Oh!" I answered.

"Later today we have a somewhat more dangerous task. We must collect acorns, a sack full for the pigs. The remaining pigs. I might add, there are only two boars left; the sow and her litter disappeared about the same time the dogs did."

"Oh," I repeated, and then was mindful of the child. "Mercy me!"

I felt Treise against my shirt and then she clutched my left hand in a hard grip. My lady thought my subdued expletive very funny and let out a peal of laughter.

I said, "Treise, you stay close to me. I will need your help today. Let's go out and water the garden."

Treise let go of my hand but followed me as closely as a shadow.

The garden was on a gentle, well-drained slope near the house. The stream ran past it, moving downhill toward the sea.

This man was a very good farmer. I like gardens, and Kyra and I had built one using terraces near our home on the coast. We grew leeks, onions, turnips, garlic, rosemary, sage, a variety of greens, and carrots. Here, he had a much warmer climate and deeper, richer soil than we had. And he'd done well with it.

The crops were planted in high rows and I saw why when I reached the fence. He had built a small dam that could be lowered into the water to divert the stream into the garden to water his crop when it was hot and a bit dry, as it was now. On the other side of the stream, he had constructed a fish stew, this being an earthen pond for raising table fish.

It was a pretty but rather treacherous place, ringed with cattails, cress, and yellow wild water lilies. A stand of osier willows grew at one end near the forest. It was dark under the trees.

I gave a shiver and set my mind on my task. I dropped the dam and the water began to flow through a trench into the garden.

I began looking for a gate. The fence was a tangle of berry vines covered with thorns and white flowers. I took Treise's hand and began walking along, looking. I didn't find one and the path began to press close to the dark forest. So I turned and retraced my steps until we reached the trench. I was thinking that I must judge if the garden got enough water from the outside and find the way in later, when Treise's hand tugged mine.

"Look, that's funny. I never saw any like that before," she said, looking up at me. "What made them?" She pointed to some big three-toed footprints in the mud beside the flowing water.

I'll give myself this. I can believe that it would have taken anyone a short time to study those tracks and reach the obvious conclusion. And I was still puzzling when I caught the movement from the corner of my eye and I saw the big reptilian head dropping down not at me, at the much more tender morsel at my side—Treise.

My hand tightened on Treise's and I flung her under the thick, thorny berry canes that twined in the fence.

"Crawl under the thorns!" I screamed.

Then the thing's teeth closed on my right shoulder and one wiry, clawed hand seized my body at the waist.

Death! I thought. *But I'm going to hurt it before I go.*

I am not very big. I could see the eye, in the sunlight, nacreous yellow as molten gold, pupil slit like an adder's. The jaws engulfed my whole shoulder and right breast. I fancied I felt the long, sharp, triangular yellow teeth grate on bone.

They did grate on something, but it was not bone.

I was dead. I knew even if the thing didn't eat me, damage done by those jaws would kill me.

Hurt it! The command drummed in my brain. *Make it pay!*

My right arm moved in the creature's jaws and I felt the thing's leathery neck. My vision darkened as I threw everything I had into my fire hand.

The world vanished. How does a bolt of lightning feel when it flashes through the clouds into the earth? I know, because that is what I was for a moment, a channel for raw, ravening, blazing power!

Even from whatever hiding place my soul had flown I heard it scream.

I hit the ground hard, realizing that, like a predator that takes a noxious insect into its mouth and realizes too late that it isn't edible, it had spat me out and fled, crashing through the fish pond into the forest.

I sat up. I wanted to be sure I still could. Then I saw that the green armor that protected my right hand from the thorns now extended over my whole body. A princely patrimony. If my father left me nothing else, this would suffice as a mark of his acknowledgment.

I was almost afraid to look at my right shoulder and hand. They were not unmarked. My shoulder and breast were deeply bruised, the red already turning an angry purple.

As I watched, the green vines faded from my skin and it returned to its natural, rather pale color.

When I looked up, she was standing there holding Treise and gazing at me in some astonishment.

"In all the years I have tracked that beast and tried to destroy it, I have never seen a champion do it so much damage."

"It is alive and thus can be killed," I said. "And I think I can find a way to do that. But I will need your help."

She helped me to my feet, and I walked to the house. When I entered the door, Treise cried out and held her arms toward me.

I took her and kissed her.

"Make the sacrifices," my lady told me.

"Come, Treise," I said to the child. "We must give thanks." I carried her to the tree that rose just beyond the hearth.

An ancient oak, its roots clutched the ground like claws or thick, knotted fingers. At the center of the house, it enjoyed a space of its own, paved hearth cobbles that looked as if they had been collected from the beach. Above the roots the gigantic trunk rose, as wide at the center as a tall man's body from head to foot. Between two of the roots, the cobbles formed an offering basin.

The lady brought honey, oil, and mead.

I knelt and seated Treise on one of the roots. I raised my arms in the position of invocation. My body was still shaking. The dress she had given me was torn away at the right shoulder and terrible bruises covered my right shoulder and breast. The teeth of the beast hadn't penetrated, but they had scratched the skin in a number of places and blood ran down from my shoulder and breast and trickled over my stomach and groin. In places it dripped on the stones.

"I live," I said, "and for that I am thankful."

Outside the wind sobbed in the trees, and it was as if I were being answered.

"Now, I must kill it," I continued, "but I will not call down your blessings on death. Yet you know as well as I that it is sometimes necessary."

Then I made the offering of mead, honey, and oil at the roots. They are a token, no more than a token, of what we owe, to what the tree represents.

Treise was quiet. She sat still, looking at me with wide, dark eyes.

When I was finished, I picked her up, rose, and faced the woman.

She nodded her approval. As a virgin child I belonged to her, and, in a way, she to me.

"Is there a workshop?" I asked.

"Certainly," she answered. "Every farm has one. But, remember, you have not much time."

"How so?" I asked. "And how much?"

"How so?" she mused. "Have you ever seen a sapling bent to make a snare?"

"Yes," I answered, much mystified.

"Well, that's something like what I did to the world in order to bring you here. Although the forces involved are much greater, they strain against my grip. Sooner or later they will pull free and, like the bent sapling, spring back and carry you home. How long—a few days at most."

"Then we must hurry," I said. "Where is the workshop?"

Treise led me to it.

There must be such a place on all farms. Tools must be repaired, harnesses mended, soap made, osiers dried and cut to useful lengths, logs formed into timber and beams, wood cured for fence posts, hides tanned, nets woven, and fishhooks hammered out—the million and one tasks that arise on a working farm.

The king was a neat man. His tools hung over one bench clean and shining, each one in its place. Along another wall were piled things left over from the butchering and brush cutting that routinely goes on every day on a farm—wood, hides, horns, sinew, bones, jars of rendered fat; odds and ends of wood too good to burn, too small to be made into furniture.

This was just what I wanted.

I described to her the thing I wanted to make.

"Never," she answered, "have I seen such a weapon."

"I think there may be none in the world yet. Or if there are, only a few and very far away."

She nodded. "That's why I sent for you. I needed fresh ideas."

We got to work.

There was a lathe. I began to make the first and most important part from an ash butt I found with the other scrap. She began shaping the sinew and horn. Treise sat on the floor and made mud bread.

The ash was hard wood and like stone. I kept having to sharpen the bronze knife. But at length, I got it into the shape I wanted.

She had managed the sinew and horn. I hunched down next to Treise and stacked the parts laid out on the floor, trying to remember exactly how Maeniel put them together.

"I need glue," I said. "Now I need glue."

"How is glue made?" Treise asked.

"From the horns, hides, and hooves of animals," I answered. "Especially the hooves."

Risderd had quite a large pile of them.

"We will need a pot," I said.

The lady looked at me in exasperation. I was grimy and perspiring. So was she.

"Now glue," she said.

"It's the only way I know how to make it."

"Then glue it is," she answered. "But come. We must tend the family."

Risderd was up walking around. When she saw him near the fire, she repaired my dress and hair.

"I came to find you, Eline," he said to her. "My wife is very bad and she has a high fever."

We both went to her sleeping platform immediately. She was tossing and turning, the bandages on her arm and side loose and bloody.

"Be still, now," my lady said, and rested her hand on the woman's forehead.

The chief's wife reached up and took the hand. "You are kind," she said, "and when you touch me, the fever leaves my body."

"But"—the woman looked up in wonder at her face—"I have no sister."

"Yes, yes, you do," she assured her. "But at this time, when the moment of her incarnation came, she did not live long enough to draw breath. But she loves you and has been long your sister and will be again, in due time. She asked me to help you. And it is time. I am engaged in duel with the dark being, Bade. This is his creature."

"Why does it harry us so?"

"Hush, my sister. Do not trouble your soul." Then she kissed Aine on the forehead and turned to me.

"Fetch me some soup and fresh water."

Soup was easy. I had put some on to be ready for supper. Fresh water, I had some trepidation as to that.

I went to the hearth and ladled some of the soup into a bowl. I gave it to Treise, telling her to bring it to her mother, then picked up a wooden bucket.

Risderd was sitting at the low table where the family took its meals.

"I would not go out there, were I you," he told me. "Something, I cannot say what, is living in the reeds near the pond. It likes fish."

"We will see," I said, and strode out into the yard.

I went to the stream, but not to where it flowed past the garden. I dipped the bucket into the water just above the duck pond, then returned to the house. I felt its eyes on me and a cold, guarded intelligence behind them. And indeed the chief was right: the reeds did move as though something watched me from among them.

But perhaps the fish were easier prey. I had hurt him.

I brought water to her, and she washed Aine's face with it.

She and I prepared a meal for the men. Finn, the elder boy, came out. I noticed the chief blocked the door that looked west to the mountains, where the carrion birds were flying, and I remembered the other son.

"What was his name?" I asked her.

"Ardal. 'Mighty in Valor.' And his courage suited his name. For had he not sacrificed himself, none of them would have survived."

When we served the chief and his son, he rose and bowed to us.

"My lady," he addressed her, "and also you the helper." He bowed to me. "I ask that you join us at our supper, in token of gratitude for your assistance to me and my wife."

She sent Treise away to be with her mother, telling the child to call us if Aine needed anything.

We sat on linen cushions that surrounded the low table.

I had made curd cheese, soup, and bread, and we drank—as was proper at the table of a distinguished man—mead.

Mead, yes—well, mead—there are many kinds. This was the mead of autumn, laced with the flavors of crab apple, cherry, and quince and even some wheat and barley, though there was enough honey to be sure it was not beer. It was a rich, heady brew, more fitted for a festival than a funeral.

The chief complimented our womanly skills. He thanked me for watering the kitchen garden, but did not comment on what happened while I was doing so. He must have known my whole right side was covered with bruises. We spoke of the chase. There was in fact a hare in the stew pot. Small game and large to be found hereabout, and how to hunt or trap it. The livestock, he expressed pleasure at, the cow's new she-calf, a valuable addition to his herd.

I had begun to think his troubles had turned his brain. He no longer quite grasped the situation into which he and his family had been plunged.

Yet there was one thing Dugald, the Gray Watcher, and Kyra always agreed on and that was courtesy. One owed it to oneself and others.

He played the genial host—we in turn were the pleased guests. And between us, we kept the conversation both light and amusing until the end of the meal.

When the chief presented us with an assortment of nuts fried with salt, Finn rose to his feet, trembling, strode to the western door, and threw it open and gazed out toward the mountains.

"I propose," he told his father in a voice that rang out across the room, "I propose to go up there and join him."

I felt the hairs prickle at the nape of my neck. You see, I knew what he meant. It doesn't happen often. Dugald had told me it was never very common a custom, more frequent in ancient times. Sometimes a person close to the dead man or woman would not let them journey forth alone but went to the place of passage and joined him. The method I cannot say—usually it was left to the voyager to choose.

I can't think it mattered, being all one to the crows, the eagles, and flies. The rite is always voluntary, Dugald said. Even in the very oldest accounts he has never heard tell of any coercion being applied.

"No!" the chief said in equally ringing tones. "You know what I must do. And you will obey me in this if you are my true son, because you are all they will have left."

The hall was flooded by the light of the westering sun. It brought its beauty to light and its strength. The black trunk of its guardian oak, the jeweled colors of the banners and wall hangings, the polished floors and the sparse intricately carved furniture that captures the eternal oneness of life's web.

Finn walked back toward the table and stood behind us, facing his father, fists clenched. "That thing will kill you."

Risderd smiled, looking every inch the chieftain he was. "That well may be. In fact, it almost certainly will be, but honor demands I take the mead of springtime and greet my bride. I will have my honor. If death is but a sleep, one wakes from a sleep. If not, why, then the sleeper is forever at peace. Either way, it doesn't matter.

"As you are my true son, you will obey me in this. As I am your king, you will obey me in this."

And then he added more softly, "As you love me, you will obey me in this."

Finn was silent and hung his head. Risderd's face was a study in power and beauty in the golden light. "When it is done," he told his son, "you will lead your mother and sister to whatever place my people now live. And you may carry yourself with pride, being the last of such a line. Your mother and sister will marry well. Now go and rest, because tomorrow we will gather what possessions we might, and the day after, I will begin my journey. If I do not return, you will know what to do."

Expressions chased one another across Finn's face. He looked as though he wanted to say a lot of things, but Risderd had caught him in front of, as he saw it, two female guests. The boy was too shy to speak his mind or grieve terribly for—again as we saw it—his father's pointless death.

She rose; I followed quickly. It doesn't do to be disrespectful of them.

"My lord, will you require another meal tonight?" she asked.

"I don't think so," he said. I could tell he was stiff and favored his injured side. "I believe I would like to sleep and save my strength for the morning. I will have much to do . . . then."

The sun was pouring through the western doorway now, the light so bright I could not look into it, as it poured from the sky over the crag where his eldest son lay.

"They have almost stopped flying," he said in a carefully neutral tone.

I knew the boy's bones must be a red cleaned scatter in the grass.

"We will put him under the hearth," Finn said.

"No," Risderd answered. *"You"*—he emphasized the word—"you and I know he didn't plan to be there. You will mix them with honey, mead, oil, and the remaining spices—sandalwood and myrrh—pound them to dust and burn them. Then send the ash into the wind from the shore. I would not have him come here past the broken roof and fallen walls and search for us in vain."

The light streaming through the house began to fail as the sun slowly moved behind a mountain in the distance.

"If you will, my lady, bar the doors against the darkness."

"I will, my lord." She curtsied.

I curtsied also, and Risderd departed with his hand on his son's shoulder.

"Oh, God," I said.

"Yes," she answered.

"I have an idea," I said.

"Good. It's about time. I have none. Let's get the doors and go back to the workshop before this fool kills himself. He's working on doing it faster than I can save him."

"I've heard of that spring mead. A good long drink of that stuff and that horror won't have to eat him," I said. "Besides, I've been wondering all day why the thing isn't in the house with us."

"It can't come within the shadow of the tree. The tree is a sacred thing and can't be defiled, even by Bademagus."

"It's night," I said. "The tree isn't casting any shadows."

"Doesn't matter," she answered. "Everything the tree shadows at one time or another during the day is safe."

"Good," I said. "I'd hate to rely on the doors. They don't seem that strong."

"It can't get us in the workshop either," she told me. "Come on."

I did. We made glue. Glue is disgusting stuff. It stinks, gets in your hair, under your nails, on your skin, on your clothes. She was a help cleaning up, though. She could make unpleasant things disappear by waving her hand. She did that when she got a big, nasty spot on her dress.

"You're a goddess," I said. "Why can't you just kill it?"

"A goddess," she repeated, interested, while I braided sinew and then braided the braids with rawhide. "That's what those Greeks called me. I lived in a cave on the rock where they founded their city. A goddess—no name—just a goddess. A-thena. The A is feminine."

"I know," I said. "Dugald tried to teach me Greek. Did you really turn that dumb girl into a spider?"

"No, not guilty," she said. "I won't say I haven't done a lot of unpleasant things. No good reason to be a goddess if you can't make life unpleasant and even short for some shitasses. Like Bademagus, for instance, trying to steal one of my sacred wells."

She ground her teeth. "He won't come within arm's reach of me. And I don't blame him. I'd melt him down into a little puddle of piss. If I ever get the chance, of course."

"You're pretty far from home," I said.

"Distance is as distance does. What would you know?"

She had me there.

"The girl said she was a better weaver than you are."

She chuckled. "Not difficult. Any human is. Look at you."

"Lend me a finger," I asked. "I've got to tie this bow together. Mae-niel taught me," I said.

"Yes, but you are clever enough to build the thing without any experience when you need to."

"Let's hope," I answered.

"Yes."

She put her finger on the string. I tied.

"That's half. Let me do the other."

"The only thing I did for those Greeks was keep the peace. I didn't fool with turning anyone into anything. Do you know what a goddess is good for?"

"No," I answered, braiding away.

"There is always something that needs to be done so that events may take their proper course. A rock balanced at the top of a ridge might fall to the right or the left unless . . . what?"

My skin grew cold.

"Unless you give it a push," I said even while I was thinking this one might push mountains.

"Poor child." She patted my cheek. "I'm not comfortable company, am I? Well, the simplest way of putting it is that I gave those talented, exasperating Greeks a push. I created a truce at my shrine, because those fools reminded me a little of your people—when they weren't talking, they were fighting. They needed to give their bellicose dispositions a rest, so they could concentrate on other matters. And my plan worked. Otherwise, I feasted on my sacrifices, enjoyed my new dresses—the women made me a new one every year—and in general enjoyed their company. They were very stimulating individuals, and when nothing much was happening, I gazed out over the very beautiful Aegean Sea.

"They asked me to tell them the future. I am no better than average at that. Unfortunately, sometimes it's not difficult. I remember one sweet thing, she had a husband and not one but three lovers."

I began laughing.

"As you can see," she told me, "some things ought to be obvious."

"Then explain to me why Risderd has to die if I can't kill the monster."

She walked away from me, out of the circle of lamplight.

"Because he is a *king, chief, husband*—words are limiting."

"Try to transcend them," I said.

She laughed.

I set the bow down on the floor and crouched, arms around my knees, wiggling my toes on the dusty floor.

"Where to begin?" She half turned toward me, her face in profile. "With an explanation for kings?" she asked. "No, too long and complex," she answered her own question. "I'll keep it simple. He must wed the Flower Bride. That was what he was trying to do when Bade sent the monster to destroy him. His people, the Atrovinties, are great warriors, but they fled like thistledown before a wind when Risderd could not complete his task. Only he remains, with his family.

"His wedding the Flower Bride seals his people's title to their holdings here. Their land, in other words. His failure means they cannot ask sustenance of this earth."

She stamped her foot and pointed down. "This earth here. The embraces of the Flower Bride confer title to them. She is sovereignty. For him to fail her maims him. Makes him like the Fisher King, one who cannot draw sustenance from the earth at all. And if he can't, his people can't either.

"He feels it is better for him to die. That way, they can choose another chief—perhaps one who can face down the monster. So he will drink the spring mead, go to her dwelling. . . ."

"That horror will tear him limb from limb," I filled in the sentence.

"Yes," she answered.

"What will happen then?"

"Umm," she considered carefully. "When he is dead, his people will flee, leaving Bade in sole possession. They will try to begin life somewhere else."

I looked down at the bow. It was fully tied, the center post connected to the elastic horn and sinew, and the laths at each end were also tied on and fastened with glue. In the normal course of manufacture, the ties that held it together would be cut off once the glue was set, but I had constructed them to be left on. It took a week or more for the glue to fully harden, and I was pretty sure after the day's events that I wouldn't have that much time.

"A very powerful instrument, that," she said, pointing to it.

"Yes," I answered. "It will drive in an arrow with tremendous force. Especially if you use it close up, like I'm going to. I need arrows."

I had spent some time considering the matter and decided to favor quality over quantity. I needed to put those arrows in deep. This was no deer that would run away. I suspected that I could pepper this thing with enough shafts to make it look like a pincushion and it would be still attacking and still dangerous—no, lethal.

We began making arrows, and we didn't talk much, because both of us were busy. I carved the heads from bone in the way Maeniel had taught me was the best for spear points if we can't forge metal. And I couldn't—not where I was now.

Bone or stone is worked into wide but very thin triangles, then sharpened at the tip and sides. They resemble leaves, only the edges are razor sharp. You don't bother with a barb, because they penetrate deeply, and shock and swelling keep them from being easily removed.

My lady worked, too. Bronze is the very devil to keep sharp, so she sharpened while I carved.

When we were done, it was close to dawn, and I had only four arrows. But I reasoned that might be enough. I didn't bother to notch the shafts, because they weren't going to travel far and I didn't want them to spin.

"You had best get some sleep," she said, turning away from the grindstone.

I looked down at my fingers, blistered and bloody from my task, and set the arrows on the workbench.

She handed me a mantle. I wrapped myself in it and prepared to lie down right there.

Something floated to the top of my memory. "They say it takes a hero to rescue the Fisher King."

I looked up and her eyes glowed strangely, a little the way the dragon's did in the sunlight, an opalescent fire in the last light of the guttering lamp.

"Why do you think Dis Pater sent the boar for you?" she asked.

I didn't answer.

I don't remember lying down. Only that her eyes were pools of light and darkness both—a sea of nightmares and dreams. I fell into them and went down.

CHAPTER TEN

HE WOKE, KNOWING HE WAS BEING WATCHED, the fear like a stone in his gut, closing his throat. He was lying under a bush, a holly bush, the sharpened points of its leaves pricking through the homespun shirt he wore. He was lying on his stomach. He moved and the prickly leaves wounded him again.

When he woke, he wiggled forward on his stomach until he was clear of the bush, then rose to his knees. He pushed up with his left hand instinctively. And when he looked at his right, he saw why. It was swollen and had two oozing marks surrounded by angry red tissue on the back where the fangs went in.

Experimentally, he moved his fingers—it hurt. And he knew he wouldn't have much use of it for some time.

He had been bitten by a snake.

Had he been bitten by a snake? He didn't know, his mind wasn't clear. He was having a lot of trouble thinking. Thinking and seeing both. When he tried to look around, the light pained his eyes. But he did see enough to know he was in a forest.

He was kneeling next to the holly bush that was growing out of a pile of fallen limbs near the trunk of a giant oak, resting on its side, broken by lightning.

Just beyond the tangle of dead wood that had been the tree's crown was a pool. He could see the glint of the sky's reflection in the water from where he knelt.

He staggered to his feet, not out of any confidence that he could walk but because he couldn't crawl. He was certain his damaged right hand wouldn't support him. He wanted water badly. His tongue felt like a file in his mouth.

He was right. On his feet he was so dizzy he could barely stand. But his thirst was so great that he managed to stagger to the pool, fall to his knees, then lie down and drink.

It looked up at him from the bottom of the pool.

He jerked back so quickly that inadvertently he used his right hand to push himself, and a blast of raw agony lanced up his arm to his shoulder, followed by a terrible wave of nausea.

He lay down again, rolled over on his back, and closed his eyes.

She was there.

He could see her face as clearly as if she stood before him. Young, the woman's features still a bit blurred by the child's. Almost, not quite, ready for love. Rose-petal skin, spun gold hair, lips like autumn rose hips, and eyes warm and blue as a summer sky.

Somewhere in his mind he laughed at himself. All the poetic banalities, and yet all love.

Women, he remembered someone in the warrior society saying. *Oh, yes, there are always women. Women for pleasure, women for breeding—very important that. Women for work, all the ceaseless cooking, washing, and cleaning. All the worrisome, monotonous tasks women are so good at. Women. Don't worry about women.*

Her eyes looked into his. Oh, yes, they were the summer sky, an arch of cloud-filled crystalline light over a green, warm world. The smell of horses, saddle leather, dogs for the chase. Woodsmoke rising from cooking fires, venison, wild boar on the spit; salmon leaping in the streams or smoking over an ash fire. All good things. Comrades, friends, food, drink, and even deadly quarrels. The glitter of edged steel in knives, swords, spears glowing, drinking in the light as it sang in their blades. All . . . all in those warm, sky-blue eyes.

For a moment, fear, anxiety, and dread vanished and he was at peace. Then he remembered what he had seen in the water, and the fear returned with a rush.

His eyes opened; he looked over and down into the pool.

He wondered if the water could be poisonous, because there was more than one—at least a dozen skulls looked up at him from the bottom with the empty stare of the dead.

He remembered a bleak joke someone had told him once: they cannot choose but stare because they cannot close their eyes.

A small bird, very like a finch clad in gray and black, landed on a lily pad and drank. Then, with a flick of its wings, flew away.

The water was very clear and that was how he knew they were there in the first place. He could see to the bottom.

They were all scattered among the stones, looking up at him. At least a dozen skulls. Odd that they should all look up at him. None were on their side or facedown. He was sure he could tell them from the rocks that covered the bottom if they were mispositioned. But none were. Each one gazed up through the clear water at the sky or at his face. He drank again.

No, the long-ago deaths hadn't polluted the water. He felt better, much better. Then he thought the water might help his hand, so he slowly eased it below the surface.

Yes, it did, cooling the angry heat in the tissues and soothing away the throbbing that accompanied every moment.

He sighed, a forlorn breath of relief, but then he noticed the forest had gone quiet around him.

No, no, that wasn't good. He was an alert woodsman, having been brought up in a world where the ancient forests were still a viable presence and large, almost endless tracts were as yet untouched by the human banes of an ax and fire. Where hunting was an avowed necessity, serving as an important source of meat harvested to keep his scattered people fed.

He knew the forest.

Birdsong ceased, and in a tree nearby a flock flew up as though frightened by some distant sound. He did the human thing. He stood.

He was in a brushy, open woodland with rather thin, stony soil. He could see nothing except perhaps a waver in the air of the sort that appears above hot fire.

It was coming. And he was shaking inside.

A small deer flashed past him, leaping the oblong end of the forest pool. And in the distance, he could hear the tearing of brush and trees as it moved through the undergrowth, steadily ever toward him.

He went to one knee and drank quickly, sucking the water from his cupped hands. The wind changed briefly, bringing the thick, heavy odor of decay to his nostrils. An owl, awakened from its midday sleep, glided past him on silent wings, and he knew whatever path it chose to take, everything fled before it.

But he was the special one. The person it was bent on catching.

He had been here before. Through this particular awakening before. But his mind was fogged with illness or drugs.

He couldn't remember.

Something like wind but not wind began to twist and fling the branches of a stand of aspen saplings across the pool, and he knew *it* was here. The stench was a thick, almost gaseous, cloud over the water and so strong in his nostrils it gagged him.

A dilatory hare burst from a copse nearby and tried to run around the pool. In its flight, it ran directly in front of the horror.

Something of the creature's terrible substance must have touched it, because the hare exploded into a red ruin. Blood and bits of flesh flung into the air, spattered his face.

Without wasting any more time, he turned and fled at a dead run through the trees. The thing couldn't move very fast. He had ascertained that . . . yesterday?

He dimly perceived that he had expended much too much energy trying to get away from it. So when he was well clear of the pool and on a game trail leading away from the water, he dropped his pace to a walk and began to think again.

He tried to remember, but looking into his memory was like peering down a long, dimly lit corridor drenched in fog. Some things from yesterday were clear—his own nightmare terror, for instance. But others were only shadows, images that faded in and out like a sea bottom seen from a cliff.

She wouldn't like this, he thought. She? Who? What she? All he could remember was that she would tell him to use his brain—think, not simply flee mindlessly from the ghastly darkness that hunted him.

He looked down at himself as he walked along. His shirt was nothing unusual. Most men wore something like this for everyday wear, a linen shirt that was almost a tunic. It hung to just above his knees. Trousers reinforced at knees and rear with deer hide, the trousers reached to just below his knees. His lower legs were wrapped in wool held in place by deer-hide crossed garters.

He wore good boots, several thicknesses of leather tanned to softness and held in place by the same cross gartering that tied his leggings.

The thing was slow, yes. And as long as he maintained a fast walk, he could keep well ahead of it.

He licked his lips and found blood on them and was alarmed for a second. Then he remembered the unfortunate hare.

What to do now?

The answer came back as if she had spoken it. First, stay alive. He laughed a bit and was surprised by the sound of his own voice.

He looked around, but in this mixed woodland he couldn't see much. Climb a tree.

A wave of fear swept over him. No. It might catch him aloft. He didn't know if it could climb, and "didn't know" wasn't a good enough guarantee that it couldn't. He must avoid being cornered at all costs.

Aside from that, he couldn't think of anything productive to do but what he was already doing—following the game trail.

She'd taught him to do another thing, a difficult thing. But she'd begun young. How young was another thing his buzzing head wouldn't tell him. But she had taught him to push his fears into the back of his mind while he did what was necessary at the moment. So he did.

The trail wound on through a thick copse of birches, through an almost evilly dark growth of scrub pine, down into a dry creek bed, where it continued along the bottom for perhaps a half mile. Then it emptied into what must have been a small lake in springtime and was now a bog. Large clumps of tall reeds and cattails replaced the trees. He couldn't see any more of his surroundings than he had in the forest.

But again he was used to wet ground. And the trail went on.

Cress grew in the shallows, and he saw that was because the water in the black lake, as his people called bogs, was running sluggishly downhill. He plucked a bunch of the cress, washed it off in a shallow pool, and ate it as he walked, threading his way around deeper pools. He could tell where these were, because clumps of yellow iris and water lily pads grew in them. Above the water, dragonflies hovered, their transparent wings glinting in the sunlight.

A beautiful place, this black lake. He would have liked to linger here if he hadn't so feared the terror behind him. He would have fished in the deep pools and caught frogs in the shallows.

His boot kicked something, and he saw it was the trunk of a downed tree. It occupied a ridge of high ground between two deeper pools.

He kicked at it again and opened a nest of grubs tunneling in the rotten tree. He didn't give it a second thought. He paired them with the cress and ate both.

Why not? he asked in his mind. *Bears do and am I not a bear?*

Then he shook his head. *How am I a bear?* But both cress and grubs were food, and he was quite literally starving.

He picked the rotten log clean. But by then he heard the cries of birds fleeing the creature that pursued him.

And he found he must hurry.

A little farther on, he came to a nest of duck eggs, the mother having fled ahead, frightened by what hunted him. They were fresh, and he consumed them greedily.

The bog began to become a rain forest. Wet, dank, but cool and thickly overgrown with moss and so many kinds of ferns he couldn't put names to them. It was an achingly green place that glowed in the distant sun like a scattering of emeralds dusted with diamond dew.

Behind him, he heard the wild, sawing cry of an alarmed waterbird, and its shadow covered him briefly as it flew. He had taken time with that log, and now he knew he must run again.

He did, and so the day went. He found his way to a higher pine forest, and since this was a patch of climax forest, he was able to make better time. But the ground was rising and he found that on the steeper grades the effort drained him.

By late afternoon, he was nearly to the point of falling but knew he must press on. Soaking his hand had eased the pain for him, but the day's walking and his sometimes inadvertent use of his fingers, and sometimes the whole hand, brought back the swelling and much of the pain.

He tried to ignore it, then told himself he was a fool. If he lost the use of it, he might be in dire straits indeed. So he improvised a sling from a piece of vine and found his discomfort much relieved.

Then he ran into the skulls again.

The last one was set on a post made from the trunk of a young birch. The assaulted tree, its top cut off, had begun to grow again, and the skull stared out at him from a nest of branches. Some had come out through the jaws and the eye holes.

The thing was toothless, and the man who must have been its living embodiment looked to have been very old. The rising bark from the broken tree was growing up to cover it.

He found himself saluting it.

I am but young, he thought, *and will never have the privilege of your years.*

To his surprise, he found himself answered, as a sigh like the breath of a powerful wind went through the trees. But there was no wind. The air was still and the sun was hot on his back.

He thought of the girl again, those warm eyes.

How sad, he thought. *I may never see her again.*

He was sure she was not the one who had taught him the craft of survival.

He went forward then, and saw his cage.

The forest ended at a cliff with at least a half-mile drop to the valley below.

He climbed quickly to the top of a cluster of boulders near the spot where the skull was being engulfed by the birch tree and saw nothing that reassured him that he might eventually escape. He was on the edge of a plateau that backed up to a sheer cliff so high its top was lost in the shadows of misty blue cloud.

The plateau formed a shelf. It held water, a bog, and the small forest, because there was a depression in the middle. But then it rose at the edges and tall cliffs fell away into a fair green valley below.

Beyond the valley the red ball of the sun was going down over another mountain range. The peaks were tall, higher than any he had ever seen in his life. Their tops were white and clad in thick fog.

From where he stood, he could look back at the thing pursuing him.

As the sun sank lower, it ceased shining directly into the trees on the plateau. It flared on the treetops and the mountain behind them.

The shadow of horror began to waver, then lift. The thing seemed to lose energy as the light failed.

And he heard a sort of screaming rise from it, as though it protested the encroaching night. A screaming like the sound of so many voices. Not one single word could be understood, but rather a cacophony of rage rising toward the pale moon that had begun to show at the horizon.

His memory told him the hunter was impotent at night and must return to whatever place it had come from until the sun rose. But he remained, his eyes searching the distant valley below for some sign of human presence.

In the twilight, he thought he saw a faint light in the distance and a wisp of smoke. It just increased the loneliness that was an abysmal ache of sorrow in his heart.

On his way back, he took the path the thing had worn through the forest while pursuing him. Occasionally he passed the carcass of some bird or animal that hadn't been swift enough to get out of the thing's way. None were salvageable as food, until he came to a fawn. The thing was practically dismembered, the head was missing, but the body was intact.

He made a knife quickly, using a cobble to flake a bit of granite. The flakes offered sharp edges, and he was able to butcher the carcass.

He consumed such organ meats as he could find in the viscera, some of the heart and liver, then ate the raw muscle meat of the young animal. Raw meat is tender, and he was crouched single-mindedly over his meal when he heard the sound of distant laughter.

He looked up abruptly.

"Can he hear us?" The whisper was female and full of delight.

"Look at his face, my dear. Of course, he can," another voice chimed in.

"How very cruel—he knows he's being watched."

"That's because I want him to know." This voice was masculine.

A volley of feminine giggles followed. But then, like a curtain dropping, the voices and the sense of presence disappeared.

And he knew that he was being tortured, subtly, cleverly but brutally and skillfully. Tortured—and someone was very amused by the process.

A victim has to shoulder the burden of another's hate, and it lay heavy on his mind as he finished eating his fill and then collected the long strips of meat he'd managed to cut from the carcass. He would hang them in the holly bush to dry. He wished for a little salt. They would cure better with salt. But salt or not, cure they would, if the sun shone, so he hurried on with his plunder. He was too tired to think through the ramifications of what he'd been allowed to know.

He sank down into the pile of dead leaves under the holly bush. But before he slept, he remembered the girl with the sky in her eyes. And her image followed him into darkness.

He didn't know who he was, and except in the most general terms, didn't know where he was. The next three days were perhaps the most hellish of his life.

He woke knowing the thing would be after him again. The only respite he received from it came in the gray hours of morning, before sunrise, and during the cool blue dusk when the sun went behind the distant mountains. Whenever the sun was high in the sky, he must run. And he did.

It materialized in the open forest as the long rays poured down past the treetops by the new light of morning.

It made noises, sometimes a muttering as of many voices speaking in tones too low to discern words.

At other times, when it was frustrated, it screamed, also in many voices. The things that most often frustrated it were the skulls, and Arthur understood they warded it. It could not sink into the pool or the bog because they looked up at it through the dark water. It could not pass the edges of the cliffs that bounded the edges of the plateau because the skulls were distributed all along the precipice.

He knew, because for the next week, he crisscrossed the plateau and explored every inch of the forest cover on top in search of a way down. But he found there was none.

He even thought of destroying one of the skulls on the edge and hoping it would leave. But he was reasonably sure he saw plowed fields and sometimes smoke rising in the distance. So for the time being, he shouldered the responsibility of being the evil thing's keeper.

It didn't move very fast, so any alert animal could avoid it. But this didn't hold true for infant creatures—fledgling birds, baby rabbits, fox kits, fawns, or even wildcat kittens. It destroyed those and anything else it touched, even trees, although in most instances it seemed to find its way around them. This didn't prevent it from ripping off limbs or, more commonly, denuding them of leaves, fruit, or flowers.

He improvised a sling from the fawn skin and tried rocks against the writhing ball of movement he saw at its core. It looked very much like the air over a fire, troubled by the rising heat, and he sensed it must be the heart of the terror.

The first rocks simply bounced away, or were bounced away.

But then he stood his ground and took better aim.

The thing gave a wild series of hideous shrieks, and the rock exploded, as the rabbit he'd seen killed by it, sending sharp fragments in all directions. One sliced open his cheek and another just missed putting out one of his eyes. A third laid open a two-inch gash on his arm.

He tucked the sling in his belt and ran, flying through the forest until the thing was only a soft growl in the distance. He crouched down near a dry ravine and cleaned his bloody arm and face with some dried moss, panting and wondering how long he could survive this endless chase. And wondering if he had the courage to do one of the two things that would end it—either waiting until the twisted core of diabolical energies overtook him or, as an alternative, leaping from one of the broken, rocky ledges that edged the plateau.

No! His mind formed the word, then he said it aloud. "No!"

Still preternaturally alert, his eyes scanned the brown carpet of oak leaves laid down by the gnarled, twisted old trees all around him. He saw acorns. Where he came from, they fed pigs. But they would feed men, also. He picked one up and smacked it with a rock. The shell broke, and he ate the nut. It was oddly sweet, and he remembered that not all acorns were bitter.

He easily found five or six more and broke them open. He soon was well on his way to a good meal, when the soft muttering of the oak leaves told him the thing was approaching, moving deliberately through the trees, and he must flee.

But he knew then he need not die without a fight.

Twice that day he doubled back into the oak wood to collect more acorns, putting them inside his shirt next to his skin. At dusk, when the thing was quiescent, he made another trip, this time stripping off his shirt to use it as a collection bag. He carried a few pounds back to his bed under the holly bush. Between the acorns and the meat he'd salvaged from the fawn, he went to sleep with a full stomach for the first time in a week.

But he woke in the morning with a vile taste in his mouth and discovered, when he turned to rise, that his hand was swollen again and he couldn't use it. Water from the pool revived him a little, and he found he could look past the screen of bushes on the other side and into the long aisles of a stand of pines behind. The tall trunks, like earth-colored pillars, stretched away into the gray haze of first light. Nothing moved.

He soaked his hand in the cold water, wary, his eyes searching the forest for the moment of the thing's first coming. The light brightened, but only a mist moved among the trees. There was a blessed silence. Above the trees, the sky was clouded over.

The blustery wind moved the tallest trees in a continuous, agitated sigh, and big raindrops troubled the surface of the pool. The skulls stared up at him with their usual indifference.

When there is no sun, perhaps it must sleep.

He lay still, resting his cheek against the rocks at the edge of the pool until the shirt covering his back was soaked. Then he went to a nearby pine that offered some shelter from the shower and fell asleep again, with his back against the tiled bark.

He woke near noon, or he was sure it must be noon, since he could just faintly see the orb of the sun, grayed by the fleeing storm clouds moving past above. He began to think, putting his needs in order in his mind.

Then he rose again, improvised a sling for his injured hand, and returned to the deer carcass. He managed to scavenge more hide, sinew, and bone. He went back to the pool.

Something, a badger perhaps, had dug a burrow near the holly bush. A little widening of the entrance made it a safe place to cache the acorns and his other useful objects.

He visited the spot where the rock had exploded and found a good many shards with sharp edges. He fashioned a fish spear from one of the long leg bones of the deer and went hunting.

A half hour later, he was crouched on a fallen tree near the bog, watching the shadows of carp moving over the bottom of the sometimes rain-ruffled pool. It had been two days since his meal of raw deer meat, and he didn't think the acorns would see him through another day, however many there were. But his very desperation made his hands tremble as he tried to select his target.

Just as one fish moved into position against the green-coated, submerged wood of the tree trunk he knelt on, another flurry of rain troubled the wet forest around him and the water. The silvery light changed, and he saw his own face reflected in the still water against the gray sky. Pale, thin, hollow-eyed, hollow-cheeked, almost as dead looking as the skulls nailed to the trees warding the monster in this lost place of torment.

He felt detached from himself, his struggle.

But then his image wavered as the fish rose from the bottom and approached the surface. He swung his spear down hard. At first, he thought he'd scored a clean miss. But then the fish floated to the top of the pond, gills still working, with a hole punched through its head. He reached out, got it behind the gills, and pulled it in. He reminded himself to put a barb on the fish spear. He knew he would live.

He ate the fish raw, as he had the fawn. He had a lot of work to do.

The acorns, some hazelnuts, and a lot of berries he found ripening on vines near the cliffs completed his meal. Soaking the hand in water this morning and the extra hours of sleep had helped bring the swelling down to manageable proportions. So, with the hand in its sling again, he made a circuit of the plateau.

As he feared, the cliffs were sheer as far down as he could see. But there were some places where natural chimneys occurred. A man could go down a long way using his hands and feet to hold his position against the rocks. But he would need two strong hands to negotiate them. It wasn't possible right now.

In a few other places, rock falls created fans of scree that broke the sheer rock face into a steep slope. But none were anywhere near the top. If he could make a rope, he might be able to slide down and reach one. From there he could climb down among the broken boulders until he got to the bottom.

The storm clouds stretched from horizon to horizon. But he felt a certain fear that at sunset, light might slip beneath the cloud shield and bring the thing to dangerous, if temporary, life again. He didn't want to be in the pine wood near the center of the plateau if that happened, so he continued his walk along the rim.

At last he reached the skull grown into the birch tree. As before, he saluted it.

When he did, the light brightened alarmingly, and he noticed that one of the branches hung almost horizontal, pointing into a grove of poplars at the cliff's edge. He looked more closely at it and noticed that it was in flower.

The birch, willow, oak, ash, and poplar bloom, but many simply don't notice their curious, nude flowers. They don't need to make a show of themselves, for they are not pollinated by birds or insects, but they give their generative powder into the spring winds before their own leaves appear or any other flowers push through the wet, mucky earth or snow-filled defiles of the colder lands. They are, in their austere way, the first to recognize the end of winter and the beginning of nature's period of joy. And often they cast their pollen under gray skies and amid sluicing rains long, long before the orchards bloom. They study to ensure the continuance of life even in the shadows of a killing frost.

But it is summer here, Arthur thought. *And no tree should be blooming.*

The branch was laden with moisture from the rain. It soaked the catkins of the male flowers, and they glowed like tiny silver wands.

I am Arthur, he thought. But there was nothing else to tie the knowledge to. He couldn't remember who Arthur was.

I am Arthur, he thought, *and I don't know what that means.*

But the branch pointed the way, so he went, wondering as he did if the poplar grove was a trap that would betray him into a treacherous spot where he might lose his footing and fall over the cliff.

But it didn't. When he was past the first ring of trees, the grove opened out, facing a pile of boulders at the very edge of the abyss. Beyond the barrier of dark stone, he saw the sweep of the misty valley, and beyond, more mountains wrapped in gray cloud.

Through the gauzy cloud, the glowing orb of the sun shimmered darkly, now bright, now hidden by the vast inchoate shapes of moisture. These rocks were blackened, and they looked as though they had endured the unleashed wrath of forces so powerful they were not even dimly comprehensible to the young man gazing at them in amazement.

What could liquefy and twist the very bones of the earth herself?

He could not imagine the terror of such a weapon. The rocks were old, worn, cracked by the water and cold, expanded by the summer heat. The flow of once-liquid stone had begun to crumble. Lichens, part plant, part who knows what, almost as old as life itself, had crusted the surfaces. They were green, black, and rust. And over the centuries, the spring had returned. It flowed from a crack in the rock near the apex of the monument.

Arthur knew it was a monument, for the water fanned out over the stone and the letters of a script he'd never seen before stood out, black against the gray.

He'd seen various alphabets—Greek, Latin, runes, and even ogam. He knew this must be another.

But he had little opportunity to speculate, because the trick of the light that made the script visible for a few seconds passed quickly and the letters vanished into an ebony shimmer that marked the passage of water over the shadowed stone.

The water trickled onto more shattered stone at the foot of the spring and vanished as strangely as it had come into an underground passage that must carry it toward the pool at the center of the plateau. He crossed the few last steps to the spring and put his hand, his injured hand, into the silent water pouring down the rock.

She had said once, "Such things heal. That is why they are. I can discern only one reason they exist: to heal us of our grievous wounds."

The water diverted by the touch of his hand flowed across the back, past and over the puncture wounds and down his forearm to drip to the ground from his bent elbow.

Cold! Cold! he thought. It was like the water dripping from the big icicles that formed at the edge of the roof after a winter storm.

His body jerked as a spasm ran through it. Involuntarily, his fingers spread, pressing his hand against the cold stone and sending an unbroken flow of water over the swollen back of his hand.

Time stopped.

He turned his head to one side and saw *her.*

I thought, his mind whispered into the silence, *I thought you were only an old story.*

She was green, gray, black, and russet, the colors of autumn and springtime. Green as the fruiting tree. A thousand shades, textures, and shimmer of gray clouds, storms, falling water, rain. The whisper and throb of the winter sea. Black as the opening of a well, a forest pool over dead leaves, the black lake of bogs, the black north wind, as the eyes of death in an empty skull.

Russet, red with its mixture of gray, green, and black. The dead leaves of autumn, the first new leaves of spring, a coiled fern frond before it unrolls, the red-orange casing of a bud before it unfurls its starburst of beauty. The tips of an another, thick with life-giving pollen, ready to embrace the moist receptive she.

God, she was old. Older than the other brides formed of flowers.

She was the wind, and he felt her caress his cheek with those oh-so-soft fingers. And he knew she had first opened her eyes in a dawn world where mankind was not even an idea, presided over vast forests cropped by monsters, and felt every spring. It is always spring somewhere. The ancient trees gave their souls into the wind and, borne by it, yielded up their life and created the poetry of the forests.

"Drink," was the only command. And he obeyed, quenching his thirst at the icy spring.

The Flower Bride will make a man a king. He remembered the words, without remembering who spoke them.

When he looked again, she was gone, and far beyond the hazy valley beneath, he saw the shadowed orb of the sun slip behind the lowest ridge of a mountain. Then he turned and walked back toward the birch that partially imprisoned—or was it protected?—the skull.

He was returned into time, and hurried back toward his bed beneath the holly bush. His hand seemed much improved by being bathed in the spring water.

Arthur, he thought. Whatever that means. *The past is coming back.*

He spoke aloud to himself. "I'm not sure I want it to. But will or nill, it comes." He paused to look up at the first stars appearing above the forest.

"My hand is healing," he said. "Soon I can use a bow drill."

CHAPTER ELEVEN

SHE WOKE ME AT DAWN. I WAS STILL VERY WEARY and looked up at her through matted eyelashes.

She placed her fingers on her lips. "Be quiet. It comes to hunt fish in the pool. You must know your opponent."

She brought me to the east-facing doors and pointed out to the garden. I was shocked. It was hard to see. Striped from the belly up in yellow and green, it seemed to melt into the sunlit forest beyond.

I will try to tell you what it looked like, but since I have never seen anything like it before or since, this is difficult. It had the three-toed feet, as I had seen the prints of earlier. The hips were slung under the body, not spradled like a lizard's. It looked like it could run fast. The upright body did most resemble a lizard, with its green and yellow stripes beginning at a line in the center of the torso and curving up over the back. It had two long arms. They were thin but muscular, with four claws where we have fingers and a large, opposable claw where we have a thumb.

The head, neck, and face were a nightmare, very much like a snake's but you cannot see a snake's teeth unless it opens its mouth. I know. Maeniel caught one, a poisonous one, an adder, and showed me the fangs and forked tongue. The tongue is a sensory organ, he told me, and can measure heat and cold. The fangs have the poison, and he even showed me where it drips from the fangs before he released the creature.

He said it cursed him in detail as it flowed back into the rocks where he found it. Snakes don't have much in the way of voices. They communicate by motion and the subtle patterns of their bodies in the dust. They also speak from the scales when the light falls on them in certain ways.

Maeniel doesn't speak much Snake. But he knows a few words. He said this one ill-wished him and let fly with a string of rhythmic obscenities. Very peculiar obscenities, he said.

I asked him how peculiar. But he wouldn't tell me, only shook his head and said, "You're too young."

I told him I thought it should have appreciated his mercy in letting it go. But he told me mercy was too complex a concept for a reptile. "They see things very much in black and white, kill or be killed, eater and meal, bite or be bitten. Don't look to them for equivocation. Simply prove you are stronger and move on. Don't eat them, either. The flesh is vile to all but birds, who savor them."

This thing's face resembled a snake's except that its eyes looked forward and the fangs protruded from the mouth around the jawline. As I watched, one hand and arm dropped into the pond and came out with a wiggling fish, which it immediately popped into a mouth awesomely well furnished with teeth.

The long torso of the thing was a prime target.

"The belly," I whispered. "Are the ribs where they are on a human? It is upright like one."

"Yes, they are," she said.

"The gut is a dangerous spot, but very sure in the end. Almost every deer or horse I ever killed bled to death from there—but sometimes it took days. That's one reason I became such a good shot. I got tired of running them down. Only in this instance, I will be doing the running and it will be chasing me. I must be sure I see it in time. With those colors, I might have looked directly at it yesterday and not known what I was looking at."

"It is quite likely that you did," she answered. "You will need your strength. Not today. Risderd is still too weak. But tomorrow."

———————

Morgana lived in an old-fashioned ring fort. It was set in the middle of a lake, so close to the coast that its lower environs were sometimes invaded by salt water during the winter storms. It was on a salmon river, and the fish were the staple diet of the people living near her. They took them all year round.

Morgana was as Igrane. Sovereignty of her people, the Silures, was to be found between her legs. But there was no king. Uther was high king, and she initiated the chieftains of the wild, the rulers of it—the warrior societies. They passed through her bed, a sought-after honor. She was known so long as a mighty sorceress that even churchmen were afraid of her curses.

When they reached her estates, that's what the Saxons would call them, Ena thought. None of these wild people seemed to know anything about cities. Ena was more frightened than she had ever been in her life.

She reflected that she'd only thought she was frightened when she had to face Uther and tell him his son was gone. She hadn't known what fear was until they entered this oak forest. Never had she seen such trees. They were monstrous, and the road wove in and out among them for miles. Huge, stark, squat oaks with sprawling branches that blocked the sun.

They had left level ground behind long ago, and the road not only went in and out among the giant trees, it moved up and down disconcertingly. Sometimes they would top a rise and see the massed green shining clouds of treetops and perhaps an emerald and gold water meadow surrounding an azure lake.

Someone always seemed to live on the lakes. Natural and artificial islands abounded, and they held the round houses Cai's people built. They were much more comfortable within than the Saxons gave them credit for being. But it made her uneasy that they simply incorporated the massive trees that grew hereabouts. And the tree's well-being was as carefully looked after as that of the livestock. It received, in addition to water and sacrifices, feedings of compost, usually buried among the roots and covered by river cobbles that formed the floors near the roots. The house roofs served as kitchen gardens. Vegetables, herbs, onions, and greens were grown on the still-green turf that covered them.

At the first stop, the king's oath men began leaving. "Most of their families live nearby," Cai explained. "And some . . ." His speech slowed. "I can't . . . I'm not sure . . . how can I tell you?"

"Tell me what?" she asked.

He saw how dilated her pupils were. They were standing just inside the door of the first house, where they planned to spend the night. And he saw her eyes had drifted to the rafters. He took the heads for granted. All established families of every rank had them. But the custom of taking heads was new to her.

"They don't have any odor," she said. But he could see she was upset.

"No. They are treated with cedar oil," he said.

This household was headed by a woman with five sons. She was tattooed in the fashion of an owl and wore a silver chain headdress that suggested owl feathers. But it was the richness of the place that impressed Ena. The richness and the rank—to her—barbarity of the inhabitants.

The tables were, as usual, put up around the circular hearth. They were, as at Tintigal, beautifully carved and polished to a high gloss. But then they were covered with a cloth decorated with owl's wings done in some sort of cut-lace embroidery. The tableware was silver, beautifully trimmed with gold filigree.

The maidens who attended her wore soft, white linen. They poured warm water over her hands and helped her scrub her face. She was seated next to Cai.

She glanced up at the heads in the rafters once or twice, then decided to solve her problem by pretending not to see them. The entire household was seated in two concentric rings around the tables, which in turn surrounded the fire pit. After a few moments, she found herself yawning, so weary was she.

The night after the summer king had been found to be a semblance, they had camped in the forest. It wasn't quiet, and Uther's oath men built large fires and kept everyone close to them. Ena woke in the night. Cai's arms were around her, but she was sure she had heard the scream of a panther.

She nudged Cai with her elbow and he awakened.

"There aren't any panthers hereabouts, are there?" she asked.

"Yes," he said. "There are."

"I think I heard one scream."

"It's very possible that you did," he said. "Arthur and I have killed them."

"What will I do when I have to pee? I can't go all night without . . . the baby is pressing down. . . ." She began to pant.

"Stop that," Cai said. "Wake me when you have to go."

She was reassured.

"Then it can eat both of us," he said.

She tried to slap his face, but couldn't reach him and only waved her arms.

"Hush. Go to sleep," he said.

She did, but true to her word, she woke him three times—twice was more usual, but panther screams made her nervous.

Now tonight, after a restless night and a long day in the saddle, she was very tired. *Unusually tired*, she thought. But then she remembered she had never been pregnant before.

Uther had a slightly higher chair than the rest. The sons of the house came and bowed before him, one asking to become one of his oath men.

To Ena's surprise, the king asked the owl woman—that was how Ena thought of her—for her permission. She gave it very graciously. Ena felt that everything had probably been arranged beforehand.

The feast went forward. The king received the champion's portion. He shared it with his new oath man and his more prominent followers, Cai included.

Ena's eyes roamed the hall. The supper was a quiet one. The drunkenness and boasts Ena was used to in her father's hall didn't happen here. What impressed Ena most was the staggering amount of food. There were four kinds of roast meats: pork, mutton, beef, and venison. Fowl were not absent: there were goose, duck, and even swan. There were roast vegetables: leeks with butter and cream, onions, greens of all kinds—cress, a cabbage sort of thing cooked with bacon, and some sort of thistle cleaned of its prickles and steamed with cooked barley. Wine, mead, and beer finished off the list.

A pregnant woman, when she is not vomiting, is an eating machine. After she mopped up the pork with some sort of apple bread and then cleaned the bones of half a duck cooked with preserved quince and started on a large slice of venison with bread and gravy, Cai asked if she was sure there was only one baby in her womb.

She gazed at him, a searing look, and was about to give him a scolding when her hostess appeared in front of her. The owl woman was walking along, offering each of her guests a drink from one of the most impressive vessels Ena had ever seen.

She paused in front of Cai. "My sweet one," she addressed him very intimately. "Who is your friend?"

"Her name is Ena," Cai replied.

"A Saxon by her looks," the owl woman said.

"Yes," Cai answered.

"She is pregnant with your child?"

"Yes," Cai said.

Ena blushed. "What are you doing? We're not married. I disgraced myself. . . ."

"Hush," the owl woman said, looking around quickly. "Be quiet. What you have done is not a disgrace among us. Don't mark yourself as a foolish foreigner among your beloved's people by letting your mouth rattle like an empty gourd."

Ena gulped and glanced at Cai, who was grinning.

"Now," she said. "Tell Niamh, owl warrior priestess, how you came to lie with the Seal. But first, take a sip from my cup."

For the first time, Cai looked alarmed. "Niamh, she doesn't know. . . ."

"You hush also. Don't mark yourself as a fool before your own people! Here, take a sip."

She presented the cup to Ena. Ena rolled her eyes, then looked at Cai, then back to Niamh.

"It's not poison, Ena," Cai said. "Here, I will drink first." He took the cup from Niamh, sipped, and swallowed, then placed the cup in Ena's hands.

"Only a sip, mind," he cautioned as he directed a glare at Niamh.

Ena first touched the liquid with her lips, then licked them. The liquid was fragrant but not unpleasant, rather like strong wine with herbs steeped in it.

Ena sipped and felt the heat spread through her body, followed by a curious relaxation. She could feel the child in her womb. It moved, its first movement—quickening, it is called. And for the first time she sensed it would become another person, a being like her, from her, but not her, with hopes, loves, experiences, loyalties, and finally memories of its own. She felt guilt because it was not conceived in love but out of her own desperate need.

"Now!" Niamh said. "Tell me!"

"We were seven. Ten, if you count the ones who died. Five boys. There was enough for them. My sister had property through my grandmother. No man will look at a woman without property. Not as a wife. I became afraid they would dedicate me to the gods. So I kept my legs crossed tight. They can't do that to a virgin."

"Yes," Niamh said, "they can't hang a virgin."

Ena felt an icy cold course through her at the word *hang*. She shivered.

Niamh handed her the cup again. At the first touch of its contents to her lips, she felt the cold being driven out of her body by something like a warm wind.

"But," she continued, "they sent me to the queen."

"Igrane?" Niamh asked.

"Yes. It didn't take me long to . . ."

"Fear her?" Niamh asked. "Or hate her?"

"Fear, fear, fear," Ena said. "I was afraid of her and her lover by day, by night, under the sun, moon, and stars."

"That bad?" Niamh asked.

"That bad," Ena echoed.

"And Cai?" Niamh asked.

"No!" the boy said firmly. "No!" He pushed the cup away. "No more! I will not hear it, Niamh. Certainly not here, in front of the guests."

"Yes," Niamh said. Then handed the cup to an attendant and clapped her hands.

A lady hurried over to her, and she spoke a few words into her ear. Ena was with her child again, feeling a deep communion no man ever knows. A full awareness of the life within her, a sense of an existence without thought or emotion yet but coming into being. And simple being is pleasure.

I am, I was, I will . . . I love, Ena thought, *in return. Ride my love into the light.* Then she opened her eyes and Niamh was placing a chain of golden flowers around her neck. They smelled like linden.

Ena lifted the chain with one finger. "From the tree," Ena said, "the other tree."

Everyone within earshot looked mystified, except Niamh. Yes, the hall had the usual tree to the right of the firepit, but there were no others.

"You are aware of the other tree?" Niamh asked.

"Yes," Ena said.

Niamh nodded. "Good, but say no more about it."

"No. The chain is very beautiful. Thank you," Ena said.

Then Niamh passed on to the next guest.

Cai put his arm around Ena. "Ready for bed?" he asked.

"Oh, yes," Ena said, or rather sighed.

Cai helped her to her feet and led her away.

The king was seated nearby. "I'm sure they wouldn't have—" he began.

"And I'm sure they would," Niamh said. "We expected to find calculation, but not such pain. She's talented. Dangerously talented. She doesn't know it yet, but she is. Get her to Morgana as soon as possible. I cannot think how she escaped Igrane, but I suppose all she and her lover felt was fear from the girl. She sensed their evil and it frightened her. You said she touched the semblance of Arthur and it collapsed?"

"Yes," Uther said.

Niamh nodded. "Power such as hers would dissolve most minor spells. She radiates it. You have her to thank that you did not continue long in ignorance of the true state of affairs. They would, you know, have destroyed the semblance in such a way as to make you think Arthur died. Or at least, that's what I would have done. That little-regarded girl put a period to their plotting, my king. Watch her closely and keep her safe."

Uther's eyes widened in amazement. "I hadn't thought of that at all."

"No? I did. So did Gawain. He rode through here last night. The summer king! This is war, my lord! War!"

Ena woke in the night thirsty. Cai was sleeping beside her, one arm thrown protectively over her. She wiggled herself out from under it and rose to her feet.

The sleeping rooms were off the big, ceremonial hall. It was a semicircle, with its own fire. They used the Roman method, a double wall that carried smells and smoke up through a grate set in the first wall, into the hollow created by the second. The floor was warm, covered by clean animal hides.

She rose and walked past the fire, toward a carved lattice that opened into the central hall. She blinked as her hand stretched out to touch it, because the writhing dragons that formed it seemed to bear human faces.

She blinked again, and her vision cleared. She pushed the lattice aside and entered the hall.

Some of Uther's oath men and a few of the dinner guests who didn't care to make the trip home had settled for the night on the floor. They all seemed to be sleeping deeply.

She could see well in the dark always, and she threaded her way among the prone sleepers as softly as a vagrant wisp of mist. The central fireplace glowed under its veil of white ash. She circled it, looking for a jug with water and a dipper. No luck.

Outside, she could hear the faint whisper and slap of water on the lake. But there was nothing in here to assuage her thirst.

Then her attention was drawn by the other tree. It stood well beyond the giant oak—at the edge of the building. And it looked as though it might once have been coppiced, that is, the trunk taken and used for timber but the stump allowed to sprout out into multiple trunks. The bark was fair and pale. *Not oak*, she thought, *linden*.

So that was where the necklace Niamh had given her drew its odor—the oil recovered from the flowers. It seemed she saw light creeping in among the multiple trunks of the giant tree.

Thinking it must be later than she thought at first, she hurried toward it. And found herself walking on a riverbed, smooth pebbles at the foot of the tree. And then felt a wetness at her toes.

The linden was planted among giant moss-covered rocks, and the water trickled from among them, down into a pool at the foot, deep enough to reflect the star road, the Milky Way, that threw a scarf of light across the night sky. There was a clay cup nearby, resting casually on its side on the gravel near the spring.

She knelt, rinsed the cup in the pool with its silent stars, refilled it and then drank. The bush bore sprays of white flowers. *Odd*, she thought. *I didn't notice it before.* The scent of the tiny flowers filled her nostrils; the petals caressed her cheek.

She set the cup down. *God*, she thought. *Where did it come from?* But, of course, that was where it came from—God. Not the terrible, dark, blood-drinking gods her people worshipped, who spoke through the oak, the tree that drew down lightning, or the shadow beings her lover Cai's people worshipped, enigmatic dreamers who shared not themselves but their dreams with man.

The branch was a hand, the fingers touching her cheek. She clasped it the way one clasps a hand. God, the mother. Not a goddess, who is, after all, only the other gender of godhead.

But god the Mother.

Ena's eyes opened, and she looked past a V formed by two of the trunks into morning. The clear, golden light of morning slanted through the trees, turning the pale spring grass to shimmering gold. The child in her womb stirred, then seemed to leap.

A second later, a pair of arms like iron bands lifted her away from the spring tree and some eternal morning. And she was back in the dark hall. And the arms around her were Cai's. He was crushing her against his body, and Niamh was beside him.

Cai's body was shaking. She could feel the quivering as he carried her toward the fire pit and the ancient oak.

"Thank God," he whispered. "Thank God. Tell me quickly."

She was standing in front of him. He was bruising her arms with his grip.

He is tremendously strong, she thought, and liked the idea, even as she had feared that strength when she first met him.

He had asked her to meet him alone, and when he did, she had known what he had in mind. *What else?* she thought. When she did sneak off to go to him, he wasted no time in exploring her charms, as he put it. Which, she decided, was as poetic as he was ever going to get. In a short time, he had her on her back, with her skirt up.

She began to struggle.

"What's wrong?"

"My honor."

"I won't tell anyone."

"Like hell! Everyone will know. Besides, they say it hurts."

"Only if you're a virgin."

"I'm a virgin."

"Well, I'll take care of that."

He did.

"There," he said. "What do you think now?"

She shrugged. "I'm not impressed."

"Well, try moving a little."

She did.

"That feels good."

"It gets better. A lot better."

It had.

Now he was staring down at her, like she was his most precious possession.

"Tell me. Tell me, did you eat or drink anything while you were there?"

"What are you talking about?" She jerked back away from him. "I didn't go anywhere. I was here all the time. What did you think? I was sneaking off to meet some man? I wasn't. I was just thirsty. I took a drink of water. See? The tree." She spun around and found herself pointing at a blank wall near the door.

She blinked. "It's gone."

"That's because it was never there," Cai snarled.

"Cai, be quiet," Niamh said. "You're frightening her. You drank water and then what?" Niamh asked.

"I felt love." Ena was still staring at the wall, bewildered. "I looked into the morning."

Ena turned toward Niamh. The old woman reached up and touched her cheek.

"I think you must have been dreaming," she said softly. "You weren't completely awake and you dreamed."

Ena turned in a circle, looking first at Cai, then Niamh, and then the wall.

"I . . . I suppose I must have."

He embraced her. This time it was a comforting one, not the fierce grip of a few moments before. He lifted her from the floor. "Let me take you to bed."

She sighed, put her arms around his neck, and rested her head on his shoulder like a tired child. Her eyes drifted shut.

Neither of them was prepared for what happened next.

Her head lifted from Cai's shoulder, her eyes opened, her face changed. To Cai, it was supremely horrible, because the woman in his arms wasn't Ena. The features changed, formed themselves into a mask of maturity, and firmed with an iron will. The being in Ena glanced at him, dismissed him, and then turned to Niamh.

"Tell Morgana he is in the cage of bones. As am I." The voice was a man's, the cadence of its speech, the sound, the expression, were all masculine. The face, seeming almost superimposed over Ena's softer features, looked at Cai. "Fear not for your love. I—can—not—return."

CHAPTER TWELVE

THE DAY DAWNED CLOUDY, AND THE WIND WAS from the north. The cold woke me. I was sleeping in a nest I had made in the workshop.

She had made it for me, using wood shavings as a mattress, topped by linen sheets and an old, woolen mantle.

She was already stirring. Up, standing in the doorway, looking out to the sea. The wind was at our backs.

"A last touch of winter," she said.

"Will it rain?" I asked anxiously.

"I don't know," she said, turning away from her view of the outdoors. "Why?"

"The bow," I said. "The string is sinew. It isn't tight when it's damp, and it's unusable when it's wet. Warriors who carry such bows always have very fancy bow cases to carry them in, and they try to waterproof them as much as possible. I didn't have time to make one."

She nodded.

The bow was on a frame just in front of the fire on the workshop's small hearth. I lifted it, hoping I had not given it too strong a pull. If I had, I couldn't even string it.

One must kneel, throw a leg over the bow to hold it while you pull down the top, and set the string over the curved piece at the end. In a few minutes, I was snorting and whispering a few words I wasn't supposed to know as I tried to accomplish this tolerably difficult process.

"What's wrong?" she asked.

"This dratted dress, that's what's wrong," I snapped.

She reached out and touched my shoulder. And I found I was dressed in the same clothing I had worn when I was brought to Tintigal—my old tunic, mantle, and breeches reinforced with leather. Only now they were much cleaner than they had been when I was stripped by Igrane's maids.

"How's that?" she asked.

"Fine," I said, looking down at myself. "Someone washed them."

She directed a dark look at me. "They needed it," she said. Then looked away at nothingness and said, "Thank you."

I looked around the dim workshop and whispered, "I appreciate your efforts on my behalf." I didn't see anything, but then, who knows?

I resumed my struggles with the bow and almost decided I had given it too strong a pull. When she touched my arm, strength poured into it, the way the new sun fills a darkened room with light.

"That is all I can give you," she said, "but if you survive this day, you will carry great strength in your arm for the rest of your life. My gifts don't fade or disappear."

The bow strung easily, and the sinew ties that held wood to horn and the larger pieces of sinew were firm.

I lifted my four arrows—Cretan arrowheads, Maeniel would have called them—and placed them in the small quiver I had improvised the day before. I handed the bow to her. Beginning at the end, she ran her fingers along its curves, from the end, over the arch that led to the grip at the center, then up over the second arch to the bottom.

"I am putting it into my memory," she said, "and seeing if it is somehow flawed."

She shook her head. "No! The glue is dried, the parts are firm, the sinew is tight. The bow will serve for at least four shots. But I can tell this is a terrible weapon."

Suddenly I felt dizzy and had to sit down. I did, right there on the floor. The world wavered before my eyes.

Her face took on a look of intense concentration.

"What happened?" I asked.

She strode toward the open door. The breeze ruffled her gown. She took a deep breath, then turned and looked at me. "Someone, some thing, is trying very hard to pull you back."

I thought of Kyra, hunched over the fire, staring at Cymry. She was toasting him just over the flame. He was whimpering like a sick dog.

"She . . . she . . . my nurse, my mother. No, Mother was . . . my . . . Kyra wants me," I finally finished up in a rush.

"She is very strong, this Kyra!"

"I—I'm sorry," I stammered. "I didn't know."

"Well, you have your choice," she snapped. "You can't fight with her interfering like that. If you must, I will let you go."

"No!" I answered loudly.

A second later, I was looking out through Cymry's dead eyes at Kyra. Her face was suffused with anger, her teeth bare.

"Kyra," I said. "Kyra, it's me. Pull the head away from the flames . . . please!"

She did. She had it on the end of a string like a landed fish, hanging from a pole.

"Who are you?" Kyra said. "This filth never said please to anyone in his entire life."

"Guinevere," I said.

"My dear." Kyra's agitation turned to sorrow. "Where are you? We have been trying to find you for weeks, Dugald and I. The wolves have ranged all along the coast, down as far as Tintigal. But that cursed, arrogant bird Magetsky says you are no longer a prisoner of the queen. And the dragons say that the one sent to fetch you disappeared along with you. Tell me what happened."

"I'm not sure," I answered, "just exactly where I am. But wherever it is, I must perform a task for *her*."

"Her?" Kyra replied, sounding mystified. "Her?" she repeated.

"Oh." She sounded enlightened. "Oh! *Her!*"

"Yes. Now, let me go!" I insisted.

"She can be . . ." Kyra began.

"She's standing right here," I said frantically.

A second later, Kyra was gone. And she was laughing.

"I believe everything is all right now," I said as I pulled myself together.

She nodded. "Poor Kyra, whoever she is, has a lot of power. To get here, she had to traverse time and space. She was trying to warn you that for a mortal to become involved with the business of immortals can be very dangerous. That's what she was about to tell you."

I gave her a look with a lot of feeling in it. "I think I know that," I told her.

"Would you like to go back?" she asked. "The line your Kyra created is still open. You may leave, if you like. I won't compel you."

"Please!" I said, thinking of Risderd and his family, and especially, for some reason, Treise. "I'm in too deep to back out now, and besides, I belong to you."

She chuckled. "An oath woman."

"If you like," I answered, trying to keep my dignity. "I suppose it's the same thing."

"Yes," she said, turning to gaze into the misty, gray dawn outside. "Many of the warriors have been and will be women. Though men would often not care to acknowledge it."

Then she turned back again and gazed into my eyes. "Soon you will bleed and cease to be mine any longer."

"No," I said, and extended my hands pressed against each other toward her palms. Her hands enfolded mine in the age-old gesture of one who accepts the homage of a house carl.

"I am," she said, "Inanna, Diana, Mother Holle, the Hag of the Mill. I have had so many names, I have forgotten them all. But I will remember yours, Gwynaver. And so will all mankind. Men have died for everlasting fame, but I can't think of any woman who ever has."

"Yes," I replied. "You're making fun of me. Besides, there was that girl who buried her brother. What was her name?"

"Antigone," she answered. "But I don't think she had everlasting fame in mind. Only her own sorrow. He was her brother."

"Yes," I said, thinking of Black Leg. "Love is important, and women being shrewd bargainers probably know fame is not worth much. I'd much rather have something I can spend, eat, or love, thank you very much."

"And you will, my daughter. So you will," she promised. "But I think you will need the food first." Then she let go of my hands. "I'll fetch you some breakfast," she said as she left the workshop.

I sat down cross-legged on the floor. Treise stumbled in. She had been crying. She walked over to me, climbed into my lap, and began to cry some more.

"What's wrong?" I asked.

"Everything! Ardal is dead, and now Father wants to go where the monster is. I could hear him and Mother talking about it last night. She begged him not to go."

"Hush!" I said, and began to stroke the fine, soft hair that curled everywhere. I cradled her and crooned. "I'll be with him, and he will come back safe, I promise."

She stiffened and drew back. "You? Protect him? How?"

"Hush!" I said. I reached out and got a handful of shavings that had been part of my bed. I held them in front of Treise. They formed a light clump of yellow in my cupped palm.

I called the fire.

I don't know how I do this. It is as simple and natural as the flight of a bird, and I probably understand it as little as birds understand flight or the Gray Watcher how he changes from wolf to man and back again.

The wood shavings stank, smoked, and then burst into flame, flared, then fell to black ash before they even had time to warm my skin.

When I looked back at Treise, she was gazing at me wide-eyed with awe.

"Is that what you did to it the last time?" she asked. "When it screamed and ran away?"

"Yes. And I can protect your father the same way I protected you. Now, don't worry," I said, and bedded her down on my abandoned nest.

She stuck her thumb in her mouth, closed her eyes, and lay quiet. In a few moments, I heard her breathing change. She slept.

My lady returned with porridge and bread. I ate it standing near the door, gazing into the misty forest. "The dragon?" I asked.

She closed her eyes. "He is dining on a small shark. It was shadowing a school of dolphins with several pregnant females. They do go after the babies. The sharks, that is. The mothers asked his help, and quite obviously received it. He likes shark. I will alert him to your needs."

I nodded. I was dry-mouthed. "I doubt if there's much he can do."

"True," she whispered. "The dragons are clumsy on land. Helpless, really. I don't think he will be much help."

"Well and good," I said. "It also means he won't come to any harm. If it should happen that I don't return, thank him for his help. Now, if possible, can you tell me where the fish eater is?"

She closed her eyes and touched her temples with both forefingers. "He is hidden from my eyes by a cloud of magic, but I can narrow it down and tell you where the cloud is." A second later, she whispered, "Predictable. He has concealed himself near the well, to . . . to . . . ah, yes, to the landward side. He is watching the Flower Bride."

"Near the path?" I asked.

"Yes. Near the path. For that is the way Risderd will come."

"Fine. Then I'll—"

"Shush," she said. "Other ears than mine may hear you."

Then she kissed me on the forehead. "Daughter mine, good fortune attend you."

And I went, hurrying into the misty, green gloom under the trees.

The early morning forest was hushed, and the soft sea mist blurred the edges of everything. The place I chose to pass through was trackless. Most deer and other beasts didn't venture here. I followed the slope of the ground as it began to turn down toward the sea.

There were a lot of trees, but most of them were small pines, and the fallen needles formed a thick carpet that blunted the edges of the rocky ground. The wind blew softly, but constantly, driving the sea fog among the slender, brown, rough-barked trunks. Above, the green needles were brilliant as polished stone with moisture.

I moved first down, blessing Talorcan's shoes because they seemed able to adapt to every surface I crossed, from spongy drifts of brown needles to slippery, wet, gray granite boulders that poked up through the trees to form strange, open spaces walled by fog at this hour. When I had to climb, I did, clutching the bow and arrows tightly in my left hand. Moving downward all the while, until a moment came when I paused and saw the huge pile of driftwood stranded in the angle where the node of rock that would become Tintigal projected into the sea.

The driftwood gave me an idea. It was a risky one, but it might work.

I skirted the top of the pile, half walking, half crawling across bare rock, feeling very exposed and vulnerable until I reached the forest clothing the slope on the other side. The sun was rising by then out over the water, the orange disk still half obscured by the night fog. I pushed myself hard, knowing that Risderd would take the path to the well at sunrise.

I couldn't go very fast, though, because I had to take care lest I alert the creature by making too much noise. *It would be hell*, I thought, *if I reached the well only to find the bridegroom killed and eaten by that monster.*

I climbed frantically up through the trees again as the pines gave way to a lighter growth of birch and poplar that clothed the knob of rock near the well. At length, I saw the glint of the pool near the spring through the trees.

I slowed and moved as silently as I could, until I was in the thick brush on the side where I had seen the monster take the deer that had come down to drink. I knelt, concealed at the edge of the wood.

I saw the first sunlight strike the pool, turning the water flowing from the spring to crystal and the pool to a shimmering gem. I could sense the beauty of the place but couldn't really see it because I was too busy looking for the serpent in this Eden.

And then, almost at the same moment, I saw the monster and the Flower Bride.

She was waiting upright for her lover, near the small waterfall that fed into the pool. She was one with the water itself. The tall flowers of the poisonous hemlock and the drape of falling water were her skirt. Above her bare breasts were the shadows thrown by a clump of white birch on the dark rock, and her face glowed in the new sun just clearing the horizon.

You don't see her, not really. She only suggests herself to you. Your mind fills in the details.

That is why she is always so beautiful. She forms herself from the transient but eternal glories that fill the world around us everywhere. Look at new leaves, bursting out from the rough buds on a branch, you see her. Alike and equally her are the orchards both in bloom and with branches laden with the heavy autumn fruit. She creates herself anew in desert, swamp, forest, or heath. In summer, winter, spring, and fall, she is eternal and yet ever new, as is a flower.

For a moment, I envied her lover, and wondered what such a union would be like. And then I saw it.

The monster showed himself to me. At the end of the path at the spring was an ancient oak. The thick, black trunk was dappled with gold by the morning sun. No doubt the creature thought it was being clever. It stood to one side in the black shadow cast by the tree. I picked it out by its silhouette against the brightening sky.

Did it see me? I remained very still.

No, the big-toothed head was turned, looking down the path.

Should I try for a shot? I have always wondered since if I might not have ended it here, had I dared. But the problem was, I couldn't judge the location of the creature. I could see its outline, but how far back was it?

Four arrows. I had only four. The forest was damp, damp and cold. I couldn't be sure the bow would hold together for four shots.

I hesitated. And then it was too late. I heard Risderd walking, without any attempt at concealment, up the path.

CHAPTER THIRTEEN

I AM BEING TORTURED, HE THOUGHT, IN THE shadow land we all visit just before waking.

He remembered her. No longer young but still beautiful. The helmet of tawny hair that shadowed her face and rested like a small cape at her shoulders. The fair, strongly marked face with a straight nose and generous mouth. Alabaster, fine-grained skin, highlighted with a roseate flush.

He was afraid of women. Had been afraid of women. But this one was nothing like the bitter witch that cast such a dark shadow over his mind. He was conscious of those past encounters that made his body shake when she touched him. Still, his father was there and had promised nothing would happen to him. So he allowed her to place him on her lap, while he glared defiance up at her face.

She stroked his cheek lightly with one finger, and the anger and fear dissolved and vanished, the way salt does in water, leaving the memory of both anger and fear behind, changing the nature of experience in the same way salt changes the taste of water.

"What a dreadful, dreadful thing," the magnificent woman whispered. And he knew the words went unheard by the others gathered around the big carved chair where she sat before the fire.

Then she spoke up and called, "Cai! Cai! Come here to me!"

The boy who approached the chair was just a little older than he was. But unlike him, this child was swarthy in complexion, with thick hair that grew straight back from a pronounced widow's peak on his forehead. He was thickset, with a sturdy build.

"Cai," she said, "long have you reproached me for giving you no brother in the comitatus, among the young lions. You are training to learn the warrior way. And bitterly have you complained to me of your solitude. I told you that it was foreordained that you stand isolated. That you were not chosen for fellowship. And you have borne your hardship well and have no peer among your age mates."

She extended her hand to the boy. He knelt and kissed it.

"But now the one who is to be your brother has come."

Looking down, he had seen happiness fill the child's face. They were both too young for any artifice. He knew he was the cause of that happiness and even then wondered if he deserved to be the cause of such happiness for anyone.

But he clambered down from her lap and embraced his new brother. And from that day forward, they hunted, played, studied, and fought together. And neither had any secrets from the other.

He felt a piercing sense of grief, so painful that it was almost intolerable. So how, then, did he find himself so alone?

Her face came back to him then. She would have said, "Think."

Torture. Why go to such elaborate lengths to cause him pain? The torturer always wants something, even if only to derive satisfaction from the struggles of his victim. His suffering was desired. The less he suffered, the more futile the torture was. And if he could find out what, if any, other satisfactions were wanted, he could study how to deny his captors those also.

He opened his eyes. His pursuer must still be dormant, since the sun wasn't up yet. The air was clear, but with a slight touch of frost in it.

He had no idea what season it was here. He and Cai had wandered in the mountains, and this had all the indications of a high-altitude place. But did it get very cold here? And, if so, when and how cold?

He crawled out from under the holly bush and went to drink at the pool. He saluted the skulls staring up at him. They were beginning to acquire personalities. The structure beneath the skin is, after all, as distinctive as the envelope of flesh it supports. This one, the one closest to the place he drank, was likely male and young. He had all his teeth, and the bones were robust and powerful.

Arthur shivered. The air was as cold as the water. He went to his cache and ate some of the dry deer meat, then folded several lengths of the jerky and hooked them around his belt.

The sun poured its new light through the trees. *Now,* he thought. *Now, just stay alive.*

He heard the thing yammering beyond the trees. He didn't run, just began walking. He thought he heard distant laughter, but now he schooled himself to indifference and allowed no expression of fear or disgust to cross his face.

I need a yew.

The thing seemed to be gaining on him, so he broke into a jog, wondering if it were refreshed by its rest also. *I need a yew,* he thought, *for the fire drill.*

Hunted as usual, he crisscrossed the plateau that day. But he couldn't find the sort of tree he wanted.

The task of evading the creature was now routine. When he reached the swamp, he kicked another rotten log to pieces and ate what he found inside. Again he heard the laughter, and as before, he steeled himself to pretend he hadn't.

He searched the tall cattails near the forest, found a few more eggs, and ate them in much the same way an animal would, crunching the shells. He discovered that by wandering along the edge of the plateau he could slow the horror down—the reason being that it was ringed by skulls that warded the creature. It also provided a certain challenge for him, since he had to pick his path carefully to avoid being trapped at the edge. The path at the rim was far from even. At times, his forward progress was blocked by piles of rock and he had to double back through the forest, sometimes coming perilously close to the monster. But this gave him an opportunity to study the thing.

It was a wavering column; shadows circled its core. And the sounds it made were almost universally those of anger and sorrow. But it was conscious of him, and when he came close to it, the thing seemed to destroy nearby objects in the hope of burying him in the debris.

A sheet of mud near the swamp fanned out, almost blinding him. But the creature stranded a few fish. When he doubled back to get them, he found himself pelted with fist-size rocks from a dry streambed.

This really frightened him and taught him not to underrate the thing's clumsy pursuit. If one of those flying stones got him in the head, or broke a leg, he would be finished.

Taking to his heels, he quickly outdistanced it again. After caching the fish, he returned to the rim, thinking he needed a refuge in case he became ill or otherwise incapacitated. Somewhere to hide where the thing couldn't get to him.

Near sunset, he found the tree. It clung to the plateau at the very edge. The prevailing winds lashed the outermost point of the plateau here. The tree was rooted in the slope at the very edge, just before it fell away into the valley. A skull, the warding skull for this place, was nailed to one of the upper branches.

She? Was it a she? He couldn't be sure. The skull was gracile, delicate with a full set of teeth. A young woman, perhaps?

Since the tree was rooted in the slope, her empty eyes stared into his directly, on the same level. He saluted her as he had the one on the birch.

A yew, just what he wanted. It was very old, and it looked as though the tree had been dislodged from the plateau by a landslide. Enough roots remained to continue to form a hold fast, even though the remains of the tree jutted out perpendicular to the cliff.

Yews do not give up easily, and over half the tree still sported the narrow, dark, gray-green leaves. It was thickly adorned with red berries. The breeze from over the valley below was cool on his face, and the westering sun was half masked by the haze drifting over the distant mountains.

He went down the slope and climbed out on the trunk. The tree was even bigger than he thought when looking at it from above.

I want . . . what do I want? he thought, alarmed. Inadvertently, he looked down.

No! All at once he was dizzy and wracked by nausea. He had refused to admit to himself how weak he was, how drained by hunger, exertion, and his wounded hand. The only thing that kept him conscious was sheer will. He trembled violently, feeling his trembling shake the tree trunk, knowing that if he slipped, he would fall to his death in the abyss below.

His hands clutched the small branches angling out from the trunk so tightly that twigs popped through his skin. At the same moment, the horror reached the edge of the plateau above him.

It screamed, voice echoing out over the rim, ringing with inchoate rage, and it seemed to want to drill into the ground. The force of its fury showered him with dirt, stones, twigs, and detritus of all kinds from the ground as it seemed to want to tear through the earth itself, rip the tree's roots loose, and send it and him plunging to the rocks below.

It might have succeeded, for the thick, knotted roots weren't that far below the surface, but he felt rather than saw searing rage from the skull. And he knew it had been she and in some sense she was still here. Vengeful and protective of . . .

The thing gave a truly dreadful scream and fled, just as the sun began to slip behind the peak in the distance. Arthur laid his cheek against the loose scrappy bark for what seemed a long time, until the light turned blue. He remembered what he wanted. She, the woman of the skull, had given him that.

He wondered who and what they had been; and found he couldn't imagine but knew, whatever their origins, he was not alone. He had allies in his struggle.

Cai! Yes, Cai taught him. Almost his first lesson was how to make fire. They had gone hunting in the omnipresent oak wood that covered their country. They had gone after geese, and they both carried longbows.

They got lost. Not very lost; both boys knew if they followed the coast, it would bring them home. But the night was moonless and the darkness thick under the trees. They had bread and cheese, enough to content them until morning, but no fire. Cai hadn't been in the least worried. Everyone, he told Arthur in a lofty fashion, carried fire with them at all times.

Then Cai unstrung his long yew bow and demonstrated how easy it was to create a comforting blaze with a bow drill. Hunkered down over the fire in a thickly overgrown hollow near a stream, Arthur immediately demanded that Cai teach him. And he quickly found out it wasn't as easy as it looked.

After a few tries, his arms and hands were sore and he was winded but no fire. Cai laughed at him.

Then Arthur was seized by rage, a fury almost as forceful as an artesian spring, a kind of evil madness. Nothing as simple as a piece of wood and a string could defeat him. He would not permit it.

He gritted his teeth and went after his task with a vengeful ferocity that frightened Cai. He worked bow and string until he had blisters and the blisters burst and bled. Until his arms felt as though they were on fire and he had a stitch in his side from the exertion. But he got his fire; then in a fury, kicked it in Cai's face.

They were both children, and Cai forgave him after they put out the fire that was running through the dead oak leaves in a thoroughly alarming way. But Arthur noticed Cai took care never to laugh at him again.

He looked up at the remains of the tree and saw a nice section that would make a bow—heartwood on the outside, sapwood on the inside. He got to his knees, still trembling with fatigue and strong emotion. The stave—because that's what it looked like, a stave—snapped off in his hand.

The light was gone, as was the terror that pursued him. He crawled back up to the rim, stave in hand. He saluted the skull again. He spoke aloud. "I thank you, my lady."

Then he stumbled back the way he had come to his bed under the holly bush. He collapsed on his stomach on the dead leaves and slept for several hours. Hunger and cold woke him.

The stave he had chosen was practically a bow. It didn't take long to rig it with a cloth string from his leggings, and he had good reason to be thankful for his long practice with the bow drill as a boy. He was highly skilled at bringing fire into being. And in a short time, he had one going in the dead leaves under the holly bush.

He swept it out, away from his improvised hearth, and surrounded it with a circle of stones. Then he added some knots of oak he'd found nearby.

Then he simply sat, looking at what he had wrought for a long time.

Then he went back to where he had cached the fish, improvised a grill from green branches, and cooked them. He was starting on the second, cleaning the ribs with his teeth, when he heard the yell of rage.

Arthur began laughing, because he knew he had baffled his captors and infuriated them by being far better at taking care of himself than they had expected him to be. He felt an ugly sense of self-satisfaction, and then the lights went out.

CHAPTER FOURTEEN

OW! I THOUGHT. NOW!

I don't remember drawing the bow and nocking the arrow. I felt only the sting as the bowstring snapped past my wrist and the sinew slashed my knuckles.

Then, almost without willing it, the second arrow was in position and the thing was coming fast, right toward me. The creature, running on his hind legs, was clear of the darkness under the oak. I saw the sheet of spray rise as its feet hit the water. I could see it now clearly, as yellow-and-green-striped as the sunstruck foliage around it, with two arrows in its midsection.

Odd, some part of my mind commented. *I never felt myself loose the second one.*

But the third was in position, and I felt the bow fling it free, even as it fell apart.

Just as well it did. I might have remained rooted where I stood and fired the fourth, and so met my doom. Because as the third landed, it penetrated the lower abdomen, near the thing's left hip.

The first two were only making streaks of red, crossing the creature's stomach. But when the third struck, the fish eater staggered, let out a terrible scream, and the scarlet blood gushed.

I threw down what remained of the bow and ran.

Down! Down toward the sea.

The thing was on my heels, propelled by its fury at the savage violation. And I knew it would overtake me soon, for it was faster than I was.

I cleared the forest. Just ahead and downhill was the massive driftwood pile. As I saw it, I felt the creature's claws on my back. Felt them slip on the armor given to me by my father.

I leaped for the brush pile. This was taking a horrible risk, but no worse than slowing down. If ever there was the devil on one side and the deep blue sea on the other, this was it. The deadwood in the brush pile might give way, sending me down into its depth where broken branches waited like sharpened stakes in a pit, ready to impale me. Or drop me into the deepest part, where I might suffocate under the windblown sand and years of compacted dead leaves.

But somehow, if I wanted to live, I must slow the creature down. I might be its last meal, but meal I would be if I failed.

I landed on the thick trunk of a broken oak, weathered to silver by wind and rain. It held, and I sprang into the air again when I felt the dead tree shudder as the creature landed beside me.

I felt, I swear, its breath on my neck and the claws on my shoulders as it tore away my old shirt.

I gave a fighting yell as I sprang into the air, again to land on a network of broken willow withes. They gave under my weight, but sprang back and didn't break. I heard my own whoop of delight when I realized the creature wouldn't be so fortunate.

And indeed, it wasn't. I was in the air again when I heard the willow branches shatter and the creature's bellow of fury as it was plunged down into the deadwood.

I aimed for the thick trunk of a decaying log near the bottom of the pile. It was both rotten and slippery. It gave way under my weight, pitching me forward and down.

I rolled to my back just in time to avoid the jutting, broken branches that might have put out my eyes, torn my breasts, and slashed my face to ribbons. As it was, the armor of fairy wasn't enough to protect me, and I fetched up on the beach, my back torn and bleeding and with deep scratches on my arms and legs. But I no sooner hit the sand than I was on my feet and moving.

Above me, the creature fought to free himself from the tangle that surrounded him. I turned and, heedless of further injuries, thrust my arm into the brush pile, seized a broken branch with my fingers, and thought, *flame!*

And I got it.

I had to jump back to avoid the inferno I created. Again, I turned and ran along the beach toward the cove where I had landed and spent the first night. Beyond it, the beach turned rocky, and beyond that, I didn't know.

I wasn't fool enough to believe the creature would be killed by the fire. The stuff in that brush pile might make a monstrously hot fire, but it was so dampened by sea fog and rain that it would take some time to fully ignite. And I was pretty sure the thing would manage to free itself before then. So I flew along the beach, running as fast as I could.

And indeed I was right. Halfway to the cove I glanced back in time to see it emerge from the smoke and begin trying to overtake me, running with long, bounding strides.

Oh, but I had marked it. I could see enough to tell that. The magnificent striped yellow and green hide was darkened by soot and smoke here and there. I saw the charred, red-black burns on the neck, shoulder, and forearms. Blood sheeted down the thing's stomach, and it left a trail of it as it ran—big, scarlet splashes on the bright sand.

Well and good, but I was leaving a trail of blood also. And it was bigger and stronger than I ever thought about being. If it was mortally injured, and I hoped it was, did I stand a chance of outlasting it?

CHAPTER FIFTEEN

HEN ENA WOKE, HER BLADDER WAS FULL AND the baby was kicking. She had been thrilled when she felt the first stirring last night, but she knew the joy would probably be succeeded by annoyance. She sat up slowly to find that Cai was already up and, with some of the other men, outside. They were saying their good-byes, since most lived hereabouts and would return to their families before attending the court ceremonies Uther would hold at Morgana's stronghold.

A serving woman brought Ena a towel and some warm water. She washed her face and hands, then brushed her teeth with a twig.

Niamh called that a dream. But Ena didn't remember it the way she remembered a dream. The touch of the flower petals on her cheek. The aroma they gave off when her fingers brushed them. The taste of clear water. The look of morning beyond the linden tree.

But then when Cai came, it was all gone and she felt a stir of anger that he had awakened her and taken her from such comfort and beauty. A second later, she found herself crying and tried to compose herself before Cai returned.

It was nice she had beautiful dreams, because today was going to be horrible. They must ride to Morgana's stronghold and bring her the report that Arthur was missing. She hoped Gawain had gone on ahead and prepared the old woman for the bad news.

And then there was the matter of the child. God! Couldn't anything go right for her? Couldn't she do anything right? She knew when her consciousness touched the thing in her womb that it was the wrong sex. She was torn by the sorrow she felt. She loved it and wanted to love it more. But she didn't dare. It was a girl. And she might find herself abandoned when it was born. Then what would she do? And to her horror, she began weeping.

Cai came in. "What's wrong?" he asked.

"Everything! Nothing!" she spat like an angry cat. "Being pregnant! Being sick to my stomach and not able to eat!"

He went to call Niamh, who came and dosed her with something surprisingly good-tasting, with mint in it. Then she served her sliced boiled chicken and plain porridge with bread and fresh butter.

When it was time to mount their horses Ena felt better.

Once on the road, she calmed, feeling better than she had in a long time. Now in her mind she was able to analyze the night's events. *No, she thought stubbornly. That was no dream.* The tree had been there, and Cai had pulled her away from a real place. Someone called her, and she had followed the voice.

She had no idea if it was a trap or not. Cai might have thought it was, and Niamh, too. But she was no baby to be soothed by comforting words. What she had seen and experienced while she was there had been real, more real in a way than anything she had known before.

My child! she thought. *My child. How can I care for it alone?*

She was trailing the rest, since it was safe here, so close to the Silurian stronghold. No one had bothered to order her to close up with the rest, as they had riding through more perilous lands. Instead, they lazed along, much as she did, enjoying the cool breath that whispered over the forest from the nearby sea and luxuriating in the golden morning. Cai and the men rode in a knot in front of her.

She was chewing over the problem of parenthood, worrying it the way a dog does an old dry bone—thinking that when Cai knew the baby was female he might not want to acknowledge it even as a bastard. Then she saw the rider leave the woods, move easily through the roadside brush, and pace her horse, riding beside her. He was unremarkable-looking, dark as many of these people were, and he carried no weapons. This alone surprised her. She knew of no one, man or woman, who went about unarmed. He carried a harp in a case strapped to his back.

Oh, she thought, *that explains it.* She had heard many times that the poets and singers belonging to these people were sacred and even the vilest brigands would not harm them. For to do so would call down the most damning curses from both gods and men. Those who committed such a crime were as dead to their closest family and friends. Left without shelter, food, or clothing and driven from place to place without mercy until they died. This as much as anything else guaranteed the safety of bards.

She seemed to hear in her mind the trickle of silver notes wrought by the instrument under the player's skilled fingers. Ena smiled and forgot her worries in the joy of the moment, wondering as she did if he were traveling to Morgana's stronghold, and if so, might he perhaps sing for them tonight.

She was surprised that no one had greeted him or spoken a word. She caught his eye and smiled as if to make him welcome. He looked wary and increased his pace until he drew slightly ahead of her. But he returned the smile.

Just at that moment the party rode out of the dappled leaf shadows and into a patch of golden morning sun. And Ena saw clearly that the sun shone through him.

Then she began to wonder. Being exposed to the spells Merlin and Igrane wove around themselves; the strange semblance of Arthur that she had broken, revealing the truth. The violent casting out of Merlin's magic by her and Cai at Gawain's instigation. The pleasure of it thrummed in her body yet.

She stretched these new, strange senses toward the child. It was fine, enjoying the rhythm of the ambling mare she rode—as much as it was doing anything. It was far from awareness yet and therefore content.

Then she stretched her senses toward the man riding ahead. He was dead, long dead. But he would wake, half wake, from some pleasant dream and try to go home.

Once he had lived nearby, down a road. But he couldn't find the road; the countryside was greatly changed.

She knew where the road was.

Necromancy, they called it. Only those with a natural talent excelled in it. She had heard both Merlin and Igrane speak about the procedures involved. They roused a sort of horror in her mind. She was not at all prepared for this calm sadness.

He had died loving them and they thought he betrayed them. He had to get back and tell them he hadn't. Then he could go on with a . . . ? She wasn't sure what.

Ena remembered there were questions. Merlin had told Igrane questions you shouldn't ask the dead. Questions they were forbidden to answer. She didn't know what they were.

"All right." She shrugged. She wouldn't ask him anything.

She prodded her horse a bit, and it drew up next to his. She studied him narrowly. A pleasant enough young man, if you didn't pay attention to the fact that you could see through him.

He glanced around quickly and then registered surprise. *Most can't see us.* The words formed themselves in her mind.

I know, she answered. She didn't speak aloud either, not wanting to alarm the men riding with Cai. *But I can. The tree is down many winters. Lightning struck it in a storm. It burned, and then someone carried away what remained of the timber. The person who did that didn't care that it was sacred.*

Here! she said, turning her horse. It staggered slightly as it had to scramble down into a ditch and up the other side. She guided the horse past a tangle of deadfalls and found, as she had thought, a narrow trace running along a hillside. When she looked up, he was beside her.

Yes, he said quietly. *Yes.*

Below them, a thickly grown water meadow bloomed brightly, supporting a lush growth of furze, golden broom, and tall purple thistles. High up on the hill, mixed stands of giant pines grew. But farther down, toward the meadow, the ground was more open and a sprinkling of white birches shaded the road as it wound away among the trees.

Thank you, he said. Then drifted into the haze of sunlight and was gone.

Just then she heard Cai calling her name. "Ena! Ena!"

He pushed his horse with some difficulty over the soft bracken-covered ground. "What are you doing here?"

"What do you think?" she said, dismounting.

"Oh, that. Ena, it's safe enough this close to Morgana to wander off, but there are still dangers for a woman alone. And . . ."

He was turning his back to allow her some privacy as she squatted.

"I wasn't alone," she muttered.

"What?" he asked.

"Nothing," she answered in artificially dulcet tones. "Love me or not, you louse." She was in a bad mood. "When the child is born, I bet I can make a living at this."

It was true. There was a lot of call in the world for the services of someone who could ask the dead questions. She remembered her parents visiting the vovulas, as they were called among her people. They left a big offering in the ladies' pot for news of their family back in Frisia. And the women had been right, too, because her uncle stopped by, having taken service with a Veneti captain. And he confirmed everything the women said.

Ena felt a lot better already. And, yes, she hadn't been in too much discomfort, but it was nice to get her bladder emptied. She didn't know what kind of a woman this Morgana was or how long she would be kept standing around. If her court was anything like Igrane's, there would be a lot of that.

But it wasn't, and she didn't have to wait long.

Morgana's stronghold was near the sea, on an island in the center of a lake. It gleamed in the sun. Ena had seen the glass-domed feasting hall at Tintigal, but this thing was completely foreign to her experience.

"A Roman built it for us," Cai explained. It was an explanation that didn't explain.

The island held three ancient trees: an oak, an ash, and a linden. The stronghold was triangular, with three massive halls, one at each tree. The tree trunks supported the roof of each hall. They came up very high on the tree, but it didn't matter. The trees were able to get all the light they wanted, because the halls were roofed with glass. Or rather, as Ena looked more closely, she saw the roofs were half glass. A strip of glass and then an equal-size strip of wood. The multipaned windows were held together by lead, a new process, now beginning to be used in churches.

A causeway, narrow to be sure but still stone, stretched out over the lake to the island. The guards at the entrance to the causeway hailed the king. He returned their salutes and rode past, over the lake, toward the stronghold.

Women—at first Ena didn't recognize them as women because they were armed and armored as men would have been—greeted them in the courtyard before the door. They took the horses, and one, a tall, dark-haired one with her hair coiled in braids at her ears, helped Ena to dismount. She was perfectly courteous but gave Ena a look of appreciative appraisal such as a man might have, and Ena found herself blushing violently.

They ushered the party through richly carved double doors into the hall. Ena took a long, neck-craning look at it and thought, *No matter how long I live, I will never see anything as magnificent as this again. I must study to see it all and remember it.*

The tree was at the center, as it had been in the other strongholds. More of the tree was enclosed than in the other halls, but the alternating solid and glass segments of the roof let in a blaze of light. This was the brightest dwelling she had ever been in. Indeed, it was a garden, more beautiful than the terrace gardens at Tintigal.

All inside was part of a garden. They crossed a footbridge over a water-filled canal, which ran on the inside of the building and irrigated the gardens.

"This is a wonderful place," Cai said. "It is never too hot or too cold here, and anything grows in my grandmother's gardens."

And indeed, they passed a blooming tree in a tub near the water. The flowers were orange, and the fruit scarlet. Cai told Ena it was a pomegranate.

Beyond the gardens, the floor was dark, polished stone, as at Tintigal. And in the center a fire pit seethed, the ash a white crust over the coals. Beyond the fire pit, the big river cobbles floored the area around the massive tree trunk.

The woman stood there. She wore white, a soft linen-silk weave of some kind. Ena had expected someone dark like Cai. But she was fair, though not blond, as Ena was. Her hair color was more tawny, and her eyes were green. Ena was reminded uncomfortably of a lioness. She'd seen one once. The Romano-British aristocrats still held games in the amphitheater at Aquae Sulis, and the lioness had been exhibited as a curiosity by a troop of traveling gladiators.

Once a *bestiarius* might have fought one, but now importing them from whatever lands they frequented was far too expensive for the big cats to be so lightly slaughtered. They had given it a runaway slave from her father's lands, but the lioness hadn't been hungry enough to finish the man off right away. Halfway through the spectacle, Ena got sick and lost her lunch. The rest of her family laughed at her squeamishness and the antics of the cat as she played with her victim. And Ena had come away convinced that they would offer her to the gods just as lightly as they enjoyed the ferocity of the cat and feel her loss no more than they did the killing of the runaway.

Ena felt hot, dizzy, and sick as she watched Morgana approach the king. For she knew this was Morgana. No one had to tell her. It didn't help one bit that the first person she beckoned to come to her was Ena.

"Come here, Ena. That is your name, is it not? Come here to me."

Ena gritted her teeth and whispered, "Hell!"

Then she approached Morgana. The closer she got, the more frightened she became. But her hardhanded father could have told her there was virtue in laughing and poking fun at weakness, because Ena was determined now to face this woman down, no matter what she had to do.

Ena stopped just in front of her. Morgana said, "Ha," a puff of breath, and she placed her hand on Ena's belly. It was protruding only slightly.

"You know what you've got there?"

"Yes," Ena said. "And if you're as good as your reputation suggests, you know, too. It's a girl."

Morgana nodded. "A strong, healthy girl, at that."

"I take after my mother," Ena told her. "She was born to birth babies. She had eleven and came to no harm through it. And I won't, either." She bared her teeth at Morgana, but it wasn't a smile.

"When did you decide to get pregnant by the highest-ranking man you could get to share your bed?" Morgana asked.

"As soon as I set foot in that witch bitch's court," Ena snapped back. "Why Cai?"

"Take your pick. The rest of them were too young, too old, too drunken, too mean, uninterested or just plain too damn married to bother with. Though in the case of your people, marriage doesn't seem all that important."

Morgana snorted. "Now, there's the pot calling the kettle black. Our people indeed. How many concubines did your father have?"

"Only one," Ena answered sourly. "That was all he could afford. But he kept the house slaves busy. His little by-blows are all over the place."

Morgana chuckled. "A realist. I see you are a realist. Are you in love with my grandson?"

"No!" Ena said. "I stopped loving him when I knew it was a girl. When it's birthed, he won't come back to my bed."

"Yes. Yes, I think he will," Morgana said. "I can tell by the anxious look on his face right now. He can tell by our expressions that this is a spirited exchange."

Ena relaxed a little. "You think he will still have feelings for me?"

"Yes," Morgana said. "And so will I. In fact, if you wanted to sit on a silk velvet cushion, eat wheaten porridge sweetened with honey and butter—for the rest of your days—you could do no better than bring me a great-granddaughter. I have several grandsons, but no granddaughters. And whatever my straying Cai might do, come or go, you have a place in my home forever. And make no mistake. I rule here."

"Then we will get along," Ena said, "so long as you remember she's your great-granddaughter but my child."

Morgana laughed. "Full of yourself, aren't you?"

"Today, yes!" Ena said.

"Found out what you can do, have you?"

"Yes!" Ena said. "I am a vovula."

"That's what your people call us?" Morgana asked.

"Yes. That's how I knew it was a girl. Things have been happening all along the road."

Morgana's hand was still resting on Ena's stomach. It was a large hand and the nails were long, like claws.

"Night before last, I heard a panther scream," Ena said.

Morgana smiled. "Yes. Yes, you did, didn't you?"

Ena felt a chill ripple over her whole body and gooseflesh covered her arms.

"We will speak of these matters later," Morgana said, "not before the assembled company."

Ena's mouth was suddenly dry. Morgana radiated raw power. Whatever her own abilities, this woman must be immeasurably stronger than she was. Ena stepped back and dropped into a curtsey, but Morgana raised her and kissed her on the cheek. Ena made her shaky way back to Cai.

When Uther approached her, Morgana bowed. But he kissed her hand.

Cai made as if to conduct Ena away. "No," Morgana said. "Stay! Bring chairs and set them around the fire pit."

Ena looked up. The hall was filled with long shafts of light from the glass roof. The roof was so high that Ena saw a bird leave the giant oak above and soar down through the doors to the outside. The glass was not clear but tinted a greenish color; and the tint blocked some of the sunlight the way the canopy of a forest would, giving the hall a look like that of a sunlit glade. There were no heads except those carved on the tall rafter posts that soared to the top of the roof near the tree trunk.

Morgana was silent until the hall emptied of servants and hangers-on. Then each member of the party took up a position at the edge of the fire pit.

Uther and Morgana faced each other. Ena was horrified to see Uther was weeping silently, the tears trickling down past his nose to disappear into his mustache and beard. She and Cai faced each other. He smiled at her, and she felt uncomfortable as she always did when he showed her affection as opposed to lust. Lust she expected from a man but not affection. The men in her life, her brothers and father, had not been affectionate; and lust would have been inappropriate, though she saw them direct that at other women, usually women of low rank, ripe to be used and cast aside.

Of Uther, she thought, the loss of his son grieves him. Maybe he loves him. She found this a bit astonishing. Some parents must love their children, but who would believe the stern winter king was troubled by this weakness?

"Compose yourself, my lord," Morgana said.

"The thought of what they might be doing to him troubles me beyond words, Morgana," the king replied.

"Whatever it is," Cai said, "it won't work. No matter what they do, it won't break him. I know. We were constant companions since I was nine and he was seven. He will let them kill him before he will yield to either one of them."

"I'm not sure your sentiments offer much comfort to your king," Morgana said.

"I don't intend to comfort him," Cai answered. "I'm simply stating a fact. If Arthur lives to rule, he will be no one's puppet or surrogate. That's why we have to pry him out of their hands before they come to that realization."

"Ena?" Morgana asked. "Are you ready?"

"For what?" Cai asked, alarmed.

"Be quiet," Ena said. "I've been part of this since the beginning. And if you want the truth, I don't know for what, and I'll wager neither does she."

"Stand close to the coals, Ena," Morgana commanded.

Morgana threw a handful of something into the fire pit. Ena took a deep breath of the smoke. For a second, it blinded her, then she backed away from the smoke and saw visions.

The first was a lioness. As tawny as Morgana, she crouched at the edge of the fire pit, one big paw on the polished floor. Her jaws were crusted with blood, the way Ena had last seen her, and she roared, showing the red-smeared fangs of a killer.

"You sent that!" Ena said accusingly to Morgana.

"No!" Morgana said. "You get only what you call."

"Yes," Ena admitted. "She, the lioness, would be dead by now, too."

The lioness faded, the way a cloud changes its shape at the force of the wind, and became the face of the dead young man she'd offered directions to today. He seemed sad, and Ena wondered what he'd found when he returned home. But when he saw her, he smiled.

"Oh," Ena whispered, because he brought a message. A complex one. She was afraid of men, with good reason, but she need not fear all of them. Cai loved her and somehow always would. But above all, she could trust him, because dishonesty wasn't in him. Not always a good trait but a part of his nature. He kept faith without thinking about it at all. He couldn't imagine not doing so.

Then the face was gone, and the smoke hung between her and the world like a veil. When it cleared, she was at the edge of a forest, and the grass around her was filled with small songbirds, finches and wrens, in all shades of green, gray, and brown. She cried out loudly in surprise at finding herself in some other place. Or was it even she who cried out?

The birds flew, and a second later she was back in Morgana's hall. But she had a name.

"Vareen!" she said.

Uther whispered, "God!"

Morgana looked triumphant.

"Vareen," Uther said, surprised. "But he's long dead. Long dead," he repeated.

"Sometimes with one of them, that's not enough," Cai said.

"What are you talking about?" Ena snapped.

"Vareen was Vortigen's druid," Morgana explained.

"But Vortigen was high king long before our time. He was a criminal. He stole from the church."

Cai, Morgana, and Uther all laughed.

"Is that the Saxon version?" Cai asked.

"That's what I was told," Ena said. She sounded exculpatory. "I'm just a woman. I don't know anything about war and politics."

"You're learning fast," Uther said. Then he continued, "Whatever may be said of Vortigen, he was a good king. And, no, he did not steal from the church. He demanded money from the monastic orders, who have a lot of it. The church is always accusing someone of stealing from it. In any case, Vareen was his druid. All kings have a personal druid, advisers. Mine is Morgana."

"She's a woman," Ena said.

Morgana laughed. "You noticed."

Ena blushed violently.

"Yes. Well, sometimes the gray mare is the better horse," Uther said.

Morgana laughed again. "Such compliments, Uther."

"Vortigen perished along with Vareen due to Merlin's treachery," Cai said. "They were murdered when they tried to make peace with the Saxons. Merlin is a supporter of the southern landowners, who keep them as mercenaries. He felt that the office of high king should be abolished."

"He miscalculated," Morgana added. "He and his followers were nearly wiped out in the resulting backlash. The Picts attacked, bypassing Hadrian's wall. The Veneti refused to man the supply lines of the Saxon troops. The Silures, our people, rose in revolt, and Merlin had to invoke the high kingship to end the war. Uther's father was elected high king, and he and his oath men were able to impose a peace on the kingdom."

"Peace. Hardly a peace," Uther said. "Say, more a truce. We won't kill them if they don't try to kill us."

Ena still didn't understand, but she didn't care to draw another lecture from the parties involved.

"We will need money," Uther said.

"Time for you to rob the church," Morgana said.

Uther looked sour. "I suppose so. I'd rather take their money than impoverish our own hearths."

"Niamh said war, and war it is," Morgana told him.

"What has money to do with war?" Ena asked.

"Everything," the three—Cai, Morgana, and Uther—chorused.

"When you talk war, the first thing you had better worry about is money," Morgana said. "Why the hell do you think those cursed Romans were so successful in their conquests?"

Cai and Ena both looked mystified.

"Because," Uther answered the question, "every Roman soldier had a better sword than most of our aristocrats could afford to buy. The Romans armed their legionnaires well and fed them well. Maybe some of those senatorial politicians were rotten soldiers, but they outlasted us. And in the end, we were driven back to our forests and swamps, into one futile revolt after another. Luckily, we had our forests and swamps here. In the south, in open country, stronghold after stronghold fell, and the people were enslaved. Enslaved by those chiefs clever enough to make common cause with the Romans and become traitors to their own people. In that part of Britannia, you served the Romans or you died.

"Here we managed to maintain some independence. The Romans are gone, but their Saxon troops remain. The archdruid is in the pay of the powerful ruling landowning nobles in the south, and, as always, he serves their ends.

"He wants control of my son," Uther snarled. "There is only one, thanks to my own abstinence. . . ."

Morgana directed an amused look at Uther.

"Well," he continued stubbornly, "if not abstinence, at least intelligent planning. No other eligible candidate for the high kingship. Besides, he has had the summer crown placed on his head."

"I know," Cai said. "Gawain wove it from wheat, barley, rye, and oats. And the warrior assemblies feasted him as he wore it."

"I blessed it myself," Morgana said. She wore a look of exultation. "*She* possessed me . . . that day."

"He is sacred—and cannot be set aside," Uther said. "But can he resist Merlin and Igrane? It always comes back to that. What say you, Cai? Of all of us, you know him best. Can he withstand them?"

The fire roared. Bounding in one jump from gray ash to a roaring blaze.

All four of them cringed from the sudden heat and light. Ena spoke, but not in Ena's voice. Vareen used her mouth and tongue! She answered for Cai. "He would not know how *not* to resist them."

He woke at Tintigal, lying on the floor, looking up at Igrane.

"You stink!" she said.

"So do you, Mother," he replied. "At least I don't smell of corruption and treachery. I can't say the same for you . . . or your lover."

She turned and swept away from him. He was in her apartments. It was day; the sky outside was thick with dark, rolling clouds.

She strode past the divan with its invisible drape and toward her glowing mirror. She postured and preened herself in front of the glass.

"Young as ever, I see," he said as he sat up.

"No thanks to you or that little bitch . . . of yours."

"Mine, Mother? Mine in what way? You brought her here. Don't blame me if you bit off more than you or even your inamorata could chew. You should have left well enough alone."

He was dizzy with both hunger and the shock of transition. But all his memory was intact, which was more than he could say for himself since he had been bitten by *her* serpent.

Igrane was wearing an almost transparent coan silk gown. He could clearly see both her nipples and the dark triangle of her sex through it. He felt the heat in his face and looked away. She was his mother, after all. And then he remembered that the other function of sex is punishment—men use it to humiliate women. And since turnabout is fair play, women often use it to humiliate men.

When he glanced back at her, she smiled at him maliciously. Then stretched herself as luxuriously as a cat, making the best of all her attributes. He wondered what might have happened to him if Uther hadn't violently removed him from her when he was seven years old. He didn't much like to think about it.

His attraction faded, and he felt sick with self-disgust. But then, that was the point, wasn't it? That was what she and her lover wanted—to control him.

She seemed to grasp that he had slipped through her fingers again, because she turned shrewish. "Will you never learn?"

All right. I'll play, he thought. Better shrewish than seductive.

"Learn what, Mother?"

"Learn who is master here," she snapped.

He managed a tolerant smile. "Who might that be, Mother? Odd. I thought I was the summer king." He looked up again, his gaze challenging her.

She spat on him.

He was delighted. He wiped the saliva from his cheek and looked at it. "Nice to know your honest opinion of me."

Smart enough to know her anger was playing into his hands, she dropped the beautiful mask of power down over her face. The angry eyes hooded themselves.

"Go bathe," she commanded in an icy voice, "lest you disgust my women. They are preparing a meal for you."

She pointed to the tub behind its alabaster screen. But before he did, he walked to the mirror on its stand, near the other end of the room. As a child he had heard many tales about mirrors and the things that could be seen in them. He had put such stories down to the fact that they were a foreign luxury and only the very wealthy could afford them. But then Morgana had told him that a people who lived near Rome used them to read the future.

He had laughed. "How?" he'd asked.

"I don't know," she'd said. "It was one of the secrets they never taught the Romans. The women did it. Scrying in a glass, they called it."

"What happened to them?" he had asked.

"The Romans," she said, as if that were explanation enough.

And when he thought about it, he agreed.

But this mirror showed him only his reflection. He was pale and had lost weight. His mother was right. He was dirty, filthy in fact. A week's growth of stubble covered his face. But he found himself reminded of a fine sword in a battered sheath. His body was lean and hard; his fine-drawn features were a mask of resolution and courage. He was a different man already from the young king Merlin and Igrane had placed in their prison. And he wondered what sort of man would emerge if he were able ever to escape their malice.

He stretched out his left hand and touched the glass with his fingertips. A face looked over his shoulder into his eyes. He flinched and recoiled, then glanced quickly at Igrane to see if she had noticed his reaction.

She hadn't and was in conversation with her women near the bath. Just as well. When he looked back at the mirror, the face was gone.

He kept secrets from her reflexively. He turned away from the mirror and went to the bath. Her women tried to accompany him, and he ordered them away in a tone of voice that brooked no disobedience. When they were gone, he stripped and immersed himself in the warm water, leaning back, his neck pressing against the edge of the marble tub.

He was a young man and hadn't had time to trouble himself about sex during her imprisonment. When he sank into the warm water, desire shook him like a fever. He pressed his eyelids tightly together and whispered a curse. Desire was only another weapon, like hunger, loneliness, and cold arrayed against him by his tormentors. He spent the next few moments spending that sexual energy as quickly as he could.

When he opened his eyes, he saw the bird perched on top of the alabaster screen, looking down at him with what seemed to be prurient curiosity. It cocked its head, studied him with one eye, then the other, then both.

"Is that an entertaining sight, bird? One of the struggles of a desperate man?"

To his great surprise, the bird said, "No!"

No, a corner of his rational mind told him. *Birds don't talk.* But this bird was a raven and might be an escaped pet.

With a flip of his wings, the raven flew down and began to circle the curious set of inlays around the pool. It strutted along with a rather pompous air, until it reached the yew, then pecked at it.

It looked at him, one eye, then the other eye, then both, and said, "Arthur."

He started upright in the water. The bird took wing.

He remembered the yew—today? It seemed a thousand years ago. And the face in the mirror behind him.

He had decided his mind was playing tricks on him. Pressure, starvation, fear. Now he concluded that he might be wrong.

He despised magic and most of its practitioners, Morgana being the one exception, and he had never felt drawn to the art. His mind strayed back to his youth, when he had feared the things Igrane and Merlin could do to him, like death. His face grew hot with remembered rage, rage at his own abasement and shame at his powerlessness, and knew this situation was a repeat of the first.

He had thought then that they derived pleasure from his sufferings. Now he knew they did. And further, they despised as weak those who were not skilled in their deadly art.

But maybe, maybe they had overreached themselves this time.

He sat in the water and clenched his fists until his ragged nails made his palms bleed. Then he deliberately made himself relax and began to wash his hair, skin, beard, everything. A few moments later, one of Igrane's women brought him fresh clothing. He didn't don it, with the exception of the shirt. He put his riding pants and boots back on, tearing the hem from the shirt to restore the cross gartering on his leggings. Nor would he let them trim his hair and shave the stubble on his face.

"You're hardly what I would call presentable," Igrane said as he left the shelter of the walled bath. "And you still stink." She turned away and, almost too late, he felt the presence behind him. The shaft of pain was simply blinding, the sort of pain a man feels when he bites down and feels a tooth break, then air hits an exposed nerve.

"Piss yourself, you little shit," Merlin said.

And Arthur remembered when he was a child, he had done so on command.

"Piss yourself, and I'll let you go."

He never afterward knew how he did it. Never! He was on his knees, next to the wizard's legs, but he was no longer a helpless seven-year-old. He spun around, still on his knees, and drove his left fist into the man's groin as hard as he could.

Merlin screamed. Igrane screamed. He saw the merciless rage in her face and the savage gesture her right hand made as she flung the darkness at his face.

He was blind.

But even if he couldn't make them kill him, maybe he could do it himself. Blindness would break him, but he would never let them win.

He scrambled to his feet and bolted for the spot where he remembered the rail to be. If he flung himself over, the drop to the next level of the fortress might be enough to kill him.

The rail caught him in the midsection. He used both hands to vault into a somersault over it.

Break my neck, was his last thought. *Please! Please! Let me break my neck.*

The worst of it was that I was running out of beach. I was very close to the cove where I spent my first night on land. Beyond it, the shore turned rocky. But that didn't matter. I had to keep on running.

When I reached the rocky barrier that ended the beach, I plunged into the surf. I managed to glance back.

The thing was slowing or having trouble running in the sand. Slowing, I thought. The arrows and the fire had wounded it deeply. The belly was streaked with blood, and charred areas on its shoulders and long, clawed arms testified that the wall of flame left behind in the mass of driftwood had taken its toll. I began to think I stood a pretty good chance of surviving.

Then I was in the sea and what I saw ahead of me along the shore made my heart sink again. I had hoped to swim around the rock, dog-paddling in the surf. But within seconds, I found myself in water so deep I had to swim for my life. Then I was caught in a riptide and sucked down.

For a second I panicked and fought the suction. Then I knew from Kyra and Maeniel's teachings that was the surest way to death in the water. Try to ride it, and the movement of the waves will bring you onshore again. You hope. Then again, maybe not. But fear will kill you more quickly than suffocation.

I held my breath and, sure enough, I bobbed up like a cork as the current weakened in deeper water. God, to breathe. Air. You don't know what it means until you cannot take a breath.

I coughed, and the salt water stung my eyes. They teared, and my vision cleared.

I had lost ground, and the thing was closing the gap between us. Beyond the low headland I had just rounded, the beach was gone and only a rocky shelf stretched between land and water. It was hammered by the waves, overgrown with barnacles and sea moss, a hell of a dangerous thing to run on. I had no choice, for the currents were trying to sweep me back toward the cove and the sandy beach where the thing could intercept me as I tried to get ashore.

I threw all my strength into swimming for the rocks and found my fatigue had become a factor. Even as I struggled to get ashore amid the breaking seas, I could feel my strength ebbing. But I experienced one piece of good fortune in that the rocks extended out farther than the sand spits did, and I found myself able to run, not swim, a lot more quickly than I thought I would be able to. I also blessed Talorcan, because his gift of shoes kept my feet from being cut to ribbons by the barnacles on the rocks.

I looked back and saw that the monster had taken to the water, and it was coming around the headland toward me. It was a wonderful swimmer. It moved through the water with the undulating stroke of a snake crossing sand, in a series of broad S-curves. The tide was coming in, I knew, and unless I could find high ground, the water would sweep me away and the thing would get me.

There is a moment in every struggle when defeat looms. I was tired, and I had begun to feel pain. My body was covered with cuts and bruises. My shirt hung in shreds from my arms and shoulders, and the lower part of my pants were torn away. The salt water stung every raw spot on my body and every wave that broke over me felt like the cut of a whip.

But I had regained my footing on the rocky shore, and I was able to speed across the flat stone table at a run. It was a strange place, and I could feel its power as I made my way across the surface. The thousands of years the sea had lashed it had worn channels in the stone surface. The breaking waves filled and emptied them with a force that could knock the feet from under you as you crossed them and sometimes sent me rolling, battered by the sea and the projections of the granite that I was flung across.

The stone was gray, silver in the light, old silver, harsh, tarnished by time and abuse. The waves were a continuous thunder and sometimes a deafening roar as the surf filled potholes from above and below and sent water geysering up into towering plumes, which crashed into roaring waves that threatened to wash me back into the monster's maw. Each immersion ended in pain, as my torn flesh was bathed by the sea.

I looked back again and saw the thing had landed, climbed up from the water, and now stood on the same broad stone I did, the gigantic ledge that projected out from the coast. I didn't know how much longer I could last. But I was heartened by the fact that the monster was flagging, also. Washed by the waves, I could see how much I had hurt him. His wounds, both those areas of skin scorched by the fire and the arrow wounds in his midsection, were still running blood. At the one near his groin, the flow pulsed with each beat of his heart. His mouth was open, spade-shaped tongue visible, as he panted. We were not far apart, and had he been as strong as he was at first, one rush and he would have had me.

302

But he hesitated, I think to get his breath after his struggle with the sea. Then he lifted one powerful, three-clawed foot and came at me.

God, he was fast.

I spun around and bolted. I found I'd left the sea behind and was running across a broken, pitted but level surface toward the face of a cliff I could see ahead.

Fear is a wonderful thing; so is youth. I flew along, but I knew it could not last. I was exhausted; the stitch in my side was agony. My lungs were burning. I could hear the steady slap of the three-clawed foot on the wet stone behind me.

And then we both ran out of running room. I flew over the edge and into the sea again. I went under. The currents took me at once. The level stone I had been running on looked oddly like the top of a sea wall.

Yes, we build them, or at least the Romans did—though no doubt my people did the heavy lifting. But this was a bigger sea wall than even the Romans could have created. Yet at last the sea breached it and cut a pass through the ruined stone bulwarks to the remnants of something almost unimaginable. At first I thought it a gigantic cave. And indeed it must once have been domed, much as those Roman buildings Maeniel and Dugald told me about. I would not have believed them either, had they not vouched for each other.

But this domed opening was larger than anything the Romans ever dreamed of. It stretched from sea level to the top of the cliffs, a vast, broken arch that ended where the fallen roof made a hole at the top.

Light swept it and seemed to propagate inside along the curving walls, flashing in a wave along them. This light was gray and blue, a mirrored shimmer that reflected the colors of the sea.

The current had me. I didn't need to be told not to fight it. I no longer had the strength to do anything; and so it swept me into the broken bowl, because that's what it looked like—a vast egg with a broken shell. The sun came out just then and shone between the clouds, and it was as though someone had struck the strings of a harp that sang in light and color, not sound.

The glow swept over the shattered walls like a moving rainbow. The dominant colors now were yellow-gold and glitter-white, glitter like the sparkle of uncounted stars or the winter sun on a frozen wood. Then as quickly as the brightness came, it faded. The sun went behind a cloud and a dreaming glow of a thousand blues, purples, amethysts, violets, and even dark reds flowed over the walls and vanished into uncounted shades of silver, and then a storm cloud's mixture of gray and white.

I knew I had picked an uncommon place to die. Because die I would. The thing had outlasted me and entered the swirling water that formed a pool under that magical dome. True, I had the fairy armor my father had given me. Yes, and a tortoise has its shell. But when an eagle catches one up in his talons and lets it fall to the stony earth, the eagle dines. The tortoise takes longer to die than a rat or rabbit in the bird's talons, but I doubt if the tortoise is glad of the fact. I would die hard, but in the end, the fangs would prevail and the monster's raw strength would wrench me limb from limb.

The current swept me around the vast chamber, but once it flooded through the channel it had cut from the sea, it became a gentle swirl, the kind you get in your porridge in the morning as you cool it with a spoon. The light was unaffected by the water. It propagated all along the walls, whether open to the air or submerged. I thought about Treise, for I was minded to breathe water rather than let the monster rend me. But no, I would not do that. Maybe I could finish my work in spite of death. My hand still contained fire. I would punish it even as it destroyed me.

It was close. I could see the yellow eyes, slit pupils, in the burgeoning light from the rainbow temple as its beauty swept along the walls around me. Then something blotted out the light from below. My mind was fuzzy and I was unable to comprehend what could dim such radiance.

The dragon surfaced under the thing. The orca dragon exploded from the ocean like a broaching whale, with the horror clenched in its jaws the way a hunting cat takes a careless mouse. The monster screamed, but the dragon had it across the body, fangs buried in its midsection.

The thing screamed again, the sound echoing under the high splendor of the arching roof. The sun struck again down. The horror was limp in the dragon's jaws, blood a scarlet flood down its white chest, dripping from the fangs. The light was a blinding whirl—yellow, red, dashed with sheet gold, then green and blue as another cloud drifted over the sun.

The thing went limp. A toss of the dragon's head threw it back to the rocks, where it lay at the edge of the pool, a torn, red ruin. The dragon ducked his head to wash away blood and bits of flesh, then swam toward me. Swam under my limp body and surfaced with me on his back. Just as well he did. I clung to the row of spines on each side of his neck and gave way to total exhaustion as he scolded me all the way back to land.

"I've been tracking you all along the coast. I kept hoping you would see me and lead the hideous thing into deep water. But no. You were so intent on putting distance between yourself and that horror that I could never get you to listen to my calls. I nearly got him when he swam around the headland, but the tide wasn't fully in and . . . what!"

That wasn't what he said, but it's the best approximation I can make in my human language.

It seemed as though a shadow passed over the shell of light around us, and the broken creature lying on the stone shifted and changed, becoming something smaller and much less menacing. A little brown man.

But as the dragon drew closer, I saw that all that remained of the murderous terror that had haunted the holy well could not be human either. The brown I saw was a pelt, light and soft at the top but more furry than any human ever is. Where the fur extended below the waist, it was long and thick, protectively covering the legs and genitals. The feet were hard, clawed as the monster's had been, but with more digits. They seemed molded together and had a thick, horny covering like a hoof.

But it was the monster, wounded in the belly by my arrows, charred by the fire, and torn by the dragon's fangs. It lay in a pool of blood.

"A faun," the dragon whispered sadly. "A faun. I had not known any still lived. And I have killed it."

"No," I said. "This thing needed killing. Don't reproach yourself, my friend."

How did a faun, the gentlest of creatures, become the terrible monster I saw? What gave it the skin of the fish eaters that once hunted along these shores? I had not heard that fauns could change shape.

The dragon's murmurs must have awakened consciousness in the dying creature, because it opened its eyes and looked at me. They were soft and brown, the eyes of a deer or some other shy, wild creature like a hare or squirrel.

The dragon had come to the stone edge of the pool. I stood and climbed off its back and approached my fallen adversary.

Yes, it was certainly dying. Too weak to move, it studied me in an almost gentle silence. Just above its forehead, I saw the two horn buds. They just cleared its rather spiky hair. Even though dying, it managed to recoil when I stretched out my hand toward one.

The light around me sang in silver, but it seemed to darken for a second, and I heard a sound as though the blow of an enormous clapper struck the side of a great bell. Suddenly I stood where I had last seen Mother, in the dark forest near the waterfall that glowed in its own light and emptied into a pool of stars at its base. In the intervening years, I had forgotten how beautiful the place was—the cool, peaceful presence of the giant pines around us, the only sound the deep-throated sigh of the wind among them and the trickling of the brook formed by the overflow of the basin beside me.

The faun stood in front of me. I could see him clearly in the light borne by the water into the basin and in the occasional flashes of illumination when the wind took the column of falling water, spreading it into a curtain of glowing lace.

"I didn't know," I said.

"Of course," he answered. "She didn't tell you. Would it have made any difference?"

"No," I answered. "Probably not." But I could feel the tears on my cheeks.

"Don't cry," he whispered softly and stretched out one hairy hand toward my face. "Think! It almost went the other way."

"Yes." And I wiped away my tears.

Above, the wind brushed the pale column of water, spraying me with a mist. As Maeniel had told me, the whisper of its touch healed my hurts. It also made the fairy armor shimmer with a slight glow.

I was clothed in it. It spiraled around my bare breasts, covered my arms in the meander's coils and delicate vining traceries of the holy and everlasting union of not simply all life but a universe into which life is woven, one thread among the rest, many and one forever. A mystery my people comprehended and left its paths in their being once, now, and forevermore.

I saw those pathways echoed in the casings of the tiny horns, and I comprehended they were not for defense but sensory organs, allowing us to speak to each other. To bridge the chasm placed between us by time, language, and breeding.

"I'm glad it's over," he said. "I have missed myself, my soul so."

"Your soul?" I asked.

"Yes. You see, that is the one thing you must never barter away. I did, and have regretted it bitterly ever since. I have not had speech with a flower or a butterfly or a star an age agone. But I was jealous and angry that such as *she*"—and I knew of whom he spoke—"had life eternal while we lesser mortal creatures die."

I understood his sorrow, and, in the course of time, I was sure I would know more.

He continued, "So I bartered away what I was—that is what your soul is—for power and immortality. And I became the creature you saw. You freed me from an eternity of regret. An eternity of sorrow."

"How will I know if someone demands my soul?" I asked.

"You will know," he said as he turned toward the fountain.

Then he went to one knee beside it and scooped up the water in one big, furry hand. "She will tell you what to do," he said. "I may tarry no longer."

"Wait!" I said. But he was already drinking. And a second later, I stood before her, back in the world I had left in the splendor of the light.

She had a double-edged, bronze ax in her hand. She looked down into the sad, brown eyes of the faun.

"My son," she whispered in tones of deepest grief. "My son. My son." Then she pressed the double ax into my hand.

"Take his head before he dies," she commanded.

"No!"

"Fool!" she snapped. "This is not the time to falter. Would you have him be lost? Do you hate him so much?"

I looked down and met my adversary's gaze.

"She is ever wise," the dragon said. "Do it."

I swung the ax. Its edge rang against the stone.

She helped me wrap the head in white linen. Then we put it in a sack.

"I will need to know his name to command him," I said.

"You will not need to command him," she said. "And when you awaken him, he will tell you his name. After he has served you for a time, let him go. Give him his freedom. Then be his transgressions forgotten, and he may forget his suffering, have life again, and use it to do good."

The tide was at the flood, and the sun was resting among the clouds. The half dome was showing me the beauties of gray, white, and, at times when the sun peered through, a golden haze. I cannot describe how wild, strange, and beautiful the place was at the end of the long platform of rock, looking out over the ocean. Where could the time have gone? Had I struggled so long with the monster? It seemed late afternoon.

I shivered and realized I was naked. The last struggle and my transition to the antechamber of death had torn away the last few rags from my body. Only the wild swirls of the green armor clothed me, yet I was modest in a sense, for it covered my sex and breast tips. I had fastened my hair up to keep it out of my way. But the braids had long come undone and, except for the two warrior braids that descended from a part just above my forehead and hung down on either side of my face, my hair floated free down my back.

Kyra taught me how to prepare it when on the hunt. She said the fighting women among her people always wore it thus, to be sure that even when taken by surprise or awakened abruptly from sleep, it wouldn't get in their faces. I had, you see, after the manner of her people, never cut it. Uncut hair proclaimed my virgin status. A man who interfered with me without my consent would face a dreadful curse. And even my husband might not be so bold as to take my maidenhead. Sometimes a virgin girl was first offered to a powerful lord or a chief, so that any ill luck would be turned aside from her husband. Kyra told me that such a rite was uncommon, but in my case, I would certainly frighten my future in-laws and I needed to be prepared to make the best of things if such a proposal was made as part of the marriage contract. To endure the rite with dignity.

I had thought men being what they are, jealous as rutting stags or bulls, that such magic would be highly unlikely, but now . . . .

Given the characteristics of my armor—I touched my belly and the complex curves and meanders leaped out and hardened—how would I ever be able to make love to anyone? Would I, like Gydden's daughters, need to be forced the first time?

Then I looked down and saw the blood running down my legs. I was puzzled. How had I hurt myself there of all places?

I frowned, then looked up at her.

"You are now a woman," she said. "I put my hand on you when you cut off the faun's head."

I surprised myself by beginning to cry. It had been a long, hard day.

Then a soft haze, wearing the colors of sunset, surrounded her and me. Someone, again I did not see who, gave her clothing—my old tunic and pants, now repaired, and another outfit, a white tunic and leggings. Then she showed me, as Kyra would have, how to wash and pad myself so that the womanly purification would be neat, and told me that I must wash myself and how often during my courses.

I was still trembling and weeping. "The daughters of Gydden," I said. "The choosers of the slain. I don't . . . I won't. . . ."

"No," she said. "You need not fear that rite, but only one man is your true destiny. You are horribly dangerous to all others—avoid them."

"I think I know who . . ." I began.

"Yes. He is already known to you," she said. Then she touched my forehead with all five fingers.

I felt her arm around me as I went limp. Even now, I cannot say what happened. A wave went through me.

"What was that?" I said as I regained my senses.

"The reward of your labors," she said. "When you need it, you will know it."

"What is this place?" I asked.

Beyond the rocky shelf, the sun was sinking close to the water. The haze around us had faded once I was clothed, but the colors danced and sang in the walls.

The dragon drifted in the pool under the dome of light. He was fishing. His black and white was reflected in the walls, an unending dialogue between the permanent and the ephemeral, being and potential met as one.

"Oh," I said. "I see."

"No. No, you don't. But you come as close to grasping the concept that ruled its makers as any I have ever known," she said.

"What was the faun?" I asked.

The dragon lifted his head from the water. He answered me. "The world you live in is cruel. Once it was—" he glanced at her "—less cruel. We tied the sea creatures together. He and his kind ruled the forests. They could speak the language of . . . bees tumbling among the flowers. The flowers themselves as their poignant solitude was fulfilled told him of their enrichment. Ferns spoke of their explorations among damp leaf mold. Even the spreading fungi constructing their webs through soil and damp, dissolving wood, spoke to him of the world's endless cycles of renewal. He could follow the butterfly's anxious search for the proper plant host for her young and understand the ecstasy of the crawling leaf eater's epiphany as she wore her wings in the sun. He had all of those things and bartered them for . . ."

The dragon paused. "I cannot think what," he said sadly.

"He is still my son," she said. "Be kind to him," she cautioned me. "And one day, set him free."

The dragon paddled close to shore. A beautiful golden haze began to rise from the water. I climbed to the dragon's back.

"Treise," I said.

"Treise will be fine. In fact, had you shown fear and let the creature eat her, you would have vanished immediately. She is an important ancestress of yours."

The haze was thick as fog now, hiding the domed room, the sea, and even the water.

"Take her home!" she commanded.

And the dragon obeyed.

CHAPTER SIXTEEN

E WOKE LOOKING AT THE FIRE. HIS EYES BURNED
and he knew he was not blind. His face was wet. He ran
his tongue over his lips and tasted wine. That's where
the illusion of blindness came from. Igrane had thrown wine in his face
when he savaged her lover's groin.

He blinked and sat up, still shaking with reaction and some fear. The
fire was warm and bright. All he could think, though, was, *How can I keep
from letting them get me again?*

But then, there had been that face looking at him from the mirror.
And the fire—someone must have tended it while he was absent. Left to
itself, it would have gone out.

He sat with his head bowed, simply letting the warmth soak into his
body. Then at length, he asked the silence, "Am I alone here? If I should
happen not to be, who are you?"

He didn't really expect an answer, but he got one in the form of a
sigh. A little like the wind, he thought, but there was no wind. Only the
tall, black outlines of the trees against a sky pearled with moonlight.

She rode high above the horizon, the full moon, on a sea of low clouds hovering over the distant mountains, a luminous vessel, adrift on phantom waves. The air was still. A voice followed the sigh; it was faint and every word articulated carefully, as though the speaker had limits set on his ability to communicate.

"At last. I was beginning to think I would never be able to persuade you to take the hints we kept dropping."

"The bird," Arthur said, "and your face in the mirror."

A woman's laugh trilled from the shadows. "I sent the bird."

Her voice was as faint and cool as the whisper of a breeze over a water meadow on a hot day. "You are in the yew."

"Yes," she whispered, "and he is in the birch."

"This is?" he asked.

"The summer country," was the answer. The man's voice spoke.

"The land belongs to King Bademagus," Arthur finished the sentence for him. "Morgana taught me well. But what took you so long?"

"We take our energy from you," was the answer in the woman's voice. "We feared to drain your strength."

"I must escape this place," Arthur said.

"And do so quickly, before Merlin can lay hands on you again," the woman's voice said.

"I would rather die than let that happen," Arthur said.

"That may be the choice," the man's voice supplied.

"Then I will take it," Arthur said, rising to his feet.

"Don't be in such a hurry," the woman said. "You have a little time." She laughed, a strange sound in the shadows around the fire. "Your adversary is still in a lot of pain."

"I certainly hope so," Arthur said.

"Yes, you have gotten a little revenge. Below the yew, the deepest roots claw their way into a fissure in the rocks. It forms a chimney. It doesn't run all the way to the ground, but it terminates at the top of a rock slide that will provide you with a slope of sorts until you reach the floor of the valley."

"I don't like it," the man's voice said. "It is a terrible risk."

"What? Will you wait? Until they drive him mad?"

"I don't know about him, but I won't," Arthur said. "A few weeks of their sport and I'll be a drooling, whimpering wreck."

"I think not," the man's voice said. "They have not got as much power over you as even they believe they have. You bore their torments as a child."

"Yes, and they have poisoned my life."

"See?" the woman's voice whispered. "I told you. We must get him out of this cage."

"Is this then a cage?"

"The cage of bones," the man said, "and escape from this part of it won't set you free. Not completely. But he will not find it as easy to seize hold of you when he wants you."

"Good enough," Arthur said. He slung the bow over his shoulder. "I want to keep it. Show me the way."

"Leave the fire burning," she whispered. "He will search near it first. You have nearly mastered this prison. You came here with nothing, and now have fire, food, and a vision of the eldest Flower Bride."

Arthur's breath caught in his throat thinking of her. "I had not known," he said.

"Had not known what?" the man's voice asked.

"That anything could be so beautiful," was his reply. "Is she really the eldest?"

"Yes. She came into being long ago in a colder, wetter time, when forests ruled the world. A forest such as man has never known. This place pens her, also. Defeat the monster, the thing that haunts this cage, and you may lie in her arms. It is her jailer."

"He is yet some years from that," the woman's voice broke in, sounding ruthlessly practical. "And he will not learn the skills he needs here."

"He may die," the man warned.

"Yes," Arthur said. "I may, but that is always a risk." He was kicking away anything near the fire that might spread the flame. "I'll leave it burning, though it goes against my instincts, woodsman that I am. Now, lead on."

A short time later, they reached the edge of the plateau. He stood looking down into the valley. The moon was bright, and when he climbed out on the branches of the tree, he could look down and see the black void where the fissure in the rock formed the chimney leading down to the valley.

He lay on his stomach on the rough-barked branch and closed his eyes.

"He will fall," the male voice complained.

"He will not." The woman spoke with as much certainty as the man had.

"Let us not debate the issue," Arthur said. "One way or another, I will get down, won't I?"

"I'm pleased that you find your plight a source of amusement," the man's voice said.

"Take your chance. You will not get a better," the woman said. "The moon is full, the sky is free of clouds. There is but little wind. The air is warm. Even here in the summer country, the winter brings chill and buckets of rain."

"I thank you, my lady," Arthur said. "I need no further encouragement."

"But—" the man's voice began.

"No!" Arthur cut him off. "Some things don't repay too much thought."

With that, he swung down and, clinging to the stubby branches near the tree trunk, he dropped toward the mass of twisted roots struggling into the fissure.

At first he found the going was easy. In some places the rock fissure sloped down without being too steep. It was also fairly deep, and he could work his way along, feet on one side, back against the other. Plant life had colonized the fractured stone, and the small trees, ferns, and clumps of moss offered convenient handholds as he climbed, moving from ledge to ledge inside the crack.

But about halfway down, the character of the stone changed. It became darker, harder, and more weathered; and therefore, more slippery than the jagged sedimentary rock above. The farther down he got, the worse it got. He began to feel blood on his fingers as the skin on them wore away against the silicates in the granite. Then, about two-thirds of the way down, the fissure, which had been becoming more and more shallow, played out. He lay, held by only two shallow handholds and the pressure of his knees against the stone on a bulge of bare rock—over the catastrophically shattered mass of stone on the valley floor.

He paused, hands bleeding, sobbing for breath, staring down at what he was sure would be his death.

"Shush." He heard Vareen's companion's voice. "Shush. Rest. Rest. Then work your way to one side. The rock slide shattered the stone into a series of narrow ledges. They will support you as you climb the rest of the way down.

"I must tell you what Vareen did not." The words were a whisper, soft as the breeze, the dawn wind just beginning to blow. "You are magic. No, you cannot do magic, as Igrane or Merlin or even your sky-eyed queen-to-be can. But you *are* magic."

"I've always hated them," he whispered. "Always hated them."

"I know. But that's why they tortured you and want to control you. Because of the magic in your being. It was your magic that drew the Flower Bride."

He began to laugh. He could feel his stomach muscles quiver against the stone. "Women and directions," he said. "To my right or to my left, these ledges?"

"Umm . . . the ones on the left are closer. The ones on the right might be better, because you're stronger on that side."

Arthur sighed and chose the right. A few minutes later, he was feeling for a ledge lower down. He found an extraordinarily flat and strong one. It took him a few minutes to turn his head carefully and check, but when he did, he realized it wasn't a ledge. He was on the ground.

He had barely strength enough to stagger away from the cliff into the fan-shaped rock pile that led into the valley. It wasn't as hard going as he thought it might be. The boulders of the rock slide were a lot bigger than they had looked from the top, and he could walk among them without difficulty.

He knew they must have fallen from the cliff, where the orange-red rocks formed the floor of the plateau. The blocks were square and almost regular enough to have been shaped by human hands. And he remembered the sense of seeing writing carved into the wall near the spring where he had seen the Flower Bride. Whatever their origin, their regular, smooth shapes made it comfortable to sit on one and rest his back against another. It was rather like sitting on a flight of giant steps—broad, spreading steps, like those in front of the basilica he had seen in London, now given over to Christian worship. Or the fallen part of a very big wall.

Various sensations warred in his body and mind. Fear—Igrane and Merlin were bound to pursue him. Exhaustion—he had had an arduous twenty-four hours, and the days before that had drained him of strength. Cold—the sweat on his body was drying in the cool air, and he was shivering with the chill. Somewhere deep in his mind, he knew that he should be hungry and thirsty, but he had passed beyond those sensations.

"I will rest," he said to himself, "just for a few minutes, and then push on."

She came in the dawn's first hush. He awakened just long enough to know she was present, his Flower Bride. He saw the waters in her eyes, rivers rushing over floodplains. The forest was her voice. The ancient, immortal, complex forest, that lives as much in the disintegration of its components as in the lives of trees or in the sun-kissed canopy above.

She was the wind of a winter midnight or the coating of frost on an autumn morning, cleansing the trees of the summer's last leaves.

The Flower Bride. For what is a flower but life's expressed passion for itself. Sudden and brief, but certain and eternal at the same time.

She embraced him and brought him closer to the knowledge of what it must be like to be loved by one of them. His troubled, angry yet courageous spirit stumbled and cried out in pain and rebellion. But her soft lips were on his and her kiss . . . was the kiss of peace.

When he woke, the sun was at its zenith. He had slept away the morning, but he was at peace and felt certain of his destiny. He knew he was dreadfully weak, and if he didn't find food and shelter soon, he would die. But his sense of freedom was so joyous that in spite of all his aches and weariness, he was filled with a dear, bright happiness.

Why? he wondered. Am I going mad? But no, it was simply so joyous to be free and alive.

He hurried down the stepped blocks until he reached the bottom. He wouldn't let himself think about Merlin and Igrane. He didn't want anything to disturb the peace he had achieved in his dreams.

At the foot of the tumbled stone blocks, he found a pool of rainwater in something that almost seemed a broken rock basin. The rock was basalt, and it looked as though it had been cooked in unimaginable fires. But the shape was such that he was sure it must have been worked by human hands.

The water was clear, but a little silt had settled and coated the bottom of the bowl. He drank deep. The water was clean and sweet, but his fingers stirred the silt and he saw the symbols worked in gold at its center.

He reached in and tried to explore it with his fingers. A second later, he stood in the presence of Merlin and Igrane. They were standing together in her apartments beside the pool where he had bathed the night before.

Igrane looked at him and screamed. Merlin's eyes widened in shock and, surprisingly to Arthur, terror.

Arthur jerked his hand out of the water and fell back on the ground next to the basin and the rocks, his vision of the pair gone. But he scrambled to his feet and ran as fast as he could into the forest.

After about a hundred yards, he was forced to slow down by his own weakness and a painful stitch in his side. He dropped to a walk. After a time, he began to wonder if he had only imagined what he saw.

The woods around him were silent except for the normal sounds of wind, birdsong, and insects. Nothing pursued him. As before, the sense of peace he had found in his dream returned, filling him the way water does an empty cup.

The woodland was open pines, some of them giants, mixed with hardwoods—oak, ash, maple—and in the low places, poplar and willow. He kept to the trees because the clearings were thick with wildflowers— white and red daisies, blue ironweed, and goldenrod were rampant among blackberry vines covered with white flowers and thorns. Here and there crab apple, wild plum, medlar, and gooseberry formed almost impenetrable thickets.

A rich place, this, he thought. Then he came to an ancient linden. It had definitely been coppiced.

Someone lives around hereabouts, he thought. And sure enough, a few yards farther on, he came to a winding road.

It was little but a wagon trace, two ruts in the grass. He followed it to the edge of the forest. He smelled woodsmoke before he saw the house.

He paused at the last tree to take in his surroundings. He liked what he saw. The house stood on a small knoll in the center of the clearing. It wasn't round, as his people's were, but crescent-shaped. The building surrounded a courtyard that was open on one side. The shed, with a milk cow chewing her cud, was on one side of the house. Near the forest, a barn stood in the shadow of the trees.

A fenced garden a dozen yards beyond the house was on high ground overlooking the river and a water meadow where two draft horses grazed. Beyond the house was a field, thick with the mixture of wheat, barley, and oats his people commonly grew. It was hard to tell what cereal predominated here, but on casual inspection, it appeared to be wheat. That meant cool nights, warm-to-hot days, and probably, from the look of the burgeoning root crops in the kitchen garden—they were ready for harvest—rather mild winters.

If the winter included long stretches of freezing cold and a lot of snow, the abundance of the kitchen garden wouldn't have been possible this early in the year. The wheat crop in the field was still very green and as yet no higher than his calves.

Chickens pecked in the courtyard. Beyond the water meadow, he saw plenty of ducks and geese feeding along the edge of the river.

Guinea hens near the back door of the house set up a prodigious cackling as he stepped out of the woods and began to walk toward the house.

She greeted him at the back door with a pike in her hand and no friendliness in her eyes. The pike looked home-forged, a savage, hooked blade sharpened on both sides, the metal dark with age and pitted with rust. But the edges had recently seen the attentions of a file, and they were bright and razor-sharp.

But he was more disturbed by the mastiff she held back with the other hand. A big-jawed, heavy-shouldered fighter of a dog that snarled and strained against her grip, trying to get to him.

"Go!" she spat. "Get off our land or I'll set the dog on you."

Arthur backed up. Then went to one knee. "Mistress," he said. "Please. I'm starving."

"No!" She was clearly very frightened and unsteady. She backed up, pulling dog and pike with her, and kicked the door shut.

He rose to his feet and staggered away. When he and Cai hunted, they often stopped with the people who lived on the land. They were always hospitable.

But then he considered that he must look like hell, like a brigand in fact. His clothing had suffered from his time in the forest, and the climb down the cliff left him battered, covered with bruises, scrapes, and cuts. His fingers were raw, nails worn to the quick. His face was covered with what must now be over a week's growth of beard. And he had not lied. He was quite literally starving.

Near the house, a log lay under a tree and a stump near it was smoothed off to form a rude table. He collapsed on the log to consider what to do now.

He didn't know he had fainted until he awakened in the grass with her looking down at him. When she saw he was conscious, she backed away very quickly.

"I didn't know," she said, "that . . . things had gone so hard for you. Forgive me. I would never refuse food to a starving man. I thought. . . . I was afraid. . . . I . . . please eat and go! We have troubles of our own here."

He saw a cloth-covered dish resting on the stump, and next to it, three loaves of the small, flat breads baked on a griddle by country people. When he sat up, she hurried away toward the door. The dog was chained near it, and the pike leaned against the wall beside the door frame. She took both dog and pike into the house with her, and he heard the bar fall inside.

He fell on the food. Until he was half finished, he didn't realize what he was eating, and then he wasn't sure. Chicken? Pork? But it didn't matter; he was ready to eat anything he could get his hands on. He did notice that the stew was mostly vegetables—onions, leeks, cabbage, turnips, carrots— all things that could be collected quickly in her garden. The bread did have butter on it, and he was grateful for that.

He found he had to slow himself down to be sure he didn't upset his stomach with the unaccustomed bounty of a full meal. When he finished, he leaned back against the log. He dozed for a time, and when he woke, he found he felt human again for the first time since the beginning of his ordeal.

He studied the farm. She was alone. He was almost sure of that. And it was possible she was running out of food. Also, the woodpile was almost empty.

He found an ax hanging on the wall of the house next to its file. He sharpened the ax and spent two hours replenishing the wood supply. The chores on such a place as this were no mystery to him. He and Cai had been sternly taught that the open-handed generosity of the poor was not to be trifled with. If they could not repay with the game they brought in, they must make some other offering, and most often this involved work of some kind.

Noble or not, at Morgana's stronghold everyone worked, and he was never spared his share of the chores. Besides, there was in his nature a strong tendency toward the keeping of order. When he saw that something needed to be done, he felt gratified by being able to do it. Sometimes when that was the only reward he got, the satisfaction of a job well done was enough for him.

These chores were lined up before him, beckoning, and he attacked them with a will. After he felt the woodpile was sufficiently full, he went to the stable and cleared the stalls of the two draft horses and dumped the manure in the compost pit near the forest. He filled the stall floors with sweet, clean hay and the mangers with feed.

Not the best, he thought. *Spelt, but better than ordinary hay or the grass from the water meadow.*

He was worried about catching the horses, but they greeted him with cries of joy. It was plain they were used to human tending. When he got them on dry ground, he checked their hooves for damage from having been on the damp ground so long. They were not massive draft horses that he'd sometimes seen shown off by prosperous farmers but simply square, sturdy cobs. Their coats were a mass of tangles, manes and tails snaked and knotted with weeds and burrs.

He spent a rewarding two hours grooming them and trimming hooves. When he came out of the barn, there was another bowl of food and more bread on the stump, this time clearly a chicken stew. Again he ate ravenously.

He went to the house and stood by the wall. It was stone, he noticed with some surprise, worked cobbles held together with mortar. There were few windows, and they were high up, just under the eaves.

"I'm going to the river to bathe," he said, "and I will return and sleep in the barn. I am feeling better now, and I am very grateful for the food and shelter. But I will leave tomorrow, if you wish."

There was no reply. The only sound he heard was the brief wailing of a child that stopped abruptly, as though it had been put to the breast.

When he returned, he found some bread and cheese on the stump. He sat and ate it quietly, watching the sunset, the river painted gold in the fading light.

He was a king on exile but still a king. Yet he knew he wouldn't have minded if he had been born a humble man and had the privilege of settling in a place like this. To know this was his land and sit quietly, as he was now, overlooking the house, fields, and pastures. If they were his own, it would have given him abiding pleasure.

He watched as the light slowly changed from yellow to rose to gold, and at last into purple and blue. The stars flung their pathway across the sky.

He remembered walking into the barn but never remembered crawling into the hay. He was so weary that he slept this night without dreams, in absolute peace. Or at least in a peace as absolute as he had ever known.

He woke before first light. When he and Cai spent time with people on the land, most families were up and stirring at their chores before the sun crossed the horizon.

He dropped down easily from the loft. The horses were restless in their open stalls, tethered to the walls by ropes. He saw they had finished the hay he had put in their mangers yesterday. He checked their hooves and saw they were dry. So he released them and turned them out into the water meadow to graze.

He followed them more slowly. As he did, he passed the smokehouse.

He paused. Yes, there was a wisp coming from the chimney. But there was no firewood stacked beside it. He comprehended that she must have used what was there when the wood box at the house was empty.

He shrugged. Such an expedient was a desperate one for a farm wife. The fire in the smokehouse must be maintained to cure the ham and sausage necessary to overwinter the family. But then he remembered she'd looked none too steady on her legs when she'd hurried back into the house.

If there was a child . . . she might have borne it after her husband left and had no means of going for help. *Bad,* he thought. *Very bad.*

He opened the smokehouse door. It was almost empty. Damn! What kind of man was her husband to leave his wife without food or fuel? And pregnant in the bargain.

It was none of his business, and he had problems of his own. But another possibility occurred to him. Perhaps the man was in the house, lying ill or injured.

He told himself sternly that it was none of his business . . . but . . . well, he could kill a pig. A spear was leaning against the wall just outside the smokehouse.

He closed the smokehouse door and hefted it. It had a brutal, wide, razor-sharp blade, and a crosspiece just below the blade. Its maker had equipped it with a stout handle that could be used to hold the pig back in case the spear missed a vital organ and the animal lived for some while until it bled to death. Pigs were most dangerous then. When suffering mortal wounds, they turned on their attackers.

He left the spear where it was and walked up to the house. As before, he spoke to the wall. "My lady, I cannot know what your trouble is. But if food would be a help to you, before I go I can kill a pig and you can fill your smokehouse."

This time he got a reply. It took so long that he was about to turn and walk away when she spoke.

"Yes . . . I would like that. I need food . . . meat . . . badly. The garden helps now, but . . ."

"Say no more," he said. "I understand." He didn't, but he said he did, afraid she might shame herself by breaking down. "I will return with the pig."

He relieved himself in the shadows by the compost pit, then washed in the river. He stood on the bank holding the spear and considered.

Beyond the water meadow, the forest stretched down to the river. The sun was up and the morning chill was beginning to depart, but mist still drifted in the shallows on both banks. He rolled up both sleeves of his heavy linen shirt and dusted his hands in the fine, dry dirt above the water. Along the river's edge ran a trail, a very faint track, and he suspected it led to pig wallows near the water.

The first was empty. But he saw traces, troubled reeds and cattails where the pigs had been feeding. The second held a sow and a half-dozen piglets. He had no desire to tackle her. Suckling pig was a delicacy among his people, but he had no mind to sacrifice a productive sow—correction, the farmer's productive sow—for a brief feast, however juicy.

The third held another sow, no piglets. She lay in the wallow, blowing bubbles contentedly.

He slowed his pace. *Yes*, he thought. *They will be somewhere close by.*

He heard the crashing in the bushes before he saw it coming. Then a second later, it came, moving right toward him, charging him, head down, tusks bared, foam at the open jaws. At the last instant, he sidestepped and drove the spear into the left flank, just behind the left foreleg.

The hit was perfect. The boar spear entered the animal's body without scraping anything as it would have if it struck a rib.

The boar crashed into the ground and slid for a few feet, dragging him along with it, already dead almost before its legs folded. He pulled the spear out and allowed the boar to bleed for a time, while he slit the throat, using the spear. Then he lifted the hindquarters to drain the body of blood.

He hated that. Wasting the blood. It made wonderful sausage. But no help for it. In the normal course of events, he and his men would have caught it in a net, stunned the animal with a wooden hammer, then strung it up and slit the throat. But here he was alone and must do the best he could.

When he was relatively sure the boar was bled out, he slung the carcass over his shoulder, picked up the spear, and started back to the house. He sighed, knowing the real work was only beginning.

When he returned, she was ready, one fire blazing in a pit in the courtyard, another under a kettle. A coil of rope and a long knife rested on the stump near the log. And, yes, there was a tree close by. Another tree section stood in the center by the courtyard. It would be suitable for a chopping block.

She held another knife in her hand. It was about fourteen inches long.

"I lost the blood," he said, dumping the pig carcass under the tree.

"Can't be helped, but I wasn't hoping for it," she said. "We must do the best we can."

"Just so," he answered, slinging the pig by the heels from the lowest branch of the tree.

"May I know your name?" she asked.

"Arthur," he said.

"Dea Arto?" she asked.

"Yes," was the laconic answer.

"Are you a bear?"

He looked away from the pig he was beginning to butcher.

"Yes." He set down the knife, lifted his shirt, and showed her.

She relaxed. "How did you die?" she asked.

The question hung in the air between them.

"I didn't," he answered, "but was sent here alive."

"You can't do that," she told him.

"But I did," he answered. "Or rather, it was done to me. Now, shall we get on with this? How did you get here?"

She looked away at the river in the distance, not wanting to stare at his face. She held the knife blade between the thumb and forefinger of her left hand; the fingers of her right opened and closed on the hilt.

"I was little, not more than seven or eight, running wild with the children of our village near the Severn River. A man came. He was handsome and beautifully dressed. He and a half-dozen others rounded us up like sheep, then they drove in a dozen or more from the village.

"A few he discarded—the ones who were crippled or slow. But then he took the rest of us. My memory of the next few days is cloudy, but when I really woke, I was here."

Was he dead? he wondered. No, he had gone back and spoken with Igrane and Merlin. They had tried to torture him. He didn't think she was dead, either, but for some reason, she believed she was.

"May I know your name?" he asked in return.

"Eline," she said. "That's all I remember. My father called me that—little fawn."

Arthur nodded. "So you have heard of the Bears."

"Heard," she said, "but never met one. So I do not know if what is said of them is true."

"It probably is," Arthur told her.

Then they both worked. And there was a lot to be done. He butchered; she chopped and stuffed.

Such a good thing as a whole pig could not be wasted. The hams would be rubbed with salt and placed in the smokehouse. A lot of meat must be cooked and then made into one type of sausage or another. Some uncooked portions would be made into other types of sausage. Large cuts would be salted down for later use to flavor beans and stews. By the by, it would provide a fine meat meal for the two of them.

Arthur cleared the fire pit and laid fresh sage branches. The rocks inside were almost red hot; the odor of sage filled the air. Then they both placed the meat on the sage, covered it with more sage, and then threw a hide over it to keep in the heat.

She toiled over the kettle and the chopping block. He cut more wood for the fire and washed the pig's intestines in a bucket, readying them to be used as sausage casings.

It was midmorning when the baby began to cry. She looked up from her task of seasoning and chopping meat and fat. He paused his butchering; he had been rubbing salt into the hams.

"I must feed him," she said. "You should go into the springhouse and drink some milk, since you had no breakfast. I have some cooling in the water there."

He nodded.

The curved house was much the same shape as a quarter moon, and they were working in the courtyard caught within the crescent. One horn was the springhouse.

The dog was chained before the door. When she spoke, his head lifted and he stared at her in mute adoration.

She took a deep breath. "I have always heard that Bears are men of honor," she said.

"We are," he answered.

"Bax!" she said, addressing the dog.

He rose to his feet and was even bigger than Arthur had supposed. He was black, with brown-gold markings and the massive frame and big jaws of a fighting animal.

"Bax," she said. "Greet my friend Arthur."

Arthur walked toward the animal, paused in front of him, and offered a hand. The big yellow eyes studied him, and Bax sniffed the outstretched hand. Then the dog stood and placed his front paws on Arthur's shoulders. He was half a head taller than the man. Solemnly, he licked his face.

"Thank you, Bax," Arthur said as the dog went back down on all fours and sat quietly.

"I was one of the dog handlers at King Bade's villa," she said. "Bax is the reason we got away. He helped us."

"What is King Bade like?" he asked.

"I don't know," she said. "I never saw him."

Arthur bowed as he passed the dog, Bax. Bax acknowledged him with a low grunt. It wasn't quite a growl and didn't sound unfriendly.

The springhouse was cool and dim. There was a spring, only a trickle dripping from a pipe in a rock wall. It filled a basin. In the basin were a crock of milk, butter, and a jug of wine. The milk cow was tethered to a wall on the other end of the cool room.

Wine, he thought, lifting his eyebrows. *An expensive treat for small farmers.* He didn't think further about it, but drank the rich milk he dipped from the jar.

He tried to remember what Morgana told him about the summer country. Very little, only that they had a sort of treaty with King Bade. A treaty pretty much honored when the king felt like it. But most often, the king did as he pleased. He could be very dangerous.

Merlin had a lot of friends, Arthur reflected. Some of them powerful. Yes, it was true he had escaped one trap only to wander into another. He shook his head, washed his face quickly in the cold water, and sternly ordered himself to tend to business. Now!

Whatever happened to him, he intended to leave her with enough meat to survive for a time. She was not yet completely healed. The birth must have been a difficult one.

He returned to the courtyard and continued salting the hams. Then he carried them to the smokehouse. There, the fire must be relaid and more wood cut, so that she could keep it going for the time necessary to cure the meat.

When he returned, bread and butter were waiting for him on the stump. Then they both settled down to the task of rendering the lard.

When they were finished, they had a meat feast. Arthur was surprised at his own greed. But then, it was true he hadn't had many full meals in the last few weeks, and she must have suffered considerable blood loss birthing the baby.

They both ate and ate of the tender, sage-fragrant ribs and loin until they could hold no more. Bax got his share, a plate piled high with bones and trimmings. Then they lazed in the afternoon sun.

"In the morning," Arthur said, "I will leave. First, I'll chop more wood, but then I'll go. Is there any place nearby where I would be accepted into the household for the work I can contribute?"

"You're a good worker," she said. She wouldn't look at him but studied the stones of the courtyard at her feet. "But I don't know."

He saw she was unable or unwilling to say more, so he rose, went down to the river, bathed, and went back to the barn. He lay down in the loft and immediately fell asleep.

The voices woke him at sunset. "Make us a bed now, dearie."

She was standing with three men below the loft where he had been sleeping. The barn was only a lean-to, and there was more than enough light in the gathering dusk to see all three of them.

She was weeping. "Why are you doing this?" she asked. "The wine is the only thing of value we have. Take it and go. I was badly torn when the child came. . . . I'm no good to you."

The one Arthur picked out as leader patted her cheek almost gently, then backhanded her a savage swipe across the face. She didn't scream but went backward into the straw, nose and mouth running blood.

"Sweet tits, you promised to be nice to us when we came on you in

the vegetable garden. Now turn over and pile the straw into a nice bed."
He was a big, dark, powerful man, with a sharp widow's peak in the center
of his forehead.

She rolled over, wiped her face with her skirt, and began to obey. The
leader looked like he might be dangerous; the other two Arthur dis-
counted as not much. One had a knife and a mace with a stone head.
The other had only a knife and a quilted overshirt. The dark man wore
chain mail and had a dirk and a sword.

The leader carried the wine jug. The one with the mace tapped it
with a cup he held in his hand. "Give me some more."

The leader poured some of the wine into the cup, then took a long
pull on the jug. Quilted Jerkin snarled, "You're getting two times as much
as the rest of us."

"No, I'm not!" Hairy and Dark slammed an elbow into his ribs.

The quilted one didn't give up appreciable ground. But he didn't re-
taliate, either.

"There is plenty here for all of us." Then he reached down and jerked
the woman to her feet. "There's plenty *here* for all of us, too," he said as he
shook her. "Now, dearie, it's time to drop your skirt or raise it, whichever
you prefer. Now, both of you get her arms and hold her while I—"

"I want some wine. I'm sick of your hogging all the best things for
yourself. Then we draw lots to see who gets to try her out first," Quilted
Jerkin spat.

The dark one reached for his sword.

Arthur acted.

He jumped from the loft to the floor behind them, landing lightly on
his feet. The dark one spun around, hand still on his sword hilt.

Arthur didn't bother with the sword. He jerked the short knife in his
opponent's belt free of its sheath. Armored men were fools, he reflected
as he drove the dirk up through the man's lower jaw, the base of the
tongue. He felt the resistance, then snapping as the blade passed the thin
bone that protects the brain from below. Then the mushy feel as at least
two inches of blade entered the brain itself.

The dark one didn't die at once; he had at least thirty seconds to contemplate his fate. But he couldn't do much, since the final two inches of

steel destroyed his neural sight center. He couldn't even really scream, since his tongue was cut off at the root. He made some noises, but Arthur didn't pay any attention. He was still busy.

The one with the mace tried to swing it. Arthur got him by the hair and pulled his head down to meet the top of his rising knee. His nose pulped and the septum was driven back and up into the frontal lobe of his brain. To be sure this was sufficient, Arthur popped both eyes out of their sockets with his thumbs.

The one in the quilted jerkin tried to run. The dark one was down, dying, his body convulsing in a bow as it stood on its neck and heels. Arthur snatched the sword from its sheath and drove it through Quilted Jerkin's back, savaging one lung, slicing both the abdominal aorta and the interior vina cava in half. He was dead of massive blood loss before he hit the floor.

"Are there any more?" Arthur asked.

She shook her head. Then she pointed at the dark one. "He's still alive."

Arthur glanced at him, then back at her. Something flickered in his eyes that frightened her more than anything she had ever seen, even the three he had just dealt with. Then it vanished, to be replaced with indifference.

"Not for long," he said.

"Take care of the baby," she whispered.

"Did they harm you?" he asked.

"No, but the wine was a trap. To get them to drink it, I had to taste some. I pretended to try to bribe them with it. I hoped they would finish it before they started on me. I hoped I would be safe in the house when they came in the first place. But they caught me in the garden. The wine is poisoned. I didn't tell them, and even drank some. I was hoping even if I died, they would die, too."

She bit him when he stuck his fingers down her throat to make her vomit. In the next few hours, she found he could be as remorseless with her as he had been with her attackers. But to a completely different end.

He ignored the bite and forced her to vomit until her stomach was empty. Then he ordered her to tell him what the poison was.

"Opium!"

He was relieved. Opium was a well-known drug. The Egyptian pharaohs had taken it to help them sleep, and the spectacular deterioration of a few of the more unpleasant Roman emperors was, by some, laid at its door. He understood how it did its deadly work, and for the next eight hours, he wouldn't let her sleep. And he absolutely, positively, would not let her die.

The next morning, he assisted her in wrapping a breast binder around her body to squeeze out the milk contaminated by the opium. Then he milked the cows and fed the baby the milk a spoon at a time, until he was satisfied and no longer squalling.

At this inconvenient time, her husband arrived home.

The house was neat and tidy. Arthur was sitting at the table, feeding the baby a puree of mashed carrots, turnips, and milk. He knew enough not to include onions; they give infants gas.

Bax, who never left her side for long, was sitting near the door. She stepped back from the central hearth, seized the dog by the collar, and stepped between Arthur and her husband, standing in the doorway. His sword was half out of its sheath.

"Before you make the worst mistake of your life," she said, "go look in the barn."

"Think that will convince him?" Arthur asked.

"It had better," she said. She spoke a word softly to the dog. Bax walked over and sat in front of Arthur.

The man was in the barn for some time. When he returned, he sat down at the table across from Arthur. He was no longer wearing the sword or the makeshift boiled leather armor.

"You lost?" she said, placing a plate before her husband.

"Yes," he said. "We tried, but we failed."

"What else?" she said. "I told you—"

The man's fist slammed down hard on the table. "Christ and the devil both, Eline—"

"Stop it!" Arthur's voice cracked with the unmistakable ring of command. "Eline, let the man eat. You, whatever your name is, your wife is a woman of honor. You need not suspect her of any impropriety."

"You did it with your bare hands. You were unarmed, weren't you?"

Arthur leaned across the table and showed his teeth in nothing like a smile. "They behaved in an insulting manner toward your good lady," he snarled. "I corrected them."

"Obviously," the husband said. And added, "Permanently."

"Yes," Arthur said. "They will be guilty of no further ill-natured behavior. I was in your lady's debt. She offered me the hospitality of food and a bed . . . in the barn!"

Eline placed a bowl of soup before her husband. "Arthur, this is my husband, Balin." She looked from her husband to Arthur. "Arthur, Balin."

"How do we know you don't belong to the king?" Balin asked.

Arthur bared his teeth again. "You don't!" he said. "But if I did belong to this king of yours, how likely would it be that I would slaughter his men?"

"I suppose it wouldn't be—"

"He came from the wild," Eline said, "and he was starving. I don't think he belongs to the king."

"No," Arthur said. "I don't belong to the king. I can't tell how much any word is worth here, but in other places, I am considered absolutely truthful. And I will give you my word I neither know this king of yours nor do I serve him in any way."

Eline brought a platter of flat breads to the table and some butter. Then she took the child, who was asleep in Arthur's arms, put him in the cradle, turned, came back, and sat down on the bench beside her husband. Neither would meet Arthur's eyes. Balin concentrated on the food on his plate; Eline played with her fingers in her lap.

"He can really fight well," she said to her husband.

"What's that to me?" Balin snapped back.

"You need him!"

"No!" Balin said, shooting a dark look at Arthur.

"If you can't get the cattle back, we are all done."

"Where are the cattle?" Arthur asked patiently.

"Across the river," Balin said. "We can't get them because someone is guarding the bridge."

Balin shot a guilty look at his wife, then continued, "He . . . he is too strong for us."

Arthur said, "Umm." Then got up, swinging his leg around the bench. "Are the three in the barn getting ripe?"

Balin shook his head. "Not yet."

"Better bury them, though," Arthur said.

Balin looked up. "No! I know a place where they can go. If we put them near here, they might . . . walk."

Arthur nodded. "Sometimes they do that."

"Here, it's not some time; it's all the time," Eline said. "Do you want a bath and clean clothes?" she asked Arthur.

He was a bit mystified, but he said, "Yes."

"We have a sweathouse down by the river," Balin said. To Arthur's eye, he still looked guilty. "I think you can wear my clothes."

Arthur nodded again. They began talking as soon as he left the house, before he was out of earshot.

"I can't believe," Eline spat, "that you're going to let him go up against that monster without even—"

"You said he could fight, and I saw what he did to those three in the barn," Balin hissed. "I'll warn him tomorrow . . ."

It felt good to be clean, Arthur thought when he climbed the hill back to the barn and lay down in the straw.

Balin and he left early, before first light. Balin tried to put him on one of the horses, but Arthur resisted this and said he could walk very well. Eline filled a knapsack with food, shooting unhappy looks at her husband while she did so.

"Remember," she told Balin. "You promised."

As they took the road farther into the forest, Arthur looked back once at the plateau where he had come from. Where he had been imprisoned. They were going in the opposite direction.

"Where do you come from?" Balin asked.

"There," Arthur said, pointing to the mountain and the nearby plateau.

Balin crossed himself.

Arthur studied him for a moment but didn't ask for an explanation. They continued walking. It was one of those mornings when it's hard to believe there is any evil in the world. Cool, clear, golden, with new sunlight, green with the abundant beauty of the wooded country-side. Wildflowers bloomed in profusion at the roadside—daisies, colts-foot, cornflower, violets—white, purple, and yellow, peeped out of the grass. Grass that was lush, long, and green.

The woods were not thickly overgrown or darkened by tall, high, canopied trees. This wood was open—mixed oak, ash, hazel, hawthorn, and willow. Sometimes through the trees Arthur could see the blue glint of oxbow lakes left by the river flowing through the bottom land.

Rich country, this, Arthur thought. *And not thickly settled.* The land around the lakes was clear, and there was good grazing for cattle.

"Does it get cold in winter?" Arthur asked.

"No," Balin said, "but there's lots of rain. That's why I built the house so high."

They stopped to eat near noon, and Arthur realized he and Balin were no longer alone. At least a dozen men were following them. In dress and appearance, they much resembled Balin. They wore homespun clothing, had raggedly trimmed hair and beards, and carried a variety of improvised weapons ranging from slings tucked into their belts to clubs, wooden spears, knives, and a few true swords like the one Balin wore.

Among them, Arthur felt as he had when, one late evening off on a hunt, he had blundered into someone's cow pasture. He stood up in the tall grass and had been startled to see a dozen cows studying him with stolid, bovine inquiry. These men seemed no more ready to speak than the cows had been. They kept their distance as the cows had, and showed no indication of aggression.

Balin cleared his throat nervously. "We have all lost cattle," he ex-plained, "when the king closed the river."

Arthur nodded. Most carried food, as he and Balin did. They shared it out among themselves without argument and fell to.

It was mid-afternoon when they came to the first corpse. He was sit-ting against a tree trunk, head bowed.

For a moment Arthur believed it alive; it still wore clothing. But then he noticed how tight the skin on the half-hidden face was and the grotesque way the few rags of clothing hung from the bones.

"Don't touch it," Balin warned. "That's why none of them are buried. Sometimes he takes exception."

"I don't know," a big, black-bearded man commented. "They usually have to be fresher than that."

"Anybody know his name?" Balin asked.

Those who answered, only a few, said, "No." The rest looked as though they didn't want to be included in the conversation.

They were walking downhill toward the river. As they drew closer to the water's edge, the numbers of the dead increased. They were in all stages of decomposition, except, Arthur noted, the stinking, disgusting, wet one. These were all dry, the oldest shrunken to brown bone with fragments of parchment skin to fresher corpses, shrunken, eyeless, but still recognizable to their kin. A few, very few, were pointed out to Arthur by their kin. In whispers.

Before they came out of the forest, Arthur could hear a yammering. "Puff up, pt, pt, yup, tup, whup, whup, pa, pa, pa, pa. . . ." Nonsense syllables, repeated over and over again.

There had once been a bridge over the river here, a well-traveled one, if Arthur was any judge. The arching spans were of considerable size. They were made of the same black basaltic rock Arthur had seen at the bottom of the plateau. They looked as though they might have grown out of the riverbed. Arthur had seen Roman bridges and roads, whole Roman cities, some abandoned when Roman rule collapsed in Britain. But he had never seen anything like these spans. They were solid, with no sign of separation between the blocks. No people he had ever known or heard of could build anything like these arches.

The bridge was usable, because the low arches had been spanned by planks tied in place. The thing danced on them, leaping, jumping, hopping, cartwheeling, all the while spewing the garbled sounds that resembled but never quite were words.

Arthur hunkered down on his heels at the edge of the wood and tried to get a good look at the thing. Difficult to do, because it was in continuous motion. The uniform was that of a Roman cavalry officer, silver helmet with a mask—a female mask. Chain-mail shirt over a tunic and trousers, shin guards, and boots.

He wondered what woman the mask represented. Bodiccia? He had been treated to a performance in Brittany where the cavalry had dramatized the defeat of the Iceni queen. He had known it was an insult while watching, probably aimed directly at him. So he had been very careful to applaud vigorously and pay effusive compliments to the cavalry commander.

Another favorite showpiece was the destruction of the queen of the Amazons at Troy. So it might be Penthesilea so depicted.

In any case, he could see nothing of its body. Indeed, he doubted it had one, because he noticed the same shimmer in the air around the figure he'd noticed around the monster that pursued him on the plateau.

"Have you tried at night?" he asked Balin.

"Yes, we have. We tried to sneak across. The one up in the woods thought he was clever enough not to be seen."

"Moving to another ford?"

"He is there as soon as we arrive," a black-bearded man contributed.

"Spear?" Arthur asked.

"They crumble and sometimes burn," Balin said. "The man wielding them is— What's it like?" he asked the rest.

"Like being taken by a spider . . . sucked dry," was the reply. There was general agreement.

"Your slings?"

Balin pulled his out. A second later, lead shot flew toward the figure on the bridge. Everyone scurried for cover when it came whistling back and imbedded itself in a pine tree.

"He has more trouble with that," Balin said, "but all of us have tried at one time. He just waits until we try to cross the bridge—and trust me, when you get halfway across the clearing in front of the bridge when that thing is stirred up, you're a dead man. Yes, we can even drive him off the bridge, but we can't hold him back long enough."

"We believe," Black Beard said, "that he feeds on the ones he kills and whatever animals stray near the river to drink."

The grass in the clearing leading to the bridge was long, but when Arthur stood, he saw that it grew up through the bones of skeletons, both animal and human. As he rose, the horror on the bridge began to kick and stamp more loudly. "Ot, yut, dut, art, ar, ar, ar, Arthur, ru, ru, ru, do, die, die, die, die, de, de, de, eee . . ." The yammering petered out, a thud of the thing's boots now the only sound.

"Christ and the one-eyed both," Balin whispered. "I never heard it call anyone's name before." He crossed himself, and then he and the rest drew back into the shelter of the trees.

Arthur remained where he was, hunkered down, eyes narrowed, thinking.

"Are you going to fight it?" someone asked.

"No," Arthur said. "It wants me to fight it."

Balin sighed sadly. "I don't blame you. But I was hoping. . . ."

Arthur stood, then drew back under the trees with the rest. "Does it stink?" he asked.

"All to hell and gone," Balin said. "Why?"

"You'll see," Arthur said.

It took him a while to find the right size stones. Then a bit more time to cut the rawhide ropes. Balin's friends understood the principle of the bow drill. Then someone had to procure fat for the torches.

He missed the first tree he tried for with his new weapon, cursed under his breath, but went on trying, and within an hour was reasonably accurate. Not the best—he was something of a perfectionist—but probably good enough.

He made several of the new weapons. He gave Balin and the black-bearded one the others. They were both fast learners. By then, the rest of the men had a fire going well away from the bridge and its guardian.

"I go first," he told them. "Even if I perish, the principle is, I think, sound. You might be able to still kill it. But don't, whatever you do, engage in hand-to-hand combat. That's the mistake its other adversaries made, and it's how it feels."

He glanced briefly at the circle of faces around him. They all nodded.

Enough said. Then he rose and started downhill toward the bridge. He didn't look back to see if they were following him. He had his mind set on killing it. Whether they thought his plan had any merit or not didn't concern him.

When he drew close to the clearing in front of the bridge, he broke into a jogging run. He could hear it—"pop, pot, poot, up, yu, mup"—stomping up and down the bridge planks.

When it saw him break cover, it gave a scream, a sound more like metal on metal than anything rising from a human throat. He ran diagonally across the clearing rather than toward the bridge. The grass was up to his knees, and a second after he began, he knew he was running on the dead. He could feel the snapping of rib cages and long bones beneath his feet. But there was no time to think about it, because the creature seemed to fly toward him, skimming over the ground.

He barely had time to get the bolo in motion before he must let fly. It took the thing around the chest, not at the legs, the preferred target, the stones and thongs wrapping around the muscle cuirass it was wearing. And ripped it in half.

The head and struggling arms went one way, followed by what looked like dried intestines. Blackened, stinking coils of entrails were strewn across the grass, connecting both halves of the body. On the other end, the legs kicked wildly.

For a split second, Arthur was transfixed by disgust. But only for a second, because as gross as these remains were, the torso had swung around and begun to crawl toward the writhing legs.

Arthur could only hope the second part of his plan would work.

He ran toward the head and torso, and when he was only a step away, he hurled the torch. It landed on the thing's armored kilt and the arms seized it. For a second, Arthur believed he must have been wrong.

He leaped away, and just as well. The whoosh of flame almost got him. When he looked toward the legs, he saw Balin and Black Beard burning them.

The blackened mask rolled away from the skull it had concealed and lay facedown in the grass. When it was gone, the flames consumed what looked like the fragments of a skull. It was hard to see, because the immensity of fire was out of proportion to the amount of fuel offered by the shattered fragments of the guardian of the bridge. It burned above the remains the way a pitch fire burns, Arthur thought, as though something gaseous were being consumed.

Yes, Arthur thought. He had been about to defeat the horror on the plateau when his mother and her lover drew him back. He picked up the silver mask with the end of a stick and hung it from a hawthorn bush nearby at the forest's edge.

I must make an offering, he thought and then couldn't understand where the thought came from. But then he had looked on the woman's face, visoring the putrid thing within. He had put the solution together all at once. Possibly, just possibly, he had some help.

The flames were quickly turning into a pyre at the hands of the men who had followed him. They were burning the dead, the remains of those humans as well as animals that had lost their lives at the touch of the life-draining horror. They dragged them in from everywhere—the woods, the meadow, the riverbank, the tall grass at his feet. Two fires, both burning about ten feet apart. The guts of the thing were still strung out between them, twisted, blackened, dead.

But they moved when he poked them with a stick, and he could feel the pull as these wretched remains still tried to exert their strength to suck the life out of his body. With one motion, he swept them up and threw his burden, stick and all, into the fire.

It roared anew as it consumed the relics of the dead thing.

No one rested until any creature the thing had killed was given into the flames. It was late evening, though the sun was still up, when at last the fire died down. Still, no one ventured to cross the bridge.

"I think you should get your cattle before dark," Arthur said.

There was a considerable crowd now. More men and a few women had arrived from the surrounding countryside. A few of the women carried weapons, as the men did. Others accompanied contingents of their male kin. These had started fires and were preparing to feed the assembled company. But most of the men lingered near Arthur at the edge of the river. The water was low, and except at the center, it could be waded.

The women were fishing in the shallows. They were using their bare hands. One woman splashed in and drove the fish into the pools of low water, while another scooped them up, catching them behind the gills and tossing them into a basket. The men around Arthur stared at the bridge, showing some trepidation.

"Well?" Arthur asked. "Will you settle down for a comfortable supper and then go by night?"

Black Beard and Balin looked guilty. Neither one would meet Arthur's eye.

"It might happen that King Bade's men are guarding the cattle."

Arthur was annoyed. "You didn't tell me about this. There was no mention of human soldiers."

"No," Balin said. "We didn't think you could get rid of the masked warrior. Last time we attacked, using our slings, they came up behind us. We had to flee. They are much better armed than we are."

Arthur blew out a breath slowly through his nose. "Why didn't you come up behind them?" he asked.

"We didn't know they were coming," Balin said.

"Why didn't you set a watch?"

"We never thought of it," Balin murmured.

"Why not? You are in revolt against this King Bade, are you not?"

"Yessss," Balin said slowly.

Then Arthur said, "It is necessary to think of such things."

They exchanged more guilty glances. "We're not exactly in revolt," Balin said.

"What are you then?" Arthur asked.

The group around him looked positively shamefaced. Balin didn't look at him and murmured in a very low voice, "Runaway slaves."

Ah, Arthur thought. *This is the nub of all their difficulties. Shame. Yes, shame is a powerful thing.*

Her face caught his eye. The silver cavalry mask still hung from the hawthorn tree, where he had placed it. The hawthorn tree was not in bloom. Indeed, it had no business to flower; it carried ripening fruit on its branches. But the white, soft petals clothed the branches, setting off the smooth, green leaves in much the same way white mist drifts over a mountain forest.

Merlin thought he had imprisoned him, but in reality Arthur had been summoned here for some purpose. A more powerful hand even than Merlin's had ordered the events of his life.

"I am a king," he said. "And I have worn the three crowns. True, I am only the summer king, for my father, Uther, yet rules. But I have been crowned with flowers, wheat, and acorns in token of sovereignty over the forest, meadow, and sown. I was taught the ancient laws of our people at my father's knee. A king's first obligation is to that law. So let us bring your case to judgment."

He strode toward the tree, and when he turned to one side of it, he saw they had all followed. Not just them, but everyone else in the clearing. Even the fishing women set their basket in the shallows and joined the outskirts of the crowd. The silver mask looked over his shoulder at the gathering.

"It is in bloom," Balin said, pointing to the tree.

"The mask is not profaned," Arthur said, "in spite of the evil use to which it was put."

He could smell the faint, exquisite perfume of the blossoms, a very pure thing. He closed his eyes for a second. He felt as though fingers, soft as flowers, stroked his cheek, and he knew his soon-to-be bride was present. She of the first trees.

Then he opened his eyes and turned. "Will you trust my judgment?" he asked.

He accepted slavery. All the peoples he knew about kept human beings in bondage. But the lawmakers had seen fit to limit its use and the circumstances in which it could be applied to any individual. In some cases they imposed limitations as to its duration and enforced a reciprocal obligation on slave owners. Slaves had a right to fair treatment; and they could not be sold off when old and no longer fit for labor but must be supported by the household as other dependent, aged persons were.

The people in the crowd looked at each other. There was a growing murmur of assent.

He raised his hand and silence fell.

"The law is that there are only three ways a man or woman may be taken and forced to labor for another: capture in war, in compensation for debt that cannot be repaid by labor, or lastly as punishment for a capital crime, a crime for which the usual punishment would be death. The death penalty may be remanded, and the person sold away from his people, into slavery. Do any of these three circumstances apply to any of you?"

The silence was vast. Arthur could hear in the distance the whisper of the wind among the trees, the long, slow afternoon sigh of the forest. The water flowing over the river cobbles near the banks sparkled in the slanted sunlight, a glittering ribbon of gold.

He didn't look into their faces, because he knew there would be too many tears. His mind stretched back to the broken feast from which the sky-eyed girl fled into the unknown. He knew many of the landowners at that feast harvested children the way they did calves or chickens from their estates, selling these surplus children into slavery. This, in part, was where these people had come from. Sent to the king of the summer country as tribute to work his lands. Never mind that the practice was illegal. It was convenient for the powerful.

He remembered Eline's tale of the children being rounded up and driven away from their homes by the "well-dressed man." Merlin, if he was any judge, or one of his minions. In return, King Bade probably gave him leave to imprison Arthur in the cage of bones, and, if this king prevailed, he would return Arthur to his prison. Between Arthur and Merlin and this King Bade, whatever he was, there could be only war.

CHAPTER SEVENTEEN

AN YOU IMAGINE A RIVER THAT FLOWS
through the vistas of the sky? Well, the one the dragon
and I were on did. Sunstruck clouds flowed around and
below us. Magnificent shapes in crystalline white, violet, amethyst, gold,
and shades of blue, their edges dabbled in blood as the sun set.

Below, I could smell and hear the storms: the clamor of the thunder,
the breathless hush after a lightning bolt hit, and the roar of the air when
it rushes back into the void the fierce discharge makes. Maeniel told me
about this place. It is neither dawn nor sunset here, yet the light is drawn
from both. The mountains of vapor hide the horizon, drifting wraiths of
mist dampen your skin, and birds pass in flight. Hawks, eagles, swans, and
geese drift by, borne on the rising air.

We swam through cold, dark clouds and out the other side, into the
splendor of thunderheads massing above us, surrounding us on all sides,
gleaming with all the colors of the rainbow in the sunlight. We rode the
waves among them, waves of air or water, I couldn't tell. At times we entered many-pillared halls, the storm clouds a roof above, a floor below,
while in between a dozen suns refracted from the one danced over the
ever-changing shapes around us, tracing in their presence all the glories

of the day. From dawn to dusk, the gift of God. Each one. All perfect, yet unique.

"Where are we going?" I asked the dragon.

"I don't know," he said.

"How are we getting to wherever we're going?"

"I have absolutely no idea," was the answer.

A second later, the spray from a wave got me in the eyes. When I cleared them, I saw the shore of Cornwall. We were, however, well away from Tintigal Castle.

I was no sooner finished drawing breath in a sigh of relief when I became aware I was being hailed from the beach . . . and I saw my family there. Until that moment, I had not known how much I loved them or had the slightest idea how much I missed them.

The dragon turned and swam toward them. He had little sympathy for me.

"Stop your bawling," he said sharply. "All the time on this long—and I might add trying—voyage, you have shown yourself calm, clear-headed, brave, and bold. Now at the sight of your family, you shatter my delicate ears with sniffling and squalling. Compose yourself."

Not being human, he continued, "I have never had the experience of bringing someone home who has too freely imbibed an intoxicant of some kind—but I have the feeling that I'm about to find out what that is like. No doubt I and all our kind will be blamed by that old scold, Dugald, for your adventures and misadventures. You don't have to compound my problem by arriving in a state of collapse. Endeavor to compose yourself and do it now!

"I am appointed your guardian and companion. Don't—I repeat, don't—make my life any more difficult than the nature of such an arduous task demands."

The dragon was right. The brawl started when we hit the beach. I think that's what families are for.

Where had I been? Well, Tintigal was one place. After that, I wasn't quite sure.

How did I get to wherever I'd gone? I had absolutely no idea.

Dugald, furious, berated the dragon and all dragonkind and kin. The dragon showed his excellent teeth and gave as good as he got, threatening to dine on Dugald if he continued to abuse him. And since the dragon floated just a little offshore in the shallows, held in place by gentle vibrations of his fins and tail, the threat was not an idle one.

Kyra embraced me, and it felt good to be in her arms, for a moment pretending I was a child again. The Gray Watcher kissed me on the forehead. But Black Leg looked at me resentfully and said, "You even smell wrong."

Dugald looked away from his argument with the dragon and said, "Eh! What?"

"Shut up!" I spat at Black Leg. "Just shut up!"

"Hush," Kyra said, and pressed my head against her breast. "You men set up a bathhouse and do it right now," she commanded. "And you, you old fool." She rounded on Dugald. "Stop jawing with your betters. Maybe they took her, but he brought her back safe and sound.

"And as for you, whatever your name is—" she pointed at the dragon "—make yourself useful and catch some fish for supper. Hear me. Do it now. Dugald wouldn't make a good meal for a dragon anyway—too old and tough."

Dugald looked outraged. "Woman . . ." he began.

The Gray Watcher took him by the arm. "Let's go fix the sweat bath. Gray and I will help."

"Gray's here?" I said to Kyra. "Why did he leave home?"

"We have no home," Black Leg said dolefully.

"Be quiet," Kyra commanded as she led me off. I don't know which of us she was speaking to, because she gave both of us a stern look.

Black Leg slunk away. I followed her, thinking I was more than ready for a bath. Not just because I felt sticky; I was having a new experience . . . cramps.

I felt better when the heat began to drive the chill out of my bones as the steam rose around us. I had padded myself with a linen cloth, but it was already stained. I studied the blood creeping out and marking my thighs.

"Looks as though I'm not a child any longer."

"Hush," Kyra said, pouring more water on the rocks. "You are now and always will be the child of my heart. My first comfort after I lost all I had. If I was ever harsh and sharp-tongued with you during those first few years, I'm sorry. It is hard to lose all and then open your heart and love again. But with you, I have." She kissed me on the forehead and began to unbraid my hair.

"You have never been unkind to me," I told her. "I have been very lucky. I have you, the Gray Watcher, Dugald, Black Leg, and Mother. Once I took all the love showered on me for granted. But having met Merlin and Igrane, I understand now how lucky I have been. They, that pair of snakes, are all he has."

"He, who?" she asked.

"Arthur."

"So you met the young king?"

"Yes," I said, looking up at her. She stepped back and met my eyes. "He is my destiny."

Kyra looked troubled, deeply troubled. "Are you sure?"

"*She* said so."

"Ah." Kyra sighed and then took her seat on the bench opposite me.

She was still beautiful, my Kyra, though gray threads were beginning to appear in her hair. But her figure had not begun to thicken, and she had wide hips and ample, handsome, upright breasts above a narrow waist.

As I said before, she was marked as all the Painted People are, tattooed with vines and flowers patterned like the Celtic knot work that covers all our creations, the testament that the world is one. Yet she had, after she came to us, placed an adder among the flowers. Her art was colored red, black, and blue.

"Look," I said, slapping my own arm hard. The green armor leaped out against my skin.

Kyra gave a loud cry and jumped to her feet. "What happened? You are marked as I am. But that must be the work of months. There hasn't been time, and how did you hide it?"

"No!" I said. "Silly, it's armor. See?" And I snatched a burning brand from the fire.

Kyra looked up at me in awe. I was naked, but clothed at the same time, my fairy armor glowing in the firelight of the sweat lodge.

Then I threw the flaming brand back into the fire. The armor wasn't perfect. After a few moments, the heat of the flames had begun to percolate through my protection.

"So she did what Dugald thought she did," Kyra said.

"Did what?" I asked.

"Your mother," Kyra whispered. "Dugald swore she lay with the Sidhe. She did."

I paused. The green coils, meanders, spirals on my flesh faded. No, I hadn't put it all together. But . . . I felt a chill.

"They looked like men," I said. "I thought they were Irish, drui— At first, they seemed ugly, dirty scoundrels, drunken fools. But when I drew closer, their aspect changed."

Kyra nodded. "They appeared as they wished to appear. Drunken ruffians to the eyes of Merlin and Igrane."

"They wanted to shame me, bring me to heel like a dog." I nodded. "The Sidhe lords played into their hands, or seemed to," I continued, seeing it whole for the first time.

"Possibly the test was also directed at you. You, my lady, were supposed to turn up your nose at them. I take it you didn't."

"No," I said. "I didn't. When I approached them, I saw what they really were. One of them, the one who said he was my father, later made a remark that I thought cast aspersions on my mother's honor. I took them to task."

Kyra looked away from me. "Honor as humans know it is meaningless to them. They understand little of jealousy or regret. Our rules mean less than nothing to them. Though it is said they have their own, still, their customs are not ours."

"He said she had more than one of . . . them."

"I hope none of them tempted you."

I felt surprised. Had I felt the powerful magnetism of such lusty males? The answer was yes, yes, I had. But I was still protected by childhood. If we met again . . .

Kyra stood and caught me by the shoulders, her grip so tight the green armor leaped out of my skin. She shook me lightly.

"Listen, girl, and listen well. To love them is . . . death. That mother of yours made a heathcomb of herself in order to bring you into being. She gave her own life willingly into the fire of the gods, the altar fire. Father or not, he, the chieftain who sired you, would lie with you willingly if you invited him."

"They weren't sure which of them was my father," I told Kyra.

"This I can believe. Mortal flesh doesn't find it easy to commingle with immortal. No doubt she had to make a great many tries before she got a child of them. Shut them out of your mind. Be warned, here and now, never, never look on one of them with desire. It is a great danger to you. Because you have part of them in you and it might try to draw you . . . home."

I shrugged and smiled at Kyra's frightened face. "They said I was the mare's own foal. And it is Arthur that I desire. As I said, *she* told me he was my destiny. I think I'm human enough. Besides, it may be that all those who passed through my mother's bed weren't gods. Seems more likely I sprang from the seed of some brave mortal, who was bold enough to pretend."

And indeed, I was frightened by all this loose talk of gods, the Sidhe, who knows what they are. The Christians say the Sidhe are not gods but heroes who may be "honored" but not worshipped. What a masterpiece of self-deception, that. It was clear to me the Irish wanted the new God, but they didn't want to let go of the old ones. So they compromised and kept both. Don't laugh. It's clear the Romans did the same. Whatever they could successfully dust off and slide sideways into the Christian religion— and it was a lot—they placed there, so that we are still encumbered with both old and new.

Although Dugald insists it all hangs together—it doesn't. And I'm surprised the whole thing hasn't been torn apart by its own internal contradictions. However, given the massive human capacity for self-deception, willful blindness allows our churches to stagger along from century to century— sometimes doing good, at other times causing great harm; and possibly only God himself can tell the difference.

I decided I would engage in a little self-deception myself. I didn't like the look on her face. She reminded me of a hen who has just discovered one of the eggs in her nest is a hawk's.

We did that once, Black Leg and I, when we were younger, just to see what the hen would do. Maeniel was in a fury about it, especially after Black Leg admitted it was his idea. Maeniel said that it was irresponsible and cruel to both chicken and hawk, and humans were just naturally cruel anyway. Then he punished us by forcing us to raise the baby hawk until it was fledged.

Then we found out we must teach it how to hunt. We were both nervous wrecks when it finally flew away to join its own kind. Maeniel said we deserved it.

In any case, Kyra began to remind me too much of that hen. So I embraced her and said I was sure that was what happened; some rapscallion was convincing enough to persuade my mother to believe he was of the Sidhe and that was how I was gotten. Or begotten, as the case may be.

Then I sat back and tried to find out what happened after the dragons took me away to Tintigal. Kyra had mixed me a drink that eased the cramps. I was getting over the feeling of being drained and tired the first day leaves me with, and I felt better.

"What is this stuff about not having a home?" I asked.

Kyra threw up her hands. Then explained, "It was all the fault of that stupid Bain," she said. "He looked, it seems, to get into the archdruid's good graces."

"As if Merlin would look at him twice," I said.

"Yes," Kyra said. "But he looked to capture us and deliver us in person to Merlin. What we would be doing in the meantime, he hadn't quite thought out. In any case, he found a few souls as foolhardy as he was and they set out one night to surprise us while we slept. But that brother of yours decided he must go night fishing, so he had slipped away after we were all asleep and, as a wolf, went down toward the sea.

"As fate would have it, he met Bain and his friends sneaking up through the forest. Black Leg said we would have heard them coming, since they made so much noise sneaking through the woods that they might have awakened the dead. The boy thought the whole thing a huge joke. Dugald did not."

I sighed and rolled my eyes. "He was probably furious."

"More than furious. Much more. Black Leg woke Maeniel, who woke the rest of us. Dugald was in an absolute fury. He pulled on his robes, picked up his staff, and threw the Druid Mist on them. They never reached the house."

Now, the Druid Mist is a terrible punishment. I must tell you this before I go further. We all have nightmares about being lost or being unable to complete an important task for which we are responsible. The Druid Mist is this nightmare made real.

Bain and his friends found themselves wandering in the wilderness without being able to go backward or forward. The victim of the mist exhausts himself trying to escape it, and like one caught in a bog, his struggles only drive him in deeper. As time passes, hunger and thirst begin to torment him, then cold, because, as it is told, this foggy place has no sun. Springs are dry; rivers won't run. The searcher blunders on and on, lost, until despair, exposure, and exhaustion claim him.

"Oh, God," I whispered. "What happened?"

"Oh, the next day," Kyra said with a sigh, "Dunnel came, begging Dugald for mercy. He said he had no knowledge of what Bain had planned to do. But the boy was his son-in-law. Dugald said that, given the marks on his daughter's face, marks seen by all, not just him, Dunnel should be glad to be rid of him.

"Dunnel left angry and despairing. Then Bain's wife came, with her child at her breast, I might add. She begged Dugald to spare its father. She had no better success with that vile-tempered old curmudgeon. And she left weeping, as if her heart would break."

"No," I said. "This is bad news. He shouldn't have—"

Kyra lifted a hand. "At last, Gray came. He was angry, and he said matters were becoming serious. He said if the boy died, Dunnel was his kin and had a duty to avenge him. Was Dugald fool enough to engender a blood feud over such trash as Bain? We all took Gray's side, and at last Dugald relented. And the whole gang of them wandered out of the fog along the shore that evening."

"Good God!" I whispered.

"You don't know the half of it," she said. "Two or three of them were close to mad, Bain among them. The rest, half dead with terror, hunger, and thirst."

"It made bad blood," I said.

"Yes." Kyra sagged back, hands on her knees, eyes closed. "The village is a small place. If you mistreat others, word gets around very quickly. People take sides. Though most people probably sympathized with Dugald, what he did frightened them. They had thought him a tame wise man, who could be counted on in time of trouble. Then he turned and showed them his teeth."

Kyra shook her head. "We can't go back. Too much has happened."

I agreed. "What now?" I asked.

The fire was low; the steam had died down. We were beginning to feel the evening chill. Kyra didn't answer my question until we dressed and left the sweat bath. I had clothes from her, but I put on my old deerskin britches and a white shirt.

The Gray Watcher had set up a table in a bowl-shaped clearing under the trees. There was a whole boar on the spit, several fresh fish cooked in seaweed, fresh bread, butter, and curd cheese.

I asked Kyra where they had gotten the milk. "We traded for it," she told me.

Yes. Black Leg and Maeniel were wonderful hunters.

Even if I wasn't completely happy with Black Leg, I still wanted his company. So we climbed the green, grassy bank that surrounded the clearing until we got to the top. From there, we could look down at the rest and out beyond the woods to the shore. The dragon was still there riding the swells, his head tucked back like a bird's.

I tried to tell Black Leg what happened to me, but when he heard about Arthur, he became very disgruntled.

"Now you have met a king," he said. "What do you think?"

I remembered Arthur's eyes on me, on the terrace, near his mother's rooms. They had caressed me.

"He was wonderful," I said.

"And I suppose I'm not wonderful."

I elbowed him in the ribs. I couldn't believe it. He was jealous. I loved it.

"Yes, you're wonderful," I said. "But not . . ." I leaned back a little to study him, and I realized he was beginning to attain his growth. He was taller than I am now but rawboned and gawky. So I continued, "But you're not as handsome as he is."

I was sorry the minute I said it. I could see my words had bitten deep. But before I could apologize, he said, "I don't know if I can believe you. Gray says you can't trust women. Any women."

I was a little stung. "Why not?"

Black Leg grinned. "How can you trust anything that bleeds for a week and doesn't die?"

I walked right into it. But I'll give myself credit. He never saw what was coming his way, either.

My right fist.

It connected with the side of his jaw a second later. My armor helped, of course, as did the extra strength the lady put in my right arm. I knew I'd hurt him when he went wolf in the air, then landed in a heap at the foot of the high bank without his breeches. His tunic was long enough to cover him, so he was still modest.

He let out a yell and scrambled to his feet, in position to climb up the bank and go for me. Our eyes met, and I flashed on his growing maturity. He was as big as his father now, and though still gangly and a bit awkward, he was powerfully muscled and, wolflike, very, very fast. He was in the process of becoming a dangerous warrior, and I knew I'd stirred a hornet's nest by attacking him unexpectedly.

But we were not alone, and I was a woman he loved. I knew this as I saw the rage die out of his eyes. He loved me very much and always would. And in a number of ways. As a friend, a sister, a companion, and now at last as a woman. I knew all this in the frozen moment in time when we were alone together. Before the present rushed back to confront us.

He was thinking about coming back up that bank and teaching me a lesson about smacking him without warning. There would be a scuffle, all right, but no one would get hurt. And we would find out how each other's bodies felt.

That would be good. Yes, and do neither of us any good at all.

In the feasting hall at Tintigal, I had exchanged pledges with the king. And she had said I was to be a queen. Or much the same thing when she told me he was my destiny. I was shaken by the knowledge of his love, a complication I hadn't thought of.

But then, Maeniel had his son by the arm and was towing him from the field of honor. And the rest were staring at me standing on the little hill as though I'd turned into a wild bull, horns and all.

I knew my hair was down, and I could feel it on my back. The green armor was flashing from my skin. They were looking at me the way Kyra had in the bath.

Anna, Gray's wife, made the sign of the cross. Gray stared at me in open-mouthed awe. Maeniel, restraining hand on his son's arm, studied me appraisingly. Only Dugald didn't seem surprised.

"Come down," he said. "Get some more pork." Then, apropos of nothing, he added, "The Beltane fair, the Beltane fair, indeed. Maeniel, give your son a talking to."

"Don't crow too quickly, old man," Maeniel said. "You don't know what this portends."

"He might not, but I do," Kyra said quietly. "Dugald is right. She will marry a king, and even before that, she will be a queen."

That night, I slept with Kyra as I always have. We went a little apart form the men, closer to the beach, where we could watch the wheeling stars. After her statement this evening, no one had questioned Kyra's words. Maeniel pulled Black Leg aside. He was a boy again, and we could both pretend nothing had happened.

"She used to think things like that were funny," he complained to Maeniel.

"Obviously, times have changed," Maeniel told him as they walked together. "She's sensitive about certain changes taking place. . . ."

And that was all I heard, because they went into the woods together. The rest of us sat down at the table to eat. There was no further quarreling, and when darkness fell, we all went in search of our beds.

I was wakeful. I had too much thinking to do. Kyra had said I would become a queen even before I married a king, and I was wondering how that was to be accomplished. Then I thought about the quarrel between Black Leg and myself. I remembered what he had said, and he was right. It was funny. He was right about another thing, also. In the past, I would have laughed. I laughed now, but at the moment my initiation into womanhood had been too new a burden to bear. So I was sorry and wanted to make up when I heard faint noises in the undergrowth around the space where Kyra and I were sleeping. I knew I had been allowed to hear the noises, and Black Leg was probably out there moving around, wanting to talk.

I tossed my blankets aside and crawled quietly toward the noises. I could smell him—woodsmoke, warm bread, young skin, and a musk that said male animal. I can't describe it. But ever since I could remember, he'd always carried that odor with him. Only it was stronger now, much stronger than it had been when we parted in the realm of Dis.

Yes, I thought. *I am a woman, and he is becoming a man.*

His arms went around me. "I'm sorry," he whispered.

"So am I." I giggled a little. It was funny.

Then we kissed. He was warm, but uncertain. I heated in his embrace, and for the first time understood all the wiggling and crying out of the couples we had seen making love.

He did, also, because I felt his shock and then urgency as his prick responded to my length of body against his own. We were both clothed. I still had my britches on, and so did he. But it came up hard and stiff, right between my thighs.

I broke the kiss and threw back my head. Not to escape him; I didn't want to. But to concentrate more completely on what was happening below.

My legs tightened on the shaft. I saw in the starlight his mouth open. Wolflike, he made no sound, but I felt his whole body stiffen.

The power of his embrace was so strong, it was painful. I felt my ribs give, but I didn't care. He could hurt me like that all he wanted. He could hurt me like that all night.

At the same moment, I felt my nails dig into his shoulder and back. Another second and we would both have been down on the pile of dead leaves where we were standing, clawing at each other, crazy with a pitiless hunger. I felt as though I were caught in a riptide. I had wandered into still waters, thinking them calm, and been seized from below and pulled down. I was helpless against this maelstrom.

The flames leaping between us scorched, blinded, and terrified us. Kyra parted us with a log from the fire. We separated to escape the heat, and seconds later were scrambling alone, parted, struggling on the forest's loamy floor.

I jumped to my feet and ran across our bed ground, ran, slapped at the embers smoldering on my shirt. I had a glimpse of Black Leg, his shirt scorched and smoldering, his body thrown back against the trunk of a low, twisted, windblown pine, fists clenched, eyes closed. Kyra stood between us, torch blazing in her hand.

The Gray Watcher stepped out of the darkness. His and Kyra's eyes met.

"That was a very near thing," he said.

Kyra nodded. "I had no idea things had gotten this far."

Black Leg came away from the tree and took a solid swing at his father. His fist landed with a loud crack in Maeniel's left palm as he fended his son off with his right hand.

I was crying so hard, I could barely see. "Stop! Oh, stop!" I spoke to Black Leg. "He hasn't done anything but what he had to do."

"Yes." Kyra spoke softly. "I can see you two didn't know how matters stood between you, either."

"No," Black Leg said. "I didn't. At least I just came to apologize and maybe ask her if she wanted to do a little night fishing."

"Night fishing, eh?" Kyra said. "And what did you hope to catch?"

"Not what I got. Only fish, Kyra, only fish," he said dismally.

She shook her head. "What a pair of innocents you are—the both of you. Come." She gestured toward the fire. "Come. We need to talk."

Black Leg looked at his father. "Yes," Maeniel said, "you, too." Then he vanished silently into the darkness.

We couldn't look at each other. We both sat down by the fire. Kyra joined us.

"Once," she said, "men obeyed their mothers and the world was good."

Black Leg blinked and stared at her truculently. "What has that to do with anything?"

"A lot," Kyra replied. "And you will shut up and listen. As I said, once we women ruled the world. At that time, there was but little meadow and no plowed land. People moved from place to place, harvesting the great bounty of the earth. Near waters, we fished. Among the trees, we gathered acorns and hazelnuts. Both of you know they make good bread.

"Among the trees, we hunted deer, elk, and the wild aurochs. All bellies were filled, and no man could call himself better than another because he wore a crown or his father bore a famous name. When decisions needed to be made, the people called on the dream walkers, and they read the future and told the people what they must do. Then one day the dreams of some of the women turned to nightmares."

Kyra was silent for a space, and for the first time I realized she was growing old and had begun to grow old among us.

"It was their duty," she continued, "to see the future, and they saw it too well. They saw human hands stretched out to control what was once freely given. A man planted crops, saw the crop mature, and harvested it for himself. Most saw that as a good thing. But one diviner understood that, while a good thing at first, it would turn bad in the end. And that once started down this road, we would not be able to turn back. There would be too many of us. The broad fabric of the ancient covenant between ourselves and the earth was torn open, and our lives would spill out through the ruined veil.

"So she and her sisters created a kingdom of women. The paradise of women. I was taught there. Taught magic, war, and law by the Scathatch and her daughters."

"This is a real place?" Black Leg asked.

"Real as the earth I sit on now," Kyra answered. "We have all heard the stories about how the ancient sorceress saw the sea rise and drown the land. So she led her people north to the mountains, where they might found their own kingdom and keep alive the splendor of the old ways. And they became the Painted People, ruling in their mountain fastness for uncountable centuries."

"The land is poor there," Black Leg said. "They have good reason to keep to the old ways."

"True," Kyra said. "They do. But their life ways work. Most among them live in dignity and peace. On the Isle of Women, we are taught how to make them work, what we must do."

"War, law, and magic," I said.

"Yes," Kyra answered. "War because envy, cruelty, and greed are universal. Sad to say, all good things must be defended. I forgot that, and my family died. Law so that disputes may be resolved and justice done."

"But magic, that's another thing," I said.

Kyra smiled. "You are both creatures of magic. Magic protects the life of the universe. Because the universe is alive in its own way, and life and meaning are part of it, the way color is part of a flower or the fingers part of a hand.

"Because you are magic, it matters very much what both of you do now. You must choose your lives. It is time. I thrust the torch between you to give you that choice before you were both swept up too far into the currents of desire."

"First," I said, "I want to know why you believe your own mistakes caused your family's deaths."

Kyra's eyes turned inward. "Fair enough," she answered. "The first sorceress who saw the land flood and the perishing of the good order of the world was one of a large family. Her line did not fail. I know; I am one of them, and so are you—as was your mother and even Merlin and Igrane. Power is, of course, not devoted to good or, for that matter, to evil. Earth, air, fire, and water are the components of everything. Both of you understand that."

"Yes. But what does that mean in practical terms?" I asked.

"In practical terms, it means we of the Painted People have a tradition of training our leaders and choosing them from among those we think would be best suited to the task. I was one so chosen and so trained by the high priestess, known as Scathatch, on the Isle of Women. We are needed in times of crisis to deal with any problems that might arise."

"And what happened?" Black Leg asked.

Kyra was silent for a space, and I could hear the fire burn and the wind sigh in the trees.

"A great catastrophe happened among the Seal people. The queen's line failed. There was a sickness and the women died—all of them—a terrible omen. A delegation was sent to Scathatch's isle to find out what to do.

"I was proud of my skill in divination. I almost always could point out a productive course of action. Indeed, when summoned by the Scathatch, I knew without being told what was wrong. You see, there were five women; that was why no one thought the line could fail. When the ship drew up to the quay, I turned to go up to her seat in the fortress. I saw the first woman. I thought she was simply a child. I didn't know. She passed me coming down. Then I saw her small feet left no footprints in the wet sand.

"The second met me at a bend in the path. She was gazing out over the sea, but I could see the rock she sat on through her body. The third was only a shadow. I could see the fourth, but she cast two shadows. They died together. The fifth stood at the head of the path and glared at me with eyes of flame. She alone of them all spoke. 'Choose well,' she said.

"I stopped because I didn't want to pass through her, but as she spoke, she vanished."

"Did you?" I asked. "Choose well?"

"No!" Kyra said very sharply. "I didn't. That's why I'm warning you now. Black Leg cannot be a king."

For the first time, Black Leg and I looked at each other.

"No," Black Leg said slowly. "No, I can't."

"Is that what they wanted you for—to choose a king?" I asked.

Kyra nodded. "This is the business of the royal line among the Painted People—to choose a king. And this is why your mother lay with the lords of the Sidhe and took on herself the curse of an early death—so that you might carry within your body sovereignty not just of the land but of the spirit of a whole people. On your body you carry the tokens of sovereignty. To you, it is but a gift of your father and an acknowledgment of paternity. But it speaks to the legitimacy of your claim to be known by right of blood as the king's Flower Bride. Tell me, have you pledged your faith with the young king?"

I was silent for a space. Then I turned and met Black Leg's eyes. "I have!" I answered proudly.

Kyra rose and walked away, out of the circle of firelight, leaving us alone.

"Why?" Black Leg asked.

"He is my other half," I answered. I don't know even now where the words came from, only that as I spoke them, I understood in some profound way their truth.

"What would you have me do?" I asked.

Black Leg's eyes were fierce as a hawk's or a wolf's on the hunt. "Come with me," he said. "We can live and love with humans, wolves, or both. I will be a hunter of great renown among the packs and a magnificent warrior among men. I know." He struck his chest with his fist. "I know. I feel it here."

"This is what you want?"

"Yes!" he answered. "Everything I want except . . . you."

"It cannot be," I answered. "And you know why."

We both knew why.

"Vortigen," I said, "is dead these hundred years. Yet your father, Maeniel, spoke to him, came to ask his help for the Bagaudae in France. I think you will take after your father."

"No," he said, scrambling to his feet. "I won't just be a watcher."

"Then seek the Isle of Women," I said. "They will teach you to become the most dangerous warrior of all."

"Where is the Isle of Women?" he asked.

"East of the sun, west of the moon. Follow the coast and they will call you."

Again, I didn't know where the words came from. But again I knew they were important and that it was important that I speak them. I wondered if this was part of the gift she had given me, the power to sometimes see into the souls of my companions and advise them well.

I doubt, you see, that the first queen of the people wanted to leave her pleasant, well-watered valley, where she and her people hunted in the winter and in the summer allowed the sea's bounty to smile upon them, and journey to the cold crags, where they now made their home. But she knew the pleasant choice was not the wisest one, and so she accepted her fate.

A second later, my friend, my playmate, my foster brother was gone, and a big, gray wolf stood beside me. I turned toward him, tears swimming in my eyes. His nose touched mine. Then he was gone.

CHAPTER EIGHTEEN

I CAN'T FIND HIM," MERLIN SAID TO IGRANE.

She chuckled.

"Don't you dare," he said.

She tried, a bit unsuccessfully, to suppress a smile. His eyes lingered on her. The hag's magic had worked well. She was beautiful again. It was a lean sort of beauty; her breasts were hardly bigger than ripe apples, cherry-topped. Her stomach was so flat it was concave, and her ribs were visible. Her skin was gardenia white, protected from the sun by unguents, oils, and a little of her own magic. Her legs were so long as to make other women's seem stubby by comparison, her sex a mound of soft curls.

As he watched, she spread her legs slightly, showing a bit, just a bit, of warm, scarlet flesh between them.

"Cover yourself!" he commanded and averted his eyes. His nostrils distended, but he knew he couldn't afford this right now. He needed all his energies, his power. She distracted him. She always had. His had been a downhill course since he had met her.

Before that he had been able to concentrate all his energies on matters of state. He had dominated the politics of several successive kings and protected his power base among the great landowners of Britain. Protected them and their possessions.

Now this boy looked to slip through his fingers. He'd aided and abetted her in torturing her child, Arthur, but he sensed she'd gone too far. Her own tendencies toward cruelty and domination had betrayed her. A somewhat lighter touch and he would have wound up her slave, but she enjoyed tormenting the child too much. She hadn't had the discretion to refrain from or limit her pleasures when the king was present, and he had caught her.

When Merlin arrived, she had a broken jaw and arm, and the boy was gone. He'd punished her; he liked punishing her. In fact, before the night was out, he would probably punish her again. But he wouldn't kill her. He ought to, but he wouldn't. And she knew it.

Hearing the genuine anger in his voice, she sighed and pulled on a long silk robe. "I thought you told me he couldn't get out of that cage." She sounded snappish.

"I didn't think he could," Merlin admitted. "But somehow he found the courage to climb down the cliff."

"He never lacked courage," she said, belting the robe. "I told you not to underestimate him. I can remember his eyes on me as a child. It was as though even while he was screaming, reduced to tears and fouling his clothing, some part of him stood aside, reckoning up the injuries and waiting for his chance to repay them in kind. I wish you had killed him."

"He's your son." Even Merlin was a little horrified.

"What is that to me?" She spoke over her shoulder. Some distance away, near the terrace, her women were waiting like a bouquet of brightly colored flowers to do her hair and dress her for dinner. Watching her body undulate across the floor, part of Merlin's mind considered his pleasures for the night, while the other part mulled over the problem of the young king. The politics of this country had been a problem since before the Romans. In a sense, they had only compounded the difficulties.

The Romans had been interested in the low, fertile lands centered around London. This wealthy agricultural land was what had drawn Caesar. The loot he extracted from the coastal tribes, the human merchandise collected by the slave dealers who followed him, and the tribute extorted from the rest of the country went far to pay his debts in Rome and make him its first full-time emperor. When Claudius followed and began a conquest of the country, a permanent conquest this time, it was primarily these warm, southern lowlands he was interested in, also.

But to the Romans' dismay, they found the deeper they ventured into the countryside, the harder the going got. Most of this never made it into the historical chronicles the Romans kept. But the mountains of Cornwall and Wales were higher; the forests denser; the tribes wilder, more dangerous, and less submissive than groups from the richer, coastal basin. Still there was gold and silver to be mined and much rich farmland to be exploited, easily worked by slaves or *coloni*—semifree serfs—for their new masters. From the less settled or exploitable parts of the country, furs, amber, and slaves generated by the endemic state of warfare between the tribes were valuable commodities.

All in all the Roman nobility were well satisfied with the situation. Bodiccia's revolt was the first indication that things wouldn't go entirely their way.

The Roman garrisons were lucky to crush it before the Roman presence was completely stamped out. But after that it was all downhill. Slowly downhill perhaps, but nevertheless a constant erosion took place. Six legions had to be stationed here to ensure the safety of the by now Romano-British landowners. Wales could never be completely subdued. In the end, after many violent campaigns, the Roman garrisons were content to extract tribute.

Hadrian's wall was at last a magnificent achievement and a confession of failure. The Romans were nothing if not ruthless bottom liners, and the bottom line was that Roman conquests had to pay for themselves. And there was no way that the legions could extract enough good land, silver, gold, or sellable slaves to repay them for the blood and treasure they had to pour out to finally and forever break the resistance of the native peoples.

What they did succeed in doing was dividing the country into two groups: the free tribes—people who ran their affairs according to customs that had been practices quite literally time out of mind—and the civilized Romano-British landowners and their downtrodden slaves.

The slaves always had before their eyes the example of the freemen holding firm in the mountains of Wales and the ancient peoples of the highlands, whose claim to sovereignty was not just over the land of Britain but also over its religious life. Their claim to have been the first originators of law and governance for the entire island was hallowed not by centuries but by millennia. He didn't know whether or not he believed the tales that they went to the mountains when the sea began to fill the valley between England and France. The story seemed like foolishness to him. But he knew he always came out second best when he crossed swords with their witch queens and sorcerers.

Like the little bitch who humbled Igrane and himself.

When the Romans left, he had cast his lot with the Romano-British. God, they were civilized. They lived in houses, read books, had table manners. These wild men and women on the fen, moor, mountain, and deepest forests, who wore out short lives in loving, fighting, feasting, sailing, fishing on the deep seas, singing, and storytelling—what had any truly civilized man to do with them?

He loved his comforts, was a connoisseur of women, food, wine, and he had the best of everything. They went to bed on the floor, on skins, scratching their lice. And sometimes endured two seasons of famine a year, one in spring before the sheep dropped lambs and another near autumn before the crops came in. If he could have what he wished at the expense of others, why so much the worse for them. In any case, most of them were second-rate material, better winnowed out the way a barren cow is by a harsh winter or an old hen fit only for the pot.

He admired the Romans. They brought civilization and law and order to the island. And the conquest of the drunk, disorderly rabble they crushed beneath their heel could only be a good thing. Twice the civilized south had made a bid to conquer the barbarian north. The second time, he had "arranged" the death of Vortigen and his powerful druid, Vareen. But he had failed. The Veneti had betrayed him by refusing to resupply the Saxon levies left behind by the legions, and he had found he had to back a new high king to halt the ever-widening chaos that threatened to bring down the powerful southern landowners, his civilized allies.

Uther Pendragon was that king. Now he, the chief druid of Britain, was faced with another rebel in his son, Arthur. Igrane *would* torture the boy! It hadn't been wise. Though Merlin agreed he could be broken and brought to heel by that means. He should have had her poisoned and taken over the child's education himself. He understood the use of subtler means to control others. But he had fallen into his own trap. She was like a drug. *Luxuria*, the Romans called it. A descent into forbidden pleasures. He could feel the tightening in his loins at the mere thought.

Her women were setting a table for two among the flowers on the terrace. Wine, Roman wine in glass goblets. Dishes of crystal, gold, and silver would hold the fruits the glassed-in chambers of his dwelling produced in such abundance summer and winter alike. There would be venison, wild boar, squab stuffed with strawberries taken from the open hilltops of Cornwall. And to top off the meal, pastries redolent of saffron and myrrh.

And afterward, Igrane was dessert. He couldn't wait.

I cried all night. But at dawn, Kyra made me do up my hair and put on a scarlet silk tunic embroidered with gold and a pair of trousers made of the same material. We had a brief, violent debate about shoes.

"You aren't going to wear those horrible things," she said, pointing to the rough leather sandals Talorcan made for me.

"I certainly am," I said.

Kyra picked them up and reacted much the same way Igrane had. They fell from her hands as though red hot.

"My God," she whispered. "Where in heaven or hell's halls did you get those?"

"Hell's halls," I said. "Torc Trywth made them for me. His name is Talorcan. They change to fit what I'm doing or wearing."

And they did, too—becoming gold with many laces that came up to my calves and tied just below the knee.

Then the whole lot of us—all but Black Leg, who was gone—I, Kyra,

Dugald, the Gray Watcher, Gray, and Anna went down to the shelter of a quiet cove, where a ship was waiting. Farry was the captain.

"You have your own ship now?" I said, surprised to see him.

"Yes, and you have become as lovely as I thought you might," he said. I offered my cheek, but he only took my hand and kissed it.

"So formal?" I asked.

"The occasion calls for formality," he said gravely. He, too, looked older. He had a short, curly beard and his hair was long now and hung to his shoulders. All in all, a fine-looking man. He wore a beautiful, woolen mantle of Irish weave. The underlying color was black, but it was striped with soft blue, green, and a dark red like wine. Only our people know how to make such things. I have never seen Greek, Roman, or Eastern cloth woven in this way. It is one of the more profitable trade goods the Veneti, Farry's people, carry even now to the east, where it is still in demand.

"When did you get your own ship?" I asked.

Farry flushed and answered, "My father gave it to me when I acknowledged my first son."

"How wonderful," I said, congratulating him. I wondered how many wives he had by now. The Veneti, especially a captain with his own ship, would have several. They tied him along his personal trade route with guest friendship, ensuring his safety while in port.

That was why they were so influential a people. Yes, Caesar had killed many of those who plied the French coast when he destroyed Ohene, port city in Brittany. Dishonor to his name, the Romans always persecuted trading peoples. But few cared to open disputes with traders. They were useful to everyone. There are always things that even relative self-sufficiency can't supply. Spices, cloth, metals, gemstones, walrus ivory, and sometimes honey and salt; we must trade for those things. And Farry's people supplied them, occasionally in quantity when famine threatened or war increased the need for weapons. It was best to keep friends with them.

"I'm here," he told me, "to bring you to the great assembly of the Painted People. When I have completed my business here, we will sail north."

Kyra nodded to me.

"So soon?" I asked.

Her mouth was tight, a thin line. "The sooner, the better."

"Yes," Farry said.

A lot of business was being transacted around us, on both the deck and the beach. As I watched, a local smith came to an agreement about a heap of scrap metal and one of Farry's men began to load it into sacks to bring it to the beach. A nearby carpet was covered with packets of spices and odds and ends of jewelry. At least a half-dozen men and women were haggling with the crewman in charge of the merchandise.

There were stoneware crocks of honey and oil, and a rack of wine amphoras under an awning shaded from the sun's heat. I desperately wanted to stop and look, but Maeniel and Dugald flanked me on either side and ushered me gently but firmly past small bales of linen and silk toward a pavilion on the stern of the boat.

"We have business here," Dugald said. "Important business."

"Oh, stop," I said. "At least you could let me—"

"Paw through those trinkets?" Dugald snapped. "They are beneath you. You will be a queen."

Farry suppressed a grin.

I sighed deeply. "I saw a pretty silver ring . . ." I began.

"I'll buy it for you," Maeniel said. "Now, move. The lady is waiting. Please, captain, whatever she wants," he added, hustling me along.

"It has a moonstone, very appropriate," Farry said, and stooped down to pick it up when we passed the carpet.

Maeniel slid the heavy, silver circlet on my finger.

"Too large," Kyra said.

"She will grow into it," Farry said confidently.

I noticed the pavilion had a curtain that shielded the inhabitants from the prying eyes of Farry's customers at the front of the ship. He pushed it aside and ushered me in.

I knew who she was the moment I saw her. He favored his father's side of the family.

She was legend.

Morgana. Said to be the most powerful of all enchantresses. So joined to her goddess the two were almost one in the same body.

I started to kneel, but Dugald tightened his grip on my arm and said, "Don't—you—dare."

I didn't.

"To what do we owe the honor?" Dugald asked.

She drifted forward. She surprised me by being plainly dressed, until I realized the subtlety of the silk brocade dalmatic and the deerskin, suede britches. It was an opalescent shimmering blue gown covered with a pattern of black raven's wings. The torc around her neck probably had a couple of pounds of pure gold in it, as did her belt, shining black hematite, gold, and real opal.

She was tawny, not blond. I have never seen coloring like that before and not since. I knew . . . she was like her grandson Cai. Shape-strong, but in what way I couldn't tell.

"Kyra? Dugald?" she said, looking at each one.

"You know my guardians?" I asked.

"I don't see anything special about you," she said directly to me.

"I don't know that there is," I answered.

"Yes, nothing that would make you someone he would have married. I was told you pledged yourself to him."

"I thought it was the other way around. He pledged himself to me."

"You exchanged vows," Maeniel said.

"I suppose we did," I answered.

"Are you sorry?" Morgana asked.

"No," I said. "He is what I want."

"Are you so sure?" Maeniel asked.

I turned and looked at him. "I'm sorry about Black Leg, but, yes, yes, I am sure."

"Well and good," Morgana said. "But it may all come to nothing. He is gone."

"Gone!" I said and stepped away from my family toward her. "Gone where?"

"Merlin made some dreadful magic and sent him to the summer country," she replied. "He is in another world. A world from which the only passage back is death."

Maeniel whistled, and Magetsky landed on the ship's rail. The raven hissed and made that farting sound it had learned.

"Be silent," I said, "or I'll burn off every feather you have. If you know something about Arthur, tell it to us now."

"How can she do that and be silent? Don't be so anxious to use that talented right hand of yours. Keep it in reserve for serious matters," Maeniel said.

The bird pecked with her beak on the rail and called Maeniel a nasty name. Then swung her backside around—it had been over the water. She aimed it at the deck, and what was worse, the carpet Morgana stood on.

Maeniel swatted her into the air, out over the water, and she didn't get to do the damage she wanted to. She gave a screech.

Kyra said, "Bird, I'm having sausage for supper. Keep on, and I won't give you any."

Magetsky circled the ship and came in for a landing where she had been sitting moments before. She hunched down. Fluffed her feathers, and looked sulky.

"Sausage," Kyra said.

Magetsky began to talk to Maeniel. She had seen Arthur at Tintigal, not long ago, Maeniel told Morgana. She has been watching the place.

He glanced suspiciously at Magetsky. I don't know why.

"She is a devious and dishonest creature," Dugald said self-righteously. Magetsky made more kissie noises and a few more wet fart sounds at Dugald.

"At any rate," Maeniel plowed on, "she says she is glad she is a bird, because his mother was tormenting him with her beauty."

Morgana's lips curled in disgust.

"But he—no, I won't say that in the presence of his kin," Maeniel told Magetsky, who cackled raucously.

"In any case," Maeniel continued, "according to the bird, Merlin joined the party and the boy hit him . . . in—in—a very tender spot."

Morgana laughed. "I hope he ruined him."

Maeniel continued, "The wizard did magic and sent the boy back where he came from."

A manservant stood near Morgana.

"Bird, I thank you." She turned to the servant and said, "Give the bird some of what we had for lunch. This information is most useful. Merlin must have made an alliance with King Bade. Otherwise, Arthur couldn't come and go so easily. The two have connived together to imprison him."

Magetsky strutted to and fro on the rail, until the servant returned with a bowl. Then she hopped down to the deck and attacked the meat ravenously.

Farry brought cushions, and we all sat down together on the carpet and shared some wine, bread, and porridge.

"This is a dangerous situation," Morgana said. "Uther is furious and preparing for war."

Dugald and Maeniel nodded.

"The way I found you was that your friend Farry here—he wouldn't tell me where you were because he said Merlin was hunting you and that you had to flee the people of your village. But he said he would bring me to you. So, I am here. Tell me, girl, did you actually exchange any promises?"

"What is your reason for wanting to know?" Dugald asked in a self-important manner.

Morgana looked annoyed. "If they formed a tie, I might be able to use her to help me retrieve him. King Bade of the summer land is no trivial opponent, and reaching out into another world isn't all that easy."

"No," I answered. "No, it can't be. But tell me how—"

That was as far as I got, because Dugald snapped, "Be quiet. In this, you should be guided by your elders."

Kyra rolled her eyes. "Old man, the girl is wise enough about matters. . . ."

That was all she said, because Magetsky saw a chance to get her licks in at Dugald. She has really hated him since that trip to Ireland. She made a quick hop away from the food and drove her beak into Dugald's thigh.

He let out a yell. Magetsky cackled loudly and went *yrrrrrp*. She took wing and hovered just over his head.

I leaped to my feet and snatched her out of the air. She gave another outraged screech and drove her beak into my wrist. The armor leaped out all along my arm. It partially protected me, but even so, blood ran down the back of my hand. It was my fire hand.

Magetsky knew she had gone too far. She stopped struggling, hunched down, and said, *yek!* She studied me with one onyx eye. She looked very frightened. I shook with anger, and the armor leaped out all over my body.

"Certain it is," Dugald said, "that vile denizen of the air will be no loss to the world."

Funny, I had threatened her without meaning it. Now I frightened her without meaning to threaten her. I folded my legs and sat down on my cushion, and plunked Magetsky back by her bowl.

"Eat," I said. "And trouble me no more for the rest of the afternoon, at least."

Magetsky put the bowl between me and her, then went back to her dinner, unruffled, as far as I could tell, except that occasionally she cast a wary eye in my direction.

"I think I can speak for myself," I told Dugald.

Morgana nodded.

"No," I said. "We exchanged no vows, but he told me he wanted me. And as far as I dared, I told him his . . . his . . . attentions were very welcome."

This sounded a bit stiff, but I didn't know how to tell a distinguished stranger that my knees weakened whenever he so much as touched my hand.

"So there is a tie," she said.

"Yes," I answered. "There is. I cannot say how much of it is our doing or how much is . . . the work of the veiled ones."

She nodded, because she knew of whom I spoke. I have not known any who do not believe in the veiled ones, though they call them different things. Certain it is the Romans did, the Greeks, the Saxons, and certainly my people. The fates, so called, they are *her* eldest servants, but it is not known if even she commands them.

"So," Morgana said. "Give me your hand."

"No!" Dugald roared.

"No," Kyra said. "My lady, with all due respect . . ."

"Yes," I said. They both started to speak, but Maeniel lifted his hand.

"The choice is hers," he said, "as it was last night. Though I would she had chosen otherwise, none of us can force the issue."

They were silent.

I stretched out both hands to Morgana. "Which one?" I asked.

"The left," Morgana said without hesitation. "Though likely you believe otherwise, it is the ruling one."

Yes, I thought. *I healed Gray with it and used it to comfort Talorcan.*

So I rose and walked toward her. We clasped hands, standing face-to-face, our fingers laced together. Her right held my left. Then she bent her elbow, and I mine, and our hands were lifted between us, the palm of mine facing my heart, the palm of hers facing her heart.

I felt the abyss. Dugald had told me about it. The abyss is the greatest barrier to magic. It is the nothingness from which everything came. Called up in some unknowable fashion. That is the question, the one permanent, eternal question, unendurable and unanswerable: why anything at all—why not nothing?

If practitioners get caught in the contemplation of that question for too long, it drains their power and they fail in whatever task they have undertaken.

Look away, she said. *I have found it's the best way to handle that particular problem.*

Dugald says it must be overcome, I answered.

A daunting task, that, she replied. We were not speaking in words, you understand, and I felt the humor of her reply. *One might say an impossible one. No! It cannot be overcome. Men, they place such trust in brute force. I've found simple avoidance works much better. That is the danger of dealing with Merlin. He thinks like a woman. He merely distracted Uther for a short time, and his net fell over Arthur while we weren't looking. His stratagems are endless and brilliant, but his subtlety suggests his powers may at length be waning.*

Truly? I asked.

I believe so, she answered.

I tried to close my mind to the abyss by calling up Arthur's face. Very easily, it seemed, I found myself beside him.

He had just finished speaking. I knew that. The crowd around him seemed stunned by his words. Many wept. Others stood silent yet with a light in their eyes that suggested a great burden had been lifted from their souls. But he seemed uninterested in what they thought or felt, as if he wanted to evade their gratitude at all costs.

He spoke to a man-at-arms near him. "It is growing late. We must cross the river. If, as you say, this place grows more dangerous after dark, we haven't much time."

Then he strode toward the bridge. The women moved back to the shallows to fish. The men fell in behind Arthur, who took point and led them away.

"Law, Balin," he said as the group marched, "is all well and good. But cattle are how we live."

"Don't try to make what you just did less," a black-bearded man said. "That we are not free men haunts us all. Much of what we think of ourselves is defined by what others tell us. And all our lives we have been told we were slaves and the property of this King Bade."

I could sense Arthur was surprised at this man's acuity. His brows rose. "May I know your name?" he asked.

"Caradog Freichfras," the black-beard answered. "I was one of the chief's sons caught in the sweep. Will you now become our king and lead us?"

Arthur looked uncomfortable. "I have . . ." he began, but then broke off because they were well beyond the bridge and into the trees. And they had reached a point where they could see the cattle and far out into the valley beyond.

I heard Arthur gasp and I understood why. Long have I lived, but not before or since have I seen such beauty. Near the river, a mountain torrent flowed over a cliff, watering the first meadow where the cattle—pale buff beasts with red ears, hooves, and tails—grazed. Beyond the first meadow, the river flowed over a slope of giant boulders, into a second meadow a bit below it. And from there, into a third. Like giant steps, the meadows fell away toward a valley, sunstruck and hazy with distance.

"Ah, God," Arthur whispered. "Never have I seen so fair a place as this. The realm of King Bade."

The meadows were surrounded by mountains, but they were not unapproachable snow-covered peaks in the distance rising sharp as pale knives against the sky. These were low hummocks of dark stone slopes covered by forests of ancient hardwoods stretching down into the open meadowed valleys. The long, rich green grass brushed Arthur's kneecaps, and the cattle were fat with it.

"Eden!" Arthur said, "before Eve took the serpent's apple and gave it to her lover."

"Well and good," Balin said, "but there was a serpent in Eden after all. And there is one here." He pointed to the dark tower.

Arthur's first thought was that the thing was a ruin. But it wasn't. It simply flowed out of the earth the way the supports for the bridge had. Trees grew out of it, and some of them seemed to be part of it. An incredibly old oak was set close to the ground, and the roots, rather than tearing up the stones—boulders, really—at the base of the tower, seemed to be holding them together. A willow farther on had a hollow trunk that formed a catchment basin for water that fed vines, flowering vines that grew in and out between smaller stones like mortar.

The mixture of trees and other plants covered a round tower that rose beside the waterfall, up and up, until it looked out over the falls, the river, and all the valleys beyond.

"They say she rules here as much as Bade does," Balin said.

"Who?" Arthur asked.

"The Queen of the Dead," Balin answered.

"The Queen of the Dead," Arthur repeated.

"She rules *them*," Balin said, and pointed to three horsemen herding the cattle. They were the three Arthur had killed in the barn.

"She heard the flies, smelled the stink, and called them," Balin whispered.

"Ah!" Arthur said. "I see."

He didn't, I was sure, but you must appear confident when you lead men. An army is as liable to panic as a flock of children. Or so Maeniel tells me. I expressed doubt about this when he said it. But even Dugald agreed with him, and they did not have their usual acrimonious debate.

This is one of the reasons the Romans were so successful—military discipline. It keeps them headed in the right direction and obeying their officers' orders.

The herdsmen were a grisly crew, pale, the washed-out gray that corpses show when the blood is gone. One's throat had been cut and sewn back together with sinew; another had no eyes—only reddish paste in the sockets. The third looked well enough but for the dreadful wound in his back. They had been gutted, and their bellies had been sewn together to keep them from rotting quickly.

"They can do simple tasks," Balin said, "until they decay and fall to pieces. There will be men nearby to supervise them."

"Let us go and find the—" Arthur said.

The water hit me square in the face. I screamed, and the connection between me and Arthur was broken. I found myself standing on the deck of the ship, the sun burning my neck, blinded by what seemed like the deluge that poured over me.

"You were in too deep," Dugald complained. "In a short time, you might have been drawn into—" he made the sign of the cross, and I remembered he was a Christian priest, also "—into God knows where," he finished.

Morgana was sitting on a cushion, looking exhausted. One of her attendants handed me a towel, and I dried my face and body. Morgana was panting as if she had run a long race, and I felt drained and exhausted also.

"He has escaped Bade and Merlin both," I said, "and is free, though I think in peril. But I believe Bade will find him a troublesome guest. A very troublesome guest."

Morgana couldn't speak yet, but she grinned wolfishly. I saw she agreed with me.

We returned to our encampment without telling Morgana what our plans were. She said she didn't want to know. And Maeniel and Dugald agreed that was probably for the best.

I said a kind farewell to Farry at the dock. He did kiss my cheek then, and told me to keep him informed of our movements. To this end, he gave me a cage with four birds in it.

"You know how to use them," he said.

I did. They are an old trick of the Veneti, one way a dispersed people can communicate quickly. Carrier pigeons.

Then we returned to camp.

That night, I lay in my blankets near Kyra, looking up at the stars. I was surprised that I couldn't sleep. The half cup of wine I had with dinner had nearly knocked me out, and I turned in almost at sunset, not the usual custom with me. Normally, even when we were at home, we sat up late.

Sometimes Kyra told us a story or Maeniel and Dugald argued and debated whatever of the world's events they had disagreed on during the day. And they seldom agreed to disagree. Instead, after nightfall, the dispute usually became louder and more heated, until the Gray Watcher went wolf and Dugald stalked away to his bed, muttering to himself loudly.

Kyra, Black Leg, and I took sides, sometimes supporting the wolf, at others Dugald. Now Black Leg was gone and I didn't know when I would see him again, if ever.

Thinking of him, a dark finger of grief touched my heart. If I could have, I would have wanted to have him nearby always as a friend and brother. But that wasn't possible, and it would not have been fair to him to try to keep him.

I rolled on my back and lay looking up at the stars. The bear was overhead, and I remembered that some called Arthur the Bear.

Dea Arto. The mountain goddess.

Kyra told me she was very ancient. Long ago, when her people fled the rising seas and came to the highlands, they made offerings to her of honey and oil. And also, in spring, salmon, because these were all things she loved. Among the Silures, men only offered the salmon.

The Bear society was the fiercest and best. When they fought, they drew lots, and the winner went naked into battle as an offering. The Romans thought us mad to fight naked, and, indeed, most often we don't. But those on whom the battle goddess's exultation falls do march out in the vanguard as offerings, blood offerings to the wrathful, blood-drinking daughters of Dis that they may quench their thirst and spare the rest.

Maeniel says it doesn't work, and for once Dugald agrees with him. But the Bears still follow the old custom, and it is said no Bear has ever been known to die of a wound in his back. However great the odds, they have always fallen with their faces toward the enemy. If Arthur was a Bear, he was a mighty man, a deadly man, and King Bade would have his hands full with him.

I closed my eyes and must have slept a bit, because the dragon's voice awakened me. He was singing a song of the stars. One of the songs about the houses of heaven that Kyra's people learn, that they may track the hours of the night, the days of the year, and the march of the centuries.

All people know the houses of heaven, or so Kyra tells me, but only the Veneti and the Painted People know the parts of the songs that allow them to traverse the whale road, far out of the sight of land, yet look up into the sky by night and know where they are. The queens of Kyra's people sit in their great halls, and each rules one house of the universe and one month of the year. The dragon sang of the house of the dragon.

I rose from my bed, pulled on my tunic, and walked down to the shore. The whole world was silent but for the low roar of the surf and the sea wind playing against the shore. The dragon glided back and forth in the shallows; his paddlelike fins stirred phosphorescence in the sea and the splash they made left a wake of cold fire.

He glided like a swan, neck arched, head bent down—a darker shape against a star-filled sky. Back and forth in a small bay between two rocky headlands.

I knew he felt me watching, yet he continued to swim, and as he swam, he sang. And I understood he was doing magic. He was asking the almighty powers for something.

And the something was me!

I didn't dare interrupt his singing, because I knew that whatever rules the universe was listening to him. Listening and answering.

The dragon song is a long one. Humans and dragons haven't always gotten along. They compete with humans for the basking shark, seal, and walrus; but above all, for the salmon and eel coming upriver to spawn. More than once a dragon rookery along the coast has been wiped out by angry and greedy humans who smashed their eggs and killed their young and, often as not, such females who remained to defend their children. The song spoke of all these things, and I found myself shivering, though the sea breeze wasn't unduly cold.

At length the dragon finished, turned, and glided toward shore. I felt rather than saw Kyra come up behind me.

"You go north," he said to her rather than to me. "And you, most royal lady, will sponsor her in and among the dwellings of your people."

"Yes," Kyra said.

"Half the seats in the hall of heaven are empty. Only the songs are remembered," the dragon said. "Of some, the line of the ancient seer queens have failed. In others, the dance floors are gone, swallowed by the sea. Others have nothing to do with us. We have no more truck with the archer, the wolf, or the fox. It has been how many centuries since all twelve queens were seated at once? It takes only one to bring a king to the people.

"Seven centuries, Kyra. Seven," the dragon said, "since you and your people fared forth no more, and you were content to tend your sheep, harvest the salmon, run and sit in your dark-raftered halls, telling each other tales of lost glories. Seven hundred years since you last sailed to the wine-dark seas of Greece or into the frozen north, where the seas glitter with islands of ice, in search of the ivory-tusked walrus or dark seal pelts. And buried your dead in the giant boulder tombs that dot the shores of Britain, Ireland, and Gaul.

"We mattered to you then, Kyra. We sailed the sea lanes with you, warned of storms, drove fish into your nets. The Dragon Queen was the greatest one of all. Then you didn't grudge us our tribute. Salmon, eel, ling, kelp, samphire, and sometimes even seal and whale we took to feed our young. It was only at the end, when you began to go in mortal fear of the Romans, that she, the last queen, betrayed us and thereby wrought her doom."

"No!" Kyra said. "None who ever occupied the Dragon Throne died in her bed. No, you may not have this one. No! And no again! Leave us! Go! Relations between your kind and ours are sundered. They were broken when Onbrawst danced, and the rock she danced upon was stricken by the trembling earth, and she and it fell into the sea."

"Don't I get a say in this?" I asked.

Kyra cried out, "What? Will you kill me with grief? Have I not had enough of sorrow in my life without this evil coming upon me?"

"Kyra," I said, "tonight there is a place I must go and a thing I must do."

A roar of wind came from behind me, parting my hair and blowing it out on either side of my face. The wind changed, and when I turned into the blast, I saw lightning dance over the mountains inland. The wind blew out to sea, and I knew I was being summoned.

I knew something, certainly not enough, of Kyra's grief. But I, or perhaps it, was something left by *her* to reassure Kyra, my mother in love.

"Kyra," I said, "whatever my fate, you will not live to mourn me. That grief will be mine. The sorrow at our parting."

Then I ran into the surf where the dragon waited. "Do you know . . . ?" I asked him.

"I know. The silver manes told me. They are old, and the centuries they have waited and watched are more than the stars in the sky on a clear night or the grains of sand on all the beaches throughout all the world. They do not speak to just anyone, but they will talk to you. The one called Lais promised, and they keep their word."

In moments, the only sight of the beach was the thin, pale line of the boiling surf. Then the dragon and I entered the darkness, and he began again to call down on me and his people the blessings of the star songs. And I knew that whatever might happen, I loved not just him but all his people. And they would make me a great queen and never, never, no matter what the cost to myself, would I ever betray them.

CHAPTER NINETEEN

ARTHUR HAD SENSED THEIR PRESENCE. AND, moreover, he knew in general who they were. He was aware that they were not Merlin or Igrane. He thought Morgana must have found a way to check up on him. He wasn't surprised. But he didn't think even she could get him back, not easily.

He remembered the basin at the foot of the cliff. He tried to empty his mind of the apprehension these things roused in him. Igrane's star-covered mantle had always given him chills. And in her mirror he knew she saw things that told her of the movements of others. She used it to terrorize him as a child. She told him he could never escape her gaze.

One night, waking from a nightmare about her, he confessed these fears to Morgana. He had begun to trust her a bit by then. No one at her stronghold ever laid hands on him in anger. He found out later she had forbidden anyone to touch him. It wasn't customary to correct children by beating them, not among his people, though the Saxons and the Romans both were very violent with their offspring. And so, these orders caused no resentment.

Besides, as many abused children are, he was almost frighteningly well behaved. So when he began to trust Morgana, she was careful not to betray that trust. She explained the limitations of Igrane's mirror to him, and he was reasonably sure, also, that she placed some sort of protective spell around him to keep Igrane from locating him as long as he was in her care.

He smiled a little at the memory, then returned to his consideration of the bowl, weighing the chances that it might be of some use to him. He decided he wouldn't know much, not without further investigation.

Balin broke in on his thoughts. "There they are."

Arthur saw a wavering column of white smoke rising from a grove of small oaks close by.

"They will not be expecting us," Arthur said. "How much killing will be required?"

"That's a strange question, coming from you," Balin said.

"I don't favor it unless it's necessary," Arthur replied. "Had those three been oath men of mine, I would have executed them had they abused even a captive woman the way they tried to do your wife. At worst, they were vile creatures who needed to be wiped from the face of the earth. At best, such behavior shows a dangerous lack of self-control. The first business of a warrior is self-restraint."

"Yes-s-s-s," Balin said slowly.

"I'll go see how many there are," Arthur said.

"May I accompany you?" Balin asked humbly.

"Yes. The rest of you stay here."

Arthur moved quietly. So quietly he astounded Balin. He picked his path, avoiding dead leaves, branches that might crack under his feet, and going around piles of dead leaves. A few moments later, they stood at the edge of a clearing in the long, dark shadows of the slender oaks, watching two men who sat near a small fire at the center of the grove.

Things were settled rather quickly. The two men didn't want to fight Arthur, and they handed over their weapons rather quickly.

Arthur studied the three on horseback. The dead men.

"They are truly dead?" he asked Balin.

"Yes," he answered.

One of the prisoners, a big man with a broken nose, said, "They give me the shivers. She—" he indicated the tower "—rules them now."

"She lives in the tower?" Arthur asked.

The other prisoner, a stout redhead, said, "I doubt if *live* is the word you want. I'll get a flogging for giving up so easily, but I'll live over it. I don't want any more part of this."

"I take it," Arthur said, "that neither of you is a devoted follower of this King Bade."

They looked at each other, then at Balin and Arthur.

"Where the hell is he from?" the redhead asked.

"I'm . . . not . . . sure, Firinne," Balin replied to the redhead.

"Truthful, at least," Arthur said. "I'm not sure either."

"No," Firinne continued. "No, we are not devoted followers of King Bade. We are his prisoners and slaves, the same as Balin here is . . . or was. Did Eline make it?"

"Yes," Balin said. "Bax led us through the marsh. He knows where the drowning pools are, the flesh eaters are afraid of him, and he found his way around the thorn barrier. It took us three days, but we got through."

"Good. I'm glad."

"Why don't you stay?" Balin asked.

"Yes," Arthur asked. "Why don't you? Why go back to be punished?"

"I have a wife and child there," Firinne said. "They are security held against my return. As it is, I live pretty well. The king's soldiers do. Eline was one of the king's dog handlers. He—" Firinne pointed at Balin "—was a field hand. No wife, slept in a barracks at night. If Eline hadn't taken up with him, he'd still be there. She and that dog got him out."

Balin looked shamefaced. "Firinne!"

His broken-nosed companion said, "No need to insult the man before his war chief."

"Is that what you are?" Firinne said. "A war chief? You look more like an unsuccessful brigand."

Arthur threw his head back and laughed. *How long,* he thought, *how long since I laughed like this?* It felt good.

"Well, look at him," Firinne said. "His clothes are clean enough, but they're about to rot off his body. A bird could make a nest in the hair on his face. He hasn't even got any weapons."

Arthur scratched his beard and grinned. "I don't need any," he said.

"It's the truth," Balin said. "He accounted for those three." He pointed to the mounted corpses.

Firinne and his companion fell silent.

"That's why I told you not to put up a fight," Broken Nose said. "When I saw him, I told you I had a feeling."

"Yes! Well and good," Arthur said. "I killed them. Now, how do I get rid of them? Killing doesn't seem enough."

Balin asked Arthur, "How good are you with a sling?"

"Passable," Arthur said. "Passable."

Balin handed him his and, surprisingly, some lead shot.

"Empty their skulls," Broken Nose said.

Arthur nodded and faced the one farthest away—the one with the sword wound in his back. "One."

He swung the sling.

The corpse's head exploded.

"Two." Arthur turned to the one with no eyes. He was facing them, except after the shot hit, the face vanished.

"Three," Arthur said. The stitches at the neck failed, and the head flopped grotesquely to one side, held on only by skin, before he slid from the saddle.

"You were right," Firinne said. "I don't want to fight him."

"Now," Arthur said. "Call the rest. Round up the cattle and bury that carrion or burn it—whatever it takes to get rid of it. And no shame about it, tell me about this King Bade. Tell me how he keeps his people in subjection, how he controls them, and why."

The story was surprisingly familiar to Arthur. Many of the powerful landowning families among the Romano-British behaved very little better than this King Bade. Who had, if the truth were known, at least the excusing factor of not being human.

That was one thing all present agreed upon. He wasn't a human, though none were willing to guess just what he might be. A demon? A god of some kind?

The word *demon* covered a lot of territory—fallen angels, the spirits of the malevolent dead, evil spirits in general, and a further class of beings almost everyone believed in. Earth spirits, indifferent to the good or ill of mankind, who had their own agendas.

He had heard Morgana's version of the blind men and the elephant, and he was certain none of the individuals he was speaking to had enough evidence to venture a solid guess as to the king's nature. They did agree on his treatment of them; it had been cruel in the extreme.

The sexes were kept separated. Given the nature of people, the measures taken by Bade's class of enforcers often failed. But children born of such unions were killed, usually aborted after quickening by one of the dog handlers like Eline. This was done by crushing the fetus in the woman's womb, a horribly painful procedure for the woman, who was given nothing to ease her pain, though the fetus was probably killed in advance by drugs prepared by the dog women, as they were called.

Yes, those talented individuals that Bade found more useful than the general run of children were given better treatment, privileges, such as marriage, leisure, being taught to read and write, more food, and some, even freedom of movement. Also, the right to sometimes enjoy the company of the opposite sex. No one explicitly permitted the favored dog handling women to take lovers, but often—very surreptitiously, to be sure—they did.

Eline had. Balin. They shared stolen embraces for almost a year. Then she found she was pregnant. She had an easy out. She could report the fact to the woman chief, take the drugs, and have it aborted. Or she could try to escape.

The women ruled the dogs, but the dogs were the actual fighters. They gave Bade his teeth.

"That's what the dogs are," Balin told Arthur. "The king's teeth. He thinks it's funny for some reason. No one knows why. The dogs are fixated on the women. The guard dogs are male, all male. The bitches are kept only to breed from. And they will kill in a split second on their handler's command. And they do. Oh, boy, how they do."

Everyone agreed with this assessment. By then all the men and most of the women had crossed the river also, and the cattle were being rounded up and driven home. Everyone knew their own, usually by name. Almost all were cows with calves at their udders. Almost all were strawberry with red ears, an absolutely beautiful dairy breed. In his world, such cows were held in some awe, and most herds belonged to powerful families. But Balin told him all the cattle here were marked this way, and Arthur remembered the wonderful creamy milk he'd had at the farm. This breed was a fine one.

"So the women keep order among the slaves," Arthur said.

Balin nodded. "I suppose you could put it that way." He sounded reluctant to adopt the point of view. "But that's not exactly how it works."

"Tell him," Firinne said. "Don't make us sound worse than we are. The children of the women dog handlers aren't always killed. Some, the ones who seem most reliable, are allowed to keep their babies. Their children belong to the king. I am such a one. My mother is the women's chief, my wife one of the handlers. If I don't return, my mother will lose her position. My wife will become one of the comfort women and my children, since they are too young to work—none is yet eight years of age—will be killed. I can't do that to my wife and mother. I hope to survive the flogging. But if I don't, they at least will be safe."

"Comfort women?" Arthur asked.

"Most of the men have no women of their own. What do you think?" Broken Nose asked in return.

Caradog walked up to the group of men around Arthur and complained, "You said to bury them, but those corpses are still wiggling."

"Bury them anyway," Balin said. "Snakes do the same thing when their heads are off. But they die by sundown. So will they."

Sundown was close. By now all the cattle were gone and most of their owners. Only Balin, Caradog, and Bade's two servants remained with Arthur.

Balin stared up at the tower apprehensively. "She will be unhappy with us for sure. We'd best get across that bridge by sunset. Firinne, if you're going back, best start now and get out of her valley."

Firinne and his broken-nosed friend began hurriedly collecting their possessions from the campsite. Arthur stood staring at the tower across the valley. The light was deep orange now, and the tower glowed like a golden finger draped in greenery, a thing of strange splendor and beauty in the gathering dusk.

Only when Arthur looked away from the glowing spire did he realize how close it was to night. He saw how the shadows had begun to condense in the dim places under the trees. The meadow was still bright, the long grass shimmering in the rays of the westering sun, but in the thickets, the forest was already welcoming the night.

Arthur began to walk toward the tower, his moving shadow like a finger on the shimmering grass, pointed east.

"Stop!" Balin screamed. "It is death to go there!"

"Who says?" Arthur answered without turning or slowing his pace.

"Everyone!" Balin shouted, and began running after Arthur.

As Balin neared him, Arthur spoke—again without slowing or turning. "Go home, my friend. If you try to stop me, I will hurt you. I won't kill you. I have too much respect for your good lady to do that. But I will hurt you badly. Go home. Your wife needs you. No one and nothing needs me."

"Why?" Balin shouted. "Why?" He was just behind Arthur.

"I have no time to explain," Arthur said. "It would take too long."

CHAPTER TWENTY

I MET MOTHER ON THE STAIR NEAR THE WELL. I saw her eyes as I often had seen them when we were hunting or I got up at night to relieve myself outdoors. It always made me feel better to know she was there.

She was sitting near the well where I had seen the Flower Bride. She looked calm. She sat upright on her haunches, in the starlit darkness, looking down at the sea.

"Mother," I said.

She made the sound that always meant *Yes, I'm here; it is not some other wolf.*

I was worried. "How do I get to the top?"

"The stair," she said. That's not really what she said. It was more like wolf for *path* or *the usual way.*

"The stair," I said, "is gone." I remembered the last sight I'd had of the island when I turned back to look, saw only the few broken steps on the side of the cliff, and realized I had climbed something nonexistent to get to the top.

Mother simply sighed and grunted as she always did when she was confronted with human perversity or flat-out ignorance. Then she turned and began to climb . . . something.

Mother is dead, I thought. But then, I reasoned, when had she ever led me astray?

I knew the answer. Never. By night in the wilderness on the edge of towering cliffs when we were together on the hunt, up and down rocky slopes where a misstep might mean a broken ankle or leg, into the fords of rivers and streams that might have drowned us both if she had miscalculated—I had followed her and always she led me safely to my destination.

So I followed and found myself climbing something. She marched ahead confidently until we reached the top. Then she entered the rock-cut chamber.

It was pitch-black inside. I dropped my hand to Mother's neck. Felt nothing, and then remembered in my grief she wasn't really here. But suddenly there was fur under my hand, and I heard the amused low bark she gave when she laughed at something.

Yes, wolves have a sense of humor. Sometimes a better one than most humans.

A second later, there was light in the niche where Lais's skull was, and I saw it looking out at me through a thick screen of vines. A shadowy shape in the gloom.

"How do you do that?" I asked.

"Do what?" Lais's voice asked.

"The light," I said.

She snorted. "There is no light. I made something happen in your brain so you can see where I am. The one you call Mother doesn't need light to see—her superior senses tell her all she needs to know without my help. You perceive it as light. Your brain tends to process information in terms of familiar phenomena."

"Thank you," I said. "Talking to you is like talking to Dugald."

"I know a lot more than Dugald," she said.

"Yes," I said. "That's why I'm here. Let me fill you in on what has happened since—"

387

"Don't bother," she said. "I already know. I've been watching you since your last visit. When you sought my help, it created a tie between us. The one you call Mother mediates that tie. Anything I don't happen to notice, she will tell me."

"I want Mother to have her rest," I replied stiffly.

Mother pressed her forehead against the inside of my hand and said, "Love." As I have told you, it isn't often said in wolf, but when said, it means a lot.

"Mother is happy," Lais said. "She's enjoying herself. In her present state, no one can force her to do anything. Believe me, no one can apply coercion to a ghost. You have really stirred up a broth of mischief for yourself, haven't you?"

"May I remind you I was minding my own business, trying to shoot a deer when the whole thing started. And I didn't choose to be abducted—"

"Enough!" she said. "But you have passed well beyond being the injured party. Now you have wrestled yourself to the center of this boil and are preparing to make a power play of your own. You might have done what the slippery British queen wanted you to."

"In a pig's eye," I said. "No, maybe I'm wrong, but I will choose my own life, thank you."

"You might have been happier if you hadn't been so headstrong," Lais said.

"He will be a great king," I said. "And if anyone knows how to get him back from where Merlin and Miss Snake in the Grass sent him, it will be you. And that's why I'm here."

"Yes . . . yes . . . he will be a great king. He knows no fear of anything, or he will not admit any fear to himself. Which it is, I cannot know. Even now, tonight, he challenges King Bade's rule in the summer country. A thing that hasn't happened in a mort of years. Not for many millennia. But getting him back may not be easy."

"I don't know," I said. "If Magetsky is right, they were able to bring him back themselves. What I want to know is how I can force them to—"

"No," she said. "And they didn't bring him back. That lecherous sorcerer probably thought he did. So did his paramour, Igrane. But they didn't, and I think Merlin is beginning to realize that his spells don't work.

When he can get his mind off sex, he tries to find your young king. And he can't.

"No! What happened was when they tried to pull him back, their spells worked for a little while, then he was returned from whence he came. In much the same way you returned to your proper place when you were finished killing the monster. All she had to do was let go."

"Then he belongs *there!*" I was dismayed.

"I'm not sure where or when he belongs," she answered. "He is one of the great captains, a war leader of distinction. Such leave a trail of blood and tears wherever they go."

"You were such a one yourself," I said.

"Yes. And that's why I tend to want to send him to trouble Bade. But I can tell that you won't rest until you challenge the order of things to go in search of him."

"Why does it matter what I want?" You see, I was really surprised that she obviously took my wishes into consideration in this important discussion.

"Oh, you matter," she said. "And what you want is important because if I fail, you only too quickly will go and find another way to reach your objective."

"You're right," I said. "All the way here I was exploring possibilities in my mind. I wonder if . . ."

"Ah, yes, you encountered the rainbow road."

"Does it still exist?" I asked.

She gave an ugly laugh.

"I mean," I went on hurriedly, "the sea has risen and covered the coast where we struggled, I and the faun—"

"Bosh," she said. "No earthly power could touch that splendid creation. It has survived cataclysmic events, the magnitude of which are completely beyond your imagination."

"The faun, he died there," I said.

"Yes," she answered quietly. "He did. And you swung the ax. If she was determined on his death, she could just as easily have done it herself. But she didn't."

"Oh, hell," I whispered.

"That is one of her names," Lais told me.

"I know how," I said.

"I was afraid you did," was the reply.

"You told me," I said.

"Yes, I'm afraid I did."

"Where are your friends?" I asked.

"In the dreamscape. If we had no relief, we would go mad."

"Being insane and immortal doesn't bear thinking about," I said.

"No!"

"The faun wanted immortality," I said.

"Yes. Anything that isn't a god and doesn't die pays the price. And the price is structured into the gift. We cannot live and can't die, either, but we are allowed to dream. And I and my surviving companions do that a lot. The rest were killed and were probably fortunate when the assault I engendered took place and life was wiped, or nearly wiped, off the earth. For that is what Bade's kingdom is. A place of refuge. But it wasn't quite ready when the long night fell."

"How?" I asked.

Suddenly, I was standing among the stars, looking down at the beautiful blue earth, a cloud-wrapped orb, the seas and continents dimly sketched out under the veil of air.

I gasped. "Where am I standing?" I asked dizzily.

"In the cave. As I said of the light, this is an illusion."

And, yes, we knew the world was round. For God's sake, even the Greeks knew that, and one of their philosophers even calculated the size of it. I can't remember which one. But Dugald felt it was a pretty accurate guess, though guess it was. Neither of us could follow the mathematics involved. Oddly enough, the Gray Watcher was better able to judge the truth of his speculations than either Dugald or I.

He believed the man was correct. He said truth has a taste, and this had the taste of truth. A wolf would put it that way, but I agree it does. Some things just don't hang together, but others do. And a lot of times when you encounter it, you say, "I don't want this to be right, but it probably is, even though it brings me to grief."

I thought of the faun, the rainbow chamber road, and looked down on the beautiful blue planet and understood, even as I saw the other smaller world moving down through the envelope of air glowing red-hot as it fell and exploded on impact. Even as far away as I seemed to stand, the flash nearly blinded me, and smoke and debris roared up into the sky like a black whirlwind limned in red as whole forests burned.

I saw the second and again was almost blinded when it, too, exploded on impact. When it landed, the sunset was moving over the now-gray orb beneath us. When the earth turned toward the sun again, the clouds were dark and so thick I couldn't see the surface any longer.

"It became very cold and very dark," Lais said.

I remembered that once Dugald had taken us to a remote spot to watch an eclipse of the sun. The druids have ways of calculating when such events will occur.

Black Leg and I loved to beachcomb. In a sheltered cove we found an oyster bed. Mother, Black Leg, and I were making a meal of them when the sun began to grow dark. For a few moments, I didn't remember Dugald's prediction and I understood the terror such events created in the minds of our ancestors.

It was amazing—with the darkening of the day star—how quickly the wind went from pleasant to brisk and then to cold and freezing. We lit a driftwood fire on the beach, trying to cast out the gloom that oppressed our spirits. But none of us felt really easy until the sun fully loosed its light again and brightened the world around us.

"A whole world perished under that cloud," Lais said. "And though your kind will probably never know it, a whole civilization, also."

Then the illusion vanished and I stood in the cave once more.

"Are you a bit less sure of yourself than when you entered?" Lais asked.

"Did you do this?" I asked.

"Yes . . ." She hesitated. "Yes, we did. We had our reasons. To this day, I don't know if they were satisfactory reasons or not, because we never returned to tell the tale. To find out if our strategies were successful. And no one ever tried to pick us up, which indicates we may have failed and our force perished. Our enemies abandoned us here, believing we had been punished enough, as indeed we have.

"But to continue, horrible as that happening was, that wasn't what I wanted to tell you. This refuge was created by the—they weren't human, but I will call them people—living here. But Bade is the only one who got in. The only one of them who survived. The rest of the animal and plant life that shared the planet with them perished. In order to live, he must steal from the world he left behind. So he, too, is a prisoner of his deeds, as we are.

"Now, do you still want to find your king and bring him back to your world? Do you still want to begin this war with Merlin and his allies, the Saxons? And, truth be known, he has friends in Rome and Constantinople."

"I thought they abandoned us long ago," I said. "The Romans."

"Oh, they still meddle where they can't dominate," Lais said. "And if this Arthur becomes the king I think he will, they will be anxious to seize him, also."

I chewed my lip until I tasted blood.

"Well?" she asked.

I added it up and saw the whole. Before he was born, the druids in Ireland and Britain saw a wave of omens surrounding this king. But they knew—my mother knew, I think—that his wife would be crucial. She had to bring him an army.

If I could do what Kyra wanted me to do, seat myself on the Dragon Throne, he would become the most powerful high king since the legions marched away. Between the two of us, we would have the power to crush the Saxons and bring any other faction to heel. Extend our rule over the whole country, break the power of the Romano-British landowners in the south, end the slave trade, put down piracy, and restore order throughout the realm.

It wouldn't be easy, but it could be done.

"Yes!" Lais said. "You know."

"Is he?" I asked. "Is he . . . do you think . . . able to take command of such a force and win?"

"Oh, yes. And don't give yourself too many airs and graces. He might even be able to do it without you. Though I don't like his chances if he hasn't the backing of the Painted People and a strong queen by his side.

"Well, then," she continued. "I think your time is up. Farry will sail with the tide. You haven't much time."

The light was beginning to fail. She seemed to withdraw.

"Mother!" I said, and felt the furry bulk press against my leg.

"Wait!" I said. But the light vanished. I had more questions; they weren't important, though.

Mother accompanied me down the stair. I stopped and drank from the holy well. And when I looked up from the water, Mother was gone.

A thing can be very old and still beautiful. Or, at least, beautiful was my judgment.

Dugald sniffed. "Primitive," was his.

Maeniel said the word is meaningless and is most often used as a pejorative to demean something we do not understand.

Still, looking back over the whole of my life, I think the great hall and assembly room of the Painted People is one of the most beautiful things I have ever seen. It was very big, almost as big as a small Roman amphitheater.

Farry landed us near the coast, not on it. A ship cannot dock there. The wind and wave action is too fierce, the rocks too jagged, and the climb to any habitable place too steep for a harbor. But I was surprised once we reached the cliff tops how many people were present.

Kyra said that probably every village had sent at least one person, and most came in groups to this most important Beltane assembly. All the most influential among her people would be present, men and women both, to aid in choosing the new queen.

They were a hard-looking and dangerous bunch, Kyra's people. They looked to be well off, also. Both men and women carried a variety of weapons and wore boiled-leather or quilted armor.

It was cold here, even in May, and the sky was an icy blue, hazed with high clouds crisscrossing it in pale streaks. The wind was blowing a gale, troubling the long woolen dresses of the women and the furs both men and women wrapped around their bodies.

We were known to them, and they greeted us with a mixture of suspicion and awe. Dunnel, the chieftain of the village where we once lived, was present, accompanied by Issa, his daughter, and a rather chastened Bain.

I saw no reason not to be polite, and I was cordial in my greetings to all three. Issa was swelling with her third child: the first had died; the second, a boy, survived and was walking now. I congratulated her on her present condition. She smiled and was deferential toward me.

Bain slipped away and would meet neither Dugald's nor Maeniel's eyes. But Dunnel kissed me on the cheek and asked after Black Leg. I told Dunnel he had left to begin his warrior training. Then he and Issa accompanied us to the great hall.

It is, as I have said, a magnificent thing. The people who built it long ago as a seat for the queens took advantage of a natural hollow in the ground. It stands in the midst of a mysterious oak wood. Oaks are always solid trees, but these were far stronger than any I have ever seen before or since. Given the wind and the cold, none were very big, but the boles were thick and strong as rocks, some of them, I judged, more than fifteen feet in diameter.

Each trunk gave rise to equally thick, gnarled and twisted branches, which held clusters of leaves that shone like green polished rock. The bark was deep, matte black, and the leaves glowed against them. I suppose they were tall enough; they were all over my head and the ground was thick with their leaves, acorns, and deadfall branches.

"How old?" I asked Kyra.

"No one knows," she said. "It is said that they were here long before the hall was built, when the first people to flee the rising sea came to gather acorns for their winter food. For the nuts they drop are very sweet and good. So the first people knew they would prosper even here."

We were still climbing, and the slope was steep. Then we got to the top; a wide, flat rock overlooked the surrounding countryside. We stood looking out over what seemed the whole world.

All around us the mountain slopes were covered with forest. The most rocky slopes held trees like these—oaks twisted and windblown but stubborn and hard. Like the people who live among them, I think. In places where the soil was thicker, the tall Caledonian pine clothed the slopes. It was wet here, wetter than you would think; and numerous creeks and streams tumbled down, whispering, gurgling, and sheeting over the rocky beds into lakes small and large scattered within the forest.

The rest of the way was not a difficult climb. Kyra's friend greeted us at the arched door to the hall.

This was where I first met Mondig. He was a short man, strongly built. He rather reminded me of Gray, but his face was so ugly. His eyes were slightly protuberant, his mouth weak, and he had no chin at all.

"Kyra," he said. He didn't sound at all happy. "I had believed you dead. . . ."

"Or worse," Kyra finished the sentence for him.

"Yes," he said slowly. "Yes. I suppose that's right."

He glanced at me. "I suppose this is the one."

"She is," Kyra answered.

"Yes, yes." He rubbed his hands together. They made a dusty, rasping sound. "Another God child, I suppose. Well, at least this one's pretty. The other two, the ones already here, could be set out to scare mice."

I was nettled. "What!" I asked Kyra. "Have you brought me before another fool who wants to say my mother was a loose woman?" The talk at Igrane's court had cut me more deeply than I realized. I'm not so easily angered, but I was tired of people casting aspersions on Riona, who was, by all accounts, a brave, strong woman.

Mondig drew back, looking startled. Something like respect flashed in his eyes.

"She's direct enough," he told Kyra. He still looked dubious.

Maeniel held my arm. A gust of wind hit, blowing my dress and hair wildly. It was strong enough to make everyone clutch at their clothing and duck their heads against the dust, twigs, and dead leaves set flying.

"They liked this place," Mondig muttered. "I can't think why. Don't stand outside in the cold. Come in where it's warm."

As I said, the builders of the hall had taken advantage of a natural depression when they built it. The arched door was so low even I had to duck down to enter, but once inside I was stricken with awe at its size. As I said, it resembled an amphitheater. Most of it was underground. In this climate, that made sense.

There were staggered rows of seats on each side. They were made of stone, obviously carved out of the limestone that made up this mountain. Aisles led down toward a central court around a fire pit. In that sense, it was like a conventional house, only much, much larger. The roof was braced by many posts, each bearing different carvings.

"Each tribe has a place here," Kyra told me. "They know by the carvings on the posts where they are to sit. You will be seated in the center."

The posts held up a lattice of curved beams that in turn held a woven osier dome, covered by cowhides. In turn, green turf waterproofed the roof. From the outside, it looked like our house used to—a green mound near the sea. Every exposed bit of wood was carved in the most wonderful way I have ever seen. The largest of the chiefly halls paled by comparison to it. Salmon leaped, dragons swam, wolves hunted, bears roared, trees bloomed, vines climbed; and above, stags gamboled, antlers high, holding the osier lattice that held the roof.

"Each post tells a story," Kyra said, her hand resting on the nearest one. "See? Down at the bottom kelp, samphire, dulse. There is the eel, coiling among the water plants. They are on an eel river and take their living from the sea."

Knot work spun among the living things, fishermen and women. No salmon, but shark, hake, and turbot. Above, oak leaves and hazel flowed out of the knot work toward the roof. Each pillar was different, each exquisite, each told of the life its people led.

"I never taught you how to read them completely," Kyra said with regret. "One with knowledge can tell not only the way they live but where, and even how many are in the particular village or villages."

She let her hand fall away from the post with a look of regret. We continued walking down the stair, toward the center of the hall. That's where the seats of the queens were. They were not really chairs and yet they weren't thrones either. Each marked the house of heaven they belonged to.

The salmon, painted with the colors of the breeding fish, leaped from the back of one seat, the comb held sway at another. The wolves, a whole pack, attacked over the back and at each arm of the one next to the fish. All of the houses of heaven were similarly marked. They formed a rectangle, a long, wide rectangle, around the fire pit.

The hall was filled with people, all working on the posts, painting the figures with bright enamels, putting up tables on the stone steps of the amphitheater, spreading weavings and cowhides on the stone seats and hanging banners from the roof. Though I knew some of the seats were empty, they had all been touched up with fresh enamel. All but one.

The Dragon Throne.

It stood alone at the end of the rectangle, looking past the six seats on each side. The wood, though as magnificently sculpted as the rest, was dark, dry, and blackened by age. The rather squat dragon body was part of the chair side; the long neck formed the back and coiled around to one side and above the person who would sit there.

"Thirteen months?" I asked.

Mondig stood at my elbow. "Their calendar had thirteen months. They reckoned time by the moon," he said. "Now we use the sun. The dragon has no place among them." He spoke dismissively. "And besides," he added, "it is unlucky, since the last queen took her place. She died within an hour of taking up her position."

"I thought the dance floor fell into the sea?" I asked.

"No, that was the one before her," he answered. "They wouldn't give up trying, though. The one after her died in childbirth. And still there was another. She slipped and fell on the path up to the top of the cliff. She never got to take her seat at all. By then the Dragon Throne was called the perilous seat, and we stopped trying. Besides, we are all enmity with the dragons. When we see them, we kill them. They are too fond of our salmon runs."

He scratched his stomach and looked at me sideways.

"Yes," I said. "You are not what you were."

"Girl," he said, "don't play with me and don't take that seat. If you do, you might die even more quickly than the rest."

Gray, Maeniel, and Issa had pitched a tent in the oak woods near the great hall. Kyra helped me to dress. Maeniel had found a tolerably sheltered spot, but it was still cold. I shivered, even though the water in the wash bowl had been warmed at the fire.

"How much power have the queens got?" I asked.

"A lot," Kyra said. "Don't let that little rat Mondig fool you. Most control a faction among the people, and that faction will back their decisions, if it comes down to it."

"I don't know anyone here," I said.

"Yes, you do," she said. "Maeniel is widely respected, as is Dugald. They know him for a druid and a powerful one. Gray comes from a large family. They will back him. Yes, they are poor, but good fighters. Then there's me, and I'm not completely forgotten. I have friends among Scathatch's daughters from the Isle of Women. They are widely respected, also, and sometimes feared. Your mother had kin among the people and among the Irish at Dalraida. Remember, Riona was the wife of a king, and she had the reputation of being a woman of strong character. No, you are not alone."

She made me wear a white dress trimmed with gold and combed my hair down my back. I wore the amber-and-garnet necklace Maeniel bought me, and the moonstone ring. The shoes changed to white leather with lace-up tops, low boots, sort of.

Maeniel came in. He was carrying the sword and belt under his arm. Unceremoniously, he drew the blade and folded my right hand around the hilt.

I tightened my fingers and raised the blade. It shimmered like the moon on the waters of a lake. The steel seemed to glow from within.

"I can't . . ." I began.

"Yes . . . yes, you can," he said. "I'll get it back."

"You will—worse luck," I said. "Not many things live as long as you. It's smaller than I thought."

"You have grown in more ways than one," he told me. "I'll get another belt and scabbard. These are too large for you."

"It wouldn't be seemly to wear it tonight," Kyra said.

I nodded.

"She might face a challenge," the wolf said.

Kyra turned abruptly and walked away, toward the door of the tent.

"A challenge?" I asked.

He looked at Kyra. "You didn't tell her."

"No! It so seldom happens."

"But she is not well known here, and it might," Maeniel said. "It behooves her to be ready—if and when. That's why I made her the gift of the sword now instead of waiting for a more auspicious occasion. I want her to have a good weapon at hand."

Kyra was silent and stood at the door with her head bowed. "Few women can really defeat a man in single combat," she said. "I know I couldn't. In theory, the queen who is seated should be an expert in the martial arts, and once, God knows, they were. But long ago by several hundred years, the custom fell into abeyance and has never been revived. Besides, Mondig made a promise to me that if she didn't take the Dragon Throne, he would make sure her acceptance would be voted by the people and she would be seated and welcomed as one of their own."

"What's between you and Mondig?" I asked.

"He owes me a favor," Kyra said.

"What kind of favor?" I asked.

"I was married to his brother," Kyra said.

"He was," I said, "the one you didn't choose. The right one."

Kyra threw back her head, and her face became a mask of indescribable pain. But she didn't answer.

"He's so ugly," I said.

Kyra pushed aside the curtain and left.

"No one will be seated in the chairs tonight," Maeniel told me. "Though the rest of us will join Dunnel and his family, Bain and Issa—we will sit together and you will be introduced to the company."

Dugald stepped into the tent. "In this, you will be guided by your elders, young lady. Kyra, Maeniel, and I have already spoken of this together, and our plans are made. Politics is the art of the possible, and whatever you may think, the thirteenth month and the Dragon Throne will be ignored by you. Do you understand me, young lady?" he said sternly.

"Yes," I answered quietly. "Yes, I do."

"I don't like the look in her eye," he told Maeniel. "I want your word you won't do anything foolish or provocative tonight. Do you hear me?"

"I give you my word. I won't do anything either foolish or provocative tonight," I answered.

He was wearing his robes, his ceremonial robes, the ones with the ogam symbols on them. He had the gold crown of his order. It's not really a crown, but a wreath. Gold oak leaves, acorns, the catkin flower, and the twisted roots completed it.

"You will do magic," I said.

"I'm going to have to. They must be convinced of your bona fides. You know your mother's genealogy?" he asked.

"I've known my mother's genealogy since I was five," I answered. "And all her family connections. You taught me. It was almost the first thing you taught me."

"Yes. Well, best have them at your fingertips, for you must recite them before the assembled company tonight. A lot of the people here will be relations of yours, albeit distant ones, and they will wonder how you fit into the sphere of the Painted People."

"The whole thing?" I said. "It goes back to before the Iceni queen and probably will take me an hour and a half to—"

"Yes, yes," he broke in fiercely. "All of it. Tell me," he asked Maeniel, "do you think she looks innocent enough? They will have heard of the business with Arthur . . . it wouldn't do for anyone to believe she had been compromised. An invitation to be a concubine is a slap in the face to a lady of your rank. You didn't let him take any liberties with you? Or give him anything like a . . . like a . . . you know," he said to Maeniel, "a down payment."

"What!" I screamed. "I still haven't—I wasn't—I wouldn't have been able . . . What are you saying? What are you accusing me of?"

At this minute Kyra reappeared at the door to the tent. She grabbed Dugald's arm. "Oh, for God's sake, you old fool. Belike the girl is on pins and needles. She has a terrifying ordeal ahead of her, and you have to make things worse by accusing her of all manner of nonsense. Of course she hasn't done anything like what you're suggesting. For heaven's sake, old man, they were together for only a few moments, and they were never alone."

I caught the last word on the fly, because she pulled Dugald out of the tent and dragged him away. Maeniel and I stood alone. I found I was crying. Maeniel gave me a clean linen cloth, and I wiped my face and eyes.

"They have it all arranged between them, just like Merlin, Igrane, and Arthur at Tintigal," I spat.

He made a noncommittal sound.

"Do you trust Mondig?" I asked.

"No," he answered. "He reeks of duplicity."

"He threatened to kill me," I said.

I saw Maeniel's eyes change. The shadow of the wolf was in them, and they shone like mirrors in the dim lamplight.

"How very, very foolish of him," Maeniel said. "He has Kyra and Dugald completely fooled."

"So you're thinking the same thing I am," I said.

"Yes!" Maeniel said. "He's relying on Kyra and Dugald to make you behave as he wishes."

"But it doesn't matter, because sooner or later he will kill me anyway, no matter what I do," I said.

"Probably," Maeniel said. "Once you and your people were not so wise, and the wolf taught you how to hunt. The ravens, like the wolf, led you to prey. The bear led others to colder lands, where the snow covered the ground and ice locked the mountain peaks. They watched the bear, and from him they learned how to fish, to wait until fruits and berries ripen, how to steal honey from hives, hunt among rotten logs for grubs, and kill deer.

"The boar showed them how to forage for winter food among hazelnuts and acorns, and the ducks and geese taught them to gather the seeds of wild grasses. And among the best of all were the dragons. They gave humankind the infinite resources of the sea. Led them to shellfish, dulse, and kelp. This is why they placed the friendly beasts among the stars and offered them the homage they deserved.

"But now all this is forgotten, and men believe the whole earth and all the good things thereof belong to them. They gobble and grab, kill and steal, and lay waste with both hands. Then murder anything that dares compete with them for the first place at the table of life. Do justice! This is the duty of a ruler."

"I made a promise to myself about the dragons," I said.

"Keep it," he told me. "And watch the food."

"You can tell, can't you?" I asked.

He nodded. "Usually."

But I never had to worry about the food. We entered the hall. It was alight with banners; the fire was blazing in the center. Everyone had dressed in their gaudy best. The light gleamed on a thousand pieces of jewelry on both men and women.

Each tribe, *tuath*, we call them, dyed their own cloth with their own subtle colors, a rainbow of reds, blues, greens, yellows, oranges, and even gray and black. Silk, linen, and wool flared on the people. In the center, the music had begun around the fire pit before the star seats. They were all painted and ready for their new occupants.

All but the dragon. The old oak that formed it was almost black with age, and it gleamed with the unadorned beauty that old dense-grained, fine wood has.

I saw Dunnel. Issa and Bain, Dugald and Kyra had already joined them in seats of honor at Mondig's table, along with two other young girls. Those must be the tame God's children, who would be made queens.

But I walked past the table and toward the open space around the fire pit. Then I turned, walked past the musicians as the harp, pipe, and tabor fell silent.

I didn't have to think about it. I went to the dragon chair and turned and sat down.

CHAPTER TWENTY-ONE

HE CLOSER HE GOT TO THE TOWER, THE LESS forbidding it got. Arthur knew he was looking at something nothing in his earlier experience had prepared him for. Nothing about the tower had the look of impressive arrogance most human constructions had. Instead, it seemed a part of the earth, the way the bridge did.

The vines twining the base looked almost as though they, and not human hands, had laid the foundations. In places where the stone was worn away by wind and rain, they closed the gaps with their thick, woody stems. Trees held the bigger boulders above, their roots stretched down to the ground to collect water and nutrients incidentally holding the larger stones in place like mortar.

Espaliered?

His people, like others, grew fruit trees against walls to save space. No, say rather the building was espaliered against the webwork of leaves, roots, and branches.

Yes, the stones, dark stone like the bridge abutments, were smoothed by eons of wind and rain. No, the trees rising up and up held the tower together, not the tower the trees. There was no door, only a perforated wall, because the tower was part of the world, built to embrace it, not shut it out. But the opening formed by the vines' fuzzy small, aromatic flowers was a door to darkness. And in that darkness, something laughed.

Arthur felt a chill at the nape of his neck. *No!* he thought. *I may die for it, but I must find out what this strangest of places contains.*

So he pushed the vines aside and went in.

A big tree root, part of the willow, made an inviting bench near the door. He sat down and let his eyes get used to the light. A thick, very soft moss lay like a carpet on the stone floor. The light was diffuse, greenish-blue, and strangely the chamber seemed to lead down to the sea, for he saw the waves breaking on the other side of the room.

His mind told him this was impossible, but his eyes refused to cooperate. So he rose and waded into the sea.

The waves broke around his legs and ankles, but they didn't wet him. So he walked deeper into the water, until it was up to his chin. His body continued dry, so he went a little farther, until the water was over his head.

Something armored like a crab ran into his arm. It had many legs, and it began to crawl down his arm. It was blue on the back, as some crabs are, but its many legs were a rather light yellow, paling to white at the tips. He tried to reach over and catch it, to see if it was really present. It must have been there in some sense, because he felt the hard carapace. Alarmed, it curled itself into a ball, fell to the bottom, and was pulled away by the current.

A school of fish flashed into view like flying needles, fleeing something. They turned left, then right, gleaming like tiny mirrors as they did so, then came straight ahead, breaking at the last moment to either side of him, and were gone.

The predator that followed them stunned him. It was fish or fishlike, but it was as armored as the crablike creature. But the plates were an iridescent red above, shading to gold-green at the belly.

Then Arthur drew back out of the surf and watched it foam on the nonexistent beach. Real or not, the water was as changeable and beautiful as the summer sea he remembered as a boy. Again, he felt the strange peace that had invaded his mind when he reached the bottom of the cliff below his prison. The sun glow poured in through openings in the rock, flaming red between the green branches.

Arthur saw the stair, formed from the twisting roots of the trees. Someone, only a vague shape, passed him and began to climb the stair, vanishing around the first bend.

Yes, this is a place of the dead, he thought. And found himself in the midst of a great multitude moving toward the stair and up into light so bright that his eyes wouldn't accept it. He turned away in self-defense to look back at the ocean, but it was gone.

Fingers caressed his face, neck, shoulders, and back; and something kissed him on the lips. Then, to his horror, he found the lips on his were teeth, the fingers abrasive bone, and the stink of death overpowering. He tore away from whatever it was, retching.

Beyond the flowered arch of the door, sunset glowed bloody on a meadow. "Run, little man! Run!" a voice whispered. "Spit the taste of death out of your mouth, spit away the fear that haunts you. Haunts us all. And know you are only a man."

Gagging, Arthur swallowed and staggered forward to climb the stair.

CHAPTER TWENTY-TWO

DIDN'T GET A CHANCE TO ENJOY SITTING ON the Dragon Throne, though it was a comfortable chair. An absolute dead silence fell in the assembly hall of the Painted People. Every eye in the room was fixed on me, and I could feel each one of them.

The emotions were a mixture of horror that any outsider would dare to commit such a massive transgression, anger that an ancient custom had been breached, rage and delight that some present had been given a truly wonderful excuse to kill me. And those were the ones I became concerned with first. Mondig must have packed the front benches of the assembly hall with his supporters.

As soon as he vaulted the table into the central court, I saw he was one of Merlin's men. He wore the black and silver that are the powerful chief priest's colors. His sword was drawn and ready. He tried to take my head off in one swipe.

I leaped clear of the Dragon Throne. I heard Kyra scream into the sudden silence, "Don't! She is without weapons! For shame!"

Not for long, I thought. And saw the Gray Watcher, sword in hand. It flew, hilt first, toward me.

My antagonist was no mean opponent. It took him only a second to see what was happening, pivot to face me, and attack. But he didn't try to kill me. He did worse, he tried to humiliate me before those who must judge my fitness to rule. With two quick slashes, he cut the shoulder straps that held the dress on my body.

You must understand, nakedness with us is not shameful; it is ceremonial. The sacrifice is naked when he goes into battle. The king is naked when he lies with the Flower Bride. The queen is naked when she leads the Beltane procession into the forest to ensure the fruitfulness of the land. To be naked is to call the powers. And that's what my nakedness did.

The armor leaped out all over my skin, green, shimmering in the firelight, clothing my skin in the ancient symbols of my people. The twining, ever-changing, changeless forms of all creation from the stone to the star, the earth we trod, the air we breathe, the water that changes all things, the fire that transforms them. The patterns belonging to the dance of life wound intricately and forever into one.

The look on his face when he saw the armor blaze in the firelight and cover the nakedness he courted was one of dismay and sorrow, a little doom, too, because he knew he'd loosed a force he didn't understand and that he couldn't contain. And it would kill him.

And it did, too. Because he tried for my eye, but his blade skidded on my cheek and I had to turn my face away. He thought that would stop me; he thought he found a way out. But he hadn't, because I pulled a trick Maeniel taught me. My sword flew from my right hand to my left, and I skewered him in the throat. Maeniel's blade was a fine one; it severed his spine.

He fell bonelessly, like an empty sack. I spun around, my back to the fire, and saw there were fifteen more after me. But the gray wolf was with me. He hamstrung the first, and I cut his throat going down. He landed between the shoulders of the next.

The sword of the third slammed into my side. The armor held, but I felt two ribs crack. He was a giant of a man.

I told you earlier my armor doesn't prevent me from being hurt or killed. It will turn a blade, that's all.

I turned to protect my left side, but he swung at my right. I didn't parry. I counted on the armor to block the sword's edge. The pain went through my body like a flung spear as the big man's sword hit. But my sword was already up, and I was wielding it two-handed. I brought it down as hard as I could on the top of his head. My sword sheared through helmet, skull, and brain. I split his skull to the teeth.

Another tried to stab me in the back, sending a thin-bladed knife through a chink in my fairy armor. He almost succeeded, but I twisted and the blade snapped away, a problem with a blade that thin. I spun around completely now. I got him by the throat and jerked him toward me. He had no sword, but he tried to send the broken stump of his knife (part of it was still lodged in the armor) under my left breast.

But my sword went through armor and man too quickly. He died before he could get any pressure behind the blade.

I jumped free of his falling corpse, but there were more coming at me. Maeniel had accounted for three—the first whose throat I slashed, a second whose neck he'd snapped, and on a third, the wolf's jaws shattered a thigh bone. He bled out when the bone leaped through the skin.

But as I said, there were more.

Talorcan erupted from the fire pit in a fountain of embers. None of those coming to try to finish us off reached me, because the Death Pig disemboweled the first, and the others fled back among the benches while the one the pig killed died, twisting and screaming beside the fire.

I stood there, bloody blade in one hand, the wolf snarling beside me, and the pig dancing with fury on the other. But we were faced with an even worse threat.

At least two dozen bowmen stood around Mondig, arrows nocked and pointed at us. And the hall was not a stage but an amphitheater. I was sure there were slingers behind us.

I spared a glance over my shoulder and saw I was right.

"Kill them," Mondig said. The entire hall was silent; his tone was almost conversational.

"Kill them," he repeated.

"Mondig!" Kyra shouted. "Give over! Suppose—just suppose—you can't!"

And I saw what had saved our lives so far. I saw it in the faces of the bowmen and the slingers.

They had seen our powers, and they weren't sure they could kill us.

But I looked at the rest of the fire-lit hall, and I knew they could. This was not a gathering of sheep but of wolves. Every man and most of the women had weapons in their hands.

"Dis!" Mondig hissed like a serpent. "Dis awaits you."

The giant boar stirred restlessly beside me, and I understood why he had appeared unsummoned, because I had not called him. We were going to die. We might overcome the slingers and the bowmen, but we would in the end be cut to pieces by the men and women of the Painted People. They would not let us loose to wreak ruin on their land.

CHAPTER TWENTY-THREE

I AM A KING, HE THOUGHT, AND BEGAN HIS CLIMB. Odd, he didn't remember the feast when he had been crowned, but then, he had been full of the spring mead that night. But Morgana told him the next day he hadn't spoken prophetically or otherwise the night of the feast. He had been amiable toward his companions.

Sometimes the newly crowned king could become quite violent. Spring mead was a strange mix, and its recipe was a secret of the druid masters. In the spring, bees drink from flowers dangerous even to handle— aconite, henbane, foxglove, the small dense secret flowers of mistletoe, and perhaps other, even more toxic plants. The distilled essence of honey at this time filled the king's cup with a beverage so intoxicating that some were, at times, lost to permanent madness.

It was said the new king could look into *her* soul and see *her* thoughts. And if he chose to kill a man among his companions, why it must be considered an offering to the powers who rule all things. That night he was sacred and could do no wrong.

Arthur remembered no anger that night, only a vast distance between himself and the rest of the world—a glass wall against which he pressed his face and fingers set between him and the other revelers at the feast. And a profound sorrow at the abyss of separation between him and others. A separation that he could not escape, around, under, over, or through. That's why he was in this tower now. He would never be one of them.

The trunks of the trees in the tower to one side of the stair formed a wall, so he could not look down. The branches above stretched out over his head and held up the walls. He passed a spot where one tree had died, and only dead limbs held up the wall's boulder-size stones. But vines had covered the dead tree and were nurturing saplings at its base. Beyond the wall of tree trunks on his left there was a whisper, and at times a rush. He knew the falls he had seen next to the tower must in some way flow through it, and the living vegetation that formed the tower's structure could drink from that flow.

Light still poured into the tower from beyond the thick growth of leaves on the branches clutching the stone, but in most places the sunlit leaves were so thick he couldn't see out to the world beyond. Instead, he climbed in a perpetual emerald and golden glow.

Surely, he thought, *it must be sunset by now in the world outside.* But then, he didn't know if the world outside was the one he had left behind. The things he did see between the interstices in the branches weren't such as to reassure him.

Once it seemed he looked down at a jungle of thick-trunked trees growing so close together that it didn't seem even a mouse could force its way between them. Another time he saw desert with spare plants tipped with flame, all around them barren rock and scorching sun. A beautiful wasteland—the rocks red, purple, brown, and sometimes black—seeming almost to drink in the light and reflect it in glowing pastels more suited to a butterfly's wings than the frightening barren place he looked upon. The glow of stone was textured like cloth, blue silk, velvet mountains, linen orange rocks, woolen green ravines in those few places where water collected. And the lean, long-branched plants dipped in blood.

He could appreciate the thought of the builders who created this tower. They had understood what his people knew: that life itself comes closest to immortality. He remembered at Aquae Sulis the forest creeping in, the poplars and willows tearing up the heavy flags the Romans laid. A *frigidarium* taken over by moss, a fallen wall only a mound under some sweet-flowering vine.

He could see that the very hard stones that formed the shell of the tower were worn, pitted by wind and rain. But the crusted lichens, fern, vine, and trees kept faith with its builders, more powerful than stone in their everlasting mortality and perpetual self-renewal. When even the stones returned to dust, the skeleton of trees that formed the tower would still stand.

He was growing both thirsty and weary, wondering if he was doomed to climb forever. He had a number of worries about this place. There are a lot of ways to kill a man, but if the ruler of this stronghold wanted to destroy him, a mind that could conceive the ground plan of a structure like this would have no difficulty in disposing of him.

He could feel places; it was one of his gifts. He'd felt the malice of the plateau and the thing it kept imprisoned along with him. He'd felt the innocence at the farm. Her innocence. Her honor. And Balin's.

He felt nothing wrong here—only the same strange sense of peace. Still feeling it, he reached the top of the stair.

There he saw how the waterfall was involved with the tower. There was more than one fall. The water entered from the river at the top of the slope and fell into a pool at the base. It drained down from there into the tower. Long, feeding roots from the trees hung like so many strings of a curtain into the falling water that slipped from ledge to ledge, filling basin after rock basin, all thick with roots.

The vines that formed the base grew up the walls, flowering in wild profusion—red, purple, gold, emerald, amethyst, carnelian, white—hanging in tufts, spikes, chains, ribbons, and spiraling, filling the air with fragrance. Immortal, indeed, growing forever, self-renewing, always changing yet immutable in their endless variation. Trees hung over the pool at the first falls, and it was as though whatever ruled the tower heard his unspoken concerns.

The pond at the base of the falls was green with saganella and water weed. Horsetails filled the shallows, growing thick as reeds. Arthur walked across, away from the tree staircase to the mossy verge of the pool, and drank. The water was clear, sweet, and good, reminding him of the Flower Bride's well at the top of the plateau.

This is not a place of death, he thought, *but of life.* The paradox was borne upon him. There would be no life without death. No sapling could live without the humus contributed by a fallen tree. Nothing could be born without another dying.

Something walked through the glade, past the waterfall, around the trunk of a tree fern, and into the shadows beyond. He sat on his heels, considering. Did they come here to look upon what gave way to them, or what rooted itself in their sundered flesh?

He heard voices talking, arguing in a language he didn't understand. Then they passed him again, only footsteps bending grass and sound, no sight, troubled his eyes.

He became aware that the trees whose roots crowded the edge of the pool were laden with fruit. Was it fruit, or something stranger that he had never encountered? Near his face a leaf clasped a chain of cherries. He picked one and put it in his mouth. The taste was a shock of pleasure. It had a big seed, though. He spat it out into the pool.

He was hungry. He finished the rest. The seeds floated and were carried away by the water as it emptied into the core of the tower.

The tree was pleased. That was a shock, a profound shock. He had never thought of a tree feeling anything, much less pleasure.

The other trees around the pool had fruit. Some were like large berries, roseate shading to black, blue shading into purple, beige outlined in scarlet. He made a meal of them. The blues were so sweet he could only eat a few, the red, apple-lemon, the beige almost like some spicy cheese.

Then he turned toward the path where he had heard the ghost pass. He followed it into a dark, strange forest. Tree ferns, all sizes; massive trees with leaves small, wet, and green as moss; paper-thin ferns that grew covering the trees' fronds, hanging down but so fragile they presented

CHAPTER TWENTY-FOUR

Y THOUGHT WAS THAT KYRA HAD PICKED wrong again. Mondig, with Merlin's men backing him, didn't look to let us surrender.

Talorcan, in boar form next to me, shifted, then snorted. "I come for someone," he said in his grating pig voice. "If it is you, lady, I will escort you into darkness with an honor guard."

The wolf snarled next to me, his voice thick with menace.

Kyra leaned against one of the carved roof posts, her face hidden as though she didn't want to watch my end. Dugald stood next to a white-faced Dunnel. He tried to seize the initiative and save us.

"Wait!" Dunnel shouted. "Don't let this go any further. I will give sureties for their behavior. Let this be the last of the killing."

"Bah!" Mondig spat. "You haven't a tithe of the honor price of any of the dead."

It was true. Dunnel was a poor man, chief though he was.

"Merlin's men!" I yelled back. "What! Are the Painted People ruled by the archdruid?"

"No, girl!" someone shouted back. "But only a fool shoves his head into a bear's den." There was a murmur of assent.

"There's more to be gained by being wary of the powerful than by provoking them," Mondig said.

The fire was at my back, the armor glowing on my skin, but I felt a wave of cold and I knew. I knew.

"Kyra!" I shouted. "The head. The head."

She looked up, her eyes wild.

Heads are oracles. This is why they are taken and questioned.

"Wait," I said. "Before you spend your blood to end our lives, best you find out about Mondig's motives."

Kyra had Cymry in a sack. Inside the sack, he was confined in a net bag, so he could be suspended. I pulled the head out of the sack.

With my cracked ribs searing, I ran up the nearest house post, using the carvings to climb. *I should be ashamed,* I thought. The armor set off my bare body the way an enameled setting displays a rare jewel. Even the blood streaming from the gashes Merlin's champion inflicted were part of the grim beauty of my flesh. I knew the eyes of every man, and not a few of the women, were fixed on me, and that fear alone hadn't saved my life.

I was the embodiment of desire! And the crowd felt it. To the people in the hall, I was Eros made flesh.

I slung Cymry's head from the highest rafters. It thumped heavily, just a few feet in front of the fire pit. They sacrificed to it, you know—both the Greeks and Romans—this Eros. And I, for the first time, knew why. And why the chief to be a chief and the king to be a king must lie with the Flower Bride at the flowing well, and why among Farry's people, kings and chieftains wed the sea.

Desire is the fountainhead of creation, everlasting renewal the only immortality. Mother and Father both, combined to make me what I am, the living symbol of both, creation and immortality. Imprinted on my soul at this moment was that knowledge, and I would bear it forever, even as I would bear on my body the symbols of that eternal knowledge my people saw time out of mind.

When I was finished fastening the head, I jumped, somersaulting in the air, and landed lightly on my feet near the fire pit, close to the head. I glanced at Mondig. He looked sick, my signal to proceed boldly.

Merlin's men gathered around Mondig protectively. It's the oldest game in the world I saw being played out before me. Would you capture a whole people? Take them into bondage without difficulty? Simply pick your candidate. He must be eligible to be chief—king, consul, chief magistrate, whatever he is called. You send your army to put him in power. Once he is seated in his position to rule, your army keeps him there, and he does your bidding. He knows that if you abandon him, he dies at the hands of his own subjects. He dares not disobey.

This is the trick that Merlin used to keep the Painted People quiescent. Mondig was his man, and the chieftains knew it. But Merlin did them no harm, and they were thankful to be left in peace. So they tolerated the alliance.

I was about to try to change all that, and it might cost me dear if I failed.

"Cymry," I commanded. "Come answer me. It is I, your mistress, who summons you!"

For a moment, I held my breath, and then I saw life creep into the face. The eyes opened, lips came down over the teeth bared in the rictus of death. I heard a whisper as a gasp of awe rolled through the hall.

"Wine!" Cymry whimpered.

I caught up a cup and tossed it into the flames. They flared around Cymry's face, and he cried out in pleasure and laughed.

"Drunken pig!" Kyra snarled. "Don't give him any more until he answers your questions."

Cymry whimpered and then sobbed. "Isn't it enough for you, bitch, that I suffer the torments of this dreadful slavery?"

"No!" Kyra screamed. "No! You murderer! Nothing, nothing you suffer will ever be enough!"

"Cymry," I said, "how did you find out when and how to attack the stronghold where Kyra dwelled with her husband and children?"

Cymry sighed and moaned, "More wine. Please. Please, more wine."

"No!" I said. "Answer! I command you!"

Cymry's eyes closed. I sensed he was trying to slip away. I had let him do so before when I was satisfied. *But not this time*, I thought vengefully.

I caught him by his long, dark hair and shoved the head into the fire. I was still armored, and I knew the armor would protect my arm for at least a short time.

Cymry screamed as he always did when threatened with fire. The meshes of the net bag were burned away by the flames.

"Nonononononononono, noaaa!" he screeched.

"I want the truth, and I want it now. Don't try to play with me, you vile heap of shit! Give me an answer, or I will put you on the coals and let them slowly, ever so slowly, consume you!"

"Yes! Yes! Yes! Oh, God have mercy, yes!" Then he sobbed and begged for more wine.

I was still holding him in my left hand, my fingers fixed in his hair. I lifted the cup to his lips with my right. I gave him only a sip, enough to wet his throat. My mind laughed at the thought, and I knew I was close to madness. I wondered if it would trickle from the stump of his neck.

But it didn't. His sudden, sinful death had trapped his spirit in the parchment flesh-covered skull. It could absorb any amount of wine.

I raised the head and held it high, showing its dreadful life to every person in the hall. "Now! Answer!" I said.

Cymry let out a sobbing ululation of almost mad grief. "Mondig told me! Mondig sold me his brother, his brother's wife, and the women of the household. They were rich. The storage souterrains beneath the chief's hall were filled with oil, sealskins, walrus ivory, wool, dried cod enough to keep a whole city fed! It was the richest prize I had ever taken."

"And you got greedy on the way home," Kyra whispered. She lifted another cup from the table. "Wine! I'll give you wine!"

She dashed the wine in Cymry's face and lit it with a wax light from the table. I put the screaming, sobbing thing on the floor. The briefly flaming wine wouldn't kill him, or I should say, drive the spirit from the head. She had done it before, for the same reason—to torment him. In minutes whatever virtue in wine that burns would flare away, and he would sink into the shadowy chambers of his living death.

Then she summoned the women. They took Mondig, coming down from where they sat with their men and children. They didn't kill Merlin's soldiers; they balled them. Maeniel told me bees do this to a queen they do not want; they crowd in around her until she dies of suffocation.

Most carried weapons, and they had shields. They surrounded Mondig's guard, pushing in closer and closer. In a short time, Merlin's men couldn't move, not even to draw their weapons. Then they began to peel them off one by one, passing them on to their menfolk, who disarmed and bound them. A man, even a strong man, is pretty helpless when seven or eight women have hold of him. It was a losing and, for the most part, silent struggle. At the end, Mondig stood alone.

The women took care not to hurt him, pushing him along with shields, sword hilts, spear butts, and mace handles.

Until he reached the center of the hall facing the Death Pig.

Talorcan's small red eyes were fixed on him. I pointed toward Cymry. The thing was on the floor, babbling to itself. "Did you come for him?"

"No!" Talorcan's stone-on-stone voice answered.

I pointed to Mondig.

"Yes!"

"I thought you only came for heroes," I said.

"He might have been a hero, had he so chosen."

The women had taken care not to hurt Mondig at all. But there was a lot of loose rock in the room. I said they'd chopped the hall out of the hillside. It was the men who stoned him.

The next day, Kyra got me up before dawn. She braided my hair in four plaits. She and I used the sweathouse to clean ourselves.

"I'm ashamed of last night," I told her.

She looked surprised.

"After we returned to the tent," I said.

She laughed a little—a harsh, soft laugh.

"I broke down," I said.

And I had. Broken down completely, once I no longer had to control myself. I threw myself on Kyra's neck and cried hysterically to go home.

Issa dragged Gray away. "Let her people settle it among themselves," she told him.

Dugald was in a fury. "What is this nonsense?" he roared.

"And just as well I did, too!" I screamed back at him. "That scheming traitor would have found a way to kill all of us!" I gasped out. "But the way . . . the way they killed him . . . I can't, I . . . don't want to be among these people."

"Nonsense," Dugald roared back. "A salutary lesson to those who would take his place."

Mondig didn't die with dignity. He tried to run—and did—around the fire pit. That was the problem; in an arena there is nowhere to go. As I said, the men threw the stones. They had strong arms and a good aim. Most of the stones hit him, but he kept running until he was a battered rag of flesh and couldn't run any longer. Then he staggered, and at the last, crawled, leaving a trail of blood and slime. Around and around, until I persuaded Talorcan to use his tusks and end it.

By then Kyra had found me a shift somewhere. My armor was fading.

The boar, with tusks and teeth, dispatched Mondig and led his spirit, an empty-eyed, wailing thing, into the fire. And then they were gone.

One of his women servants scooped up his remains and carried him to a high, lonely spot for the sea eagles. The Painted People will in no wise be buried. They look on it with horror—Christian or not—and want to be left exposed until the scavengers clean their bones.

I think then I sat with Dunnel and the rest, and we ate and drank. I think mostly I drank. I have no taste for it, not even now. But that night I did, and I took as much as I could of the most potent mead. And those highlanders do make a strong brew.

I think that's why I fell to pieces at the end. Kyra and Dugald tried to reason with me, but it seemed that I grew more hysterical and insistent that we leave. And leave *now*.

"In the first place, we cannot go home, as you put it," Dugald snorted. "All we would do is bring endless trouble down on Dunnel's head and the heads of everyone we know in the village. Now, stop behaving like a child . . . or I'll slap you silly."

He raised his hand, and Kyra flared back at him. "You touch her, you old fool, and I'll break your arm!"

"Stop it! Both of you!" Maeniel said. "Guinevere, stop screeching. If you want to leave, I'll take you. And now, tonight."

"No!" Dugald shouted.

"How? Where will you go?" Kyra said.

I quieted. "You will?" I asked.

"Yes," he said.

Both Kyra and Dugald started to speak, I think. But he gave both of them his most wolfish stare, and they fell silent. He handed me a towel to dry my face. My eyes were swollen and burning, my nose running. We were standing in the tent. Maeniel glanced out the door.

All through the forest, lights were scattered among the trees, marking the spots where other families attending the assembly were encamped.

"Soon most will bed down for the night," Maeniel said. "Then we can leave. We have traveled in the wilderness before. By dawn, we can be miles away. It will take some time to find a place where there are few, even no, people, but it can be done. We can go there, and I'm convinced Black Leg will find us when his warrior training is over. Guinevere, if that is what you wish, truly wish for yourself, then we will do it. I have no regrets. I grow tired of these murderous men and women.

"But remember, we came here because you chose to come. My son didn't suit you. No. You must have your fair young king. He will not be yours without cost. Kings have even less choice than most men about whom they wed."

I was silent, staring at his shadowed face in the lamplight.

"Remember," he said, raising one finger. "After tonight, there is no going back, however much you wish it. After tonight, too many lives will in all innocence be committed to your purposes for you to ever run again. This is your best chance to shake yourself free of the mantle of ambition and the possession of power. So now make your choice. Not out of disgust or fear, but in clarity of mind and strength of will. Choose . . . the direction your life will take."

Then, taking Dugald by the arm, he led him away.

Kyra got a clean cloth and some cold water and washed my face. I sat down on the side of the cot and stared up at her, aware that I was emotionally and physically exhausted, completely done in.

"Never," she said quietly, "have I seen anyone do what you did tonight. How did you know about Mondig? He had all of us fooled, and a lot of his people."

"I know you," I said. "You wouldn't make that kind of mistake. You wouldn't choose the wrong man. Tell me, was his brother, the one you chose, handsome?"

"No," she said. "He was about as ugly as Mondig. Maybe even worse looking. But there was more kindness in his face."

"Yes," I said.

I didn't remember lying down or falling asleep. She cared for my wounds while I slept.

"You can still go," she told me the next morning in the sweat bath after I apologized for my behavior the night before.

"No!" I said. "I won't be going anywhere."

"Seems," she answered, "that I didn't choose wrong the second time either." Then she patted my knee and left to bring me a dress and the oddments to wear under it.

When we came out of the sweat bath, I was rigged out like a prize horse. I had a sort of crown; seems the queens—all of them—wore one. This was just a gold circlet with a stone at the center. It fitted around my forehead.

The rest of the outfit was more elaborate. A flat, gold band from which dangled fine gold chains was set at my shoulders. Another, at my waist, was also ornamented with the same fine gold chains. The dress was silk, white raw silk, and it probably cost more than the gold chains.

Kyra told me I would wear only the gold chains when I danced tonight.

"But they don't cover . . ." I looked down at my breasts. "And they don't conceal everything down below."

"No, they don't," Kyra said. And that's all she said, except, "Prepare yourself."

Then she led me to a seat in one of the most ancient oaks in the forest. The sky was gray, as was the sea. The wind blew constantly. Dugald, as my druid, stood beside my chair. Maeniel—wolf—sat at my knee.

The seat was formed out of the tree itself, and a stern face with one eye was carved into the trunk above my head. Kyra, as my sponsor, stood behind me.

"The chiefs will be coming, and all the distinguished men and women of the Painted People," Dugald warned me. "And they will bring gifts. It behooves you to remember who brings what and what they have to say to you."

He was right; come they did, in a steady procession all day long. And he was right; they did bring gifts.

The Painted People are great artists. I cannot think they will be appreciated as the Greeks and Romans are, for they work in ephemeral materials, cloth and wood, not stone. Their silver and gold work is magnificent, and some of that may survive. They all seem to be warriors, even the women, and they wear the arts of the loom on their backs and carry a stunning array of weapons.

Never before or since have I seen such beautiful clothing. The cut, it is true, was not imaginative: a simple tunic for both men and women, leggings of wool to keep off the cold, and a mantle, sometimes with a hole cut for the head, at other times simply wrapped around the shoulders. But the endless variety of color and design was simply unbelievable.

As I said, they were marked with the sky signs. The bull, boar, snake, wolf, salmon, dragon, and the patterns of each dance, the colors of the wind and sea, were all met in their clothing. The designs picked out on their skins in blue, green, red, gray, and gold. When each approached me, the patterns my father set on my skin leaped out as though to greet a friend.

The queens came first and brought me silver torcs. They are a grim reminder of what the position of queen means if disaster should befall the people. She is, as the naked warrior, placed in the forefront of battle, the premier sacrificial offering most pleasing to the gods. In times of gravest evil—plague, famine, enemy attack—they cast lots and the chosen one dies. That's what the torc is, a strangler's cord. A mark of favor—that the chosen one may go bloodlessly and consenting to her death.

Consent is important. But I knew that and took the first, a heavy silver object with dragon heads as the finials, as I said, beautifully worked in silver, amber, and blood-colored carnelian. I placed it without hesitation around my neck.

She was the senior lady, the girls with her all young, none having chosen a man to try for the kingship. She looked at me for a long time, and I wondered if she had chosen Mondig. So I asked her.

She said, no, she had not chosen him. Nor was he king but merely the most influential of the chiefs gathered at the assembly. Since he was Merlin's cat's-paw, he had managed, with the archdruid's help, to overawe or intimidate the other chiefs. Now, that was ended. But all the omens, oracles, and prophecies were in agreement: something momentous was going to occur soon.

And something already had: my arrival with all the marks of divine favor. Then she cautioned me to listen well to what the chiefs had to say. Then turned and left, followed by the quiet young girls.

It was just dawn, and from my seat I could look out over the sea. The sun was red behind thick bands of sooty clouds. I spoke with every one of my visitors, many at length, that day. I learned a great many things.

The dragons had a large party. Many people did not share the disapproval the more salmon-dependent villages felt toward them. Others protected their rookeries near their homes, especially the merchants and the deep-sea fishermen, who esteemed their services highly.

A lot of the coastal villages were unhappy with the present situation. They were harried by pirates, Saxon and otherwise, who sailed from the continent to raid along the coast and among the islands. Many were the ports now closed to the Veneti by aggressive barbarian lords who dominated them. Further, any captain finding himself in difficulty might be taken and he and his crew robbed and slaughtered, just as the more unfortunate villages were treated.

All in all the minor chiefs were disgusted with the failure of central power. They needed a king, for that is what a king primarily did: put down the groups who raided along the coast.

The women who sat in the chairs in the great assembly hall had shown no inclination to offer their favors to anyone. Mondig had more or less controlled them, and none of the chiefs was individually powerful enough to oppose him. For various reasons, no group had chosen to combine against him until I came.

At midday, I broke and ate with Dugald, Kyra, Gray, and the Gray Watcher. We talked about what we had heard. Issa cooked and made bread and curd cheese.

"The queen must marry," I said.

No one disagreed.

"It's imperative," Kyra said. "And to a strong man. But your strong man is trapped in another world, and no one knows how to get him back."

"I think we should cross that bridge when we come to it." Everyone looked at me as though I had lost my mind, even the Gray Watcher.

"You have gone from wanting to marry a king to planning to marry a king who is not here," Maeniel said.

"I don't want to talk about it," I said. "But I'm pretty sure I can solve that problem. But the world doesn't need to know how."

True to form, Magetsky was prowling around, picking up scraps.

"Yes," the Gray Watcher said softly. "Yes, that's true."

"She's right," Kyra said. "What she has to do right now is impress them enough tonight. A lot of power here is prestige, and these girls—the 'queens'—are hardly more than the puppets of one faction or another. If you sit on the Dragon Throne, they will fall in behind you, provided their vital interests aren't affected."

"What is so special about that damned dragon chair?" Gray asked.

"The woman who sits in it is usually the first among equals," Kyra answered. "Why the hell do you think Mondig wanted it empty? Why the hell do you think this crowd of quarrelsome chiefs has conspired to keep it empty?"

"They are afraid of its inhabitant. But I can tell from the talk that there is pressure to fill it now," I said. "And I plan to do so. There are too many raids along the coast for the women to ignore their responsibilities any longer. Someone must provide a king."

Then I asked Gray where the raids were coming from.

He looked surprised. "The Saxon shore," he answered. "That's why they put down roots in the first place." Then he named two or three towns.

"Show me," I said.

He drew a map in the dust, marking the towns with dead leaves. "The ships move from Frisia in the raiding season—the spring. They dock along the coast and pick up a crew. Then they sail north."

We all knew what they were after—women, ivory, walrus, sealskins, wool. Pictish wool is the best in the world. But above all, slaves. The eastern countries had an insatiable appetite for them, and a beautiful girl would bring a dozen pounds of gold on the block in Constantinople, especially if she were blond. As the woman in Igrane's hall had suggested, the slave trade was booming.

"Do you think the war bands would follow me?" I asked.

"Ships, weapons cost money," he said.

I pawed open the bag Dugald had placed the presents in. "What does that look like?" I asked.

Gray's eyes lit up. "I knew I was right about you."

Maeniel looked at me sadly. "There is much to consider," he said.

Dugald said, "Wait! You can't—"

"Oh, be quiet," Kyra said.

"They will follow you," Gray said. "I'll see to it."

Maeniel sighed, rose, and walked away into the forest. I could see more people were gathering, waiting to talk to me. I started to get up, but Kyra hissed, "No," and straightened my dress and hair.

"There are well-worked-out ways to do these things," Gray said.

"I know," I told him. "Think you and the rest can be ready soon?"

"Very likely in a few days. But how are we going to find out which ones are ripe for plucking?"

"Need you ask?" I said.

He looked over the ocean. The sun was well up, but caught in a cloudy haze. There would be fog tonight.

"No!" he answered. "No, I don't suppose I do."

The row started as soon as I got back to the tent. It was getting crowded in there. Five heads—the men Maeniel and I killed—were slung from the ridgepole in leather sacks, soaking in cedar oil. The gifts included two wolfhounds—I didn't need those, but they got along fine with Maeniel. He confuses them so much they don't do anything. Besides, they weren't much more than big puppies. He grinned and said he'd train them.

It turned into one of those four-cornered fights we often have when everyone takes up a different position and argues it vigorously.

"You have not yet been accepted as a royal," Maeniel said, "and already you are planning a war."

I opened my mouth, but Gray answered, "If you can think of any other way to stop these raids—I'd like to hear it."

Now, I must tell you, these raids are serious. I suppose most people have always lived at the edge of survival. I know we certainly did. The coastal and island communities of the Painted People are fragile. In a raid, they lose women, livestock, and sometimes—often—all their food reserves. Those women and children not taken as slaves are often killed out of hand, and the survivors are left with nothing to maintain themselves. Often they must sell their bodies to labor in other villages for their bread.

Taking the women is sometimes worst of all. What good is a farm if there is no wife to do the dairying? Or a fishing boat if there is no one to salt or smoke the catch? And the community itself suffers when the sheep and cattle are neglected. Women protect them against predators.

Our sheep are not sheared, but the wool is combed out by the women, cleaned, dyed, spun, and woven. It is wonderful wool, but without women to turn it into cloth, it falls into the heather and thorn, and the wealth of the community is washed away by the rain and wind.

"No, the raids are very dangerous and getting worse, and I'm pretty sure I'm where I am and Mondig is dining with Dis because the people have grown weary of his neglectful ways." I know I spoke sharply to my elders and betters, but I felt I needed to have it out with them now. If I qualified for the position of Dragon Queen, I would refuse to be a mere figurehead. I intended to face up to my responsibilities.

"I can't disagree with you," Dugald said. "But why this unseemly haste? I think you should visit the important chiefly households. Feast your strongest supporters, curry favor with the rest, and judiciously sound out the more mature and intelligent—"

"I haven't got the time," I told him. "Another year of these raids and the stones that landed on Mondig will be aimed at me."

Maeniel and Gray looked at each other in a certain sort of way.

"She's right," Maeniel said. "Much as I hate to admit anyone is smarter than I, in this instance I believe she has a better grip on the problem than any of the rest of us have."

427

"But she has no experience with—" Dugald began.

"No, but we do," Maeniel said.

He and Gray exchanged looks again. They both caught Dugald's eye, and he said, "Hmm."

I looked over at Kyra. Her gray eye looked like granite and her face was set.

"I would forget the villages, and the villas are fortified," Maeniel said.

Gray nodded.

"Usually the pirates camp on the beach and the crews live under the boats."

Gray nodded, listening intently.

"Usually, in fact always, there is a strong point nearby, where they can keep prisoners and loot," Maeniel continued.

"A lot of them are more than half ruined," Gray said.

"Doesn't matter." Maeniel shook his head. "The idea is to have walls. Slingers can stand behind them and drive off anyone who tries to bother the ships. Usually they don't leave them in the water. As I said, the crews use them as houses until they want to make a raid."

"We take the strong point first," Gray said.

Maeniel smiled. "Exactly! The very early hours of the morning, just before first light. Dugald, can you think up a few things to do to a sloppy bunch of thieves?"

Dugald's eyes narrowed. "Oh, my, yes."

"What's my part?" I asked.

"You stay here," Gray said.

"I can fight . . ." I began indignantly.

"I know," Maeniel said. "And as viciously as a wounded boar. But there's no point in your risking your valuable neck in these small-time cleanup jobs. No, what you do is give a feast for the chiefs who supply us with men and ships. Give each one an expensive present. Those are sureties that they won't lose if the fighting goes against us. It won't, but they will want guarantees."

"Naturally," I said. "Who picks our targets?"

"I will," Maeniel said.

"The dragons . . ." I began.

"No," Maeniel said. "They have always remained neutral in human quarrels. I think things had best remain that way."

I did agree it was best.

Gray said, "You will tell us where to go—I've never seen anything you couldn't find out if you wanted to. We'll clean up."

"I think that's quite likely," Dugald said. "One thing though. The loot? What do we . . . ?"

"Farry's people," I said. "I'll sound him on it. The Veneti make a parade of their neutrality, but I'll bet they will buy anything you care to sell them, no questions asked."

"The slaves?" Kyra asked.

"That's a thorny one," Gray answered. "But most of them will be young women, and the boys with us will be young, unmarried men. I think they will form . . . connections. Any from among the Painted People we can send back via Farry. Most of the rest will probably melt away into the countryside if we give them the chance. Aside from not caring for the slave trade, I think it would be dangerous for us to try to transport people in our ships. We're going to use small, fast ones, paint them, and dress the rowers so they will be hard to see. In blue or gray they will look like the water. I've been talking to a cousin I have, and he said it worked against the Romans."

"Anything that worked against the Romans will work doubly well against these fools," Maeniel said.

"Disreputable!" Dugald said. "Very disreputable, but likely very lucrative."

"Disreputable!" Gray took exception to Dugald's characterization of our plans. "The king of the Franks in Gaul doesn't think so. Clovis sinks money into the Saxon treasury every year. He thinks it's a good investment."

"Serves two purposes," Maeniel said to me. "It will put a bad crimp in their plans to steal from the coastal folks, and probably incidentally make you rich. An eighth share of—"

"An eighth share?" I snapped. "I want a fourth!"

"A fourth!" Gray moaned.

"I'm putting up the money," I said.

"A sixth," Maeniel said.

"Done!" I told him. "But only because you're an old friend. And besides, you gave me your sword."

Maeniel grinned wolfishly. "I think you will do very well as a queen. A lot of women would just want to hang that gold and silver around their necks and impress everyone."

"Money is a tool," I said. "The lot of you taught me that when I was growing up."

Kyra nodded. "Not greedy," she said.

"Greedy for power," Dugald said.

"Maybe," I said. "But this is my job. These people are putting me in a position of trust. I don't plan to let them down, if at all possible."

Kyra went to the door and looked at the sun. "It's almost time. Go, all of you. She has to bathe and prepare herself for the dance. When the sun reaches the horizon, she won't be able to speak again until the dance is finished."

Maeniel came to me, put his hands on my shoulders, and then hugged me and kissed me on the cheek. Dugald embraced me, also. I held him close, the smell of his old woolen ceremonial robe strong in my nostrils. I was trembling. I'm sure he could feel it.

"I would spare you this, if I could," he said.

"No," I said. "This is what my mother wanted. She gave her life to bear me. I owe her a debt I can never repay. Without your protection, I would have perished."

"Ah, God!" he whispered. "Did I do right? I might have left you to Merlin and Igrane. They would have seen to it you were reared in a more civilized manner."

"That pair of horrors?" I answered. "Arthur barely survived them with his mind intact. And I'm as civilized as I care to be. If I have any shortcomings, I blame myself for them. All my virtues are the result of your teachings."

"Ah, God!" Dugald said. "I would that were so." He raised his hand to bless me.

Kyra said, "No! I doubt if Christ would sanction this rite. It was many thousand years old when Mother Mary wrapped his swaddling clothes around him. Don't you put Christ's seal on her tonight."

"She's right," Maeniel said, and led him away.

Gray kissed my hand, wished me good fortune, and then Kyra and I were alone together. We went to look at the sun. It was touching the horizon.

"Time now for silence," she told me. "Turn your thoughts away from worldly things. Look inward and ready yourself for a visitation of the divine."

CHAPTER TWENTY-FIVE

WHEN HE REACHED THE SEA, IT WAS SUNSET. HE walked out of the jungle and across the almost perfectly white beach to look at the water. His heart was nearly stilled by its beauty. The water was green as the combers began to break into white foam, then the green faded to crystal transparency as the wave came up the shore, until the water sank down into the alabaster sand and vanished.

Out from the shore the deep water was a clear rich blue. The sun was already high in the clouds on the horizon, and the wind, still warm, had begun slightly to chill. Not like the seas of his own land, though it wouldn't be difficult to learn to love this almost too perfect beauty as well. He and Cai had hunted near the ocean when they were boys. Often they swam out to offshore islands of rock to try to hook the deep-water giants that came by night to feed on squid in the shallows. Twice they had managed to hook fish almost as big as themselves, and the other youngsters tried to worm the secret of their success out of them. But they wouldn't tell, not only because they wouldn't give them the satisfaction but also because they were afraid if Morgana knew the risks they were taking, she would put a stop to their expeditions.

But Cai knew no fear of water, and Arthur refused to allow any companion of his to show more courage than he did. So one evening they dove in and swam to a small, rocky isle almost out of sight of land. While they were setting their lines, deep-water fog rolled in, trapping them there. Cai was frightened, not for himself but for Arthur, if the truth be known. For the young prince. The air held a damp chill, and the thin, light-skinned Arthur had no fat to keep off the cold.

One of Cai's strongest traits was his sense of responsibility. He pulled off his clothing, put it on his smaller companion, and dove in, searching for a way back to the mainland. But the water was too cold to make a long search practical, night was coming on, and it was clear they were stranded. So he returned to the rock, found the most sheltered spot, and embraced the younger boy.

No one had ever before embraced Arthur in love and protection since he could remember. Arthur stiffened and bit Cai on the arm, savagely, drawing blood. Cai was still scarred by the bite. It left a semicircle of white dots on his right forearm.

The fight was brief and ugly, but Arthur was cold and frightened of the sea, if the truth be known—and Cai and reason prevailed.

"Why are you such a fool that you won't let me keep you warm?" Cai snapped, and his charge subsided.

After a time the warmth crept through Arthur's body. They were both far too young for even a dream of passion, but Arthur found in Cai's arms what he had never found in his mother's, his father's, or even Morgana's. He couldn't put a name to it, except that it created a rich silence within him and he encountered for the first time in his brief, tormented life a sense of peace. He lay quiet in body and spirit for a long time.

He had woken still warm near dawn. He sat up in the hollow in the rocks where they had taken refuge and saw the seal by starlight. It lifted its dark head from the water and gazed at him with large, gentle dark eyes, then turned and began to slowly swim away.

Arthur slid into the cold water and followed, and in a short time reached land. Their weapons, mantles, packs, and the bow drill were wrapped up under a tree. When Arthur turned and got his footing and looked back, the seal was gone and Cai was climbing out of the water behind him.

Sleep was like a drug to Cai. He embraced it, went down the way a seal does in water, and rode it the way a seal does waves, diving deep into its silences, blessedly without dreams. Arthur woke from frequent nightmares, struggling, gasping, panting, perspiring, his heart pounding. Sometimes he could remember what they were about, but he was thankful when he couldn't. They slept in the same room; he would rise, climb into Cai's bed, press his back against Cai's warm body and drift off again. He was conscious that something in Cai's personality bolstered his confidence and allowed him to rest, to seek peace and find it. He never gave a name to it, and never spoke of it. And never, never would he have allowed himself or anyone else to call it—love.

Yet he had from that day forward been drawn to the sea, to its everchanging, changeless face, to the eternal sound: silence, sound of the breaking wave, its deep-held secret of eternities, peace.

He sat on a log. The fading light lit a spire of cloud in gold as a rainstorm moved over the jungle miles away. *She would come*, he thought. And try to do what? Destroy him?

No! Had she wanted that, it had been easily accomplished as he climbed the long stair. The accomplishment this place represented was clear to him. If sorcery, it was of a kind he had never seen. Merlin's evil tricks and Igrane's manipulations were nothing to this.

No—this greeted him with a philosophical grandeur beyond imagining. The form of the tower bespoke a thinking other than human but possessed of accomplishments that men—mankind, humankind—might admire, try to study, and ultimately emulate. Possibly he might perish in trying to yield to the Queen of Death the fruits of her desire, but then, there are many worse ways to die. And he was well acquainted with most of them, having been considered a man since his eleventh year when he made his first kill, a vandal brigand who sold his sword to a slave trader working the coast of Morgana's realm.

The warrior societies had surprised the man's ship run aground on a sand spit near her stronghold. It carried an illegal cargo, one of Morgana's women. They were highly prized in Constantinople for their fighting ability, and this devil had taken great pains to acquire this one. None but women and boys had been present, none older than fourteen. Arthur, already a Bear, was one of the ones who drew the burned cake.

The memory was a dark one. They hadn't had much time. When they received word of the abduction of a girl from the Hawk society, the Bears found their group was the closest one to the coast. Honor demanded the girl be retrieved at once, even though the young Bears might perish in the attempt.

Their captain and leader was their weapons instructor: Shela-na-gig. They ran for the coast.

The slaver captain might have shown his erstwhile hosts a clean pair of heels had he not misjudged the speed of the falling tide in the bay where he'd anchored. It stranded his heavy vessel at the mouth of the bay, near the sea. He had a full cargo of slaves. If he unchained them to see if he could lighten the ship, some would certainly try to break away across the tidal flats. Left chained, they might drown if one went under—they were chained neck to neck. She might drag the rest down with her.

He didn't think his hosts could muster an armed party between one tide and the next. He reckoned without the Bears.

They covered thirty miles in just a few hours on foot. They paused only long enough to form the cake, the flour specially mixed by their priestess leader. It contained oat, barley, wheat, and as many of the other plants and flowers of cropland and wild meadow as could be gathered and stored at one time. It was cut, separated into as many sections as there were men in the war party. Secretly, the priestess burned one section with a broken bit of firewood.

The boys crouched around the fire while she baked the flat bread on a hot rock. Each boy took a section. Arthur tasted the char in his mouth when he bit down. He chewed and swallowed without giving any indication of distress.

Shela crouched near the cooking rock and gazed at the boys sitting in a circle around her.

"I am the one!" Arthur said immediately. He remembered her savage smile, the gleam of perfect white teeth in her scarified and tattooed face. Without further ado, he began to strip.

Cai objected. Shela had Cai disarmed and tied to a tree.

"You are to be a king. You are the only heir. We can't spare you!" Cai cried in anguish, then began openly to weep.

"Your love," Shela said, "does you credit, but if 'they' want him, he must go." Then she began to mix the preparation of charcoal, fat, wood, and yellow ocher used to dedicate the sacrifice. Eros, desire, lust, her hands were all of these things when she marked his bare skin.

He was virgin. He had never known a woman—not a human one. He had no idea if the creature who had chosen him and drew his body into fire at his initiation was truly female or not, but Shela's hands and body were obviously those of a woman.

Shela-na-gig. The church hated her and feared her, yet they let the people carve her on the apse of their churches. She was too strong to deny or ignore.

The priestess's hands lingered and caressed the young warrior as she prepared him for death. Then they stamped out the fire and finished their run toward the sea.

They were children, but Shela and they thought as one. The only advantage they had was surprise.

Arthur crouched on the shore with them. In the darkness, he could smell them around him. The reek of fear and rage, old ashes, piss, hot meat, raw meat, newly dead like a bloodless kill, ready to be butchered. He knew he must lead. The sacrifice must go first, the raw rage that precedes certain death, terror, boiling into rage as liquid into vapor, filling his mind and body with exultation and a readiness to inspire others with his directed self-destruction.

His sword was in his right hand. Shela's instructions were, "Let your eyes accustom themselves to the darkness. Be sure they have accommodated well. Then pick your target and hesitate no more."

Yes, he saw the ship. There was no moon; it was a dark shape against a sea of stars. Now his eyes picked out the gunwales. Stranded, she was canted a bit to the left, her sloping deck an easy leap from the sand.

There was a light aboard, a shielded lantern or candle. Very faint. The sentry or sentries would be close to it.

He probed the shadows around the vessel, searching for an ambush, because that would occur to him, were he stranded in such a place. But no, it did not appear to have been part of the captain's thinking.

He felt a surge of raw, physical desire. His left hand was resting on his thigh. He felt his male organ move across the tips of his fingers. His death would be ecstatic.

He heard the whispered word, "Now!" without really knowing who said it. Then he was flying, flashing along like spindrift carried by the wind. The stranded ship loomed over him, and he had time to reflect that they were barely in time. The tide was rising, and he was running through the shallows.

A second later, his leap—he seemed to be flying—carried him to the deck. The sentry stood before him.

He remembered the man's face, large gray eyes, a scar on the forehead. The sentry must have heard them splash through the shallows, because his sword was in his hand. He drove it swiftly at Arthur's unprotected left chest.

Arthur felt the blow.

I'm dead, he thought. *But I have a second before my heart stops.*

He felt a jolt of raw pleasure and his mind and body rode the wave he was sure would break and spill him into eternity. He had permission to swing his own weapon now, and his descending blade split his adversary's skull to the teeth. A fountain of scarlet—warm, wet, and sticky—blinded him, and he went down.

He felt rather than saw Shela and the rest of the boys flood onto the ship. Most of the crew was still asleep and never woke up. They rescued the girl warrior of the Hawk society. They took no casualties at all.

No, not even him.

The warrior's sword thrust didn't penetrate. It skidded along his rib. He still had the scar—his first mark of valor. And he was felt to have met all the conditions of the offering, including allowing his enemy to strike the first blow.

The powers had spared him. He had other work to accomplish.

The sun was down. The stars changed places with the sea and stretched around him until he stood alone in the vast emptying of the universe. She came drifting across the star glow.

He found he knew her. Not long after he and Cai had their adventure of being trapped offshore, they returned to the gentle green valleys caught in the flanks of the mountains beside the sea. He couldn't remember what spring it had been, because when he lived in Morgana's realm time didn't seem to exist any longer. She held it at bay with her magic.

Even the Romans had found the ground shifted beneath their feet at times, and they lost a legion in her mists. She laughed at the Roman commander when he tried to get it back, so he remitted the taxes he had wanted to collect and the legion returned from the soft, wet nowhere into the world of men again. Not long after, the Romans marched away from the white isle forever as they confronted the disintegration of their particular world.

She had been born in the valley, near the sea, and so she died there. Her family were Christians, and they would not give her to the sea eagles. She was buried.

He remembered her face when his father returned to put her to rest. For she walked. Or so the other families in the valley complained. And Uther said Christian or no, her body must be burned before there were more killings.

One woman and two men were already dead. All three had seen her walking in the mist near the sea before the tide caught them in the flat open sands near the ocean.

Uther came and overruled the local bishop. She was dug up.

Arthur remembered her face, the yellow skin cleaving to the fair, delicate bone structure of the skull. The empty, dark eye hollows, and lips still full but purple-black with decay over young, even white teeth. The corpse's tallow body even more ripe, full, and curvaceous than the rather slender virgin girl buried a year ago. It radiated a cold eroticism, even discolored as it was but still draped in its silk and linen winding sheet. Like a snake, firm but cold to the touch.

She walked toward him out of the darkness along the road of stars. She held out her arms to him.

He had seen his father embrace, then kiss her and yield her to the flames. *How am I less?* he thought, and took her in his arms.

He remembered the snapping of twigs, the hiss of flesh melting in the fire, running like wax. The beautiful, dead but still beautiful, face crowned with dried flowers yielding, withering, vanishing into flame. The loathsome lady, the hag of winter's darkness, that the winter king, to be a king, must kiss.

His nostrils were drenched with the scent of putrefaction as he pressed his lips to hers.

CHAPTER TWENTY-SIX

I SAT, FOR THERE IS A SO-CALLED CHAIR WHERE the queens sit before the dance. There are a lot of these things, so old no one is sure what they mean.

A footprint at Tintigal. And yes, Uther places his foot there always when he visits. And when he does, his oath men and many others hail him with a great shout.

That would be the people's seal of approval, if my dance pleased them. A shout. A mighty shout. Then another, if my actions seemed proper in a queen. Then at last a third if I were acceptable as a ruler.

For rule I would. The young women Mondig had chosen were puppets, and Kyra was right. They would fall in behind me, provided I did not seriously inconvenience any of the factions they represented. Or, quite possibly, even if I did, since I could practice divide and rule among them, picking them off one by one at my pleasure. None were individually strong enough to defy me, *if, if, if* I could bring an end to these raids.

Kyra had given me a warm mantle, some wool-silk blend, another of the gifts I had received. It was colored with a rich blend of early spring greens, blues, and pale yellows—water, grass, and sunlight. And it was warm and almost feather-light.

That was good. I was almost naked under it. I wore the chains at my shoulders. They fell away on either side of my breasts, colored with the glowing greens of my father's gift, my fairy armor. A similar fine metal band at my hips held a skirt of fine chain, which hung almost to my knees. Eros, it gives life.

I knew that in the hall the woman they choose is ready; she is fertile. Her body is the warm, spring earth before the plow. The red translucent salmon roe glowing like fire in the icy water, waiting for the pale swirls of milt. Warm flushed as coals covering the bread baking in a pot, thick as the wheat heads bending with fruitfulness, the blush of wild autumn apples on the bough.

Eros and the watching crowd gathered on the slopes surrounding the dance floor would see it as I danced. They had a right to know the Dragon Queen could choose a king or, if necessary, bear one. And either way there would be no reason for them to be disappointed in her.

So be it.

Then I thought about war, because above all, it was my business.

"It is a lottery," Maeniel said. "The winners garner the prizes, power, wealth, women. Women are last, but they go with wealth and power or, at least, many do. To the loser, death, slavery, poverty, and ignominy. Mostly death."

"Ha!" I asked, "What about the dead on the winning side?"

That was long ago, and Black Leg was still with us. "You make it sound terrible," he accused his father.

"It is," Maeniel said. "And there is only one side in a war—that of the survivors. The others don't count, no matter what their stated affiliation might be. And, trust me, more on the winning side survive than on the losing. Slavery is often only a somewhat slower death sentence than that found on the battlefield."

"God! Why do they do it, then?" he asked his father.

We had been out after a herd of wild horses and were walking along downslope through a pine forest. Maeniel stopped and looked at both of us.

"Think about the boys in the war band."

"He's right," I said to Black Leg. For a second, he looked appalled, then, as comprehension dawned, he nodded and whispered, "Yes. I see."

None of the boys who faced the pirates that day on the beach ever went back to the wandering companies who guard the coast. Bain made a marriage to Issa, the chief's daughter. No way Dunnel would have given his only child but that Bain was able to bring the loot he stripped from the bodies of the pirates killed on the beach that day.

On the strength of his gains, Gray got Anna, the smith's daughter. Next to Dunnel, the smith was the most important and prosperous individual in our community. All of the boys got places and most got women.

"That is how the game is played," Maeniel said. "Never be misled by claims of valor, honor, or even justice or truth. Though you will find these things all deploy themselves as part of the mix from time to time and so must be dealt with. Remember this central truth. Your enemy is there because he, too, has weighed the consequences of failure and accepts them. Play always to win, because nothing else matters."

He was right. And the raids had to stop. But whatever killing Maeniel and Gray did—in the final analysis it would only win us a temporary respite. There were simply too many young men, and, yes, women, hungry sometimes only for simple survival and without the means to ensure it. They would risk all on the off chance they would draw life, wealth, and happiness in the contest of war, violence, and theft. It had been so in the time of the Romans, and the Greeks before them. And even when the sea kings battled for supremacy over the blue Mediterranean and the first Greeks were hill tribes cutting one another's throats with bronze swords and the Painted People carried iron from Etruria to Gaul and the first iron swords were smelted in the mountain fires. None even then thought any differently than they do now about war and its necessity.

Maeniel believed Christ tried to change men's minds about one another, tried to persuade them that they were brothers and sisters and owed each other the love and protection any good family owes its members. That they might live together in compassion and peace.

"He failed," I said.

"No!" Maeniel answered strongly. "He did not entirely fail. And since what he tried to do was so difficult, he may be satisfied with the work of one lifetime. I cannot say. The mind of God is a closed book to me. But he showed us which direction we must go in order to serve good. The good! And to seek it!"

I was . . . what? ten at the time he told me that, and walking through a forest in search of game to feed our family. Mother and Black Leg were beside me.

Mother snorted, a soft wolf sound only faintly audible to human ears. It said volumes.

What she replied said more volumes. All the books in the world could not be so succinct.

"We hunt whatever we need to eat, be it deer, hare, horse, or even fish or fowl. They—you, for you are one of them—hunt each other. We are avenged for their multiple cruelties and supreme madness. I can but hope we survive them." Mother was, as he said, a sarcastic bitch.

Yes—Mother—she formed my mind, and in my heart I am a she-wolf.

The sun was sinking now into the sea, so low—so lost in haze—that I could look into its circle of light reflecting burnished gold like a mirror. The wind was growing cold, and below the chair, the ocean thundered and hissed against the rocks.

Mother! She is part of the answer to the abyss. The question: Why anything? Why not nothing?

She is life and guides it from generation to generation, even as both my mothers did.

Mother had no easy life, even for a wolf. The mantle of procreation fell on her young as the last surviving female in her pack. Her first get were born when she was little more than a yearling. Not long after, Maeniel became her mate, and she was after not too many years saddled with me. A strong creature, the she-wolf, strong and wedded to her duty.

But she was also free and no wise Maeniel's property. Had he returned to Gaul the next spring, she would have danced in the moonlight with new suitors and gone on with her sacred task of ensuring the future.

"This is what we do," she told me once.

"Why?" I asked.

She laid her ears back, a sign of great displeasure. "Why does water flow downhill, a river to the sea?" she asked. "I cannot think your kind has any sense at all. Even as I remember when long ago ice and snow covered the whole world, so I know this is God in me. God the mother."

I was full of myself. "Maeniel says we must exercise discretion in the matter," I told her.

"I can do that also. I know when the weather has been bad, humans have been particularly insane or for whatever reason game is scarce. I know not to summon my lovers in springtime but wait and protect what I have. It is you—your kind—who are feckless, lecherous, and stubbornly blind. A wolf too aggressive would meet my teeth. But your men will force a woman, especially a woman they see as theirs, without a second thought. As though one could own another."

Then she left me to ponder her words.

Yes, everything they, Maeniel and Mother, said was true. And it had mattered little to me then. I was only a young girl with her way to make in the world. I could do little about such philosophical conundrums.

But now! Now! I was reaching for power. And I must give the lessons of war and love some thought. I must decide what course my life would take. As Maeniel pointed out—though as usual, Dugald did not agree with him—Christ pointed the way for the rest of us.

Could I change things?

The sun was down, but the sky was still suffused with light. Beyond the chair where I sat along the cliff, people were gathering on the slopes around the broken dance floor. Fires were leaping at the edge of the remnants of the dragon dance floor. The people arriving to watch my performance carried torches; neither candles nor lamps would stay lit in the omnipresent wind from the sea.

The sky was a bowl of bright blue above, still catching the light shining upward from the sun. But the stars were finding their way out against the glowing blackness. When the sky was fully dark and the crowd an island, a kingdom of light between the sky, the mountains, and the thundering sea, Kyra would summon me.

Could I change things? And if so—how? Need war be an eternal necessity among humans? Need lust and greed always determine the fate of men and women? Especially women?

I heard footsteps and knew Kyra was coming with the ladies of heaven, the rulers of the ancient houses set among the stars. They were here to escort me to the dance floor.

CHAPTER TWENTY-SEVEN

HE STARS VANISHED. INSTEAD, THEY WERE IN a pit.

"Congratulations," came the voice, dry and ancient. "You have won the right to face me in single combat. Few of your kind get so far. But none has ever survived this final test."

Arthur tried to see into the murk surrounding him, the not-quite darkness.

"Trying to look at me?" came the ironic question.

"We are uncomfortable when we cannot see," he answered.

"Oh, discomfort, not terror. Not pissing, shrieking madness."

"No!" Arthur replied. "Only discomfort."

"I'll see if I can remedy that."

The flame seemed to shoot from the floor near his foot, a wash of fire rather like that of a smelter fueled by the air from a bellows. It was hot. He moved away, but then another, closer, roared into life. Then another.

Now he could see, but it wasn't comforting. It seemed a vast metal dome covered them both. It was stitched together with iron bolts. But even though it seemed formed of something grayish, harder than the steel that was the hardest metal he was used to, the dome was beginning to deteriorate and shards of metal were peeling off the thick plates. Not rusting, but undergoing some much slower process, which rendered it brittle. His booted foot crunched a piece at his feet, and he watched it disintegrate.

Another flame leaped from a jet on the floor and illuminated the thrones around the walls.

The voice laughed. "See! We are all dead."

They were; and in addition, none of them was human. She sat before him, a rack of bones clothed in silk, gold mesh, and shadows. He could clearly see her hands and face. The hand bones were long, four fingers—no, three fingers—and something that looked like a very flexible thumb. The skull was simply a nightmare, longer than a human's but broad at the back with a lot of room for brain. The front was fanged with long teeth, which protruded at the jawline. It reminded him of a bird, a bird of prey, because the eyes faced the front.

The one next to her was covered by strips of something that had fallen into a pile from the seat of the chair, stretching to the floor. But between them, the rust-colored bone and some sort of almost unbreakable ligament clung together. The rest were heaps of tattered remnants, sometimes on the chairs, others scattered on the floor.

The torches roaring around him sent flickering shadows over a scene that would have done credit to the Prince of Darkness himself.

Arthur laughed. "I wouldn't have missed this for the world," he said. "But don't you think it's getting hot in here?"

It was. However large the airless place was, the fires couldn't burn like this for very long. Soon, when the heat became too great, he would fall to prostration and suffocation.

"Is that it? Am I supposed to smother?" he asked.

"You must be here long enough," she said. "Unless . . . unless you want to stay."

Arthur looked down. Some of them had. Quite a lot, in fact. They were in all stages of disintegration, a few sloppy wet and stinking, but most of the rest with dry skin clinging to the bones stretched over them like parchment. Others were shattered brown heaps of crumbling bone and a few only shadows marked by a crumbling skull, one or two long bones, or a scattering of teeth.

It was getting hotter and hotter in the shell.

"Will you ride the wheel?" she asked.

He shrugged. "Why not?"

The water was a relief. It was icy but that didn't seem to trouble him. He tried to close his eyes, but found he couldn't. He could feel the water around them, but was no more troubled by it than he would have been by air.

What? Where? he thought, looking at the pebbled streambed beneath him. The stones had a polished glow brought on by water. As he watched, a fish slipped into the field of vision belonging to his right eye. A salmon, greenish-black back, red belly.

Why isn't it afraid of me? he thought. It was close enough for him to reach over and touch it. He moved to stretch out his arm, but his muscles wouldn't obey him.

He leaned toward the fish. An extra sense from somewhere told him he was leaning as the pressure against his side changed. With an elegant and utterly inhuman motion, he righted himself.

I am, he thought, *also a fish. Yes, a man breathes, a fish swims. Neither has to think about it much.*

He willed himself to rise toward the rippled, gleaming ceiling of the stream in which he was swimming. He felt the strange sense of lessening pressure as his body approached the surface. He didn't need to see to know his depth.

Trees along the stream smothered it in dark green. The black of wet, broken rock, the brown of splintered shards of broken trees washed downstream by the winter snow melt. All crowded around the water.

Down, he thought. And his fins carried him toward the bottom.

Faster, he moved past the fish he still saw to his right. And suddenly, with a shock of fear, he found himself stranded, gravel under his belly, the air, the cold spring mountain air an icy shock of deep pain.

A few minutes more and you will die, something in the dark instinctive matter of his brain warned him, and nudged him toward panic. But he was still a man and beat back the fear. *Think!*

His eyes were clear of the water. Ahead was a death trap; the shallows continued for as far as he could see. And indeed, he saw the desiccated and scavenged bodies of those who had made the same mistake he had.

One chance. He took it. A fish can bend almost double when it wants to. He wanted to.

His powerful musculature snapped his head around toward his tail. A second later, he found himself still in the shallows but looking toward deeper water. *Now, fish, pretend you are a snake.*

He did, wiggling forward, ignoring the occasional sharp rock that poked at his soft belly. A few seconds later, he found himself part of the resting crowd in deep water, gills working. He could feel them now, relieved to be safe for the moment.

Everything eats salmon! Hawks, eagles, bears, men!

Ah, yes. But a lot of them survive.

The stream bottom was a road, a gleaming tunnel roofed by a surface that showed him broken images of an ancient forest of pine, yew, and evergreen. A path of clear water floored with glowing stone. He and some others who had rested enough started along it, this time more cautiously than before. He kept to the deeper channel.

He heard the rapids. He had ears of a rudimentary sort, but the changes in pressure, the pickup of rapid staccato swirls of movement alerted him to their presence. He moved toward the surface. He found he didn't have to will it any longer.

He saw the falls, a set of shallow stairs laced with tumbled deadfalls from upstream set in the emerald green of new leaves on the poplars, willows, and young water ash at their margins.

A beautiful place, but a lot of trouble for a fish.

He turned toward the shallows, but to do so, he must cross the deepest part of the pool below the falls.

No! No more recklessness. He did notice most of the fish entering the pool behind him broke to one side or another of the dark depths. He moved easily around them, keeping a wary eye out for movement until he reached a deep hole under a willow, an old willow, half rotted near the foot of the first falls.

Fish. I am fish, he thought as he sank toward the bottom. *Am I fish?* And he knew among the many dangers that awaited him here was one he hadn't counted on if he remained too long. Or was it that if he became too comfortable with this shape, he might forget who he was? Who he had been. And, indeed, the human memories seemed to grow dimmer as he listened more closely to what the fish told him. As the images of silver sides flashed in his mind.

Then they were crisscrossing the shallows above him. At least a dozen. He struck, felt the recurved teeth in his throat. Crush, savor, swallow. Even as he dove toward the bottom.

Not very smart above, they were still darting as before. But then his mind saw the exquisite economy of it.

The mayflies were swarming, green lacy wings landing in the water by the dozen. Some might eat and die, but the rest would eat and that was what was important. But if it was important to them, and they were important to him, might it not be that he could be important to something else?

What?

He sank deeper, belly resting in the mud, fins barely moving.

What? Nothing!

Then the pike glared out of the gloom. A fish can't stop breathing, can it? But he felt as though he had.

The first was delicious, but the second one he went for would have been his last. But then, he couldn't be the only one on the hunt. Now, could he?

A second later, he saw the hook jaw snap shut on another silver side, the red belly a scarlet splash in the light from the surface. The jaws that seized it were as long as he was. Blood crimsoned the water; he could taste it as it passed his gills. He watched the pike vanish into the depths with the still-struggling salmon in its teeth. His eyes studied the pool, much movement, all of it small fish, though.

Nothing ventured, nothing gained. He struck again, and again, until his stomach was full. Then slowly he stroked out of the shallows, then shot forward. The leap carried him out of the large pool into the smaller one at the first step of the falls.

Get to the top. The fish was taking over; all the man had to do was let go. But he wouldn't. Yet he knew he would obey the fish.

How does a fish jump? The thought made him clumsy. The salmon leap, a warrior's tactic.

Don't think! Act! Up! And he was, after a brief journey through air, in a higher pool.

The falls were a buffeting pressure wave. He didn't see the bear until the last second. It was fishing in the shallows, almost at the top. There was no time for a leap; there was no time for anything except regret and a question.

How would I have been as a fish?

The vicious jaws were falling toward him. The fish executed it, but the man invented it. One powerful slap of the muscular tail and the bear had eyes, nose, and mouth filled with icy water. It stumbled back with a roar, swinging a paw down, armed with gleaming talons.

Hero's salmon leap, and the fish fought the current at the top of the falls. He was peeled away like a bird taking wing.

She seemed no longer dead this time, and they wandered through a strange, haunted wood, dark even by day. It was achingly silent; no insect buzzed, no bird called. They were walking along the riverbed. He wondered if it could be the same river, but she, striding along beside him, said, "No! Everything here is dead. Even the river."

It was so long ago. The trees were green, smooth trunked, tall, green-black at the base but growing lighter and lighter as they approached their twisted, feathery tops as much as a hundred feet above and more. Dappled with sun, the soft canopy above moved gently in every vagrant breeze, allowing dappled light to penetrate the ferns and mosses growing with equal thickness in the rock-lined riverbed.

She was beautiful in an eerie sort of way—tall, taller than he was, her wide head covered with a crest of white feathers contoured to cover her head smoothly, the way a bird's do. Her face was covered with an even finer growth of gray feathers. The long, powerful fangs projected down from a rather small jaw. Her body—he could see enough of it through her golden mesh tunic and long pants—was covered by feathers also, all the way down to the feet, which were rather slender claws, like a bird's. Even the backs of the long-fingered hands were feathered, looking curiously

451

nude when she opened them, showing the palm and fingers. Her eyes were a bird's also, light brown with a black ring around the iris; and the pupil could contract to a pinpoint in one instant, then expand into a black well the next.

"Everything here is dead?" he asked. "Even you?"

"Yes!"

"So there is life after death," he said.

"No," she answered. "There isn't, but there is something—at least, for me there is. I cannot say what others will find, but whatever they do, it is not life. Of that you get only one. Use it well."

The wind blew a little harder and the trees murmured as the very fine, feathery leaves and branch networks were tossed around by it. Arthur rested his hand on one of the dark-green trunks. It was lightly ridged with a complex pattern of leaf scars. But then, that was how they grew and he saw they were very simple plants, because there were saplings next to the river's rocky bed. Even when small they came straight up out of the ground, the growing points at the top differentiated into many fine branches, which gave way to equally fine, soft leaves, rather like the soft, loose feathers of a plume.

As the herb . . . bush . . . tree—somehow it managed to be all three at the same time—grew, the stem at the base expanded from within, not the way a tree grows along the outer bark but at the soft curve. And the reason they could grow so close together was that they were top to bottom, even in the deep shadows of the high-canopied forest—all green.

"What are they?" he asked, caressing the smooth, ever-living trunk.

She ran her eye over the nearest, a two-hundred-foot giant decorated along its length by scattered masses of plumed foliage.

"Moss," she answered. "Moss. Not much different from the soft carpet you tread on."

He glanced down at the mosses at his feet, some as fine as deep-green velvet. Others, coarse like tufted cushions, occupied the spaces between the velvet-covered boulders. Just then the sun vanished, wrapping the world in green gloom, and the rain began sending its misty silver curtains among the tightly packed trees. The trickle of water at the center of the stream where they walked grew wider and reflected the gray above, then blue as the storm clouds passed, blown away by the wind.

A crackling, snapping sound spread through the forest, a simple statement amid the omnipresent silence. All around him the aisles and aisles of trees, dense, almost impenetrable, echoed with the sound.

"What is it?" he asked.

"They speak their souls," she said. "After the rain, the female cones—the ripe ones, that is—open and give their spores into the wind. See? If you look closely, you can pick them out against the soft leaves."

And indeed, he could. Dozens and dozens of them massed the green feathery cushions of the giant trees.

"Hush," she whispered. "Hear them."

So many cones were cracking, they echoed like a drumroll, as though an invisible army rode the wind through the moss forest.

"Life," he said. "This is a tale of life, but you are the Queen of the Dead."

"That is what death speaks to—life," she said.

He woke in the dark. The pitch dark.

I am indeed riding the wheel, he thought.

Then, when he tried to shift his body, he felt an instant thrill of re-vulsion. He tried to express this in sound; it came out a hiss.

Well, he thought. *What else can you expect if you are a snake?*

Death. She had spoken of death. Death woke the . . . snake he was.

It didn't mind dying. It didn't mind much of anything. It was far too simple.

But such stark simplicity opened the doors to other realms. It was old. The mind of the creature, even the fish's mind, hadn't seemed so terrify-ingly old.

I am, I was, I will be? were all the same to the snake. There are the many and then the one. I am the one, unless death reaches me.

There are many deaths, but all one and, like me, death is one and many. There is the death from above without warning, hawk or rock slide the same to the snake. Death from below with warning, but inescapable nonetheless. Death by predator—pig, weasel, otter, wolf, cat, human. Death by torpor and cold. This threatened the snake now.

Winter was ended. The tongue flicked out and tested the air. The den was still cold, but outside the sun was shining. The air the snake tested was warm.

Feed or die. Things are simple to a snake. But he knew the creature elevated paranoia to a high art.

Lord, this thing could move well. Point the head, the rest follows. The snake cleared the den slowly, carefully, testing, testing the air all around for the spike of heat that would indicate the approach of a large predator.

No! Nothing!

Ah, warm.

The snake coiled on a bed of brown pine needles before the den mouth. Warm, he felt his body and his senses quicken as the sun seeped into him.

Ah, warm!

Simple. The man Arthur had not known simplicity could be this absolute, this pure. The gratification so intense, the experience so all-encompassing.

Do not think, but be.

Yet, after a time, there was such a thing as enough. He moved forward toward a patch of new green grass shaded by a domed rock.

Test the air; taste the air every few seconds or so. The forked tongue and deep mind mapped the world. A rock sun-warmed on one side. A pool, not a very big one, but big enough to hold a dangerous inhabitant. On the other side, the forest. The living things there were glowing spots of heat. Birds, baby birds in a nest in the lowest branches of a pine.

Too high.

A fallen tree, still half green, a maple, branches glowing with a thousand new green leaves. That spot on the base, on the rotten side, mice—a whole family. They gnawed their way into the tree, the hole they made too small to admit him.

Keep that, and the memory was placed among the rest, only a few, like beads on a string, each discrete, complete, embodying all the meaning it would ever have. The tree was rotting; the chamber the mice inhabited was fairly large. At the moment, they were safe, the tree bark still intact. He could not gnaw. But the wood would rot.

The pond to the left of the domed rock. Winter-killed brush filled the shallows near the rock, clustered around one fallen willow sapling. Willow like it was still alive and formed a curtain of branches, cutting off the pond from the brush. The trunk was canted.

A perfect resting place? The man's mind questioned the mind of the snake.

Taste the air. No. Nothing. No bird. No otter. Cool water, warm trees, and reeds.

Moving cold—fish, frogs, insects.

Feed tonight. Feed or die.

We hate them, the man thought—Arthur thought. *We do not begin to understand them, but we hate them nonetheless.*

He peered into the deep, dark well of the snake's mind. Sought approval—found it, and moved toward the broken willow. Point the head, the body follows. Can snakes climb trees? Actually, they are rather good climbers.

He reached one of the willow branches. It was leaning against the rock. Now warmed by the sun and moved by hunger, he went quickly, head out, around and around the slender branch, his body vanishing against the gray-green bark.

Look up.

Ah, the man thought. The snake noted the bird. The tongue flicked—warm.

Arthur's mind stumbled. The snake was so wholly *other.*

Of course. That was the death without warning—he was looking at it. He knew the snake had to be faster than the bird.

No, faster is dangerous.

Drop?

No. Too much noise. Other things live in water. They can hear. He must move and hope the bird didn't see him.

He turned bonelessly as a rope, clasped the slender branch, and flowed toward the ground as his body turned around the center of the branch. First one eye, then another looked up. The bird began to fall.

But he held himself steady, understanding why now. As long as he moved at one speed, the bird's eyes might not see him clearly. Any sudden jerk would trigger a flash of certainty in the hawk's mind. The slow, steady movement managed to convince the hawk he might be mistaken, but he had seen enough to drop down and take a closer look.

The snake gambled. It must eat to live. To stop now, give in to his terror, might well be a death sentence. Stop now, and he would be caught in the open by the hawk. Even a small hawk was deadly to most snakes. Arthur had seen them kill and knew they were born knowing how. If at all possible, they landed behind the snake's neck. Even as the talons embedded themselves in the body, the sharp, efficient beak snipped off the head.

A snake was a lovely kill. No waste; they ate him nose to tail. All of him.

One thing to admire efficiency in the abstract; another to contemplate it with respect to one's self.

But the snake's cold cunning was as much inborn as the bird's skill. It commanded the pace, and he entered the water before the bird drew close enough to see the snake clearly and snap into its stoop, the closed-wing fall of a bird of prey when it strikes its chosen victim.

The snake moved through the green, watery gloom—it was warm—beyond the fringe of branches on the willow. And from the shadows, stealth dictated he could see the afternoon sun illuminating the central area of the pond. There were minnows at the surface. Water striders were already present, their feet dimpling the thin layer of molecules neither water nor air, which floats between the two worlds. Dragonflies, a lot of them, darted like the spangles of a jeweled gown.

The snake reached the recumbent willow trunk and moved, belly scales expertly catching the rough fissured surface of the bark until he rested several feet above the water, concealed by the smooth, leafy wands of branches hanging from the fallen tree. Arthur had seen them lying as he was on summer days when he forded rivers and streams. He had never bothered one, and now was glad.

The snake took a dragonfly with blinding speed. Not very good tasting. The minnows had been better. Like the fish's, his teeth were to the back.

Now! The dragonfly had been an appetizer only.

Arthur was uncomfortable. He couldn't let himself sink into the serpent the way he had into the fish. He didn't want to be part of such a being. But he sensed that if he allowed himself to become simply an observer, the creature might perish. And that was the test.

This was borne out when he saw the shadow of the viper swim past below the log through the sunstruck water. It was only an outline in the murky green translucence, but he clearly saw the flat head, broad at the back, a wedge set on a narrow neck that tapered into a thick body, wider across than high.

The venomous have their own profile. It belongs only to them.

The serpent had accepted his judgment and come to hunt here. It remained to be seen if the true proprietor of this puddle would overlook his trespass or not. The viper was twice the size of the vermilion hunter he occupied. His companion would be a good dinner.

Vipers. Now, where there was one, there usually was another. But he didn't move—even a human eye would lose him along the bark.

Where oh where was the other?

His eyes roved over the winter-killed reeds and sedges, the fading brown stalks of cattails, the faint traces of green on the knot grass growing through the water at the margin of the pond.

Then he knew. If she wasn't anywhere else, she would be . . .

Behind him.

If there's one thing snakes can do, it's move fast. The turn he made was an arc. She was already striking.

His head swung wide, toward her tail, and he hooked the very tip with his recurved teeth. She swung like a flying whip. He was in the air, but it didn't matter. He tightened every muscle and jerked his head to the left. He felt her neck snap.

There were only stars. He lay in the sea of stars, and there was no up, no down, no earth, no sky. Only the arch of the star road, the Milky Way, over him. He was very tired, but it was good to have arms and legs and be a man. He was unbelievably dirty, his clothing in rags, part of his hair and beard singed away.

She was standing not far from him. He got to his knees. His arms were shaking, and it was difficult to push himself up.

"Did the snake live?" he asked.

She laughed. "What does it matter? In the end, you won't—live, that is. No man can ride the wheel for long."

"It matters to me," he said.

"Then, yes, it did. After its struggle with the viper, it took some small fish and a frog. Not a lot, but enough to allow it to survive the next cold spell. Later that year, it mated and bred."

He looked down at his dirty clothing. Even in the starlight he could see how tattered it was.

"When we walked in the forest . . ." he began.

"We weren't really there," she said. "No more than you were with the fish or the snake."

"But I'm here now?" he asked.

"I cannot say," she answered.

"I have only a small need," he said. "But I hope I am present in such a way as to gratify it. I would like a drink of water."

Abruptly, he found himself in the forest, just below the plateau where he had first been imprisoned. He was standing in the same jumble of rocks where he had seen the strange bowl that seemed to bring him back for a moment to Tintigal. She was standing there with him.

The bowl was at his feet. He made as if to kneel.

But she said, "No. Reach down and rest your fingers on the inside of the rim. Just touch it, but don't put your hand in too deep and touch the zone of power at the bottom."

He reached down with his right hand and touched the inside of the rim. There was a soft click, and the bowl came free of its place in the rocks and stuck to his fingers as he lifted his hand.

"See," she said. "Already it knows you."

The bowl was half filled with water and the golden cross. Not quite a cross, a circle with strange symbols for arms, four arms, no two alike. One arm was a crescent and two ovals, another hooks and ovals, a third another oval and a sinuous symbol in the shape of a half S, the bottom half of an S, and on the last, the ovals were joined by curved lines. The curious marks quite clearly glowed from within but not with the cold, blue phosphorescences of the winter surf or rotten wood. They had a warm, dark umber glow, like amber in sunlight.

He transferred the bowl to a more conventional grip, holding it cradled in his two hands.

"Now drink!" she said.

He did, and the water from the bowl flowed into his body, and not only quenched his thirst but warmed him, strengthened him, and filled him with a relaxed confidence he hadn't felt before.

"Is this fair?" he asked.

"It isn't a contest," she said.

He struck out instinctively. The bird was coming directly for his eye.

The raven screeched and exploded in a tangle of black feathers. It fell toward the ground, and he realized he hadn't killed it, because it took wing and flew.

Something thumped against his shoulder, and he felt the sting of a beak on his skin. This time he moved even more quickly, and the starling died when his giant, hooked beak closed over it.

The small birds mobbing him drew back, quarreling among themselves. That put the fear of God into them.

Then a gust of truly icy wind hit him. He hunched his body and fluffed up his feathers to protect himself from the biting cold. The sun was a band of pale orange on the horizon. Night was coming over a devastated countryside. All around him the forest was blackened and dead, left that way by a fire that had burned out only a few weeks ago.

Far I flew, the bird thought. *And everywhere I saw desolation.*

It wasn't in a bird of prey to examine the motives of another species, but this was extreme even for them. And the bird knew with gritty disgust that it would soon die. It hadn't been able to find food for over a week now, and it was starving.

Not fair, Arthur thought. *This one will be the death of me.* Then he was brought up short by his companion's incomprehension.

It is not that we don't give up. We don't even think about it. But, yes, the bird, a young eagle, had exhausted all her—that one was a revelation—all her reserves. She had been on her own for a month now. Toward the mountains where she came from, the pickings had been fairly good. But she couldn't remain in her parents' territory, and all others had been taken.

So she began her journey, guided by the wheeling stars and the earth's movement on its axis. Out over the plain, and ran into the destruction caused by war.

At first at least there was carrion. She rested for several days near a battlefield, cleaning the scraps from the bones piled in wild profusion, successfully quarreling with the rest to maintain her position. Until all the available food had been eaten and the scavengers had been reduced to feeding on rodents that lived on what they could gnaw from the joints and bone piles that had once been men and horses. Feeding at last on the scraps of leather armor and horse tack that remained.

As she journeyed on, the desolation grew worse and worse. Farms and villas burned to the ground, livestock that couldn't be driven away slaughtered in their stalls, stables, corrals, and pastures. Ducks, geese, and chickens cooked and eaten to feed the army on the march.

The forest fires were set when the armies fired the crops standing in the fields. Even the orchards were felled or the trees girdled and killed with the fruit still green on the boughs. The same fate befell the people. Those unfit to be sold as slaves were cut down where they stood. Weeds were beginning to grow up through their bones.

Her last kill had been a scrawny hare, almost a week and a half ago. Now she stood clutching the highest branch of the blackened pine, looking at the burned-out forest and farm below her, enduring the cold and being buffeted by a wind that carried a hint of snow.

It was more than welcome to him to be a bird. He liked it better, though the sheer ferocity of her mind was frightening. Yet even in that, he felt somehow a connection to her, since he bore in the darkest parts of his spirit the same insatiable and unquenchable fury that waited, held by an iron control, until the moment of combat, when he could release it unchecked by conscience. A savage force, which terrorized and then destroyed his enemy.

Yes, she was like him, taking no quarter and giving none—not even to herself.

We are, he thought, *even in this extremity a fine thing.*

The growing darkness drove off the birds that were mobbing her, and they found themselves alone. What wonders she possessed. He would have killed for those talons that clenched themselves around the branch. They were armed with two-inch nails and strong enough to snap the neck of a full-grown goat. Even though her body was reduced by semi-starvation, her massive wings were intact and would carry her above the highest peak on the highest mountain in the world.

Her eyes were a miracle, and, indeed, just then they demonstrated how good they were. A shadow moved in what had been some sort of dwelling near the foot of the burned pine. Her eyes accommodated the darkness and focused on a thin wood rat scavenging among charred corn grains near the blackened remnants of a chicken coop.

The man had a second to wonder at the destruction so awesome and absolute that it encompassed even barnyard fowl. His next thought was that high intelligence isn't always an advantage—sometimes it is only a distraction. But not to her.

He was startled to realize that she had begun her swoop while he was still considering it. She was swift, silent, and deadly. She didn't bother with even one wing beat. The moment they opened, she dropped into a beautifully controlled glide, which took her only inches above the wood rat.

Arthur saw the wood rat glance up once, when she was nearly upon it. Its look was one of surprise—and that was all it had time for, surprise.

A few seconds later, she sat on her perch in the pine, dining on wood rat. It wasn't enough, but it was something. A snack for a bird her size. The wind had a bite to it. She hunched down and fluffed her feathers against the growing cold while she finished her meal. When her crop was full, she dozed for a few moments.

He realized she was glad he was present. This surprised him, until he explored her consciousness further and discovered she was capable of both love and loyalty.

Not to her young. A bird of prey is tested from the first moment it pecks open the egg. Most fail.

No, her strongest feelings were reserved for the mate she would one day join in dominating a territory and rearing young. Him, she could love. And Arthur knew they did love. He had seen it when one of the other Bears captured a young goshawk. His mate would in no way desert him, but remained nearby and even tried to feed him through the bars of his cage in the mews. This moved Arthur. Most of the rest of the boys involved themselves in an enthusiastic attempt to capture her, also.

A few days later, Arthur realized that looking at the pair of birds trying to reach past the cage bars to each other made him want to cry. So he gave the goshawk's owner a gold-hilted knife for the goshawk and released it. The bird spiraled up and up, toward the sky, and was greeted from the clouds with a cry of the purest joy he had ever heard. He had wept then. And was glad no one saw him.

What to do? What to do now . . . for her?

She was glad he was present. She had felt so . . . alone.

It was dark now, and the stars were aglow, a mesh of timeless beauty that seemed to catch eternity in its shining nets. She and his kind had lived together for a long time. Humans got respect from the birds. But no more. They couldn't be tamed but would, with some persuasion, accept a human hunting partner. To the men and women who were devoted to the pursuit of falconry, the birds were held in near godlike awe. That's what he needed: one of those fanatics right now.

We fly.

She did.

She couldn't have his knowledge of war and its limitations. For a moment he was simply lost in the joy of the mighty wings that lifted him higher and higher, up beyond the burned-out forest. The abandoned farms, the rolling hills, pastures filling with weeds, the eyeless villas of Roman occupation still standing only because they were walled with stone and would not burn. Their roofs were long, open to the rain. They had fallen first.

The few walled towns were blackening piles of rubble. From time to time he saw lights, and she obligingly dipped down and focused those magnificent eyes on the few furtive survivors of the long war. They offered little hope. Most, like the eagle, were struggling to survive amid what seemed universal catastrophe.

He asked that she turn toward the mountains. There, in the heavily forested foothills, hiding on ground so rocky and broken that it could not be farmed, were a cluster of survivors. In the summer they made a living by driving their stock to pastures in the mountains. In the winter they stole from travelers on their way across what was once the prosperous countryside to the still-functioning market at Paris. The rewards were sufficient to keep trade alive, and those thieves were usually content to let themselves be bought off.

Nothing in the forbidding little valley was in an easily accessible position. They were all fortified in some way. They were round houses, as his people built, and the eagle landed on the roof of the largest one. She took a little persuading, but finally she entered the smoke hole and climbed down to sit among the rafters.

Arthur was delighted. They were the toughest, most terrifying, most disreputable crew he had ever seen. The leader was a horse-size redhead, who wore only breeches, no shirt. But that didn't matter, since he had a pelt of red hair that would have been the envy of a bear. He wore enough jewelry to make up for his lack of a shirt. At his neck, two torcs and assorted chains hung heavy with jeweled medallions.

But best of all, at least a half-dozen hooded hawks stood on perches against the walls that ringed the room. And it was clear from the guano piles under their perches that their nutrition and comfort were favored above all else.

There was no furniture, and the chief and his men sat in a loose circle on hides around the fire pit. He was speaking to a tall, lean, powerful young man at his side. "I still cannot see why you will not tell me how you learned they were operating hereabouts."

"The question is father to the lie," the young man answered.

The rest of the ugly crew laughed at the chief. This seemed to disturb him not at all.

"Someone should teach you respect for your betters," one of them said.

"I'll respect my better when I meet him," the young man said. "He is not here."

Again gales of laughter.

"It won't do for you to be so mealymouthed," the chief said.

There were at least three animals roasting in the smoke over the fire pit. A deer, a pig, and something that looked like a horse. The chief was sampling the first course, a suckling pig cooked in clay. The dogs were scattered near the fire. A beautiful gray hound thrust her nose into his hand, and he gave her a leg from the pig. When a big coursing hound tried to pull it out of her mouth, the chief slapped him across the muzzle. The giant hound whined and covered his muzzle with his forepaws. The chief relented and gave him part of a haunch.

"You should give it up, Cregan," one of the freebooters said. "Black Leg will never tell you how he finds things out."

Cregan sighed. "It's true. But if the lot of you wouldn't get him started smarting off, I might get some truth out of him."

"There is no truth in any of you," the boy said. "Otherwise, you wouldn't be here."

"Still, we have done better since you wandered out of the forest," Cregan said.

"You told me you wanted to study war and fighting," he continued. "And I will say, you picked the best possible site to further your education. I cannot remember a peaceful year in my lifetime, nor in my father's. Nor his father's before him. Yet I think we should be grateful we survived the Romans and the Franks. Now we are left to deal with the Huns."

"Tremendous rich men they are, too," one of the others contributed. "That bunch we ambushed yesterday were dripping with gold. We got a good price for cutting their throats. Ah, well, the masters at the villas pay well, and happens it's all ours now."

And, indeed, they looked rich. Every man had at least a gold torc; most had belts, gleaming with silver and precious stones, and gold-hilted gem-encrusted knives, swords, and throwing axes. Some armor, mail shirts dripping with bullion trim, chains, rings, bracelets, and highly burnished helmets rounded out their accoutrements.

The weapons and jewelry were, however, the only clean things in the room; for the rest, most of the men looked as though they dressed their hair with lime or butter and replaced their clothing only when it grew too rotten to wear. But as far as an eagle was concerned, this was a minor affair. All she cared about were the three carcasses ready to be eaten. She was wretchedly hungry.

She dropped from the rafters onto the remains of the deer and began to fill her crop at the best speed possible. There was a loud shout from the men. A few scrambled to their feet, reaching for weapons. The ornate throwing axes troubled Arthur. But Cregan was sitting, gazing up at her with stunned delight.

"Hold!" he roared. "If any lays a hand on her or even splits a feather, I'll unman him with a hoof knife. Oh, my beauty. My fair, my lady of the peaks. How come you here?"

"Let her be," Black Leg said. "What do you trouble a highborn guest before she has eaten and drunk her fill?"

"Ah, boy," Cregan said. "It's friends we will be forever. You understand my thoughts so well."

"What is it?" someone asked. "The thing is too big to be a hawk."

"Fool! It's a she-eagle, the very queen of birds," Cregan said.

She ceased feeding and met Cregan's eyes.

"Boy," he said to Black Leg. "Get me my toughest glove."

Black Leg nodded and hurried off. He returned with a bullock-hide falconer's glove. Cregan pulled it on and waited politely until she finished her meal. Then he raised his hand and she flew to his glove.

Arthur studied the two men's faces, Black Leg's and Cregan's. So did the eagle.

"One must live," he told her. "It is not slavery but brotherhood."

Her silence was assent.

"She can no longer live off the land," Black Leg said to Cregan.

"Most can't, boy. Most can't. Not now."

Then she flew, circling the hall just over the men's heads. Then, abruptly, she rose higher and exited through the smoke hole in the roof.

"No!" Cregan cried out as if in mortal pain.

"She has something to do, that's all," Black Leg said.

"You know? You're sure?" Cregan shouted.

"I know. And I am sure," Black Leg said. "I tell you it will rain, it rains. I tell you it will snow, it snows. I tell you the Huns are coming, the next night you're eating their horses. I know."

She entered the smoke hole, dipped down, and circled Cregan. "She does him homage," several of the men gasped.

Then she rose higher and exited through the smoke hole in the roof again, spiraling upward into the night sky. She turned toward the east. Arthur was bewildered for a moment, and then he understood.

"Is that all it is?" he asked.

Again, as before, the silence was assent.

It was a long climb. Higher and higher they flew, rising beyond the hills and above the mountains that looked strangely ethereal, their tops locked in perpetual winter. But she managed to climb higher yet, into realms where ice clouds spread their dust into veils riding the wind-driven currents of the upper air, circling the earth the way water currents swirl through the oceans. And then beyond, hovering at the edges of the profound silence that lies between the worlds.

The earth was spread out beneath them. Its visions—the ugliness and darkness of war, the unending, ever-varied beauty of creation—all swallowed up in the abyss of distance until at last she must perforce level out. There alone, with God and the eagle, Arthur saw the sunrise flare across the edge of the world as they flew on out of darkness and into the sun.

He woke in what he knew must have been her throne at the top of the tower. He closed his eyes briefly, so he would know, and saw the eagle enter through the smoke hole. The hall was filled with sodden, snoring men, but Cregan and Black Leg waited up for her. Cregan stretched out his arm; she landed, and he brought her to her new home in his mews.

Arthur opened his eyes again and looked out into the morning. He had won.

The throne was set between two parts of the waterfall that entered the tower. The bowl from which he had drunk was in the center of the room where the fire pit should be, and he sensed that all he needed or ever would need in the way of material possessions was contained therein. He was tired, weary to the point of death, but filled with absolute, complete, and unutterable peace.

He had won.

What that implied or how it would play out in the scheme of things, he had no idea. But none of this mattered now; he would deal with these things as they presented themselves. For now victory was all that mattered. He must sleep.

And he carried the knowledge of his triumph with him into the darkness.

CHAPTER TWENTY-EIGHT

HE STEPS OF THE DANCE ARE A SECRET. THEY
are between the Painted People and the queens. They
and the pattern the dance floor follows inform the
watchers about the season of the dragon in the sky and what it means
day by day, month by month. And one who sails beyond sight of land
can navigate safely between landfalls even when there is only water
and sky.

Those directions were worked out long ago by the wise, and incorporated in the dance long before any could put pen to paper. The directions
for safe voyaging were handed down from generation to generation by ecstatic dance.

But that is not the only thing the dance means. As I said once,
Dugald told me that I would not understand love fully until I loved, or
war until I was in the midst of battle. The same is true of the dances
taught by the Painted People. Each of the rulers in the houses of heaven
has a different meaning. The salmon, as I have said, for both chastity and
fertility. They do not love until the appointed time, but then have many
children. The wolf is the symbol of duty and skill. Wolves seldom fail at

either. The boar bespeaks headlong valor and unsullied courage. He is not, however, very smart, but one who values these qualities above all will embrace his dance.

We—each one of the Painted People—enter the dance that seems best to that particular person. Each adopts that particular path in life. I had chosen the dragon path, and I would embark on it tonight.

The dragon is wisdom and power. That is why it is so feared and yet courted. Nothing is more powerful than the dragon, just as nothing is more chaste than the salmon or braver than the boar. And as you put your feet on the path, you hope—you pray—that somehow the wisdom is granted to your heart that allows you to deal with that great power without vainglory or selfishness. That your spirit doesn't die like a rotten tree eaten away from within by its own greatest gift turned into a fatal, tragic flaw.

This is as far as I can go in telling you what the dance means—beyond this point, you must look into your own heart and see Dugald was right. Some things can't be taught. At least, not in any words possible.

Maeniel felt this was why all the great sages never wrote anything down. And why the druids committed their wisdom to memory only. In the final analysis, scriptures are futile things, dependent as they are on the intentions of the interpreter. All too often too literal a mind can lead human students into strange follies. Sometimes it is better to allow the searchers to try to plumb the depths of the great mystery on their own and accept that not every one of those taking the road will see the same end.

There are ways to hold back, not fully commit to the journey. But I scorned those and even now, after a lifetime of sorrow and struggle, I believe I made the right choice. I never asked her to teach them to me, but yielded fully to my destiny.

When we reached the edge of the dance floor, I cast off the mantle and let the crowd look their fill at me. The dress of fine chain was not intended to conceal. The ring of chain at my shoulders fell back, baring my breasts. The one that circled my hips left me bare at the sides, and when I began to dance, I knew the moving skirt would hide nothing.

Sometimes, what we are is more important than who we are, and what we represent more important than what we are trying to accomplish. I surrendered to this truth, also.

I was the ripe apple on the highest bough, the wheat field turning from green to gold in the autumn sun. The mountain and river teeming with fish, dressed in scarlet robes of desire. The crowd was silent, and even the wind seemed to die down as I crossed the broken dance floor toward the center.

Then I heard a murmur of approval from the people gathered on the hillside. The women would want to be me, the men would want me . . . that was the point.

Then silence fell. I had passed the first test.

It was cold. I remember that. But I was young and my blood heated and brought a flush to my skin. And the armor rose, a green tracery over my breasts and hips, the most exposed parts of me, rendering me less naked.

We had the dance mapped out, Kyra and I. We practiced a method of compensating for the broken dance floor. You see, in any given dance not all of the paths in the maze are used. Each dancer finds her—or his for that matter—road along them. So I knew what I was to do. I knew each step. Each twist and turn of the pattern had been laid out for me beforehand. I could follow it in my sleep.

When I reached the center, I stood silent, facing the vast crowd standing on the hillside above the dance floor. I raised my arms and the music began. So practiced was I that my feet seemed to sweep into the repetitious first movement of the dance without my will.

It begins with the sun. They all do, the increasing and decreasing sun of summer and winter. That way the watchers know, by how many turns in the sun spiral and their direction, what design in the stars is indicated, what constellation the dance is about. Then, this and other information once given, the dancer is free to lay her interpretation of the dragon journey to the people. They could read it in the intricate in-and-out steps of the labyrinth. It was theirs to accept or reject.

I'm not sure how I can tell what happens next. I'm not sure I know how. I'm not sure if anyone would know how. But I did not dance the steps I and Kyra worked out so laboriously.

Instead, I found myself alone with the night wind, the silence, and the sea, the torchlight and the cold stone under my feet the only reality. We ask and ask the question of the abyss. We beat our fists against the wall of ignorance standing between ourselves and the ultimate meaning of the universe. The ultimate truth that lies at the heart of creation itself.

We search, call out into the darkness, and hope for an answer. Hope that somehow the ruling principle of all things, the eternal lover, will formulate an answer that would not destroy us.

I struggled. I sought. I asked. And I was answered.

Words fail here. They not only cannot come to the end of this ultimate experience, they cannot even reach the beginning of it. It is as if you lived in a world where the clouds never parted and your eyes and mind never experienced the sun. Then one day the overcast thinned for a little time and the light broke through, transforming all creation. Even if it lasted only an instant, from that instant might be drawn a lifetime of transcendent illumination and love.

For that is what God is: light. Thought that is the light of the mind and love that is the light of the heart. And they are one and there is no place in or outside creation where that light does not shine.

And for a precious few seconds, moments, it was one with me, and I it. And nothing else mattered. Nothing.

And I danced the hunger of the human spirit for the fulfillment of everlasting love. I danced the rapture which is the contemplation of the transcendent love, meaning, beauty—where the seeker, the questioner, the lover, the dreamer, for an instant knows what a purely human mind can never know. And the shape and meaning of everything in life itself changes, is changed, and we cannot look at so small a thing as a blade of grass and not experience it as part of the only mystery, the great unknown, the root and logic of creation itself.

No, words cannot describe it, cannot come to the end of it. They cannot reach even the beginning.

My friends stood and watched me, a figure glowing in gold and green, moving through the maze of rock, my body a living column of sparkling light against the gray stone.

"She is not dancing the figures we agreed upon," Kyra whispered to Maeniel and Dugald.

"I know," Dugald said. "But it is not the dance that troubles me but where it is leading."

Because I was drawing near the edge of the cliff.

"She will double back," said Kyra.

But I didn't. I danced out over the empty air.

A scream boiled up in Kyra's throat, but Dugald ended it by slapping his hand over Kyra's mouth.

"Be silent, both of you," he whispered to Maeniel and Kyra as I danced on and on in an arc where the dance floor had been, out into the wind, above the pounding surf, below the stars. And Dugald told me I carried the watching crowd with me, not into the miracle of one who dances on nothingness but into the search of mankind for the absolute and the transcendent. A search begun when the minds of human beings named the divine after the day itself, the light. A search that is not ended yet and perhaps never will be. A thirst never quenched, a hunger that may never be assuaged.

But a search without which we would be less than the dumb stones tumbled by the endless swirling of the surf until they are at last worn away.

"She might die!" Kyra whispered.

"And I tell you, fool woman, break her concentration and she surely will."

So they watched while I completed my arc out over the pounding sea, then back to the cliff and then, in a few moments, back out again, my face void of all awareness. Not only of danger, but even of where I was as I closed the final sun spiral to mark the place where the dance must end, reached the center of the dance floor again, and was still.

I didn't know what I had done. I remember only a vast silence until I heard the first shout, then the second, and at last a third. Then unbelievably, a fourth. One honored me, my effort. Two confirmed my candidacy. Three crowned me; the Dragon Throne was now my right.

The fourth—I heard only a few times a fourth—commanded me to go forward.

I threw up my arms and gave my promise in return. "It is the duty and pleasure of the queens to bring kings to the people. With all my heart, I embrace my duty. I will bring to you the greatest king of all."